Bruja

A Novel
By Chris Tolliver

Shawn,

Thanks for supporting
a hobby

C Tolli

This book is a work of fiction. Names, characters, places and incidents are products of the author's imagination or are used fictitiously. Any resemblance to actual events or locales or persons, living or dead is entirely coincidental.

ISBN: 978-1-9808-3486-1

Dedicated to my family and friends who share a love for rock and roll and a good poltergeist movie

TABLE OF CONTENTS

Part I :
The Opening Verses

Chapter 1:
She was a wicked sorceress…

Greg Palmer exuberantly sang the opening lyrics to his favorite song by the seventies rock band the Silver Blasters. He drummed the steering wheel to the rhythm and mimicked the lead singer's piercing squeal, "She had me frozen in place as she slowly undressed." He continued with the next few stanzas as his mind drifted into memory. The automatic portion of his brain took control of his car allowing him to fully embrace the CD and the associated experiences. He was completely unconscious to the fact that he tapped his brake pedal to slow down for an impending red light.

This song describes Cynthia, he thought. *She was THE perfect woman to me. She froze me in more than one way.*

His eyesight momentarily blurred as he delved deeper into his memory banks and brought forth the image of a beautiful and exotic woman that he had not seen in over twenty years. Instead of peering through a dirty wind shield of an ancient Honda Accord, he gazed upon the vivid image of a woman that he once loved and feared. The subconscious part of his mind applied his foot to the gas pedal to accelerate through the now green light while he examined the vision he held.

The first feature that his mind's eye captured was her long, jet black hair that cascaded around a slim and graceful neck. His memory eyes followed the flow of the hair to the edge of her shoulders. A thin gold necklace silently traced her neck's curve down to a few inches above her breasts. He focused on the bottom of the chain which held a striking, starburst pendant. He recalled the blood red coloring and the apparent sharpness of each point. He did not know if the ends were as sharp as they seemed because she never let him touch the pendent. Her refusal to allow him to hold the adornment became a source of entertainment for him. He often tried to poke at it when he was high (which was frequent during that stage of his life). He felt a pain of remorse as he recognized that this interplay was a great source of irritation to her. He broke from that line of memory and shifted his eyes back up to her facial features.

The thick hair framed a thin, dark complected face that was smooth of any blemishes. Her lips were full and accentuated by her trademark rich, red lipstick. She had classic high cheek bones and a slightly pointed chin. He quickly glanced over her unremarkable nose to the feature that originally (and literally) stopped him in his tracks.

In 1994 Greg was a few years removed from high school, apprenticing as an electrician and quickly advancing into a full-blown junkie. He lived in a medium sized town named Remington that was situated roughly an hour southwest of Seattle. Grunge music was dominating the airwaves and he embraced all aspects of that lifestyle; the flannel, the music of Nirvana, Soundgarden, and Alice in Chains, the don't give a fuck attitude, and most importantly, the drugs. He was only recently introduced to heroin, but he was quickly forming a terrible relationship with the substance. The drugs had yet to seriously affect his job or his relationships, but the writing was on the wall. Those closest to him, which actually only numbered a few, began to have doubts. More than likely his life would have spiraled completely out of control (or at least in a completely different direction) if Cynthia had not entered his life.

The night Greg met Cynthia he and his "friends" were at a run-down night club named Castaways enjoying one of the regular cover bands. After moshing like idiots to a cover of "Smells Like Teen Spirit" for the thousandth time, he jetted to the rest room for both release and recharging. He hit the urinal and then hit a line of blow. He looked into the mirror just before he exited and thought, *Man, you look like crap.* He was still managing to work full time, but he was also trying to maintain his second job as a party hound. His life was the epitome of burning the candle at both ends. Deep in his soul he knew this was not sustainable for the long haul, but *carpe diem damn it, Castaways is rocking tonight.*

Despite the filthy conditions of Castaways and the less than friendly staff, the locals packed it every weekend. He could never pin-point why he went to Castaways so often when so many other places were "better". The cover bands were often terrible, the drinks were not cheaper, and the facilities were markedly worse. Despite the obvious negatives, he just felt at home. The others that filled it on most nights must have shared that feeling. Romans preferred other Romans. That particular night was no different as he bumped and bounced off a dozen people while attempting to navigate back to the table where he left his friends. Many of those he fumbled into were in a condition very similar to Greg and did not note his intrusions as unusual. Those that did notice would tell you that they simply did not give a fuck. This was an establishment of unsettled apathy and moribund expression. He was in his element and enjoyed living this dark path to the fullest; at least until he returned to his friends' table in the corner.

He soon discovered that they had abandoned him (again). He cursed out loud and spun around to see if he could find them in the mass of people. That particular group lived for the moment, and at any given time they could drift out of a club into a stranger's house. They often woke up not completely sure of the chain of events that led them to their situation. Most of the time this scenario did not bother him because he was usually on the end that involved a ride in a car. He did not have a great desire to attempt to hitchhike in a cold steady rain. As he stepped away, he heard a voice say, "Is something wrong?" He turned his head and locked eyes with Cynthia for the first time. He stopped and his life instantly changed.

The first thing that captured his attention was the deepness of her large brown eyes. Solely on aesthetics her doe eyes were acutely adorable. He once attempted to describe to her that moment when their eyes connected. He wanted to use the words of poets and authors and describe in vivid detail the feeling of being absorbed into another reality. He tried to articulate to her the thoughts that raced through his mind and the atomic rush he felt the first time they met. He desperately wanted to describe the idea of something ancient and calming but yet so deeply powerful. He struggled to say that he was instantly transported away to another time and place; a place of sentient thought. He also needed to vocalize something else. He had a dark intuition of something just beyond the calmness; of something very unsettling. H. P. Lovecraft could have described what he sensed just beyond the edge but not Greg Palmer. He drunkenly blurted out, "beautiful and scary." She flashed a quick smile at him and innocently imitated the word "scary". Despite the drugs and alcohol, he actually felt real embarrassment. He let it go never to revisit, though in his soul he always felt that her eyes were a gateway to another place. He was content to not explore and potentially complicate a situation that eventually turned into the proverbial gold mine.

Greg chuckled lightly at the reminiscence. He continued to drive through his old hometown oblivious to the actual surroundings. He made a right-hand turn onto a busier four-lane street replete with restaurants and stores on each side. The traffic instantly thickened, but he obliviously continued in his own separate mental voyage.

She offered to give him a ride that evening. Greg instantly agreed. He viewed the whole situation as extremely fortunate. Once outside he steadfastly agreed that the rain was indeed something he did not want to mess with that night. The other reason was that this fabulously beautiful and sexy woman seemed genuinely interested in him. He dated a few girls in the past, but none of them were in Cynthia's category. She bought him drinks, danced with him, and made him feel like a stud. In return he stammered and slurred as he attempted to engage with her. She soothed his psyche and clutched him tighter while they slow danced. Several times he could not help to slightly sober up and begin to feel foolish. Oddly she seemed charmed by his lack of conversation skills and his overall ungainliness. As last call was being sounded Greg succumbed to a flash of frantic. He did not have the experience with the ladies to exactly know how to continue the evening. She seemed to sense his impending struggle and calmly suggested that she should give him a ride.

Cynthia never asked for his address. Instead she immediately drove out of town onto rural and narrow two-lane roads. Pines guarded each side of the road for miles and miles while they sat in silence. For the next few hours only the light chatter of the radio and slight hum of the engine interrupted the complete stillness. Occasionally he glanced in her direction. He foggily concluded that she seemed focused and distant from the current situation. Her sharp, thin eyebrows were furled, and her eyes appeared to go from brown to full blown black. Why fuck up a perfectly good situation so he said nothing, enjoyed the buzz, and her silent company. The only motion that occasionally disturbed the scene was when he shifted the radio station away from commercials to an actual song.

Shortly before sunrise he turned the knob of the radio several times in boredom. Suddenly he recognized the beginning of a song as he flipped past a station. He wrenched the knob back and excitedly broke the reverie by turning the volume dial up. He loudly announced, "Oh, this song is never on the radio and it is one of my favorites."

He realized that he spoke a little louder than intended. She was momentarily startled, but quickly recovered. She gave him an inquisitive look as the opening notes of a slow rock song filled the car.

"This is 'Radiate' by Tackles the Mute", he excitedly explained. "This is off their first album. I never hear it on the radio." She simply nodded. He could not tell if her acknowledgment was out of familiarity with the song by the nineties grunge band, or to simply humor him. He did not try to solve the puzzle. He let the music fill the car and engage his soul. As the song progressed the rhythm and the volume continued to build to a crescendo. When the soaring chorus began, he threw out his arms and crooned along,

I need you to radiate, alleviate my pain
Loving, anguish, sex, all my suffering
Comfort, torment, sex, can't you see
Radiate, please set me free

She carefully listened to the lyrics and watched Greg. She turned the volume to mute as the chorus ended and the rhythms slowed and softened to start the second verse. She abruptly stopped the car in the middle of the road and shifted the car into park. The night was moonless, and they were distant enough from manmade light to leave them surrounded by darkness. The only illumination was from the gauges on the dashboard. He could not recall the last time they passed another vehicle, and he was certain that they were the only living souls on that isolated stretch of road. She turned in her seat to square her body to completely face him. She reached up and turned on an overhead light.

"Look at me," she calmly directed.

"I am," he returned as his eyes adjusted to the influx of light.

"No," she sighed. "I mean *really* look at me."

With a slight perplexed look, he also shifted in his seat to directly face her. He looked her in the eyes and asked, "Is this better?"

"Yes," she began. "I was not positive. I was pretty sure when we left the bar, but I needed some other sign. You said the name of this song is 'Radiate'."

He nodded affirmative. She pulled out a cigarette, lit it, and continued, "I know that this does make any sense right now, but it will over time. I want you to come home with me. Our lives will never be the same."

She let out a puff of smoke and slowly continued, "As the song just said I want to set you free. Do you trust me to set you free?"

He thought, *What the hell does that mean? How is she going to set me free? Fuck it, why not? She is freaking hot and wants me to go home with her.* He reached for her cigarette, took a long draw, and nonchalantly uttered, "Sure."

She smiled and turned back around in her seat. She quickly turned off the overhead light, put the car back into gear, and aggressively applied her foot to the gas pedal. As she sped along the isolated and winding roads, he vaguely understood that they were heading back towards his hometown. He nestled back into his seat and let the sleep that he managed to stiff-arm now wash over him. The lyrics to 'Radiates' merged in and out of his consciousness; loving...sex...pain...comfort. Each lyric birthed a new image in his mind. *Sex with Cynthia?! Soon?* He glanced in her direction and clearly felt the beginning of an erection. The last coherent thought he formed before he fully passed into the sleep world was the crystal-clear opening riffs and drumbeats of his favorite Silver Blasters song. *Cynthia...She is a wicked sorceress.*

In the present time and place, the Silver Blasters had moved on from an evil woman tempting them to encouraging others to drink with them. He was still drumming the steering wheel and lightly singing about bourbon and tequila and salt. Greg broke out from his reminiscent daydream. He quickly punched the power button cutting off the Silver Blasters in mid-howl. Greg flatly and clearly spoke out loud, "She was a wicked sorceress".

He instantly felt nauseated and weak. His whole body broke into a cold sweat, and he could feel his pulse racing. He mentally told himself to breathe, but at that given moment that particular automatic function was escaping him. Traffic was bumper to bumper, and the idea registered with Greg that he was starting to become a dangerous element on this stretch of busy roadway. He was able to limply hit his blinker to try to shift over to the right-hand lane. He could see in his passenger mirror that he did not have room for this maneuver. He impatiently waited as a bright red Mustang in the right lane moved even with him. Time seemed to stall as the seconds agonizingly stretched along tic by ever slow tic. The Mustang appeared content to stay even with Greg even as he managed to lift his foot off the accelerator and let friction slow his Accord.

A sharp pain ripped through his chest and the thought of *HEART ATTACK?!* zipped through his mind. He finally was able to take a small gulp of air and look over to his right. He wanted to scream at the sight of the driver of the Mustang neck down giving full attention to his phone. He could not scream, but he was able to moan. A new thought crashed his mind and that was *PANIC ATTACK?!* He was not sure if this was what he was experiencing, but he was absolutely positive that he needed to get out of traffic and into a parking lot. He was pretty sure that he was going to lose consciousness and cause an accident in the process. A loud vulgar car horn then jumped into the scene.

Greg's Accord had now slowed enough to cause the driver behind him to respond with a hand gesture and push on the center of his steering wheel for several seconds. The blast startled the driver of the Mustang and caused him to refocus on the street and his surroundings. He glanced over at Greg for a split second and then accelerated his own car forward. Greg could see in his side mirror that some American brand piece-o-shit mini-van was racing to close the gap between himself and the Mustang. Greg looked back forward and swerved his steering wheel into the right lane. He braced for the impact that he was very concerned was going to occur. Instead he heard another car horn, and he was confident that he heard several choice obscenities. At that given moment he did not care. As a matter of fact, he reverted to the twenty-some year-old Greg and choked out," I don't give a fuck what you think." The edges of his vision were blurring, and he felt like the entire right side of his body below the waist had gone numb. *STROKE?! Just fucking great.* A quick glance into his rear-view mirror revealed that the gentleman in the minivan was not finished giving Greg a piece of his mind. He shifted his eyes back forward and thankfully saw the entrance to a convenient store less than a hundred yards ahead.

Unfortunately, he understood that he had a few problems that he still needed to resolve. The first was that his foot had relocated the gas pedal, and his car was gaining speed instead of slowing down for a turn. He had no control of that foot. The mental orders from his brain were being ignored. That was not his only issue. His left arm was also not responding to mental orders to get up onto the steering wheel so that he could use both hands to guide the Accord into the store lot.

His right hand still responded to his desires. When he was almost parallel to the convenient store, he used the working right hand to slam the wheel at a rude angle and sling shot into the lot. The tires squealed, and he violently bounced in his seat. The seat belt kept him from flying too far but the momentum freed his right foot from the accelerator and jammed it under the gas pedal. Again, milliseconds seemed to stretch for minutes as he observed the people in the lot and store twist their necks to look at the impending crash. The bullet of a car was in the lot headed towards the left-hand side of the store. Luckily no cars were parked in the furthest four parking spots in front of the store. He briefly wondered if the ice freezer at that corner would keep him from rocketing through the front window. He closed his eyes and let a silent scream escape his lips.

He heard a voice that had not touched his ears in twenty-one years. Cynthia seemed to be sitting right next him and calmly ordering him, *Put your foot on the brake.* He opened his eyes and jumped both feet onto the brake pedal. The Accord stopped with a resounding thud against the concrete parking block. He pin-balled back and forth in his seat belt for a moment. He quickly turned to the empty passenger seat and stared. The people in the store gawked for a moment longer, but since the event ended without violence and bloodshed, they quickly returned to their own lives. An elderly woman and a young girl continued to gaze intently at the Accord as they cautiously crossed the lot to the front door. When Greg made no sudden movement, they went inside and joined the others in forgetting about the unusual entrance he made.

Greg drew a deep breath and began to feel the cornucopia of emotions drain from his body. He thankfully recognized that he had regained full control of all of his limbs. He stretched his right foot and made exaggerated motions with his left hand. After a few moments he scratched serious medical ailments such as stroke and heart attack from the list of potential causes. He could feel sweat rolling down his back and legs while he wiped his brow with his hand. The perspiration made him feel uncomfortable but being uncomfortable was a thousand times better than he was a few minutes earlier. He opened the glove box and found napkins of various colors and sizes from a dozen different fast food restaurants. He toweled his forehead and face before moving onto his arms. His stomach had loosened from the sickening feeling. He marveled that nausea was being replaced by hunger pains. He sat back in his seat and asked out loud, "Cynthia, what am I doing here?"

He looked over to the passenger seat almost expecting an answer. When none came, he smirked and shook his head at his own folly. The first giggle came out as a snort. The second developed into a real laugh, and soon he was in a fit of uncontrolled guffaws. *This is so ridiculous,* he thought. *None of this is the least bit funny.*

The irony that the situation was not humorous launched him into a new wave of laughs, snorts, and tears. As the hilarity subsided, he grabbed a second group of napkins to wipe his face once again. He pulled down the visor and opened the vanity mirror hidden underneath. He stared into the face of a middle-aged man complete with crows-feet around his eyes and a large bulk of gray hair. He asked the image, "Greg, Ole Buddy, we are pushing forty-five years old. You are too old for this nonsense. She did not even give you an address. What makes you think that she is still at the same house? And do you really think you can find it after all of these years? Your sense of direction was never really good and back then you spent more time high than sober."

He paused and then scolded the reflection, "You really are an idiot. You did not even spend five minutes weighing the pros and cons. You opened that stupid card and within 48 hours you are back here. What the fuck is wrong with you?"

He watched his reflection exhibit the anger that matched the voice. He slammed the visor back into place and glanced out the passenger window. A very expecting mother and a toddler were passing a few feet from near his car to their own. The woman had a protective arm wrapped around the child and the other one across her voluminous belly as they stared at him. He realized that they had witnessed the outburst towards himself. The mother nervously shook her head and hurried the girl into her car seat.

Lady you have no idea how bat shit crazy I am to be back here in Remington, he grimaced to himself. *Ok, what am I going to do now?*

He sat in silent contemplation for several minutes. The focused, managerial side of his personality kicked into gear. He had not built a fairly successful career as a financial advisor over the past twenty years without carefully analyzing situations. He was not normally a risk taker. This little trip fell directly into the shaky category. The list of negatives quickly filled one side of the mental spread sheet.

He had no family or friends in the area. He moved to Sacramento over twenty years ago, and he never returned until today. As he sat in the Accord gazing through the front window, he searched his feelings and memories. The last two decades made him extremely analytical and he grasped that he never revisited his time with Cynthia. Their relationship was scorching, exhilarating, and dangerous. Then it ended like a flash from a roman candle. He also realized a very odd fact. He actually had to dig hard into his memory to recall the specifics of the break-up. Two decades have a way of washing away the fine details of an event, but he thought that more should jump to the forefront. The wounds should be healed, but the emotion and fire should still be able to be recalled in an instant. Instead he had vague recollections of an argument, and her throwing him out her house (by that time they were living together). He closed his eyes and strained for a moment longer before a bolt of reality and common sense struck him again.

He embarrassingly accepted the fact that he acted extremely rash after opening the card from her with an invitation to come visit. He instantly morphed into a completely different person. He fell into some kind of a spell the second he saw Cynthia's exaggerated "C" in her signature. The anger and laugher freed him from the trance. He quickly decided to ease the throttle of the current path of insanity. He knew that he was not going to try to find her house that afternoon.

The pragmatic side of himself offered a few counterpoints. He already dumped time and money on this trip. He understood that he needed more time to figure out this situation (and create more mental spread sheets). He decided that he should find a restaurant to grab an early dinner and a hotel to work out a new plan of action.

He picked up his phone and started the task of locating a nearby hotel. The app listed several places according to distance. He scrolled down the list looking for that perfect mix of cheapness without risk of sleeping with cockroaches. He found a brand name hotel that he hoped had a vacancy while simultaneously not break the bank. The map app indicated approximately four miles and eleven minutes from his current location. He hit the green go button to start the navigation and then performed a check of each mirror to before backing the car. Satisfied that no person or vehicle was behind or in a blind spot he grabbed the gearshift to put into reverse. As his eyes moved downwards to the shifter he momentarily focused on the squat, brick store through his front window.

He now noted details that escaped his attention earlier. The building was excessively decorated with spray paint and very little of the brick frontage was free of tags and ghetto art. The few square inches not tagged appeared grimy and stained. Cigarette and lottery adds covered all available window space which was also equipped with steel bars guarding the windows. The ice chest had several large dents (had others not stopped in time?) as well as the matching spray paint art. The trash cans posted on each side of the front door were free of spray paint, but rubbish was overflowing onto the ground. The aluminum sign on top of the store was battered and the blue and yellow colors were faded to resemble various shades of grey. He quickly assessed as a *dump in the poor section of town.* He cocked his head in an inquisitive manner as sense of Deja vu slowly crept upon him. He examined the store sign again and whispered the name out loud, "Fred's Market: Beer Groceries Lottery."

He thought, *I think I have been here before. I think it was called something else.*

Memories can sometimes be so very fragile. Some can be recalled with great ease and are concrete as the ground that one stands. Others require coaxing and teasing to bring out into light. For Greg nothing is as frustrating as having that specific word on the tip of his tongue, that answer that is just a second from popping into his head, or that memory that he knows only needs the slightest nudge. He furrowed his brow partly in concentration but mostly in anger.

Not only do I think I have been here, but for some reason I think I should remember this place more clearly, he urged his mental pathways. *This is fucking stupid. I think that I can envision the inside of this shit hole, but I cannot specifically remember being here.*

His hand was hovering above the gearshift for several seconds before he let it fall into his lap. He scratched an itch in his mind, but all he did was inflame a type of mental wound. A second voice in his head told him to let it go and drive to the hotel. A third voice originating from his phone was telling him to proceed to the highlighted route. He mentally told both of these intrusions to shut up. He closed his eyes and sank into his car seat. A knock on his driver door window broke his concentration.

Greg lowered the window and turned to face a pimply faced adult in baggy pants and a convenient store vest puffing on a cigarette, "Dude, my manager wants me to check on you. Every little thing crawls up her ass and you have been sitting here forever."

"I have only been here a few minutes," Greg responded. "I was getting directions from my phone."

"Well, you had your eyes shut long enough for me to smoke an entire cigarette. Bitch wanted me to bug you right away, but I waited till she went ballistic when I lit a second," the employee responded and grinned. "I didn't even want a second cigarette, but it was worth the level of anger she is in right now. I don't know why, but you are seriously fucking up her chi."

Greg started to question the length of time he sat with his eyes closed, then began to say something about the foul language, but in the end, he simply replied, "Ok. I will leave."

"Cool", the employee acknowledged. "Hey, you ever lived around here? She seemed to know you from somewhere, but I have worked here forever, and I have never seen you?"

Wonder what "forever" means to you, moron, Greg sarcastically thought. "Long time ago. Has your manager been here longer than twenty years?"

"She was here before the dinosaurs and Nirvana. She was here when this place was called something else," he replied.

Greg unthinkingly blurted, "Marco's.

"Yea, I think that is right," the kid responded as he dropped the cigarette and put it out with his foot.

Greg wondered if he was in store for another panic attack but somehow deep in his soul, he knew one wasn't going to hit him. Just the mere reconnection of memories with Cynthia sent him through a loop when he was driving. Yet now he felt perfectly calm as he gained a much clearer realization of the mystery of this convenient store. He grimly smiled as the horror flooded his memory. He put the car into drive and carefully backed away as the unrealized amnesia was ripped away. For some reason the fresh cuts did not surprise him. He made a left out of the store following his phones navigation voice and thought, *Yep, this is definitely the place. This is where the murder took place.*

Chapter 2: Hear my words…

Greg mindlessly mouthed the rest of the opening lyrics of the song as he pulled his toiletry bag from his suitcase.

She is on the edge.
If you don't pay attention,
She will end your life.

He momentarily paused to consider the words, shrugged his shoulders, and continued to softly sing "Danger Woman" along with the eighty's hair band, Rude Jones and the Manic Tide. He left his phone on the desk playing the Amazon Prime playlist as he walked into the bathroom. He quickly dropped all of his clothes onto the floor and stepped into the preheated shower. The shower noise drowned out most of Rude Jones's vocals. He stood in the shower, hands against the wall, and allowed the steamy water to wash over his head for several seconds. The music was completely masked as he began to think about the convenient store.

No not yet, he scolded himself. He blocked any serious contemplation throughout the drive to the hotel. He checked into a room, threw his suitcase on the bed and used Yelp! to help him find a restaurant. He tended to enjoy spicy Thai or Indian food whenever he traveled, but he opted for something more mundane (and less likely to cause more angst to his stomach). He found a diner a few miles away and enjoyed a quiet grilled chicken sandwich. He was still able to stiff arm terrible memories by focusing on recent work events. Before he returned to the hotel for the evening, he located a package store and picked up a twelve pack of Bud Light and threw in a couple of airplane bottles of Yukon Jack. The airplane bottles were a true spur of the moment buy. Yukon was one of his drinks of choice back in the Cynthia days and the small bottles in his hand felt like a throwback to a long-ago period. He also figured that it may be one of those nights, *so why not mix it with the past*.

As he returned through the lobby, the girl behind the desk made a point of calling him over to remind him that she was working all night long if he should need anything. He thanked her, noticed her youth and beauty for the first time, and headed to the elevator. He grimaced a little as he recalled their initial interaction. He sighed at the thought that she flirted with him. That was not a routine event in Greg's life. Women rarely hit on him since the breakup with Cynthia. The situation was completely reversed when they lived together. He could never explain it, but when they lived together females flocked to him. Not only did it seem that he had some secret magnetism, but this unnatural attraction emboldened the women. Several made it clear that they were interested in creating a Penthouse Forum story with him. He managed to push away memories of Cynthia's insane jealously until he sang out loud, "She will end your life" prior to his shower. Cynthia did not react well to the bold women that gave him attention at Castaways and the other dives he frequented. She often made him nervous during these near violent excursions with "the sluts".

He finished his shower, dried off, and put on a pair of loose running shorts and a faded Van Halen t-shirt. He turned off the music emanating from the phone. He opened a bottle of beer and one of the Yukon Jack bottles. He took a deep swallow of Yukon Jack and chased it with a swig of beer. He made a slightly twisted face and exclaimed out loud, "Did I really used to like this stuff?" He shrugged, finished the bottle of Yukon, and tossed it into the small trash can under the desk. He took another long swallow from his beer. He stood for a moment feeling a rush of warmth as the alcohol hit his system. He took another small sip from the beer, grabbed a pen and pad off the desk, and moved towards the bed. He sat on the bed with his back against the wall with pen and pad in hand.

"Ok," he flatly stated. *I am not going to talk to myself but Greg Ol Buddy, we are going to have a serious conversation about the events of this afternoon and the shit that happened twenty years ago.* He closed his eyes and concentrated on the night he and Cynthia broke up. He intended to jot notes while the memories surged into his brain like a tidal wave.

After a few seconds he opened his eyes. His mind was blank. He knew that a fight occurred, but he could not remember the details. *I feel like I have some sort of selective amnesia,* he grumbled. *Why am I just now realizing this? Only one answer. Everything always comes back to Cynthia. Three days ago I had big parts of my memories…not exactly gone but faded to the point of…well like just out of reach. I did not think about Cynthia, Remington or Marcos in any sort of detail in twenty years. Why, why, why?* He rubbed his head in frustration.

He sighed and continued, *who am I kidding? The curtains started to raise the minute I opened her card. I don't understand what is happening to me. My life is well, let's be honest, pretty dull and I never have a spur of the moment kind of event. I opened her card, read the hand-written invitation, and immediately took action to come see her. Today I suffered what I think was a panic attack. I never experienced anything like that in my life. I also have selective memory or targeted amnesia. Ok, what exactly do I remember? Maybe I can piece this together with the parts that are able to be recalled. Marcos seems like a good starting point. I am pretty sure that I went there after our fight…*

On a warm, dry summer afternoon in 1996, Greg stumbled down the long driveway of Cynthia's house. He punched the air and cursed as he weaved down the street, completely unconscious of where he was actually going. While his mind may not have consciously known the destination, his body was following a path he took many, many times in the two years he lived with Cynthia. At the end of the street he made a right turn still cursing under his breath. Two blocks later he was standing in front of Marcos and his mood instantly changed.

He did not purposely define Marcos as "home away from home", but he did spend an abnormal amount of time inside the convenient store. During the two years he lived with Cynthia he drove less and less. At first this was due to the fact that she would not allow him to drive her expensive sports cars. Internally he realized this was for the best because he was often in no condition to legally be behind the wheel. As time passed, he simply really did not have a need or even a want to drive. All of his needs, wants, and desires were being taken care of by Cynthia. She encouraged him to give up the apprenticeship. He gleefully jumped into unemployment with both feet. She was independently wealthy and had more than enough cash for the two of them. He never asked how she acquired her wealth or how she maintained it because he honestly did not care. Or as he often thought during that period, *really don't give a fuck.* Life was a grand fucking party. The only negative (besides her occasional frightening outbursts) was that they were NEVER separated. Marcos became the place to escape for more beer, cigarettes, lottery tickets, and the occasional burrito. He loved the life that was forged with Cynthia, but he also became bored. The trips to Marcos were a way of taking a break from her for a short period of time. He did not try to psychoanalyze the time he spent at Marcos. He just knew that he felt better after spending an hour or two at the store. If he was asked at the time if any of the employees in Marcos were his "friends", he would have laughed. In truth he had indeed befriended two of the employees.

Marcia Johnson was the manager of Marcos and Luke Ro was a full-time clerk. Marcia was in her late thirties, single, pudgy, pale and constantly grumpy. She really did not realize that deep in her soul she hated her life. She finished high school, but barely, so college was not going to be an option. She started working at Marcos when she was seven-teen. She began as a part time worker on nights and weekends. After high school she began working full time almost every day. She eagerly accepted a promotion to assistant manager at the age of twenty-two. She was still dating fairly frequently and was just promoted. At that time, she thought her life was on an upward trajectory. At twenty-nine she begrudgingly said yes to become the full-time manager. Each year she gained weight (which she hated) which caused undiagnosed depression, binge eating, and drinking. She went to the gym about once a month and could not understand how she continued to see her pants get tighter and tighter. She often said that genetics and life were not fair. Dates became fewer and fewer over the years and she had not been in a serious relationship in almost five years. She was not graced with natural beauty, but people often exclaimed how nice she "cleaned up". The problem was that by the time Greg started frequenting her store, she was not even trying. The kindest description of her on most days probably was that she looked unkempt. Greg did not notice nor care.

She literally swooned like a hormonal teenager the first time he spoke to her. His natural light heartedness combined with the illegal substances normally racing through his veins made being friendly to her very easy. He joked and was so at ease with her that she was completely disarmed. She grew to look forward to his visits to the store and a day without seeing him was by definition to her, "a bummer." She was still crabby most of the time and her life was unsatisfactory, but his visits momentarily brightened her. The other friend he made did not have an infatuation, but also eventually grew to enjoy Greg's routine visits.

Luke was only nineteen, loved his life, and hated his job. He was tall and lanky with a face marred by pimples and acne scars. His immediate family marked Caucasian on the census, but they all knew that one of the grandparents was Pilipino. Ironically, he did not consider himself Pilipino and often used racial slurs to describe the area's largest minority group. He had a very slight olive complexion, but he appeared much darker when standing next to the pale ghost that was Marcia.

His true calling was a musician in the vein of Pearl Jam. The problem was he could not sing nor play an instrument. He was through with high school (and likewise his high school decided it was through with Luke) when he was seven-teen. The job at Marcos was simply a way to get money. He still lived with his parents who were not overly thrilled with the living arrangements. Unfortunately for them they needed the income that Luke and his two older brothers brought into the house to make ends meet.

Luke was lazy, often rude to customers, and incompetent. His only redeemable work habit was that he actually showed up to work every day. Marcia learned early on that Luke could be depended upon to open the store at 6 AM, but his till was never right. She concluded the store was open, but he was not. She worried about shop lifting and loss of profit. When she shifted him to the afternoon and evening shifts, he came to work every day and the register also balanced correctly every day. She dealt with the frequent complaints from customers and understood that he was not going to accomplish anything except stand behind the register. Luke had no true ambitions and he continued to show up day after day. He could not think past tomorrow much less into the future. As much as he disliked the store and working, he actually appreciated his unambitious life.

He thought Marcia was a bitch and was completely befuddled when he watched the first interactions between Greg and her. Even though he was not fond of Marcia and the store, he was actually protective of the place that he despised. For the first dozen or so times that Greg was in the store Luke kept watching out of the corner of his eyes because he was positive that Greg was pulling some sort of scam.

Eventually the goofy jokes and laissez faire attitude on life won Luke over. He soon figured out that they both had an intense love of music and not an ounce of musical talent. When Greg wasn't innocently flirting with Marcia he was debating with Luke on the merits of Black Sabbath's first six albums, Nirvana's "Nevermind" vs Pearl Jam's "Ten", and why is Axl Rose destroying Guns n' Roses. They always talked about catching one of the big-time bands at the Key Arena or the King Dome, but Luke could not afford it and Greg was not reliable.

Luke also learned that Greg usually had some kind of illegal substance on him. Since money was not really a concern to Greg during those years, he willingly shared whatever he had in his pocket. Neither Greg nor Luke felt that this sharing was in any way one sided. He felt somewhat compelled to make small talk with Marcia, but he truly enjoyed the conversations with Luke. Regardless of his connection with each of them he clearly never imagined that he would hurt either of them.

Greg first peered into the glass door on that warm summer afternoon and did not immediately see any customers. He was pretty sure that this was Luke's shift, but he spent a few more seconds like a sneaky voyeur until he caught a glimpse of Luke lounging behind the register. Greg smiled as he thought, *Oh even better. Motherfucker is taking a snooze.*

He aggressively threw open the door and marched into the store like a triumphant gladiator. Luke broke from his nap with a startle. Greg assumed the posture of air guitar wielding rock star, took a step to an invisible microphone, and loudly snarled, "I am here to conquer, why do you doubt me?"

Luke jumped from his seat, leaned across the counter and continued the lyric by the metal band Pressurized, "I have all the answers, why do you question me?"

In unison they butchered the next few lines, "Jump onto my back, what could be better? Send your fears my way, who are you to judge?"

By this time Marcia broke out of the back room shouting and waving her hands, "Will you two knock it off. What have I said about doing that in the store?"

This was not the first time that they had given one of these impromptu performances. They both paused frozen in their air guitar postures. Greg smiled and quietly crooned, "My..."

Luke matched the volume and continued the chorus, "My way..."

Marcia wagged a finger at both of them, "I am warning you two."

They continued together becoming louder, "M-y....my way. M-y...my way is better!"

After the final lyric, they both fell into an exaggerated air guitar solo while wildly banging their heads up and down. Marcia could not help to feel both irritated and amused by the scene. She managed to stifle a smile as she curtly stated, "You guys are idiots."

Greg stopped in mid-swing of his invisible guitar and play pouted, "Idiot? You are hurting my feelings."

"Just please do not do those things in the store", she semi-apologized.

"Sure thing sweet cheeks," he beamed. He stepped around the counter and gave her a hug. "Hope your day is kicking ass."

He reached around Marcia's back to slap hands with Luke and said, "She treating you right today, bro?"

"You know it", Luke joked. "She is just a peach."

"Yea, yea I am peach. Greg, for the ten-thousandth time you cannot be behind the counter", she replied as she reluctantly pulled free from Greg's embrace.

He strolled around to the front and nonchalantly leaned against the counter. He asked, "How am I supposed to hug you when I come in when you are always behind the counter or in your office."

She did not want that to actually occur, but she put up a facade as she answered, "Well maybe you just won't be able to give me a hug."

"Oh crap on that", he replied. He snapped his finger and exclaimed, "Hey you know what? You usually eventually come out from your office like a rocket to check on something on a shelf. I will just wait till then and as you race by, I will just give your ass a little friendly smack."

"You will not do such a thing," she indignantly reacted. "Don't make me throw you out of the store." She turned on her heels and stormed back into her office. She wanted to appear as if the idea was revolting and beneath her, but in truth she felt her cheeks blossom in embarrassment. The thought of Greg touching her butt was wildly exciting.

She flopped down into her worn fake-leather chair and ran her fingers through her thinning hair. She could hear a conversation starting about last night's Mariner's game. Neither Greg nor Luke were sports fans, but the recent success of the Seattle's baseball drew in a few new fans including them. She herself rarely watched sports but she guessed by the animated discussion that Seattle must have won the game. She smiled as she overheard Greg describing the classic Ken Griffey Jr. home run swing. She pictured Greg in the middle of the store imitating Junior and thought about how his legs and waist would twist. She felt another rush of embarrassment. She jumped up and quickly headed out of her office.

What are you doing? she asked herself. *Don't fool yourself, you KNOW where are going.*

Greg and Luke barely noticed her as she left the office and headed to the back of the store. Her heart was racing in her chest and she thought that if either one of them asked her what she is doing that she would pass out. The twenty steps to the swinging door that marked the back of the store loomed forever far to her short legs. She burst through the door a lot harder than she intended and she hoped that no one noticed.

The back part of the side consisted of a relatively small storage area to the left with only a few shelves of store operating items such as spare coffee pots, register tape, mops and buckets. Straight ahead was a heavy, multi-locked back door which was currently shut with an illuminated red light above indicating that the security alarm was set for that door. Her destination was to the right.

She stepped into the bathroom, instantly noted the filthiness for the millionth time, pushed the door shut, and turned the lock. She often had trouble being able to pee because the room simply grossed her out. She vowed on a daily basis that she was going to make one of the employees come back and scrub it out, but some crisis always made her forget. Today she barely noted the grime.

She rapidly and impatiently fumbled with the button and zipper on her pants. She cursed until the pants were finally loosened. She normally did not want any part of her clothes touching the disgusting floor, so she usually only lowered her garments to her knees. She tugged both her pants and underwear all the way to her feet.

Have you lost your mind? she screamed inside her head. She looked down at her pants and panties and thought, *fuck it.* She sat on the toilet, reached down, and yanked her shoes off with a thud. She then pulled her clothes completely off and let them drop on the floor. She leaned back against the cold toilet tank and spread her legs.

Her mind protested again; *YOU HAVE NEVER DONE THIS BEFORE. WHY TODAY? FUCKING SNAP OUT OF IT. HAVE YOU LOST YOUR MIND?*

She ignored that part of her brain and let her hand ease down to touch herself between her legs. She felt slickness. She was able to note the irony that she was both shocked and not surprised. She was flabbergasted because she could not believe that she was about to masturbate at work. She was also not surprised to find how wet and ready she was at that moment. She was not a celibate woman, but the years of bad relationships and simple depression had rendered that part of her life pretty insignificant. If she asked point blank, she honestly could not recall the last time she experienced an orgasm.

She lightly circled her pleasure spot and instantly had her breath taken away. She had not experienced this type of pleasure in years. Her toes curled and unconsciously she lifted a leg and pushed it against the wall. She momentarily thought, *this will be a hell of a scene if one them came in right now.*

She stopped rubbing for a second to consider the idea of Greg actually seeing her in that compromising position. She opened her eyes and stared down at her exposed legs.

My legs are still not too bad, she thought. *They need to be shaved of course, but I bet Greg would love them. I think if he caught me like this that he would instantly want to fuck me.*

In her mind she imaged him opening the door and wordlessly removing his clothes. She usually did not have an active imagination, but today her senses were in overload. For a split second she almost felt that he was actually standing above her with a magnificent erection. He then kneeled to enter her. She closed her eyes and roughly inserted a finger into herself. As she built towards her climax the rational part of her pleaded one more time. *Ok you are going to go through with this, but YOU CANNOT YELL. SHUT YOUR FUCKING MOUTH.*

She was not known for being verbal or loud in the bedroom, but she recognized the wisdom being offered from her psyche. She clamped her mouth shut as a sound that she did not recognize begin to emanate from herself. She knew at that moment that she was about to experience the most intense orgasm of her life.

The climax racked her body several times over a period of twenty seconds, each orgasm more powerful than the previous. The last one did cause her to let out a small squeak. She understood she was actually in the middle of the most powerful orgasm of her entire life. Also at that exact moment she heard the first gun shot.

She instantly dropped her leg and sat up straight as an arrow. She sat holding her breathe for a few seconds wondering if she had indeed actually heard a gunshot. She counted to five, let out her breathe, and slowly leaned back against the toilet. Then two more gunshots rang in quick succession. She became instantly convinced that a shooting was occurring in the store.

If this happened any other day except today, she would have flipped the light off in the bathroom, sat in silence and fear, and prayed. Fright would have paralyzed her from taking any action much less do anything that could be considered rash or heroic. Later she wondered if some kind of left-over adrenaline was coursing through her veins. She also marveled at her next series of actions.

She leaped off the toilet to quickly grab her pants. She rapidly bent over and viciously smacked her head against the sink. She fell back stunned and angered at her own clumsiness. She held a hand against her forehead while she slowly kneeled to pick up pants. The corners of her eyesight grayed just for a second, but she shook the cobwebs away. She gazed into the mirror and saw the blood spilling between her fingers.

She thought, *Way to go dumbass.* She took her hand away from the wound to wrestle with tangled knot of panties and pants. She ripped the underwear away from the pants and tossed them away. She rammed first one leg and then a second into the pants. Blood was on her hands, rolling down her face, on her shirt, and now on her pants. She jammed her feet into her shoes while she buttoned the pants. She did not pause to pull up the zipper nor have her feet completely in the shoes. The back of the shoes flattened beneath the heels of her feet. She unlocked the door and raced into the store.

She had the same thoughts on a daily basis for the next several years. These included what exactly did she expect to do and why in the world did she leave the bathroom in the first place. Marcia gave up on the first part. No scenario that she ran through her mind ever made sense. After much deliberation and soul searching, she did arrive to a conclusion on the second question. While the two of them drove her nuts on a daily basis she was more than just fond of them. They had somehow infiltrated her defense systems. She would never go so far as to admit out loud that she loved the two of them, but she felt something deep inside of her in regard to her "idiots." She finally concluded with some embarrassment that some kind of mother instinct kicked into her blood. At the exact moment she ripped the door open she intended to save her boys.

She burst through the swinging door not knowing what lay on the other side. She actually closed within a few feet of the front counter when the scene suddenly came clear. She skidded to a stop and tried to speak. Only unintelligible and guttural sounds escaped her throat. She froze and was unable to move. Time seemed to be moving in slow motion. The shooter was standing over Luke's prone and bleeding body. She instantly knew that Luke was dead. The shooter took a slow step backward, shook his head, and turned towards Marcia. Marcia was finally able to use her vocal cords. She screamed the scream of the truly horrified. Tears instantly burst down her cheeks and she thought her vocal cords were literally being shredded by the intensity of her shriek. The shooter took two giant steps to close the gap between them. He violently swung the butt of a handgun and connected solidly on her temple. Her wild vocalizations instantly ceased as well as her consciousness. The last thought that ran through her mind before she collapsed to the floor was the same one that will cause her to have years of nightmares and sleepless nights. *Why did Greg just shoot Luke?*

Chapter 3:
Oooh that can't be real…

A few minutes after Luke was killed Greg was sitting on the curb in front of the store smoking a cigarette. He could hear the wail of sirens becoming louder and louder. He honestly wondered where they were headed. He also could not explain why he had the bluesmen JuJu Brown singing in his head. He closed his eyes and mumbled,

God sho me the way.
People tol' me doan you look off the path,
The snake guards tha secrets.
So run, run back to your house.

"PUT THE WEAPON ON THE GROUND. DO IT, DO IT NOW", a voice broke his trance. He saw that at least three police cars were parked at odd angles in the Marco's lot. The number of police officers that he could see probably numbered at least a dozen.

He slurred, "What is going on?"

So run, run back to your house.

"DON'T MAKE US TELL YOU AGAIN. PUT DOWN THE WEAPON FOR YOUR SAFETY", the nearest police officer ordered.

Nothing made sense to Greg. He weakly asked, "What?"

Run back to your house.

The directions coming from the cop became louder and more frenzied. Greg was stunned, scared, and confused about the instructions regarding a weapon.

He heard Cynthia's voice in his head, *The gun in your hand you rotten piece of shit.*

His left hand held a cigarette that was mostly ash. He glanced down to his lap and was horrified to discover a Ruger 9 mm handgun was held loosely by his right hand on the top of his right leg.

She commanded in his head, *Drop the gun or they will shoot you, you idiot.*

He quickly tossed the gun several feet in front of him. As the police swarmed to recover his weapon and to take him down, he did not hear Cynthia in his mind again but instead the clear warning of JuJu Brown,

Oooh…I warned you that snake is real.

Back in the present Greg ran not in the jungle but in the bathroom to the toilet. The chicken sandwich, Yukon Jack, and Bud Light all returned with a vengeance. He vomited two more times and dry heaved once. He flushed the commode and turned the cold-water handle on the sink. He cupped a small amount of water in his hand and lifted to his mouth. He swished the foul taste and spit back into the sink. He captured a second mouthful and this time slowly swallowed. He stood and stared at the wretch of a human being in the mirror wondering if the water would stay in his stomach. When he was pretty sure that he was not going to be immediately sick again he grabbed one the plastic wrapped paper cups from the sink. He ripped the plastic off and filled the cup with water. He took another small sip and stared back at the image in the mirror.

You look like shit, he thought. *You have dark spots under your eyes, your cheeks are sunken in, and*

your complexion is ghastly. You haven't looked this bad since your drug days.

He paused and continued, *Luke was killed, you were charged with his murder, and you spent time in jail awaiting the trial. How are these not vivid memories?*

He pondered such ideas as PTSD and suppressed memories. He had no formal education on psychology, but his gut told him that his symptoms did not match any mental illnesses currently in the books. He tried to follow a path of reasoning, but none of it made any sense to him. He did not know the "how's" but he could guess a very crazy reason for the "why's". Somehow and someway, Cynthia was the key.

He walked out of the bathroom and saw the pen and paper laying askew next to the bed. He picked up the pad, flipped the pages back to the front, and saw his poor handwriting all over the first two pages. The words were excessively large for the small sheets so only a few items in a list were on each sheet. The first page had four words, the first three were legible and read:

Marcos
Luke
Marcia

He tried to decipher the fourth scribbled word but could not. He did not recall actually writing anything. The idea of the list surprised him, but the actual content did not. He flipped the page, recognized the word on the top of the list, and flipped back to the bottom of the first page. He concluded they were the same word. He must have recognized his own chicken scratch was not useful and carried the thought to the top of the next page. The words, though, confused him. He read and spoke the fourth word aloud, "Sex?"

Why did I write that? He scanned the words on the second list looking for a connection. He read out loud,

Sex
Gun
Dead
Sally

Who the hell is Sally? And again, why the word sex? he searched in his head. He bent over to pick up the pen, scratched out the word Sally, and underneath wrote 'Patrick McCormick'. He put the cap back on the pen and thought, *ok that mystery is solved. Sally something was the public defender initially assigned to me. Mr. McCormick became my attorney for the trial. Ok, piece by piece this is slowly coming together. Might as well go down the path that sort of worked before and examine the things that are tangible. Like the interrogation. Wow, I can remember that evening real clear all of a sudden. Those guys were assholes.*

If one was ever going to break out from a daze the situation would have to be when you are roughly man-handled and literally tossed into the back of a police car. The trance that held him since he demonstrated his Ken Griffey Jr swing was completely erased. He still felt a little loopy because of the drugs, but that was a normal feeling for him. The spell he experienced was not. Feeling alert he sprang up in his seat. The closest police officer glared menacingly back at him. Greg shrunk down and cowered, but he kept his head raised enough to see out the window. The store was swarming with police officers, EMT personnel, and investigators. He watched Marcia gingerly walking out of the store with an EMT at each side and step into the back of an ambulance. He noted that she was shoeless. He thought that her lack of footwear was very odd.

Two cops entered the car and proceeded to drive him to the precinct. Throughout the drive they suggested that things would be way better for him if he just immediately told the investigators exactly what happened. They provided him several keen excuses such as Luke was fucking his woman, Luke stole from him, or that Luke owed him a bunch money for drugs. Greg quietly denied all of these ideas. They snapped at him and called him a liar. They found drugs in his pockets so according to them, the answers were crystal clear. They pulled into an underground entrance and delivered him to an administrative person who asked rote questions without once actually gazing in his direction. When finished the police officers roughly escorted him to one sour clerk after another. No one smiled during the bureaucratic process, and Greg supposed that was probably normal. At one point he requested to use the restroom. His request was soundly denied. After two hours he was unceremoniously dumped into a tiny room with two chairs and a table and told to wait. He asked again if he could use the restroom. The slamming door was his answer.

Greg understood that Luke was shot and killed. He also knew that he was holding a gun when the police found him sitting outside. He had no idea how he came to possess the gun. He never even fired a weapon much less owned one.

He remembered leaning against the counter talking to Luke. He vaguely recalled Marcia racing out of her office towards the back of the store. Luke was unable to catch the game the previous evening, so Greg stepped a few feet away from the counter and did his Griffey impersonation. They laughed and the conversation stalled as an elderly black gentleman entered the store and asked for a pack of Camel Lights. He then pulled out several scraps of paper with numbers scribbled haphazardly across them. These were the numbers he wanted for each of the various Lottery games. Greg witnessed this event enough times to know that Luke was going to be processing lottery tickets for several minutes. He left the counter and wondered down the store aisles looking at everything and nothing in particular. He bent over to grab a Twixt candy bar when he heard Cynthia's voice right behind him, *what are you doing?*

He turned to answer her and was stunned to see that she was not anywhere around him. He turned several times and peaked over the aisles, but he did not see her.

Do you know what she is doing in the bathroom right now? Cynthia hissed. This time the voice did not seem so much behind him as all around him at once. He looked toward the ceiling and shrugged. This was not the first time that he felt like she was inside his head talking to him, but this time was definitely the most intrusive.

She icily yelled in his head, *she is in the bathroom rubbing herself imagining that you are there with her.*

He mentally responded, *that is crazy.*

Somehow, he knew that the Cynthia in his head was telling the truth. He left her a short time ago in a complete rage, but he could feel that she was building up to an unprecedented new level.

I am glad I am here, he thought. *You are about to crack, and I don't need any more of that kind of shit today.*

Her voice was like venom as she commanded, *no you are not glad. I am the best fucking thing that has ever happened in your miserable life. You will leave that store right now and come home. This afternoon was bad enough, but I know you. You are getting ready to cross a line…again.*

What line? he asked.

You know what line, she screamed. *She is not one of those sluts. THEY actually serve a purpose for me, but Marcia does not. You will NOT fuck her.*

Fuck her, he gasped, somewhat revolted. *You are off your rocker. I would never…*

Suddenly a door appeared in his mind; not a figurative door but a literal wooden door. The door seemed to be standing upright directly in the center of his entire mental processes. Nothing else was visible but a solitary door. His consciousness was solely focused on that door and was completely absent from the reality of the Twixt bar, Luke, and the store.

He mentally studied the image a little closer. The door appeared to be heavy duty, weathered, and wooden. The entrance was not in a wall but simply standing free and clear of any other object. He was thoroughly paralyzed by the image and could not think about anything else at that moment. He was so perplexed on the reason for the door and why it would appear at that given moment. A distant female voice that he never heard before whispered, *she went too far this time and now you can see that you too have a door.*

He heard Cynthia yelling but as if she were a great distance from him. He could not make out her words, but he understood their intent. She wanted him to ignore the door and refocus on the Twixt bar that he held in his hand. The curiosity, though, was simply too strong. The Twixt bar was not nearly as tantalizing as this door in his mind. He wanted to open it and see the secrets on the other side but wasn't sure how to do it.

The pleasant voice returned, *just reach your hand out and turn the handle like any other door.*

What is on the other side? he asked.

I honestly do not know, the voice cooed. *Different for everyone.*

He was pleased to discover that grabbing the handle and turning were just as easy as opening the real thing. He turned the handle all the way but just before he actually opened the mental door, he queried, *who is this?*

He felt as if the voice was smiling as it replied, *my name is Sofia. I am Cynthia's mother.*

Interesting, he replied. He turned back and pushed the door wide open. He stepped through and found himself in,

A jungle. I am in mother fucking jungle, it is hot as shit, full of greenery and vines and I hear exotic birds and monkeys. What…in…the…FUCK?

The door in his mind was standing open behind him and only a few feet forward of him was another door. He instantly knew that he had to open that door too. He did not wait for confirmation from Cynthia's mother. He pushed that door open and was not surprised to see Marcia sitting on a toilet, naked from the waist down, one leg against the wall, and masturbating. He did not think about the situation. He quickly undressed and positioned himself above her. He wordlessly and gently entered her.

The position was awkward for him but as he slowly made love to her, he suddenly felt very compelled to make this all about her. Just two minutes prior he had reacted in disgust at the thought of being intimate with Marcia. Her nude appearance was as he expected and would not have normally been a turn on for him. At that moment he could not but help to feel an overwhelming rush as she gave herself completely to the experience. Her energy sparked something inside of him. He found himself incredible aroused, and he hoped that he did not finish before her (which was a new concern for him). He was amazed at how quickly and how utterly beautiful she was during her orgasm. As soon as she finished, he pulled out of her and stood. He still had a raging erection but was strangely compelled to not ruin the moment. This event was all about her. In that moment in time his body swarmed with positive emotions.

All of a sudden she jumped up as if something very wrong had occurred. He did not hear the gun shot, but he instinctively knew that something was actually very wrong in the store. He cocked his head as if he was receiving some kind of subliminal radar.

You need to get back before it is too late, Sofia lightly whispered. He saw Marcia scrambling to grab her clothes. He did the same and vaulted through the door into the jungle.

He expected the door to his mind and back to his conscious body to be the original few feet away from the bathroom. He was shocked to see the door was now down a tangled path at least two city blocks away. He was lazy, out of shape, and still pretty stoned, but he knew he had to try to run. The undergrowth grabbed at his legs and slowed his already miserable effort. The path seemed to be collapsing on either side as the jungle retook the vacant ground. The little light that originally pierced through the thick green and black was also diminishing at an alarming rate.

He caught the fleeting glimpse of something racing past him to his left. The same thing occurred again and then several times to his right. Menacing yellow eyes appeared and disappeared just at the edge of the shrinking path. He continued to stumble and run despite his exhaustion. He was truly frightened. He wondered what would happen if he did not make it back to the door.

What have I got myself into? Is this some kind of fucked up dream or bad trip? FUCK THIS. I need to get to that cock sucking door.

The door was closer, but he still had a solid twenty yards to clear when a root snagged his ankle. He tripped hard, and he made no effort whatsoever to break his fall. He landed face first with a resounding thud. His breath was momentarily knocked out of him. He rationalized that the current moment in time was not a good time to pity himself and moan at a few bumps and bruises. He knew he had to keep fighting back to the door. He took only a second to catch his breath, shake his head, and attempt to rise.

When he lifted his head, he found himself face to face with an obscenely large snake. His entire vision was blocked by copper scales and softball sized black eyes. The total immensity of the beast was difficult to estimate, but the head alone was larger than his own and the visible portion coiled around the head must have weighed hundreds of pounds. A footlong tongue slowly licked into the air a few inches from his face. He instinctively flattened himself back to the ground. He held his breath and nervously kept his eyes locked on the monster. The thing slowly turned its head left and right as if it was locking in on a bearing. The snake then seemed to focus on Greg and became extremely still. The cold black eyes seemed to bear down directly onto Greg and probe his thoughts.

He heard Sofia shriek, *be gone.*

The snake slightly turned in the direction of the voice, flicked the searching tongue a few more times, and then turn back towards Greg. The head slowly raised a few feet above his prone body into a classic attack posture. Greg swore the monster was actually smiling at him.

I said BE GONE, Sofia thunderously ordered.

The thing seemed torn between striking Greg or following the command. The tongue licked the air a few more times before slowly backing away from the almost non-existent path. The jungle seemed to swallow the giant beast in just a few seconds.

You must hurry and fight your way the last few yards, Sofia soothed. *Follow my voice.*

He jumped to his feet and commenced tearing, ripping, and pushing his way in the direction of the voice. For every vine he broke, two more seemed to grow and grab a limb. He was making slow progress, but his lifestyle was tipping the scale in the jungles' favor. *This place is alive and wants to swallow me,* he thought. *What have I done?*

He was yelling, crying, and on the brink of losing his mind when he fell against the door. He pulled it open and passed out as he fell onto the other side.

He awoke just a few moments later feeling completely wiped and groggy. He was not laying on the ground in the jungle or standing in the store. He was sitting outside smoking a cigarette. He did not remember stepping outside for a smoke and the images of doors and jungles were rapidly fading.

He thought, *What about a jungle? Seems like…*

He then heard sirens screaming in the distance. He again wondered why he was outside and then he became curious about the cause of all the commotion. Sounded like the entire police department was racing through the city. He exhaled a long stream of smoke out of the corner of his mouth and softly sang, "Ooh that can't be real…"

Several hours later two detectives entered the interrogation room and introduced themselves to Greg as Hanson and McCovey. Detective Hanson sat down, dropped a folder of papers and pulled out a tiny tape recorder. McCovey leaned back against the door and crossed his arms across his chest.

Hanson turned on the recorder and began, "My name is Detective Hanson of the Remington police department. It is 10:10 PM on June 10th, 1996. I have in the room Detective McCovey and a Mr. Gregory Palmer. Detective McCovey will you please acknowledge so that the voice is recognized on the tape?"

McCovey, "This is McCovey of the Remington murder task force."

Hanson looked pointed at Greg, "And Mr. Palmer."

Greg responded, "I really have to use the bathroom."

Greg watched as Hanson and McCovey play the role of good cop and bad cop for the next several minutes. Hanson acting as Greg's ally appeared to calm McCovey and get him to agree to start over in ten minutes after Greg used the restroom. Hanson guided him to small bathroom just a few feet from the interrogation room and winked, "Don't let McCovey upset you. He just gets cranky at the end of a long shift."

Greg acknowledged, "I will keep that in mind and thanks for letting me go to the bathroom."

"Don't mention it kid," Hanson soothed. "This will be over in short order."

Back in the interrogation room, the event was anything but over in short order. The procedure started smoothly as Hanson reminded Greg of his legal rights and inquired if Greg was willing to talk to them. He quickly nodded and verbally agreed. The two investigators gave each other a quick mental high five, and Hanson proceeded. The first question was for him to simply state his name, but the second question started the derailment.

"Please state your address for the record", Hanson absent-mindedly asked. He was deep in contemplation on the series of questions he would ask that he hoped would lead Greg to confess and quickly end the interrogation.

Greg meekly responded, “I really don't know.”

Hanson broke from his train of thought to sharply ask, “Are you fucking with me? How can you not know your address? Are you stupid or something?”

Greg responded with some indignation, “No, I am not stupid. I moved in with my girlfriend and I know where I live. I just don't remember the exact address.”

McCovey gruffly stated, “That is a thin excuse. I hope you are not playing games.”

Hanson continued, “Ok, you recently moved into her place and you don't know the correct address.”

Greg stammered, “Well it was two years ago.”

Both McCovey and Hanson responded with a string of expletives and accusations. After several minutes of brow beating, Hanson asked, “Ok, humor me. Describe where you live. How do you get home from work?”

“Well I am unemployed,” Greg began. “But I can tell you that you turn off Pleasant Avenue onto an alley. She has the only house on that alley.”

The two cops took a moment of contemplation, looked at each other, and then began berating Greg again. According to them they had worked in this city for over twenty years combined and they had no idea about ‘an alley off of Pleasant Avenue’. Greg remained silent throughout and did not try to defend himself. He walked that alley a thousand times to and from Marcos since he moved into Cynthia’s house. He actually thought the cops were stupid for not knowing about it.

After a few more minutes Hanson calmed down McCovey and began the actual meat of the interview. For over three hours the interrogators and Greg had a circle conversation over three specific points. Greg flatly denied that he killed Greg and he had no idea how he came to process the gun in his hand. Hanson thought he was moving in the right direction with the third point which was that Greg admitted that he hit Marcia in the head with the weapon.

"You admit striking Ms. Johnson in the temple with the murder weapon, but you deny shooting Mr. Ro?" Hanson sarcastically asked.

"I don't know if it was the murder weapon. I don't know who shot Luke and with what gun. I did, though, hit Marcia with a gun," Greg admitted again.

"That makes absolutely zero sense," Hanson frustratingly exclaimed. "I don't know how you can make those statements. I don't know why you are making this so difficult."

"I remember hitting Marcia. I was getting a Twixt bar when Luke was shot. When I ran to the counter, he was lying on the ground bleeding…", Greg started to choke up.

Neither interrogator had any sympathy for Greg. His anguish was genuine as was his testimony. He admitted to knocking Marcia out because he clearly remembered that part. He did not recognize that he hit her with *a gun* until he was outside. He was completely forthright when he stated that he had no idea why he did it. He remembered the action but not the reason. They repeatedly try to circle back and connect the gun in his hand to the shooting. In Greg's mind he was being completely truthful because he was in the candy aisle when the shots occurred. By the time he ran to the counter Luke was already dead, and in his version the real killer was already gone. He was convinced that he told the truth and nothing but the truth.

The interview eventually ended. He later met his young and inexperienced public defender. She was going to fail not so much because of her weak abilities, but more from a lack of effort. Deep inside she felt that this was an open and shut guilty verdict. Outwardly she began the prep work to fight for her client, but subconsciously she was not (nor would she) truly give forth the effort needed to give her client a fighting chance.

He faced a judge to announce his pledge of innocence. His bail was set at a million dollars. He had no assets nor family, so he was escorted to jail. He wondered only briefly if Cynthia would arrive and post bail. He soon, though, did not have time to think about Cynthia because he was about to experience a new type of horror.

Chapter 4:
A puppet in hell…

In the summer between elementary school and junior high Greg's family moved to Remington from Tacoma. The main reason was a job opportunity for Greg's father. His parents believed a secondary benefit was that he would have a better experience in a smaller community school. He was not particular distraught about moving because he had difficulty making friends throughout elementary school. He was excessively shy and somewhat awkward. The few friends he did have were not particularly close to him. His parents told him that moving to a new school district when he was starting junior high would be beneficial to him because as they explained, "all the kids will be new at the same time." He quickly learned that they were not exactly correct.

His first few months were not really horrible or exceptionally difficult. He liked the school as a whole and was pretty happy with all of his teachers. He was not tormented or bullied; if anything, he experienced just the opposite. Often he felt as if no one under the age of 25 noticed him. His classmates never gave him a hard time, but they also never included him in their gossip, their jokes, or their tables at lunch. He stayed quiet and made the best of the situation. He probably could have achieved a higher level of satisfaction if it were not for his parents asking on a frequent basis if he had made any new friends yet.

Josh Walters entered Remington Junior High just after Halloween that first year. He walked into Greg's English class completely decked in denim from his pants to his denim jacket that was covered in rock band patches. A brightly colored Iron Maiden the Trooper t-shirt was visible underneath the jacket. He had a red flannel bandanna tied around his leg and fingerless gloves on both hands. His high tops were not tied, and he more or less slid his feet along vice actually walking. He had shockingly long (and greasy) hair that fell to the middle of his back and the beginning of a cheesy teenage mustache. He looked to Greg like the Webster's definition of a "burn-out" which was a social class in the school that he avoided. Josh, though, was not interested in making friends with other burnouts. Greg never asked what motivated Josh to join him on that first day at lunch, but they shared lunch together every day for duration of Josh's enrollment in Remington Junior High.

They bonded together over their mutual love of eighties metal music. Josh was able to pull Greg out of shell just a little bit and soon Greg was sporting (to the horror of his parents) an extensive collection of rock and metal band t-shirts. They constantly attempted to one up each other to be the first one to discover that new, next big thing. The band or song did not always have to be "new" either. Discovering a classic sixties or seventies song or band on MTV's Classic Vault also counted. They hung out and watched videos, listened to albums together, and talked about girls and their future.

The time that they spent together was almost always at Greg's house. Stating that Josh's family was dysfunctional was an extreme understatement. Josh was not interested in exposing Greg to the daily circus and Greg's parents were familiar with the issues in Josh's family. Greg never asked many questions and Josh volunteered virtually nothing. At the end of their sophomore year of high school, the family life finally came to boil. Josh was sent to Texas to live with an alcoholic grandfather. Even at that age Greg had enough world smarts to detect that the recent events in Remington must be pretty severe for the Texas plan to be a viable alternative. Josh literally had five minutes over the phone to tell Greg that he was moving to Texas. He promised to keep in touch. He called Greg one time and they had an awkward ten-minute conversation. Greg could hear the Grandfather bitching the entire time about the cost of a long-distance call. Greg wrote Josh's new phone number down and promised to call so that his Grandpa would not have to pay for a long-distance call. A few weeks later Greg called and found the number was no longer in service. Josh never called Greg again.

Greg never knew that Josh died in car crash during his junior year in high school. He was drunk and high and doing over 90 mph when he lost control of his car. The vehicle rolled and flipped several times before coming to rest on the car's roof with a resounding and sickening thud. Witnesses went running to the car to see if any one survived. The car was dead along with the driver, though a boom box strapped in the back seat was somehow still intact and blasting out harsh metal music. The rural and very conservative Christian rescuers were extremely at ease with the violent rantings of the thrash band Sadistic Arch emanating from the back seat.

Greg's and Josh's taste in music crossed in a thousand instances. The one place that they were one-eighty apart was the dark thrashers Sadistic Arch. They took turns picking albums and Josh more times than not opted for a Sadistic Arch album. Greg sulked that he did not understand the extreme melodies, violent lyrics, or harsh vocals. He wasn't even too fond of the ghastly album covers. Josh would hype the song or album and continuously quote the same Hit Parader article that said that Sadistic Arch's *Unholy Church* was "the soundtrack of hell". That idea thrilled Josh but made Greg uncomfortable. He wasn't sure if the urban myth that the lyrics to every Sadistic Arch song were written in human blood was real or not. He was not raised in exceptionally religious family, but he attended enough church as a kid to be unnerved by the whole Sadistic Arch experience. They listened to *Unholy Church* dozens of times, but once Josh moved Greg never listened to that album alone again. Or more specifically he did not actually put on an album on a turn table or a tape into a player. He did, though, hear the songs and lyrics loud and clear on a frequent basis during his incarceration.

More specifically, Greg heard lots of lyrics during that period, but they were not from a radio or a tape player. These songs were in his head and they pounded his senses ruthlessly. He normally loved the fast and aggressive rhythms of the eighties metal, the classic riffs of the legends of the sixties and seventies, and the slow melodic tones of early nineties grunge scene. He, though, did not care for any kind of music when he could not sleep, was going through detox, and close to losing his mind.

He often marked memories of his life with an album or a song. He could hear a riff or a lyric and be instantly transported to a time and place. Most of these memories were fairly pleasant; or at a minimum, not traumatic. This trait of his personality was something that he carried for his entire life. The only time his music let him down was during his time in jail.

The first night in jail he desperately tried not to think about Cynthia, but that task was next to impossible. They were together on a daily basis for two straight years so simply closing his eyes and hoping to close his mind to her was not an option. At first he experienced anger because he blamed her for his present predicament. Within an hour that emotion softened, and he soon began to truly miss her. Right before he was about to drift asleep, the song "I Got You Babe" by Sonny and Cher popped into head. The seventies anthem by the television couple was not one of Greg's particular favorite, but he smiled at the sappy lyrics that danced in his mind.

Faster than a blink of an eye the song changed into something horrific. The words and melody were the same, but the vocals were replaced with violent shrills. Sonny and Cher now sounded as if they were murdering each other. Greg's eyes slammed open, he sat up, and he exclaimed out loud, "What the fuck is that?" The song stopped mid-screech.

The radio in his head turned on and off at random intervals all day and night long. Some of the songs were his favorites while others were ones that he heard only once or twice before on the radio or MTV. Often a crystal-clear verse or chorus was transmitted into his head for short thirty second increments. Often the volume was low, or at least started at a minimum. These specific events were unusual but not especially disturbing.

When he was feeling especially sick or tired the music would literally blast and bring him to his knees. He loved listening to music, but his favorite songs often paralyzed him when they entered his mind with the volume knob at eleven. Most songs were not distorted, just simply loud. The initial shock wore off pretty quick. He stumbled back onto his bed and waited it out. These events were annoying but not especially painful.

The lyrics that caused him physical discomfort were the ones that suddenly and without warning became distorted like the Sonny and Cher song. These shifts were random and never the same twice. The noise penetrated his senses like nails on a chalkboard and continued to deteriorate to tone of pure agony. He could not explain afterwards but when these wild renderings happened to familiar songs, he became gripped with fright. He could not exactly comprehend the reason, but he felt that the twisting of something very familiar into something else was the epitome of evil. His reality was already in a fragile state and these grotesque incursions into his mind were breaking down his loose grip on reality. As much as hated these events they were not the worst.

He knew he was in for nearly four minutes of the most abstract physical and mental torture when he heard the low strum of single violent note, a distant rumble of drums, a moment of silence, and then a fantastic explosion, Sadistic Arch's "Satanic Tornado" was being cued up. He often jumped up and ran around his cell looking for somewhere to hide. If anyone observed Greg during these instances, they would have labeled him as insane. He frantically searched for a way out but once the driving guitars and drums started for the opening lyrics, he understood that he was truly trapped. The opening line defined his life at that moment...

Puppet in hell,

He had no control of his life or his mind at these moments. He constantly told himself afterwards that it is just a song. He scolded himself that he was letting the words have too much meaning and causing imagined pain. The end of each lyric brought a bolt of searing pain that started in his head and seemed to race down to his limbs. Song lyrics do not cause physical harm in the "real" world. But of course, the situation he experienced since he reached for a Twixt bar in Marco's just didn't seem real. His reality was that like a puppet in a charade. He was,

An actor in the unreality

simply waiting for the curtain to rise and shine light on this fake reality. He cursed Cynthia and

Contemplating demise

wanted this all to end. He was clearly suffering from the DT's, but no one in the jail seemed to notice. As matter of fact he often felt that no one truly remembered he was in that cell until his lawyer came for one of his very infrequent visits. Besides the real pain he was suffering from the withdrawals, he was certain that someone (Cynthia) held a voodoo doll in his image. He wished

Denying existence

that he never touched drugs or met Cynthia. The rest of the song continued in this vein with every lyric seemingly touching his life and continuing to shoot a blast of physical pain throughout his body. He crawled on the ground, drooling, and begging for the release. After the second time he heard "Satanic Tornado" in his head, he knew exactly what to expect. He wanted to be released from his cell, released from the torture of the DT's, released from the hex of Cynthia and most of all, simply released from his life. He knew from experience that the end of the song was the worst. If a weapon somehow suddenly appeared in his cell when this song was crucifying him, he would not hesitate.

As winds began blowing in his cell (*this is not real, a storm is not building in my cell)* and blow his minimal belongings around the cell, he prayed for an end. The build-up for the climax of "Satanic Tornado" was always momentarily paused. The air in the cell seemed to instantly become still, the music ceased on a dime, and the storm clouds froze in mid-crash. The words *FUCK YOU* always then pounded into his head as hard as if he actually was struck with hammer. The frozen time restored with vengeful crescendo and

Satanic tornado

the twister formed inside the cell

Replete with the whore's blood

and tossed him into the corner and spun blood throughout the cell. He struggled to hold his hands up and cover his head. The force of the winds was deafening and took his breath from him. The spinning blood covered him in wetness and gore. He attempted to wipe his eyes with blood covered hands. If he did not keep his face toward the wall, the blood blasted into his nose and mouth and choked him with the vileness. He kept his head down and covered it with his arms, crouched in the corner, and cried. He often heard phrases such as *GOOD!! YOU BROKE MY HEART, YOU BASTARD.*

The horror on earth is pre-meditated

YOU FORCED ME ONTO THIS PATH AND NOW IT CAN'T BE STOPPED.

The puppet is crushed,
Behold! The satanic tornado

For exactly the next fifty-nine seconds his entire body was exposed to the most excruciating pain as the song spiraled out of control towards "the soundtrack of hell." Every part of his body tensed as if being shocked with thousands of volts of electricity. His agony was so intense that he was unable to articulate a sound, though tears and snot flowed freely upon his face. He was no longer praying because his mind was simply unable to try to process a single other thought. He had to ride it out. When the last note abruptly crashed and turned into a thunderclap, he was released from the vision (for now).

All sounds and all illusions of blood and the twister instantly vanished. His body and cell were dry of blood, though he was always wet from sweat and he frequently urinated on himself. The pain also ceased but he was left with a tingling sensation throughout his body. He was physically sapped of strength and to climb onto his bed required great effort. He often napped for a few hours immediately after the "Satanic Tornado" experience. When he awoke, he felt as if he had been involved in a serious car accident. He also felt disgusting from the sweat and piss that now soiled his bed sheets. He sighed with relief because he knew (at least he thought he knew) that he would not hear that particular song for a few days. He hoped that someday the music would just stop. When the nightmares, visions, and mental radio songs did stop, he was sure that his lawyer had something to do with it.

About a week into his jail time while waiting for his trial, he experienced a particular bad day. The music was incessant and the pain unrelenting. He was lying on the floor of his cell in the fetal position when the guards roughly grabbed and escorted him to a small room. They hand cuffed his hands to metal rings on the table. He wearily waited and actually started to doze when Patrick McCormick entered the room and into his life with an air of distaste. The lawyer quickly scanned Greg over, swung an expensive leather brief case onto the table, sat down across from him, and abruptly stated, "You look horrible."

McCormick opened the brief case and brought out a manilla envelope full of papers. He briefly glanced in Greg's direction and proceeded to read through the documents. Greg was unaware that

McCormick was hired to be his lawyer. He waited a few seconds assuming that the man was going introduce himself, but he soon realized that the stranger was completely absorbed in the paperwork. This gave Greg time to study and ponder his unusual visitor. Even though he still felt quite ill, the man stirred his curiosity and stemmed some of the nausea.

Greg never actually saw an expensive hand-made suit up close, but he knew he was looking at one now. The man in the suit was roughly in his early fifties, fairly handsome with a short crew-cut haircut. The short hair was peppered with distinguished gray. Both hands appeared well manicured and his left wrist was sporting a Rolex watch. He reached inside his suit jacket and produced a Cartier pen. Greg had absolutely no clue the true value of the pen in McCormick's hand, but as he watched him scribe a few notes with the device, he assumed that it must be very expensive. His eyes glanced away from the pen to the actual notes that were being created. The lawyer continued unabated for a few more minutes when he noticed Greg was attempting to read them upside down. He stopped writing, put the pen down, and bluntly asked, "Can I help you?'

Greg chuckled and said, "I don't know. Who are you? Why am I here?"

"Mr. Palmer, my name is Patrick McCormick. I have been hired to represent you with your current legal situation," he responded impatiently. "The first rule you will follow as my client is that my notes are my notes. Second rule is you will never talk to anyone else about your case except for me. Third and last rule for today is that my time is extraordinarily valuable so you will not waste it by asking me stupid questions and you will answer my questions as succinctly but as accurate as possible. Do you understand?"

Greg flatly answered, “Yes.” He started to ask a question but recalled the rules. He quickly snapped his mouth shut.

Patrick sighed and waved an impatient hand, “Go ahead. Ask your question, though it may be a waste of my time.”

“Who hired you? I am assuming that you not working pro bono,” he quickly asked taking advantage of the opportunity.

“Mr. Palmer, I do not want to come across as egoistical, but the fact is I am the most expensive lawyer on this side of the state. The person who is paying for my services is both wealthy and discrete. I am not at liberty to disclose your benefactor,” he responded. “May I continue with this review.”

Greg nodded affirmative and McCormick refocused on the papers in front of him. He gazed at Greg while jotting another note. He assessed that Greg was not paying any attention to the words on the paper for he was lost in another world.

Only Cynthia had the assets to hire someone of Mr. McCormick’s stature. The overwhelming question was, *Why?* All of his tangible physical needs for the previous two years were a non-issue for Greg. While most people worked and struggled to have a roof over their heads, the lights on, and food on the table, Greg never thought about these things since the night she asked him to go home with her. Besides the necessities, money was always at his fingertips for drugs and all other forms of leisure. Despite the positives of being with Cynthia, his knew that his life was on an out of control roller coaster always on the verge of jumping the rails. The ride that he called his life was currently way off the tracks. He foresaw a fiery crash looming directly below him. He quickly assumed that Mr. McCormick was really good and that his arguments could plant a small seed of doubt in a jury.

He surmised, though, that even Mr. McCormick could not disrupt the laws of physics; and hence, gravity was going to carry his roller coaster car straight into the ground.

He witnessed many unusual things living with Cynthia. These events seemed to disobey the laws of physics and the natural world. Early in their relationship he excitedly pointed them out to her. She responded in a motherly fashion assuring him that he was quite mistaken. She first denied and then convinced him that the things he witnessed were of the chemical inducement variety vice the supernatural. The drugs and sex were too good to truly force the issue, so these incidents were always soon forgotten. Deep in his mind he kept track of these oddities on a list that he stored in a secret mental filing cabinet. He cautiously approached this cabinet with an idea of dusting off the list and attempting to see if a possibility exists, no matter how minuscule, that Cynthia and Mr. McCormick could stop this ride. He broke from his daydream by the irritated and loud voice of his lawyer.

"Hello, Mr. Palmer, can I have your attention," said McCormick. "I need to ask a few questions to clarify a few points in my mind about the police report."

He broke from his trance and meekly said, "Ok."

For the next several minutes the lawyer and his client replayed the same circle conversation that the suspect and the interrogators already danced. The lawyer, though, did not become angry but simply asked the same question three different ways. He furiously penned notes as Greg answered each question with the exact same words. Greg grew frustrated but McCormick did not. He finally set the outrageously expensive pen across the notes and sat back in contemplation.

After a few minutes he leaned forward and stated, "I am going to be upfront with you Mr. Palmer.

This is going to a difficult case. I have a lot of work to do between now and the trial. I will be back after I have a plan of action. In the meantime, can I do anything for you?"

Greg shrugged his shoulders and unthinkingly replied, "Well, the food is horrible."

McCormick carefully placed each sheet of paper into a neat pile that was deposited into a manilla envelope. He slid the envelope in between several other similar folders in his brief case and slammed the brief case shut. As he stood to leave, he replied in a non-comital manner, "I will see what I can do."

A week passed before Greg recognized that his meal quality was indeed improved. Greg kept this information in the back of his mind during his lawyer's second visit to the jail. When McCormick again off-handedly inquired if Greg needed anything, Greg hopefully responded, "Well, I know this is a jail and not a Hilton, but the mattress and bedding are extraordinarily worn and disgusting."

McCormick again made no promises, but within a few days Greg had the newest and nicest bed in the entire jail. Greg was on the other side of weening from the drugs, and so on some nights he was actually able to sleep. That is until the radio randomly turned on. At the end of the third visit, Greg tentatively stated, "The radio is loud and keeps me awake." Greg prayed that McCormick would not ask any questions to specify which radio. His prayers were answered by his lawyer's nonchalant acknowledgement without further clarification. Two days later the evil radio in his head turned off for good.

Chapter 5:
The change in the mirror…

While shaving the next morning (in the present) Greg considered the events of the previous day and night. He relived an abundance of suppressed memories. He took the first downward strokes of his razor removing shaving cream and stubble. Several pieces fell into place over the course of the night, but he could see that many were still missing. He thought about his time in jail as he worked the razor first with the gain and then slowly against the grain. He used his hand to feel for any stragglers, quickly swiped those and then rinsed his face of the remaining shaving cream.

He stared hard into the mirror of the man looking back at him. He had aged gracefully but aged nonetheless since the last time he saw Cynthia. The previous night he thought that he looked pretty rough, but a night of awareness and good rest refreshed his psyche and restored his vigor. He slowly reached for a towel, dried his face, and snagged a tag of shaving cream trapped near his left ear. He absentmindedly dropped the towel onto the floor while thinking about which shirt he was going to wear and humming the song "Reflecting…" by the sixties psychedelic band the Driver Inn. As he silently mouthed the opening lyrics he drifted to the day of his verdict.

His lawyer provided him with a tailored suit and all the required accessories. The actual trial did not have the twists and turns that one sees on television dramas. Since the radio in his head was off and he was free of the influence of illegal substances, he was able to truly focus. He imagined the trial dozens of times in his head before he walked into court that first day. Most of the nuances, procedures, and the people were not as he invented in his head, but the essence of the arguments was pretty close. Mr. McCormick instructed him to maintain focus on the witnesses and prosecuting attorneys and to avoid scanning the jury or the extra people in the chamber. He followed his lawyer's instructions and kept a mental score. He calculated that he was losing by a significant margin.

He adjusted his tie and stared hard into the mirror. The closing arguments were today and then the jury would formally begin to determine his guilt or innocence. He could possibly know his fate before the end of the day if they returned a quick verdict. The man that looked at him was not the same one that entered jail on day one. He actually thought he looked pretty good for once in his life. He took a step back from the small vanity mirror and began to lightly sing," the change in the mirror, makes the path become clearer."

I think I have aged ten years since I was arrested, but somehow, I look better, he thought. *I am free of drugs and alcohol for the first time in a long time. I feel more focused…my path is clearer. Too bad all the goodness is going to be behind bars for a long time.*

I lost so many years,
But the future can soothe these fears.

Besides purging the poison from his body, he also bled the essence of Cynthia from his mind. Slowly day by day he thought about her less and less. For months he envisioned being released and heading straight back to the alley off Pleasant Avenue. He grew to contemplate a future where she simply was not a part. He did not think about confronting her and having "closure". Instead his new life would take place somewhere far away and without her.

For the first time in several weeks he gave her serious thought. *No,* he confidently stated in his mind, *the past is indeed gone. I loved her. The relationship was warped but I loved her. The years, as Driver Inn says, were lost.*

The closing arguments were just as dull as the rest of the trial. Greg was satisfied that his lawyer did the best he could considering the circumstances. Most of the defense was based on no actual witnesses or gun powder residue on Greg's hands. Good fortune smiled on Greg as the store recording system failed to reset at midnight the previous night resulting in no surveillance footage for that entire day. Greg felt the defense was thin at best, but as the jury was whisked away, he estimated that he had at least a tiny chance of walking out a free man. The day he was arrested he estimated his chances as zero, so a minuscule chance was better than none. McCormick and Greg were escorted to a back room by a uniformed police officer.

"Settle in," McCormick directed. "I think we have raised questions to a few of the jury members, so this is going to take some time."

Greg nodded in acknowledgement and then the lawyer turned to the police officer, "I need to make a few calls and check on a few things."

The police officer also silently nodded and gave Greg a harsh gaze. Greg assumed that the cop did not accept their defense. Greg turned away and wondered how he was going to pass the time. Before long he drifted into a dreamless nap that was rudely broken up by the police officer "accidentally" kicking his seat. Greg looked down at the watch (also provided by McCormick) and saw that almost 40 minutes passed since he was escorted into the room. *What do I do with the rest of the afternoon?* he wondered.

He did not have to wait all afternoon as his lawyer excitedly rushed back into the room and announced, “The verdict is in already.”

Greg blanched and meekly asked, “What does that mean?”

McCormick stared into space a few minutes before answering, “I was hoping for a longer deliberation.”

The door opened and a clerk whispered to the police officer. He nodded and turned to them, “Regardless what the two of you wanted, time to go back to the courtroom.” He grabbed Greg more roughly than necessary. Greg learned early in his incarceration to simply flow in the direction that the guard desired. One suffered a whole lot less pain by not fighting. They returned to the court room and waited for the judge.

McCormick quietly gave Greg instructions on the protocol for the next step in his trial. Greg nodded that he understood and waited. He knew that he should not let his eyes wonder around the courtroom, but human curiosity overtook his lawyer’s instructions. Most of the seats were empty with the majority gathered in the one corner by Luke’s friends and relatives. He quickly glanced away before he could accidentally make eye contact with one of them. He was fighting for his future, but they were present looking for justice. Greg understood that justice to them was a guilty verdict.

The bailiff ordered them all to rise, the courtroom rose and then the judge authorized them to be reseated. The judge asked a few questions to the jury foreman and a sealed envelope was passed to the judge by the bailiff. He carefully opened and read without expression. He handed the envelope back to the bailiff who redelivered to the jury foreman. The bailiff formally announced for Greg to rise. His lawyer stood up with him. As the judge was providing instructions to the court audience, Greg once again felt an uncontrollable urge to scan the courtroom. He perceived a rush of embarrassment because he knew that he should be giving his complete attention to the judge and jury foreman. The millisecond glance around the room satisfied this mental itch. He faced the jury foreman as he read the verdict. At that exact moment a few neurons connected in his head and he realized that he saw Cynthia in the audience. Before he could completely process this information, he heard the words, "Not guilty" ring loud and clear.

The next sounds were from himself as a wave of relief hit him quickly followed by cries of anguish from Luke's friends and family. The judge pounded the gavel and ordered silence. Greg still had a few more charges against him, but he instinctively knew that the rest were also going to be not-guilty verdicts. He used the distraction created by the family's angst to look in the direction of Cynthia. The outburst also enabled her to take advantage as she was quietly but quickly exiting the court. She was dressed in a conservative jumpsuit, a plain scarf covered her head, and large sunglasses hid her eyes. Her attempt to disguise herself was almost successful, but her bright red lipstick gave away her appearance. Her back was towards him as she scurried to the door. McCormick was attempting to shake Greg's hand and give verbal congratulations. He turned his head only momentarily to accept McCormick's hand. When he looked back, she was exiting the door without making any acknowledgement of Greg. As she stepped through the doorway and turned to her left, she gave the slightest glance back into the courtroom. Their eyes locked. She smiled.
She continued out the door and out of his life for the next twenty plus years.

The minute Greg walked out of the courthouse into a rare, bright and sunny, western Washington afternoon he pondered, *What the hell am I going to do now? I have no house, no car, and no money. I am screwed.*

He ran dozens of scenarios in his head about the trial before it began, but he never followed past the verdicts. The reality of the situation hit him like a brick and for a second, he felt slightly dizzy.

McCormick asked, "Are you alright?"

"Yes, yes, just...well just everything. The sun is shining, and I am free," he replied.

"Ah, I understand", McCormick responded with more sympathy than he had shown during the entire trial. "I need you to come to my office with me. I have some paperwork for you."

Greg shrugged his shoulders and agreed, *I don't have anything else to do and nowhere to be.* He followed his lawyer around the building to an expensive BMW parked in a small lot. McCormick motioned that the car was his. The only conversation throughout the drive was a short revisit of the verdict. Greg kept silent purposely focusing on the details of the outside world.

After viewing the same four walls for months the smallest facet of humanity fascinated him. He noticed things that he previously never gave a second thought. He sadly recognized the rust on the bridge underpasses and litter on the edges of the street. The colors of the vehicles were more vivid than he remembered, but he also noted the layer of dirt accumulation on most of them. He saw grass growing between cracks in the pavement and patches of brown in residential yards. He was awed by the simply but complex engineering design of the road. He was also saddened by the homeless that he knew were always visible, but he just now seemed to notice. The world and humanity had expanded and not all of it for good. This child-like investigation of the world around him also allowed him to push thoughts of Cynthia into the deepest recesses of his mind. The thoughts of her fought to surface and several times seemed to be lurking just under his consciousness like the ever-hunting shark.

They arrived at the law firm of McCormick and McCormick (Patrick's father was the first McCormick, though he was now retired) and his lawyer guided him to a conference room. He offered him a soda or coffee. Greg gratefully accepted a Coke. McCormick explained that he needed a few minutes to gather the papers for Greg to review. After half a can of soda and ten minutes later McCormick returned holding a stack of large tan envelopes and an attractive young blond woman in tow.

"Greg, this is Patricia. She is going to be the witness for a number of transactions that we are going to have," McCormick explained. Patricia sat in the chair to Greg's left.

She offered her hand which Greg shook as he inquired, "Transactions?"

"Yes, transactions. Are you ready to get started?" he asked.

"Sure", he calmly replied. He also wondered, *what the hell is this all about? Am I about to get handed a bill that I will never be able to pay?*

McCormick walked around the table and took a seat facing Greg and Patricia. He then spread the stack of tan envelopes on the table. They were of different sizes and thickness, but each one was sealed across the top by visible red tape. He also set an ornate letter opener on the table. The lawyer selected the envelope closest to Greg and used the letter opener to break the red tape seal. He ceremoniously dumped the contents onto the table. McCormick pushed a lace wrapped box towards Greg and straightened a single piece of paper in front of Greg. He reached into his vest and produced the Cartier pen which he set next to himself. Patricia's hand appeared across his line of sight as she handed him a plain black Bic pen. He noticed she was holding some kind of fine metal pen in her other hand. Greg took the pen and looked down at the paper that McCormick was pushing in his direction.

"This is a contract made between your benefactor and my law firm. If you were found innocent the contract directs me to bring you here and sign over the contents of these envelopes. I need you to initial here that I explained the purpose of this contract and then sign the bottom," McCormick clarified.

Greg signed the front of the paper and McCormick turned it over. "This signature is for taking possession of the contents of this first envelope."

"Looks like a box of cards. What's actually in it?" Greg inquired while signing.

Patricia leaned over, signed as the witness, and stated, "We have no idea. The client did not offer that information. All we know is that we are required to tell you to open it *after* you have left the premises."

Greg pulled the box to his right and said, "Ok. I understand. Well, actually I don't but let's keep going. I wonder what is inside the other envelopes."

Neither Patricia nor McCormick reacted to Greg's curiosity. In a stiff and professionally manner McCormick filed the first paper in an empty folder with Greg's full name neatly typed on the tab. He then picked up a second envelope, cut the tape, and once again emptied the contents. This time a smaller, plain white envelope, and another legal form spilled onto the table.

"This time we need you to open the envelope and state the contents. Then sign the receipt form," McCormick directed.

The envelope was not sealed but merely had the flap flipped inside. Greg pulled it open and retrieved a check. He read it and gasped, "This is a check from your law firm and is made out to me. It is for $25,000. What the fuck!"

"So as you colorfully acknowledge that it is a check made out to you for the amount of $25,000", Patricia stated. "Please sign for receipt."

Greg looked bewildered while he scribbled his name. Patricia quickly signed the witness line. McCormick repeated the procedure four more times. The third envelope contained a set of keys to a brand-new Honda Accord, the title in Greg's name paid in full and an insurance card for a year of insurance also paid in full. The fourth envelope contained a standard 8 X 11.5 envelope that appeared to contain a few sheets of papers. The lawyers informed him that he should open that envelope after he opened the box. They were authorized to tell him that he needed a place to stay and that envelope was the answer. The next tan envelope contained another 8 X 11.5 envelope that appeared to contain a very large bulk of papers. The lawyers again directed him to wait till later to open. They had no additional information on the contents of gift number five. The last envelope contained another 8 X 11.5 envelope, a business card and road maps for western Washington, western Oregon, and northern California. The lawyers had no information concerning the road maps, the business card, or the contents of the envelope.

"Patricia, I appreciate your assistance. That will be all for this client," said McCormick.

Patricia rose, extended her hand and said, "Good luck, Mr. Palmer. I hope everything works out for you. I think you have been given another chance at life."

Greg politely shook her hand and replied, "Thank-you."

She exited the room and McCormick spoke again, "I do not know the details of all of these other envelopes, but I understand enough about your benefactor to know that Patricia is likely correct. I think you have a real opportunity and a chance to put this behind you. I have one other duty to perform to complete my transaction with your benefactor and one piece of advice that I will offer free of charge."

He reached into his suit pocket and produced a hotel key. He set the key in front of Greg. He then pulled out his wallet and counted three hundred-dollar bills and four fifty-dollar bills on top of the keys. He looked at Greg and said, "The key is for the Holiday Inn off of route 51. Not the nicest place in the world but you will not be robbed. The room is paid in full for one night and one night only. The cash will enable you to get along for a few days before you find a bank to deposit the check."

He paused, sat back in chair and ran his fingers through the stubble of his crew cut. He continued, "Mr. Palmer, I am not in the business of giving life advice. I focus on the technicalities of the law and never give recommendations to a client about their life except for the details specific to a case."

He stopped for another few seconds and chuckled, "I am also not in the business of offering anything in this office for free."

Greg smiled at the lawyer's minimal attempt at humor. McCormick finished, "I think you should check into the hotel and then find yourself a place to have a decent meal and a good beer. Then you should go to the hotel and have the longest and hottest shower you have ever had in your life to try to wash away that jail smell. You should then carefully open the box and check out the contents in their entirety. You need to thoroughly read all of the papers in the other envelopes. I don't know for a fact, but I think they are going to give you very explicit directions. I think you should have a night cap of good bourbon, go to sleep, get up in the morning, and check out of the hotel. And the most important piece of advice I can offer, get into that new car and drive out of Remington, drive out of western Washington, and never return."

McCormick stood and grabbed the folder with all the signed receipts. He wordlessly motioned for Greg to follow him. They walked through the office and out the front door. At the edge of the parking lot McCormick pointed to an Accord parked in an end spot.

Greg stared at the new car for a moment before asking, "Is that my car?"

McCormick did not respond and when Greg turned around, he saw that his lawyer was already near the entrance of the building. Patrick McCormick entered the office without a pause. Greg shrugged his shoulders and thought, *only one way to figure it out.*

The key was for the Honda. Greg followed the first part of his attorney's advice to the letter. When he sat down after a great meal and long shower, he did not believe that he would actually drive out of town the next morning. The box contained a long letter from Cynthia. She did not offer any kind of apology nor give any indication that she may have been responsible for the series of events that occurred since he stumbled out her house. The letter was a series of directions for Greg to put his life back together. She claimed that she called in "many favors, plus money does talk." She wanted him to go to Sacramento and restart his life. An apartment and a job interview awaited him. He found a lease for a small condo paid in full for a year in the packets of papers. The envelopes provided a lot of background information on a company that she arranged a job interview for him. Additionally, she listed answers to all the questions that she was confident were going to be asked. The job was entry level and meant to simply get his foot in the door. She also wanted him to talk to a counselor at a small community college and start taking a few classes. Somehow, she already forwarded all of his transcripts and SAT scores to the college. Despite his pathetic effort and constant substance abuse, he breezed through high school with exceptional grades. He had potential but after his parents were killed in a car accident during his sophomore year, he never applied himself. He did not remember ever describing any of this part of his life to her, but her letter scolded him for his effort in high school and warned him against a repeat performance in college. She literally thought of everything for him to start with a clean slate. All he had to do was get in the car the next morning and drive down to Sacramento. He went to sleep (after the recommended bourbon night cap) with the intent of staying in Remington.

He awoke he next morning with a completely different thought process. By ten AM he was in his new car following the high-lighted routes on the road maps down to Sacramento. He found the fully furnished apartment and then located a nearby bank to deposit the check. He studied the notes Cynthia gave him and on the designated day arrived for the interview. He never had a job interview and he found the experience significantly more nerve racking than he anticipated. He was not surprised by any of the questions, but he was positive that he performed very poorly. He was given the job. A month later he timidly wondered into Richmond Community College and signed up for a single class. He firmly applied himself in the 100 level English class and came away with an A grade. He also met a woman in his English class. He never gave the situation any thought but his previous life *was lost,* but *fears of the future are soothed.*

Part II:
The Chorus

Chapter 6:
Over and over…

For the first six years after his trial Greg kept his nose to the grindstone and completely clean. He worked hard at his job and diligently applied himself at school. He initially took just a few courses at a time to get used to working and reacquainting himself with education. After two years of community college he transferred his credits to Sacramento State and began to work more aggressively towards completing a four-year degree in finance. The six-year effort resulted in his bachelor's degree.

While in college he earned a few minor promotions. Once he completed his degree his company rewarded him with a significant promotion. He did not know it at the time, but that was his last promotion at the firm. Even if he could see into the future, he probably would not try to find another job. He was thirty, single, making good money with little overhead. He considered buying a house or condo. He actually went a few times with a realtor to look at houses. He could afford to buy one, but he was simply comfortable. He continued to rent the same condo year after year. His building was twice sold and both times he wondered if he would be forced to move. Each time the new landlords were more than willing to keep a tenet who paid his rent on time month after month and year and after year (that is of course with a slight rent hike).

He took up biking on the weekends for exercise and relaxation. He joined the firm's softball team in the summer and the bowling team in the winter. He volunteered at least once a month at a local animal sanctuary. Sometimes he worked a booth for donations while other times he cleaned kennels. He often told his work associates that his life was full.

Eight years after he left Remington he bought a new two door Mercedes. He kept the Accord and justified it to himself by saying that he "may need it someday." Ten years later he traded his Mercedes for an upscale Audi A6. The thought of using the Accord as part of a down payment never crossed his mind. He took the Honda out for a drive at least once a month and he kept careful track to make sure the maintenance was completed on schedule. He didn't realize it, but he was more diligent with the Accord's maintenance than he was with his newer cars.

The years rolled on year after year,

Over and over,

living in the same place, going to work at the same company (without earning a promotion in years), driving (or owning the same car) and repeating the same forms of weekend entertainment. The other significant facet of his life that was cyclical (and not in the good way)

To love and lose is just a part of life

was his inability to form a long-term connection with the opposite sex.

The day after Greg suffered some sort of panic attack he was once again on the road using twenty-year-old memory as GPS with the mission of visiting Cynthia. This time the pros and cons were weighed with appropriate risk factors assigned. Much of this journey did not make sense, but a feeling of needed closure was heavily tipping the scales towards Pleasant Avenue. His analytical mind required answers, and the only way to get them was to find her house.

He glanced down on the passenger seat where a pile of CD's was scattered across the sun faded plaid fabric. When he entered into the trance like state and packed for the trip, he mindlessly grabbed almost two dozen old CD's from the dusty CD rack. Before he pulled out of the hotel that morning, he sifted through them not searching for a particular title. He held up Megadeth's *Rust in Peace*, looked at the scratched and aged plastic case, opened it up, and discovered the CD was missing. He could not recall the last time he listened to that CD, or any other actual CD for that matter before this trip. Like most other people electronic media replaced the compact disc format. He tossed the empty CD holder into the back seat and continued shuffling through the pile again. He saw a dark album cover with thin, attractive woman in stilettos kicking open a door. He held up Slippster's *Let Me In* and wondered, *this chic was in all of those eighties' hair band videos. I wonder where she is today. Man, when was the last time I listened to this?* He opened the case, found the CD inside, and slid it into the player. *How far have we come?* he smiled. *The freaking Audi doesn't even have a CD player.*

As the music filled the car, he drove out of the hotel, and headed towards the Remington city center. By the time that the chorus to "Over and Over" rang out Greg was mentally in automatic. He would never be able to backtrack the train of thought that guided him to current mental image. Her name was Chastity and he met her in the first college class he undertook.

When it came to college Greg was an absolute creature of habit. He tried to do things in an orderly fashion and as close to the same way as possible every time. This included the seat he sat in for a class. Once he parked himself on the first day of a new class, rote habit took over, and he mindlessly vectored towards the same seat every time. Chastity was the polar opposite of Greg in this regard as well as in almost every other way that mattered to Greg. Without thought she flopped herself into any seat, usually taking a different seat every class for the course. Greg noticed her a few times in the class, but he did not make any attempt to introduce himself. On one of the last sessions she arrived late (which was also fairly routine for her) and narrowed in to one of the few empty seats. One of them was directly next to Greg and chance prompted her to choose that one. She immediately began to noisily pull notepads out of a backpack and whispered to Greg, "What have I missed?"

Slightly irritated he responded, "Nothing really."

He did not go out of his way to strike up a conversation with her during a break, but she took the initiative. She was bubbly, laughed easily, and chatty. She did most of the talking, and Greg was actually surprised that he was disappointed when the break was over. He studied her (and her body) instead of the professor for the remainder of the class. As soon as the class was over, he nervously asked if she wanted to grab a cup of coffee. She declined saying that she had too much to do. She did give him her phone number and told him to call her the next morning. He told her that he worked full time so he could not call her during the day on company time. She smiled and said she had a waitressing job at a local steak house. She worked the twelve to six shift and suggested that he could pick her up, and then they could grab something to eat. Greg agreed and without intention, he had his first date since Cynthia.

Greg arrived five minutes early, but she was not ready to leave for another twenty-five minutes. As soon as they shut the car doors she asked, "Hey do you mind swinging by my house first. I want to get out these work clothes."

"Sure, just give me directions", he answered.

"Thanks", she replied and in-between "turn left here" or "swing it right", she filled him on every aspect of her day at the steak house. He was not able to say much except nod and hum.

Once at her apartment she literally hopped up the steps, excitedly burst through the door, and called out, "Hey Sheila."

A scrawny, thirty-something female entered the front room from the kitchen. She was dressed in oversized sweatpants and a loose San Francisco 49ers t-shirt. The sleeves were cut off revealing her bone thin arms and the sides of her bra. Her hair was pulled back in a tight bun and she was currently frowning. She slowly wiped her hand on a towel and in a severe tone said, "Chastity, who the hell is this?"

Nonplussed she replied, "This is Greg. We have a class together. Will you relax?"

She walked up to Greg to offer her hand and flatly replied, "Maybe."

"Ok, great," she beamed. She turned to Greg, "Just give maybe ten minutes to grab a quick shower." She skipped out of the room leaving Greg alone with Sheila. Internally Greg sighed as he understood that she was not "just changing" but now was taking a shower. He would have to deal with this stern lady, and he had no idea of her relationship to Chastity.

"Well, go ahead and have a seat", she directed. As soon as Greg sat down on the edge of the couch she continued, "How old are you?"

"Twenty-five", he answered.

She gave him an authoritative look, "Are you taking freshman English? Aren't you a bit old?"

"Yes, I am in the freshman English and no, I don't think I am too old. We have people in their thirties in the class", he stated as a matter of fact.

She waved off this answer and leaned in, "Maybe the better question is aren't you a little old for Chastity?"

"I don't know about that," he said defensively.

Sheila paused for a second and then quizzed, "How old is Chasity?"

"I honestly don't know. I didn't think she was right out of high school, but we have not gotten into too many details of each other's lives. We have only talked a few times", he replied.

She seemed to ignore his answer and quickly asked, "What is your intent with Chastity?"

"Maybe some dinner. Exactly who are you?" he quickly asked before she could continue with the third degree.

She laughed out loud and eased her tone several levels, "I am just a friend. I tend to be overprotective. I have children of my own. She is my roommate but sometimes...oh she is twenty. So, NO FUCKING BOOZE."

Her outburst startled him for a second, but he recovered to say, "No problem."

She gave a stern stare for a few moments before continuing, "Chasity is sweet girl and doesn't see the bad in anyone. Frankly, she is gullible and has been hurt a couple of times. I just don't want to see her hurt."

He gently said, "I do not intend to hurt anyone. We are just going to have some dinner and see if we have anything in common."

"Well it doesn't take a rocket scientist to see that you will have nothing in common, but I have to let her figure that kind of stuff for herself. Why don't you tell me about yourself and why you are taking freshman English at the age of twenty-five," she invited.

Greg gave a generic summary of his life purposely avoiding a few spots in his lifeline. She listened and did not interrupt. He emphasized the good things in his life since he moved to Sacramento. He kept glancing towards the bedroom hoping that Chastity would soon reappear.

When his story slowly ground to a stop, she squinted at him and pointedly stated, “I don't understand how you ended up here in Sacramento. You have no ties out of Washington. Did you throw a dart at a map and this is where you landed?”

At that moment, Chastity bounced back in the room in all her eccentric glory. She did not follow a fashion style but simply went with the things that made her feel good. She loved bright colors and odd matches. This evening she wore a pair of tight pink overalls over a floral halter top. Pink flip-flops and gaudy bright coral bracelets completed the ensemble. Besides being an overwhelming eyesore, the outfit extenuated her figure and cleavage.

Greg gawked a little bit at the voluptuous figure dancing in front of him. She was short with a thick build and well-endowed on top. Her large breasts were on the verge of breaking free from her top as she swayed through the living room. She was naturally blonde with a few sporadic highlights in her unruly and curly mess of hair. Tonight she had a sunflower hair clip holding a clump to one side.

She beamed, “Do you like me?” Before he could respond she grabbed his hand and said, “Let’s go.”

Sheila stood and said, “Wait a second Chas. Greg was going to answer a question for me.”

“Oh poop”, she waved her finger at Sheila. “You are such a *bi-atch* sometimes.”

Greg looked towards Shelia and then faced Chastity, “Well, we have not had much time to get to know each other. This wasn't really the way I envisioned this conversation but might as well get this over with.”

Shelia responded, “Hmmm.”

Greg continued, "My parents were killed in a car accident my sophomore year of high school. I did not have any other relatives as both my parents were only children. I ended up in a foster home of a nice family. I thanked them by getting involved in all kinds of juvenile delinquency including early drug and alcohol use. School was easy for me even though I was frequently using. I was able to graduate and accidentally fall into a great job as apprentice. I screwed that situation completely up too. During that period, I dated a woman named Cynthia. She grew tired of my shit and my problems. I got clean two years ago. Cynthia had some connections and even though I burned my bridges with her, she went out of her way to get me a second chance at life. I had to leave Washington and break off all the old and wrong connections. My opportunity was here in Sacramento."

He paused and gave them a second for rebuttal, "In short I moved to California to start fresh."

Shelia crossly replied, "Well, that is just great."

Chastity timidly asked, "You are good now?"

He shook his head affirmative. She smiled and hugged him, "Ok, let's get some dinner."

Shelia shook her head in disgust as they walked out of the apartment. Chastity never gave any indication that she gave his background a second thought. Their conversations that evening focused on her history and his present. She again dominated the conversation, but at this stage of his life he was simply content to be in the presence of a female. He dropped her off at her apartment and declined an invitation to watch a little television with her. He honestly enjoyed himself but also did not feel like having a second stint with Shelia. She made him promise to call after work the next day which he completely intended to do. His phone was ringing as he entered his apartment. He laughed and raced to the phone. They talked till 2 AM and a relationship started to form.

On their third date they progressed to kissing and heavy petting. When he stopped, she let him know that she was not a virgin. He could not explain but he thought that they should wait a little while longer. That restraint only enamored her even more to him. She was rapidly falling in love with him. He enjoyed her company, but he could not say that he felt love for her. He never felt the same as she felt for him.

A week later their touching progressed to love making. He loved having sex with her and was completely infatuated with her body. She loved as free and as expressive as her ward robe. Sex was never a problem.

After a few months the differences in their personality started to put dents in the relationship. Her dominance of the conversation developed into incessant chatter to Greg. He grew to hate her place of employment and every person that worked with her. Her forgetfulness and happy go lucky attitude became synonyms for flighty and ditzy. He learned that she was not very bright and more than likely she would not finish college. She was more than likely destined to be a server her entire life. He did not feel that he was “above” her and her potential was not a real issue. He just realized that her future and his did not seem to cross. After three months of dating, he admitted to himself that he did not love her. He tried to be as gentle as possible, but he broke it off. She was destroyed, and he was relieved. His life floated along

with the typical unbroken routine. Almost three months to the day that he broke up with Chastity he accepted an invitation to a dinner party of a work colleague.

Unbeknownst to him the wife of his work friend was secretly trying to set him with her recently divorced best friend. He met Sharon that night and soon fell head over heels in love with her.

Sharon had virtually nothing in common with Chastity. Sharon was tall and thin but with an athletic build. She had common brown, shoulder length hair and unremarkable facial features. In high school she frustratingly complained to her friends that she was the "plain Jane" of the circle of friends. As an adult she was comfortable in her skin. She understood that she was intelligent, caring, and would make a fine wife for a lucky guy someday. Her first husband met the requirements at first, but he had an abusive streak that he kept hidden during their courtship. She was on the verge of leaving him when she became pregnant with their daughter Chelsea. She tried to make the relationship work for the first three years of Chelsea's life, but after one particularly scary incident, Sharon decided that both she and her daughter deserved better. Greg met that bill. He treated Sharon with the upmost respect. He grew to love her for her wit and humanity. He was exceptional careful of her boundaries, especially in regard to their intimacy and her daughter. He did not press for a physical relationship and they dated nearly three months before Sharon felt comfortable enough to rekindle that part of her life. Greg also did not step in and try to be "instant Daddy". That relationship never had time to germinate. Greg allowed Chelsea and Sharon dictate the pace and by the time that Chelsea may have been ready, Sharon pulled the plug. After their first few lovemaking sessions, she came away completely satisfied. On the other hand, she also instinctively knew that she would never really love him.

Greg was completely at ease with Sharon, appreciated her intelligence and earthy approach to life.

Unlike Chastity, he found himself imaging a future with her soon after their first few dates. He grew to quickly love her, but he also sensed that she needed time. He did not press her. When he thought that the time was getting close, she blind-sided him by ending the relationship. He was greatly hurt, but he handled the situation maturely. He also harbored a secret hope that by not doing anything impulsive and stupid that she may come around. She did not. When she said good-bye, that was the end.

The cycle continued for twenty years. Every few months or so,

Over and over,
To love and lose is just a part of life.

Greg began dating a new woman. A relationship formed, but also withered away after a few months. One of them would not be content and broke it off, usually surprising the other. No easily detectable pattern could be discerned for these broken relationships, though oddly he never considered the situation anything but normal. Each of the ladies was different in a hundred different ways. He met and dated females of all builds, hair colors, races, cultures, education and backgrounds. Half the time Greg moved towards ending the relationship while half the time the ladies took the initiative. Even the times in which Greg was the dumped and he was hurt, he did not carry the pain for too long. The situation did not depress him. In the grand scheme he was never out of a relationship for very long, or at least not long enough to bother him. He simply floated through life with a deep expectation that the "right" girl was the one he just met or was one that he would meet very soon. This thought process did not change even as his twenties evolved into his thirties and then tacked into his forties. Mrs. Right was just around the corner.

As the Greg of the present drove past Fred's Market (Marco's), he absentmindedly turned off the Slippster CD. He did not fear another panic attack, but he simply wanted to concentrate on the faded memory road that he was attempting to navigate. The streets and the buildings in many ways looked just like every building and street in this part of the country. Somehow, he seemed to be viewing them differently, like the picture he saw through the windshield was from 1996 and not in the present. The things on the streets that changed during the previous twenty years were still visible but also seemed to be set into the background. The features that did not help with retracing his footsteps to Cynthia were secondary in visibility. The items similar to his past were bold, prominent and almost seem to glow; in his mental eye, the proverbial memory yellow brick road. He followed the path and did not desire distractions from the radio. He needed to concentrate to "catch" the next critical clue.

Two blocks from Fred's the street rapidly inclined up a fairly large hill. Greg gave the car more gas to overcome the gravity and the friction but then immediately took his foot off the gas.

Why did I do that? he asked himself. *Am I close?*

At the crest of the hill he applied his foot to the brake and flicked his left turn signal. He waited till the one oncoming vehicle went past him and he turned onto a narrow side street. He verified (but he already knew) that he was entering Pleasant Avenue. He was close.

The street's name did not live up to the billing. Every city and town have that one neighborhood that the police are required to frequently visit, and that regular folks do not purposely drive on after midnight.

Pleasant Avenue was Remington's Hell Street. During Greg's time with Cynthia gangs developed into a problem in this part of the country. As hair bands gave way to grunge, some of California's larger crime gangs were starting to reach into the pacific northwest. A few lower level Filipino gangs controlled the drug traffic in these areas until the California gangs entered the scene. Pleasant Avenue then was hotly contested, violent, and dangerous. The territory turned over several times over the next two decades. The constant was the drug trafficking and violence. The area was currently controlled by the Marijuanos, a gang loosely affiliated with the Mexican Mafia. This information would not have deterred him. He was in automatic and would have turned onto Pleasant Avenue if ISIS controlled the street.

Greg slowed the car nearly to a crawl desperately looking out of his driver window for the alley. His eyes searched between each of the closely set houses looking for another spark to jog his memory.

He thought, *At the beginning, I always had a hard time finding the alley when I drove. Her street just seemed…like out of place.*

He slowly applied the brakes and brought the car to a complete stop. He looked in his rearview mirror to verify that he was not blocking traffic. When he confirmed that no other cars were behind him, he stared out the front window hoping something would trigger a memory. He could see that the street slowly curved to the left. He frowned in memory strain. He recalled that the section of street that he could not see due to the curvature crossed another small street named Lazarus. If he drove to that intersection, he missed Cynthia's alley. He slowly scanned each house from the beginning of the curve to his present position.

Greg was unaware that a car slowing down on this particular street attracted attention. Some folks used this street simply to get from one area to another. Most, though, traveled these neighborhoods for other purposes and none of them were legal. A few noticed his slow entry and wordless signals were passed from house to house. While infrequent since the Mexican Mafia flexed its muscles in these parts drive-by shootings were not completely non-existent. When the Honda stopped and remained parked for a few minutes' curiosity grew. A young woman was sent to investigate.

He was so lost in retracing the lost path that he did not notice her saunter up to the Accord until she was parallel to his driver window. She leaned over and signaled for him to put down the window. Instantly Greg recognized the attention and put down his window.

"Are you lost, amigo?" she purred as she leaned into open car window. "Maybe you looking for some-thing?"

"A little lost", he admitted. "I have not been down here in long time. I am looking for someone."

"I am someone, I am Rosita," she replied as she leaned further inside the car providing him a bird's eye of her small but exposed breasts. "You looking for girlfriend?"

The male side of him could not help to take a quick glance down the open shirt before he shifted his eyes to her face. She was leering and attempting to be sexy as she purposely shifted her eyes down his to crotch. At one point in her life she was probably very beautiful. Today, though, life and probably heroin or meth turned her flirting into something very different; something ghastly. Her face was gaunt with dark bags under her eyes. Her jet black, greasy hair was pulled back into long ponytail that fell to the middle of her back. She wore oversized gold hoop earrings that deeply contrasted against her oily and pale skin. She wore dark lipstick that only accentuated the ruddy complexion. Her teeth were blackened and rotting, and the lipstick only made the unintentional goth appearance more grotesque. He saw the scabs and tracks on her inner arms. A heavy perfume floated into the car but as she leaned further into the car, a deep unpleasant smell of sweat and dirty vagina wafted in behind the perfume. He processed all of her in an instant and concluded that she gave everything over to her drug habit. She no longer cared about her body or her hygiene. She slowly ran her tongue over her blackened lips causing him to involuntarily shudder.

He blurted, “No, no you misunderstood me. I do not need a girlfriend. I am just looking for someone who lived here a long time ago.”

Undeterred she replied, “Long time ago. That person long gone. No one lives here long time. I am here right now. I get in car and we go party somewhere.”

She turned away from the driver window and loudly exclaimed, “Look at all you can have.”

With her back to the car, she leaned forward and started twerking her ass in his direction. She had long shapely legs and a firm rear. He groaned at the scene she created right on the sidewalk.

I need to get the fuck out of here, he thought. He reached to put the car in gear when she broke from her dance and ran around the front of the car. *Oh, shit, she is going to try to get into the car.*

His mind raced as he calculated the odds of her clearing the front end, putting the car in gear, and heading down the street without hitting her. As she passed the front passenger fender a memory jammed into is head. He recognized the house on the right side of the street behind her as she approached the passenger door.

The house was unremarkable compared to all the other hovels on the street; overgrown weeds for yards, falling down steel link fences, faded and peeling paint jobs, and refuse filled covered porches. The house that grabbed Greg's attention had one unique feature. The upper portion of the two-story house had scalloped shakes that were painted purple. The coloring was faded and not touched up in decades. The gaudy color still stood out and provided a landmark. Greg remembered stumbling down Cynthia's driveway on numerous occasions staring at the purple monstrosity and wondered who painted the top of the house that color. Greg immediately turned to the left and now easily spotted the narrow, hidden driveway. He forgot about Rosita as he put the car in drive and started to ease the car towards his destination. She quickly regained his attention as she banged on this hood and yelled. He stopped the car as the left front tire just entered the driveway. He could not understand her words as she cursed him in Spanish, but he gathered the gist of the meaning. She ran around to the driver side and shifted back to English.

"What are doing?" she demanded.

"At the end this alley is the house and the person I came to see", he replied.

"NO, NO, NO", she yelled. "No one you want to see at that house."

"I think an old friend is there", he answered as he put the car in gear and carefully pointed the car down the extremely narrow pass between the two houses.

As the back tires of the Honda lifted onto the driveway, she scrambled to his window once again and hissed, "Bruja", turned and ran across the street.

Huh, I haven't heard that word in twenty years, he thought as fresh memories resurfaced.

Chapter 7:
In the darkness…

In the early '90's Seattle became the music center of the world. Several bands burst onto the music scene and became giants in a short period of time. Their music was lumped together into a new genre known as grunge music. A few of these bands became extremely commercially successful and saw their albums reach platinum status. The band, and specifically the song, that seemed to launch the entire pacific northwest into the musical forefront was Nirvana and their groundbreaking song, "Smells Like Teen Spirit." This anti-everything nod to punk was original, driving, and an absolute monster. Any young person who loved rock music and lived in this part of the country at the time simply could not but have the non-sensical lyrics to "Smells Like Teen Spirit" completely ingrained into their daily lives. Greg, like many young people in the pacific northwest, began investigating every band from Seattle that snagged a record deal in an effort to find the next Nirvana.

Cynthia's long narrow driveway was a city planning anomaly. The alley/driveway to her house had a long stretch of overgrown bushes on each side that grew so high and wild that the natural light was blocked out. Many times as Greg stumbled up and down this unusual path, he stopped and embraced the minimal light. He then belted out one of his favorite songs from that era.

During this period, he constantly listened to a little-known grunge band named Sea Wretch. Their one MTV video, "Wrecks the Day", was a direct rip-off of "Smells Like Teen Spirit" in the cinematography, the aggressive and punk paced chords, and unintelligible lyrics. He didn't note the similarity, nor did he care. He simply loved the song. As he ventured to Marcos, he frequently tottered, hiccupped, and then launched into his version of "Wrecks the Day." He roared,

In the darkness,
We gorge on the limes.
Soon we will arrive,
So show us good time.

Nobody ever heard his rendition of Sea Wretch, but he also did not care. He often laughed (and farted) and felt that he was so *witty* to sing about being in the dark when hardly any sunlight could penetrate that murky alley. The sober Greg of today was not considering Sea Wretch as he tried to navigate his Accord down the alley.

Immediately Greg cursed under his breath and concluded that the alley should never have been run between these two houses. He had less than a foot on either side of the car as he passed between the two houses. Once clear of the houses the physical structures were replaced by extremely thick and tall bushes. These were planted parallel to the alley and spacing between his car and the limbs was not improved. In many places random branches reached out and scraped the length of the Honda as he slowly crept down the trail. He guessed that he must have traveled the length of another property when the path altered. The broken concrete was replaced with dirt tire tracks. Foot tall grass grew in the space between the tracks which the front fender bent over like a wave of dying soldiers. The foliage became even wilder and distinctly out of place for the pacific northwest. The branches and vines stretched up higher and higher until Greg was unable to see the tops of the foliage even when he strained his neck up against the front window.

The daylight slowly faded, and the only sounds were the Accord's low rumble and the sound of the grasses being bent over. Greg recalled that the length of the alley was excessive, but he attributed his memory due to being so out of shape at the time. As he drove another property length, he concluded that her house was indeed way hidden inside this city block. The path slowly began to curve to the right and also became littered with ruts. He bounced in his seat as the undercarriage scraped the ground on several occasions. The miserable driving experience continued for another hundred yards or so when suddenly the tires rolled up onto smooth concrete. The entranceway also immediately widened enough for two cars to pass side by side. The right side of the path remained guarded by the immense and exotic brush, but the left side was opening up by about ten degrees. He could not see a house yet, but after another fifty yards the edge of yard appeared. He drove another twenty yards when the wild mass to his right abruptly ended into waist high, finely manicured standard bushes. His eyes followed the bushes for quite a distance as the right side opened up to at least a half-acre of smooth, weed free grass. Several apple trees were spaced in the open area to the left of the driveway and Greg remembered that they hid a small, but fine house behind them. Once he cleared the trees an 1800 square foot ranch with an attached three car garage came into view. He stopped the car.

This is exactly as I remember it, he thought. *Her garage was nearly as big as the house. Wonder what kind of cars she owns today?*

He leaned back in his seat and focused, *Screw the cars. What am I going to say? Again, what am I doing here?*

He took his foot off the brake and drove up to her garage. He put the car in park and killed the engine. He sat in silence for a moment before he reached for a duffel bag in the back seat. He pulled the bag to the passenger seat and set it on top the pile of CD's. He unzipped the bag and lifted out a card that was located near the top.

The bright envelope was the invitation from Cynthia. He pulled the card from the envelope and read the contents again to prove to himself that he should be sitting in her driveway. He could recite the short correspondence from memory, but he took the time to carefully read it out loud.

"Greg", he read, "I do not know if this card will find you or not. I do not know if you will take the time to read or simply toss away. Even if you read my words, I doubt that you will take me up on my offer. After all these years I understand any reluctance on your part. I have nothing to offer and no agenda other than I would truly like to meet with you sometime. Our relationship…well you know. I have lived a full life and I am sure you have too, but you were special to me and…I think we owe each other one more visit for a sort of closure. Greg, I simply would like to see you again sometime. You don't need to make any sort of special arrangements. I am always here. Anytime you feel like it, you are welcome to come for a visit; an afternoon or a couple of days. Your call. With Love, Cynthia."

This short letter launched him to his current situation. Now that he was here, he had a very nervous feeling. He was not sure if he should turn the car around and leave or knock on the front door.

What the hell am I going to say, he thought perplexed. *She sent the card but what exactly is she going to say and feel? Will she want to see me today?*

Soon we will arrive,

So show us good time

He chuckled lightly as the rest of Sea Wretch chorus vaulted into his mind.

Kick me now,
I am the idiot.
Soon we arrive,
So show us good time.

Yea, I am an idiot, but I am here now, might as well go in and let her show us good time, he concluded. He opened the car door and exited the car before he changed his mind. He confidently strode up to the front door. He hesitated the first time he went to knock, thought, *fuck it,* and then gave a sturdy knock on the elegant, steel screen door.

For twenty years Greg's love life roller coaster at an almost predictable clip. He seldom was not involved in a relationship, but also as expected events always ended the romance. On that morning his romance plane was actually slightly off course from the historical precedents. He had not dated anyone in over eight months, and he honestly did not have a desire to meet someone new. He was simply living his life day to day, and more importantly, he was going through the grieving process.

His last girlfriend was a black lady in her early forties named Monica. She had a thin upper body with a slightly chunky lower body and relatively wide hips. She had "junk in the trunk" as she self-described her figure. She kept her hair in extensive, lengthy braids with deep red streaks. She wore little jewelry or make up and most of the time her ward robe fell in the conservative category. She did, though, sport long and expensive nails at all times.

Her life was a series of targeted goals and accomplishments. The month she met Greg she just finished her PhD and shortly thereafter was hired to be the principle of one the largest elementary schools in northern California. She had a very easy going and charming personality. While she desired to find the "right guy" she was not willing to settle. The number of offered dates was not the problem. She had a streak of quick judgment, and she often labeled men in ways that she thought would interfere with her life goals. She was an educator since graduating college and most of the men were in her own field. Her quick assessment of these men was always unfavorable. Bar-hopping or blind dates were also not her thing. The result was that she only experienced a few serious relationships prior to Greg. At her core she felt that her life was full filled. Meeting Greg was just an added bonus.

Despite the difference in the life paths they hit it off very quickly. They met through a mutual friend at a picnic, though the intent was not to set them up as a couple. After being introduced they both wondered in different directions in the park. Later they ended up next to each other in the food line. They made small talk while they filled their plates. When they turned to find an empty seat at the picnic tables, they recognized that the only empty spots were next to each other. They joked that the Gods must have wanted them to sit together. They shared BBQ chicken, potato salad, and their life stories. He was attracted to her mind and internal drive. He may not have made her "cut" the year prior, but on that day his honest and sincere interest in her life broke down her defenses. She was attracted to his candid answers, quirky worship of music, and for the first time in a long time, his wide shoulders and narrow waist. She definitely did not consider herself celibate, but for some reason she was drawn to him in a way that was not her norm. They seemed to mutual understand that at their ages they were not grab ass happy teenagers, but on the other hand, they were not getting any younger. They slept together that night, and neither felt guilty about that fact. They eased into a routine with each other. One month turned into two and before long the relationship shattered Greg's normal pattern. As they celebrated six months together, they loved each deeply and mutually. This was a first for both of them. Tentative conversations began about moving in together, possible marriage, and maybe even children.

Greg woke up one cold, drizzly November morning, sat up in bed, and concluded that he would soon ask her to marry him. They spent most nights together at each other's houses, but on this rare Wednesday morning they woke in their own beds. Monica had an early morning flight down to San Diego for a statewide educator meeting. She was her school district's representative which was a significant honor. She was very excited, and he was happy for her. As he shaved that morning, he was running marriage proposal scenarios in his head. He was expecting a text any minute to tell him that she was on the plane down to San Diego. He had no idea at the time that Monica never made it to the airport.

A drunk driver rocketed up the exit ramp of the highway in the wrong direction. She was so surprised to see a car heading directly at her that she momentarily froze. The drunk in a haze thought the *she* was going the wrong direction. He began to yell and wave his hands for her to get out the way. He never slowed nor attempted to avoid the collision. At the very last second, she tried to swerve her car to avoid an accident. The drunk's car smashed into the front driver quarter panel at nearly 45 MPH. The initial impact probably killed her. Her car was driven off the road, through the guard rail, and into a steep ravine.

He car flipped several times and caught fire. The first responders could only watch in horror.

Greg became worried when the morning turned into afternoon, and he still had not heard from her. She did not respond to his texts or calls. After work he tried calling a couple of her friends that he knew. He wanted to avoid worrying her immediate family, but by eight o'clock he was frantic. As he looked for phone number for Monica's sister, Samantha, in the contact list on his phone, Sam actually called him. She sobbed and delivered the terrible news. He was devastated.

For the next eight months a day did not pass that he did not think of Monica. He went online and read about the grieving process. He learned that the feelings he experienced were in the normal category and that everyone healed at a different rate. He did not go as far as to have suicidal thoughts, but he clearly fell into a deep depression. He considered taking some vacation from work and booking a cruise somewhere far away from Sacramento. He was looking at various cruises online on the day he received the invitation from Cynthia. As he clicked through one vacation package after another, he became frustrated that he could not make up his mind on any of them. He decided to go get his mail to break away from his mental wrestling. He vigorously promised himself that when he returned from the mailbox he would immediately choose. After he opened and read Cynthia's note he scrapped the Caribbean idea and headed north.

He waited a few moments before he knocked for a second time. He held his breathe and listened intently for the sounds of movement within the house. The second knock produced the affect he desired. He heard a slow shuffling towards the door, a series of locks being turned, and the heavy wooden door swung into the house. A very short and very elderly Hispanic women looked up at him through the screen door.

"May I help you?" she asked though a deep Spanish accent.

He fumbled, "Ah, yea…I was looking for Cynthia. Is she home?"

"Wait here", the woman returned. She shut the door behind her and reengaged a couple of the locks. He patiently stood and waited for the response. He assumed that since she did not deny that someone named Cynthia lived in the house that he would very quickly be reunited with the "wicked sorceress" from his past. He was slightly mistaken. He was able to stand still for almost two minutes before he checked the time on his phone. After a few more minutes he seriously considered knocking on the door again, but he felt that somehow fell in the rude category. He also felt being made to wait outside for an extended period of time was also not in the polite category.

Eventually the locks were undone once again, and the aged lady re-opened the door. She bluntly responded, "Yes. Ms. Cynthia is home."

Greg waited a few seconds expecting an invitation to enter the house. He curiously asked, "Can I come in and see her?"

The old women rolled her eyes and stated, "I will go check." She left the heavy door open as she turned and started to slowly shuffle from the entranceway. She took only a few steps away when she spoke again. The words did not startle Greg nearly as much as the voice. He clearly heard the voice of his recent deceased love, Monica emanating from the old lady. She said, "You should leave, Cynthia is not good for you."

He was startled and felt a shiver run through his body. He loudly asked, "What did you just say."

The minuscule old lady stopped and with effort turned half-way, “I did not say anything, Sir.” She turned back and ambled out of his sight.

What the fuck was that, he asked himself. *I know what I heard, and the voice was Monica’s.* He actually took a nervous step backward and continued, *you know this is way screwy. I must be losing my mind.*

He sighed and whispered out loud, “What am I doing here?”

Before he could answer himself, the lady returned and unlocked the screen door, “She said to send you to the pool. Do you know where it is?”

He stepped into the house and said, “Yes, I lived here a long time ago. I know the way.”

“Good”, she retorted. “My duties are done for the day and I have a long walk home.” She stepped past him clutching a small purse and started down the driveway at a remarkable fast pace. He could hear her talking to herself. He deduced by the tone that she was unhappy with Cynthia. He wondered if she actually walked the alley everyday as she scooted past his car. Her volume increased tenfold the further she walked away from the house and the ranting reverted completely to Spanish. The last word he heard was crystal clear as she ranted, “Bruja.”

“That word again”, he remarked to himself as he ventured through the entranceway, past an office to his left, and a formal living room to the right. A quick glance revealed that the decor significantly changed since the last time he was in the house. He entered the kitchen, noted much of that room seemed the same, walked past the small breakfast nook to a set of large French doors. He pushed the door open and stepped onto a colored concrete patio.

Straight off the concrete patio was a small oval pool. He recalled that the swim season in the pacific northwest was relatively short, so the pool usually had the heated pool cover installed. Today the cover was removed, and the water looked shimmering and inviting. The patio curved to the right of the pool and formed a roughly four hundred foot outside living area. In the center was a built-in brick fire pit. Pushed to the far-right hand side was a long and expensive brick and stainless-steel grill. Off centered between the grill and the pit was a small, circular glass and aluminum table with flour slingback chairs. A small outside love seat with bright floral cushions was paced to the left of the pit. At the top of the patio near the pool were two adjustable teak, pool chairs and a small table with an open briefcase. Cynthia was reclining on one of these chairs. She was holding and reading a few sheets of paper oblivious to his presence.

He stepped past the table, cleared his throat, and said, “Hello, Cynthia.”

She looked up from her papers, seemed confused for a second before she dropped the papers into the briefcase. She quickly stood up and exclaimed, “Oh my God, it’s you! Silly Esperanza, you are not Bill. Oh my God.”

She closed the gap between, stood for a second looking up into his eyes before she embraced him. At first he awkwardly stood stiffly while she hugged him. He eventually and somewhat ungainly reached around and lightly returned the affection.

She stepped back and stated, “I can’t believe you are here. You look fantastic.”

He momentarily stared at her from top to bottom. She was wearing a white swimsuit bikini top and a blue and white pin striped bikini skirt. Maroon flip flops adorned her feet and oversized sunglasses rested on her face. Her long hair was pulled back into a simple ponytail. The only jewelry she wore was the starburst pendent on the thin gold chain and a gold ankle bracelet on her left foot. The only make-up he detected was her deep red lipstick.

"You do too", he returned the compliment, but he felt troubled giving it. The idea that she aged well was an absolute understatement. He could swear on a stack of Bibles that she was *exactly* the same. He could not detect any age lines on her face, neck, or hands. Her body was still firm, and her ample breasts filled the swimsuit top without any sign of sagging. She barely looked old enough to purchase alcohol much less be solidly in middle age.

He stuttered, "I know people always say to people that have not seen in a long time that they haven't changed, but you *really* do look twenty something."

"You are so sweet," she cooed. She stood on her toes and gave him a quick peck on the cheek. She removed her sunglasses and said, "These things hide so much."

He looked down into her eyes. The first glance did not reveal any difference. She had no crow's feet, no signs of grey, or any sign of aging. He started to make a comment and right before his eyes, she aged twenty years. He blinked and rubbed his eyes. Her eyes locked onto his and her forty some year-old face remained. No movie ever had a better special effect. The longer they held each other's gaze, the more his concerns did not seem important. He shifted his eyes slightly down to her pendant, pointed, and remarked, "Oh, you still wear that."

She laughed and said, "Yes. This is one of the few things I have from my mother. Please have seat." She motioned to one of the chairs at the outside table.

He took a seat while she operated the crank for the umbrella in the center. The umbrella opened providing them with shade.

"I am going to grab us some ice teas. Are you hungry?" she asked.

"No, I am good", he replied. She turned and headed into the kitchen. Even though he knew that staring was not polite, he could not but stare at her hips and bottom as swayed thought the kitchen door. She might have aged twenty-years, but her sexiness was still vibrant.

Ok, now what? he thought. *What are we going to talk about? I can't lead off with the night of our fight, though I think we need to eventually talk about it.*

She returned balancing a tray that contained a picture of iced tea, a couple of glasses, a bowl of salsa, and chips. She carefully set the tray down onto the table and served tea to both of them. She pushed the salsa and chips into the center of the table and took a seat facing him. He marveled at her grace and beauty. He felt a rush of warmth flow through his body. He did not define the feeling as erotic, though the sensation emerging between his thighs did have a special appeal. He sank into the sling back chair relaxed and especially content. He thought that he could actually take a nap.

He shook his head and refocused. He carefully said, "The pendant. You never told me about your mother?"

"I didn't?" she asked.

"I don't think so. If you did, I don't remember. As matter of fact, I don't remember much about your parents," he added.

"Ok", she replied. "My parents were from Peru and married as teenagers. They immigrated to California in their early twenties. They had the fabled 'come to America with nothing, work hard, and become successful' story. They kept moving north as opportunities opened for my father. They settled here in western Washington when my mother was pregnant with me.

She took a drink of iced tea, wet her lips, and carefully continued, “My mother had, well, problems. I do not know the extent because she disappeared shortly before my third birthday. I barely remember her. My father was so great. I never felt that I missed something by not having a mother in the picture. My father was also a financial genius. By the time I was finishing high school, he had amassed quite a fortune. He intended to quit working before he was fifty, but cancer took him first. I was barely twenty and an heiress to a financial empire. Fortunately, my father had a few very trusted partners who guided me through the first few years. I was young and distraught and not interested in following in his footsteps. They pulled me aside and informed that some members of the board were conspiring with another company for a hostile takeover. They found a third party and recommended I take their offer. I honestly do not know if that was the right path, but I can tell you that I have never worried about money.”

She made a circle with her finger and continued, “Back to the pendent. My dad said that this belonged to my mother. She was wearing it the first time he met her. When she took off, she left the pendent. I found it in junior high. He was hesitant to tell me about it, but I coaxed him. I just knew it was hers. He said I could wear it if I wanted. I have worn it almost every day. At first the thing seemed to give me a connection to my mother, but after his death, I viewed it as a connection to both of them.”

Her voice slightly cracked as she completed the story. He reached and touched her hand and said, “Ok, I am sorry for bringing up something painful.”

She laughed and said, “You didn’t know or didn't remember. Either way, not your fault. You asked a question, now it is my turn.”

“Ok shoot”, he replied.

"What have you been doing for the past twenty years?" she teasingly quipped.

He chuckled with her and then began a summary of his life since he moved to Sacramento. She nodded and intently listened. She teased him for having the same job and same apartment. He floored her when he told her that he still had the Accord. Her watched her jaw drop open when he told her that the car was sitting in the driveway.

"You took a road trip in a twenty-year-old car. You must be crazy," she exclaimed. "How many miles do you have on it?

"Pushing two hundred thousand, and I probably am a little crazy", he agreed. In his mind he added, *driving that car here is one of the least craziest parts of this entire story.*

He continued his recollection of his past by highlighting a few of his romantic encounters. He did not go into any specific details in regard to the depth of love or sex, but she seemed to deduct the truth anyways. When she asked a question about Chastity's habits in the bedroom, he flushed with embarrassment.

"Oh my God", she exclaimed, "I think I have mortified you."

Greg flustered, "I suppose a little."

"A little", she tormented him, "You are red as a beet. You know at one time, I could have dropped my top right here and you would have instantly climbed on top of me."

She laughed out loud and grabbed his hand. "Ok, ok, I see that some things are not the same. Let's move on."

"Loud and energetic", Greg flatly replied.

"Excuse me", she asked.

"You wanted to know about Chastity. She was loud and energetic. I loved having sex with her, but I could not connect with her very much", he flatly reported.

"Greg, I sure do appreciate the honesty. I have not changed too much, at least I don't think I have. Esperanza is constantly nagging me about saying 'inappropriate things'," she sighed. "She is probably right. If I cross a line you can tell me to back off."

"Have you loved anyone? Who is Bill", he queried.

"As far as Bill, he is one of my financial advisors. He has been so good for so many years but recently he disappointed me. He was supposed to meet me yesterday and I did not get even the courtesy of a phone call. I assumed you were him when Esperanza told me that 'hombre Blanco' was at the front door", she answered. "I have loved a couple of times and I lost a couple of times. The internet has made dating risky for me anymore. People know who I am, or more specifically that I may have some money before we go out for the first time. I still have faith, but I am very guarded. Unfortunately, I had a few really bad experiences. Some people just equal shit."

Greg smiled and said, "Slipknot."

"What?" she confusedly asked.

"Ever heard of the band Slipknot? They have a song called 'People Equal Shit'," he asked.

He gave him a funny look and said, "Music was your thing, not mine. While I doubt that I have ever heard a Slipknot song, I agree with their sentiment. How about you, have you ever really loved?"

For the next two hours, they shared stories about love, sex, and romance. They laughed and made fun of each other's bad experiences. Cynthia admitted that she was engaged about seven years prior, but she broke it off when she discovered the future groom was not faithful. Since then she became even more selective and reclusive. She told him that she liked to paint.

She surprisingly shyly added, “I also like to write. I have written a few books.”

“What? That is great. What are the titles? When were they published? I would sure love to read them some day”, he responded.

“Oh, no, no, no”, she reacted. “You are actually the first human being that I have ever told that I wrote a book, well actually three books. They are not published because they are never going to see the light of day from my Mac Book. I have too much fear of rejection and won’t risk letting anyone reading a single word.”

“You have a fear? That is surprising, though I have to admit that our time together is a bit hazy. We probably have more surprises than known facts”, he concluded. “Any chance you let me read one chapter?”

“No”, she answered. “Those books are sort of a purging of bad relationships. Have you ever been in a relationship that ended really poorly?”

He did not immediately answer, and she stated, “Did I cross a line already?”

“No, you plowed through the line”, he joked. “I just wasn’t sure how to begin. Let me tell you about the love of my life, Monica.”

She listened carefully without interrupting even once. He relayed the entire story from their meeting to his decision to marry her. He choked up as he described the funeral and the pain he has felt since that day.

“Oh my God, I am so sorry. When I said ended poorly, I had no idea. I can't believe I made you drudge this all back up when she has not been gone that long”, she lamented.

“Well, like your books, I have not really told anybody about this. Coming up here is actually a welcome distraction. I was planning a trip to the Caribbean till I received your invitation", he replied.

"You should still go to the Caribbean. And to Alaska and to Europe. You should do it all while you can", she enthused.

"I have always wanted to go to Alaska", he admitted. "Maybe when I get back, I will put in for more vacation in a few months."

"That sounds like a great idea. Why don't we talk about something a little cheerier? Let's talk about dinner. I am getting pretty hungry and the salsa and chips disappeared a few hours ago," she said standing up.

He remained seated and looked completely puzzled. He glanced down at his phone and was surprised to see how long he had already spent at her house. She looked down at him and gave a quizzical expression, "Dinner? You still eat, right?"

"Well, sure," he stammered.

She picked up the empty pitcher and iced tea glasses when she stood. She seemed to sense his insecurity and slowly set the items back on the table. She kneeled down in front of him and took one of his hands. She gently asked, "Why did you come here today? I mean besides that I sent the invitation."

"I am not sure", he honestly replied. "Hard to put into words."

She stared up at him and asked, "When do you have to be back at work? How much time did you take for vacation? Do you have to be back within the next day or so?"

He shook his head and replied, "No. I really don't need to start driving back for a few days."

"Ok, as I guessed. I am going to go on a limb and say that we might have some unfinished business," she carefully stated.

"Probably", he answered.

“I think you are struggling with multiple choices. You don't know whether to leave this afternoon or to stay for dinner. I also think you don't know if you should spend your few days with me or head home,” she surmised.

“Those assumptions are pretty fair”, he returned.

“I have all sorts of great ideas”, she smiled, “But I think you need to make at least one decision. Let’s start with dinner. Why don’t we go out and have a bite? My treat. We can take your car. I can always get an Uber back to the house if you decide that you have enough answers for one day or one visit. I think you will hate yourself if you don’t”

“Dinner on you”, he smiled. “Who the hell turns down a free meal.”

“That’s the spirit”, she replied as she stood up. “Give me ten minutes to change.”

She walked past him, her hips swaying a few inches from his face. His eyes involuntarily turned and followed her around the table and towards the house. Her right hip was so close that he could smell her body spray. The visual and the fragrance launched him into thousand memories, most of them erotic. He looked down and saw the clear outline of an erection under his shorts.

Oh, that is just great, he thought somewhat embarrassed. *She is still completely hot. Give me a few minutes for this to go away.*

She called from the French door, “You don't have to sit outside, you can come in and turn on the tv or the stereo.

You are freaking kidding me, he cursed inside. “No, it is so nice outside today, I will wait till here till you are ready.”

“Are you sure?” she inquired.

She knows, he moaned inside. "No, I am good. Just gonna sit here and check out some stocks on the phone."

She gave him a knowing smile and said, "Alright then. I just need ten."

He was thankful that when she announced that she was ready that his groin was distracted enough with boring stock information. He followed her out of the house and once outside they agreed to a change of plans. They opted for one of her sport cars, specifically, her Tesla Model S instead of the Honda. She even allowed him to drive the expensive car to dinner with old-school Nirvana on the radio faintly acting as the backdrop to their conversation. In his mind, though, he heard the Sea Wretch song over the Nirvana vocals.

Chapter 8:
Oh baby, let's spark a flame…

They could not decide on a place to eat. They didn't argue, but instead neither really wanted to make a decision. They were hungry and so many places sounded appetizing to the both of them. He continued to drive as they passed place after place. She then gave instructions to the next street that had restaurants. They passed the time with more small talk with each avoiding discussions about their breakup.

After thirty-five minutes Greg announced, "Next place on this road we are stopping, even if it is a Chuck-E-Cheese."

She laughed and said, "Agreed."

He drove a few more minutes before he asked, "Why have you stayed at that small house? I think you have the money to move to a bigger house. And you could be in a slightly better neighborhood."

"You know I have actually looked at houses a few times," she sighed. "The truth is I don't need a bigger house and I am awfully content. That little place has everything I need. The neighborhood isn't that bad."

"Are you kidding me", he reacted. "Pleasant Avenue was a war zone when I lived here and by the looks, I don't think it has changed."

"You exaggerate", she defended.

"A prostitute propositioned me when I slowed down to pull into your driveway. I don't think I exaggerate," he retorted.

She stared at him and replied, "I think you are telling the truth. Well, was she hot?"

"If hepatitis and syphilis are your thing. Plus, her crotch stank", he answered.

"You checked out her vagina. She mustn't have been that horrible", she teased.

"The odor from her vagina invited itself into my car," he said.

"Pretty fortunate that we took my car then," she quipped, "I think having Esperanza as my housekeeper sort of makes my place off limits from certain elements on Pleasant Avenue. She is the elder statesmen in the neighborhood. She is a horrible housekeeper, but she keeps me company a couple of times a week. She is always trying to set me up with one of her hooligan nephews. Thinks I need to keep the Mexican blood line pure."

"You have Mexican heritage", he teased.

"Greg Palmer", she sighed, "We lived together for two years and I sometimes wonder how well you knew me."

Before he could respond she said, "Up ahead is a TGIF's on the left and Azteca's Mexican on the right."

Greg confidently replied, "Azteca's it is." He was actually not feeling very assured but more in vein of being relieved. He was not ready to have to consider the statement regarding how well he knew her. *True I lived with you for two years, but all the stuff I should probably know, I don't. What I think I know is pretty freaking wacky.*

A few weeks after Greg moved in with Cynthia, he experienced something that he could not explain. The evening started pretty normal. After they finished dinner, he left his plate on the table for her to clean up. He grabbed a beer from the refrigerator and his favorite bong from the counter and headed towards the living room.

"Hey slob, are you going to help me?" she asked.

He plopped down on a bean bag in front of the television and replied, “You got all that, right?”

She walked into the room behind him, swiped the pipe, and said, “You are a terrible roommate sometimes.”

“Hey, give me that back”, he demanded.

“Before you get totally baked and useless, how about you do something for me”, she said holding the bong out of his reach.

“What do you want? Do I need to get up?” he whined.

She sighed, “You really don't deserve me. Yes, you need to get up and go take a shower with me.”

Startled he said, “Serious.”

She was already walking out of the room simultaneously removing her top. He dropped the beer on the floor, ungracefully slid out of the bean bag chair, and raced after her. He had his arms wrapped her groping her breasts before they made it to the master bedroom. Their shower was hot and steamy, and they fell onto the bed still wet. When they finished, she announced, “The sheets are soaked. You get to help me change them.”

“I think the Sonics are on tv”, he returned. He pretended to give her Bambi eyes.

“Go on, you will just annoy me anyways”, she answered. “And put some shorts on if you are going to sit on the couch.”

“Yea, yea”, he replied while rapidly exiting the bedroom. He grabbed the remote from an end table and switched on the television. He clicked on the guide and began searching for the Sonics game while peering back into the bedroom. He actually did not know if the Sonics were playing that night. He breathed a sigh of relief when he found they were playing. He switched to the game, turned up the volume, and yelled, “Yep, they sure are on.”

"Turn it down, I don't want to hear it in here. I am going to turn on the radio", she returned.

He lowered the volume, tossed the remote onto the couch, and bent over to grab the beer on the floor. He walked into the kitchen and rifled through the silverware drawer till he found a bottle opener. He stepped outside and peaked into the house looking for Cynthia. Satisfied that she wasn't coming around the corner, he turned his attention to his beer. He used the opener to pierce a small hole and then shot gunned the entire can in less than 20 seconds. He belched, gave a little whoop, and went back into the house. He grabbed a second beer from the refrigerator. He saw that he only had a few left and figured that he may need to venture down to Marco's later that evening. He picked up his bong and then carefully loaded it. He slid back onto the bean bag with the bong in one hand and beer in the other. He put the beer between his legs. He flicked the lighter and drew several breathes off the pipe holding in the smoke as long as possible. He settled into the chair looking up at the game that he actually had no interest in viewing. The alcohol and the drugs provided him the entertainment that he desired. The plan was not to drift into a nap, but he knew that scenario was very likely. He was not overly surprised when he woke up about an hour later with the unopened beer warm in his lap.

He was stunned that instead of waking somewhat groggy, he awoke completely alert with his every hair on his body standing on edge. He never broke sleep in such a manner. He sat up in the bean bag chair still unsure why he felt so unnerved. Quietly he stood up and tiptoed out of the living room trying to figure out why he was spooked. The Sonics were still on and he could hear music emanating from their bedroom. He held his breathe while standing in the kitchen trying to block out the sports announcers and the radio from the bedroom. He turned his head in the direction of the bedroom and strained to hear something just under the other house noises. He took two large steps toward the hallway with the master bedroom. A barely audible sound was coming from the bedroom. He followed his ears all the way to the shut bedroom door. He could tell that it was Cynthia and that she was lightly singing.

Greg was what Cynthia termed “a walk-about-the-house singer”. He was not a good singer but that did not stop him when the mood struck him to sing along with the radio. She usually allowed his obnoxious vocalizations for a minute or so before the noise drove her crazy. Hearing her sing made him smile. He felt the tension that he could not explain dissipate in an instant. An evil smile crossed his face. He intended to give a little pay back for the abuse she heaped on him for his singing.

He turned the bedroom doorknob and discovered that the door was locked. They lived together for only a few months, and this was a new event. He bent over to look at the lock and saw the simple keyhole. He remembered that she kept the door lock keys above the door frames. He reached and found the straight key. He smiled again as he put the key into the knob and felt the locking mechanism release.

He froze in fright. A sixth sense was screaming for him to not open the door. He felt a cold sweat break out over his body. The unexplained fear had suddenly reappeared. He stepped away from the door leaving the key still inside the knob.

What the hell is wrong with you, he thought. *Why are you scared to open the door? Don’t be such a pussy!*

You know something is not right inside that room, he mentally argued with himself. *Take a walk down to Marco's.*

He wiped his brow. He was still unnerved as he continued the disagreement, *this is fucking ridiculous. She is in there making the bed and singing. I am doing it.*

NOOOO, he yelled as turned the unlocked doorknob and forcible swung the door open.

He was immediately hit by a wall of heat. The room was not just stuffy but was outright sizzling to the point of almost intolerable. He involuntarily took a step backwards and stuck his hands up in front of his face as if to block an invisible attacker. His body adjusted to the heat rolling from the room and he took a step forward towards the bedroom, though he kept his hands up. The unbearable temperature caused him to tilt his head to the side as he took another step through the open door. He felt every sweat gland on his body kick into action as he attempted to survey the room.

A small reading lamp was providing the only light in the room. The overhead light was off, and the curtains were pulled tightly shut. The illuminance seemed incredible dim and excessively far away instead of the ten feet straight ahead. The room somehow seemed to have expanded beyond the drywall and four by four studs. He scanned away from the table lamp and strained his eyes to make out the pile of stripped sheets in the corner on the opposite side of the bed. A little more visible was an outline of Cynthia of sitting crossed legged to the right of the bed. Her back was resting against the bed and he was facing her right-side profile. Two very strange features in the room stopped him in his tracks.

Throughout the room a phosphorus green and dark purple hazy fog settled from the floor to roughly three feet in the air. Above the haze, the rest of the room seemed somehow to be pushed out beyond the walls and her property. Scarlet red flashes randomly zig zagged from the top of the haze to the floor. One struck within a few inches of his feet and he instinctively jumped to his right further into the room and closer to Cynthia.

He looked down as the visibility of his feet faded. He tentatively said, “Babe.”

She did not respond, and she appeared to be in deep concentration. Her head was down, and her hands were in front of her appearing to hold an invisible ball. Her arms and hands were trembling as if in a great struggle. He started to try to get her attention again, but she reacted first with a loud yell. She began to sing the repetitive chorus to a fifties do-wop hit,

Oh baby, let’s spark a flame,
Oh baby, let’s spark a flame,
We need to give the evening some heat.

The lightning strikes increased tenfold throughout the room and she repeated lyric over and over again. A few of these flashes seemed to pass straight through him without causing him any harm. For a few seconds his eyes raced around the room following the rapid flashes. When he returned to the profile of Cynthia, he again took an involuntary step backward.

Her profile was no longer smooth and lifelike. Her limbs had lengthened to grotesque lengths and freakish lumps and growths covered her body like a prehistoric beast. The circumference of her head was increasing at an alarming rate and was at least three times larger than normal.

At that moment, Greg lost control and yelled, “What the fuck! What the *FUCK!* Cynthia, Cynthia, what the hell is going on.”

He took another step backward and he roughly hit the bedroom wall. He went to slide to his left and out of the room, but he discovered that he was stuck to the wall. Thousands of tiny branches seemed to be gripping his back and holding him firm. As he twisted to free himself, the wall stretched with him and he felt like he was caught in the tentacles of a gigantic octopus. He yelled nonsensical statements and curses towards the monstrosity sitting where his girlfriend had been sitting only a few moments earlier.

The red flashes ceased, and the head of the Cynthia-thing shrunk back to the normal size. He could see the outline of her mouth start to open, shut, then open again.

"GET OUT", the Cynthia-thing roared in voice that was deep and dark and unlike anything Greg ever heard except in horrendous horror movies.

The wall released him, and he stumbled forward within a few feet of the Cynthia-thing. He could now see that the growths over her body were flashing in synchronous with the red lightening. He reacted by screaming in terror. He turned and took two giant strides out of the room.

Once in the hallway, the temperature dropped by dozens of degrees. He did not have any discernible thoughts other than he needed to get out of that room; and possible out of the house as quick as possible. He rounded the hallway and into the kitchen at too great a pace for his athleticism. He started to trip, and he grabbed a chair at the table. He twisted himself around the kitchen table, but he could not stop the momentum. He hit the floor flat on his back. His head bounced off the tile sending a blast of pain through his temples and graying his vision.

He was not sure if he lay on his back for thirty seconds or thirty minutes. When he opened his eyes,

Cynthia in a normal form but nude was standing looking down over him.

"What are doing on the floor, Graceful?" she asked in a teasing manner.

He stuttered, "You…you..you".

"Yes, me", she replied.

He sat up and aggressively slid away from her, "What the hell was that?"

"In the bedroom", she casually pointed.

"YES, in the fucking bedroom, what the fuck was that shit", he yelled.

"Well that sure is nice", she replied a little crossly. "Let me teach you something about living with a woman. If a door is locked, she is doing something that she probably does not want you to see."

He pushed backwards again and hit a chair. He ungainly lifted himself onto he chairs, rubbed his hands through his hair and looked at the sweat now coating the hands. He looked at Cynthia and recognized that her body was dry.

He shook his head in disbelief and unable to form the words to protest against what he had witnessed. In an exasperated tone he muttered, "Horrible."

She took a couple of steps towards him and said, "You can be such a shit sometimes."

"I am a shit?", he scowled.

"Yes", she emphasized. "You did not finish me when me made love. I hinted that I was horny when I suggested we take a shower and you did not wait for me. Then I come in and find you passed out. I am human but we are not in the stage of our relationship where I want to masturbate in front of you. So, I took action into my own hands and you rudely unlocked the door, yelled some absurdities, and bounced out of the room."

"You call that playing with yourself", he defiantly stated.

"I don't know how you do it, but yes, that was what I was doing", she answered. "What do you think I was doing?"

"Oh, oh, you are crazy", he sputtered.

"Alright, never mind all that," she waved her hand as if to end the topic. She knelt in front of him and yanked his shorts down to his ankles.

"Have you lost your mind?" he yelled and jerked away.

She grabbed his waist and pushed him down back onto the chair with a strength that surprised him. She gazed at his limp penis and bluntly stated, "I am on my knees and naked and your cock is not ready. I still want you inside me. I can fix this."

She leaned forward and took him into her mouth. She ran her tongue around the head while rubbing her hands on his thighs. He thought, *if this bitch thinks that she can make me hard again after that shit I saw in the bedroom, she is fucking crazy. And she is doubly crazy if she thinks I am going to fuck her ever again. No fucking way.* He was wrong on both accounts.

Their dinner at Azteca's was pleasant with good food and stimulating conversation. They fell into an easy back and forth of introducing something new about themselves to the other person. He brought her up to date on his volunteer work, his favorite books, and music. She was a movie buff and seemed to have seen every major release in the past twenty years. He found that even though she was mostly a home body, she traveled an extensive part of the United States as well as several countries. The food arrived, was devoured, and they continued to sit and talk. Greg sensed that their server was becoming impatient so he suggested that the time may have arrived to pay the bill and leave. Cynthia agreed and waved for the bill. Greg excused himself to use the restroom before they headed out the door.

As he exited the bathroom, he bumped straight into a different server who was standing right outside the door.

"Oh, excuse me", he said surprised and attempted to step around her.

"Why are you in such a big hurry?" she blatantly flirted. "My name is Isabella and I am clocking out right now."

Isabella was short with wide hips and large breasts. Her long black hair cascaded around a round but very pretty face. She smiled and reached out and put her palms on his chest.

Shocked he stated, "I am with someone tonight. Sorry."

Before he could move away, she leaned forward and tried to kiss him. He ducked her aggressive move. He exclaimed, "Whoa, lady. What the crap?" He stepped backwards away from her until he cleared the hallway that held the restrooms. He turned and rapidly walked back to their table. He did not desire to sit so he stood at her side and asked, "Is the bill paid? Are you ready?"

She looked up surprised and asked, "What is the big hurry? You have a hot date tonight?"

He blanched and said, "You are not going to believe this, but another server just tried to kiss me."

A fire lit in her eyes not seen in a very long time. "Oh really", she nicely stated.

"I just want to go", he hurried her. "Are you ready?"

"As matter of fact, I am not", she declared. "I also have to use the rest room so have a seat."

He groaned and asked, "Are you going to make a scene?"

"No, I don't even know which slutty server hit on you. Besides we are not a 'couple'", she responded with using her hands in quotations. "I really have to pee before we leave."

"Oh", he replied as she pushed her seat back and headed towards the bathroom. He slowly slid back into his seat, picked up his phone, and checked his ESPN app. He did not see anything to catch his eye, so he switched the phone off. He absentmindedly played with the cloth napkin in front of him, looking around the corner for either Cynthia or the unwelcome server. He did not see either. His eyes wondered back to the remaining few items on the table. The bill was sitting face up inside the open bill holder. He could see the servers large handwritten note across the top and bottom. He randomly reached over to pick it up. Part of him instantly felt guilty that he should not be reviewing the bill paid by someone else. As he started to set the receipt back down, he noted writing on the other side. He turned it over without intending to read. He dropped it and yanked his hand back as if the paper was on fire. He saw that in large bold letters the word "BRUJA" was scrawled.

He stood up faster than he intended and actually knocked the seat over in process. The few tables that still had customers stopped their conversations for a second. He waved in embarrassment, carefully lifted the chair, and slowly pushed it under the table. Everyone returned to their affairs and Cynthia mocked him from behind, "Way to go, you are smooth".

She came up behind him and hugged him. He pointed to the receipt and said, "Did you see that written on it when you paid the bill."

She leaned around him and asked, "See what?"

He pointed again at the bill and directed, "Read it."

She stepped around him, picked it up, flipped it over a few times and curiously said, “What am I looking for?”

He grabbed the receipt from her hands and flipped it over. She retorted, “That is a little rude considering I paid for your dinner, buster.”

He dejectedly said, “I swear a word was written on the backside.”

He looked at her, back to the bill, and whispered, “What the fuck.”

She took his hand and said, “Let’s go.”

He allowed her to lead him outside to the car. She opened the passenger door for him indicating that she was going to drive back to her house. She did not say anything as she drove the car out of the parking lot. He wondered if he should break the silence, but he was still trying to decipher the strange ending to a great meal. She pulled into a package store and declared, “I am going to need a drink tonight. What about you? I know that you had a problem at one time. Are you still clean?”

“I haven't done drugs since I left Remington. I probably should not but I do have the occasional drink”, he admitted.

“Good”, she said opening the car door. “Let’s get something to drink.”

He followed her into the package store. She selected two bottles of wine while he grabbed a twelve pack of beer and a small bottle of Maker’s Mark. She insisted on paying for everything.

Once reseated in the Tesla, she turned to him and softly asked, “What word did you think you saw?”

He started to answer but noticed for the first time that the collar on her shirt was ripped and she had scratch on her neck. He gestured towards her collar and neck and asked, “What happened?”

"Nothing don't worry about it. Answer my question", she firmly insisted.

He hesitated a second. He considered pressing her about the issue a little harder but then decided to let it go, at least for now. The writing on the bill bothered him a lot more at that given time. He replied, "I will probably mispronounce so I will spell it out. B, R, U, J, A."

"Bruja", she enunciated the spelling.

"Yea", he answered, "And I have heard it a few times recently too. What does it mean?"

"It is Spanish for a witch", she answered.

"I don't understand", he said.

She sighed, "I think I do. Not everything but some of it."

"Alright", he replied.

"You remember the day we broke up", she began.

"Ha, that is the fuck of it", he exclaimed. "I actually don't remember too much from that afternoon."

"Are you driving back to Sacramento tomorrow", she inquired.

"You know I am not", he answered.

"Did you check out of your hotel?" she continued.

He shook his head negative. She put the car in gear and said, "We are going go to your hotel so that you can get all your stuff and check out. For the next few days we are going to get everything on the table. I think then that we can stay friends, or we can go our separate ways. We can't do either until we tell each other everything. Do you have any issues with this plan?"

He non-verbally agreed and she drove to his hotel. During the drive she turned on the radio and found a classic rock station in a commercial break. The first song that started after the break was the do-wop song, “Spark a Flame.” She unconsciously sang softly along the to the chorus. She gave him a confused look when he laughed out loud.

Chapter 9:
You could have it all…

Cynthia set Greg up in a small spare bedroom and they both changed into comfortable clothes. For Greg, he donned a loose pair of work out shorts and a Motley Crue Dr. Feelgood t-shirt. He finished dressing first so he helped himself to a beer and lounged on a couch. He picked a remote and turned on the television. He randomly flipped though the channels until he came across a terrible eighty's zombie movie. He watched a scene from in which a young heroine is attempting to escape a neighborhood of slow-moving zombies on a moped. She kicked, screamed, and begged the scooter to go faster as an unidentified soundtrack song played in backdrop.

You could have it all,
But you are beginning to fall.

A few minutes later Cynthia entered the kitchen and poured herself a large glass of merlot. She strolled into the living room and eased onto a love seat opposite of Greg. She was wearing a very short one-piece simple cotton night gown. When she sat the bottom creeped high on her thigh and was low cut in the front revealing her full breasts. He momentarily looked away but when he turned back his eyes immediately fell on her upper thighs and cleavage.

"Humph", he sounded.

Oblivious she took a sip of wine, set the glass on the end table, and asked, "What?"

He blushed and half pointed towards her legs. She looked down and then laughed. "Greg, what are your trying to tell me?" she teased.

"You are a distraction", he stated.

"Do I need to change my lounging shirt in my own house?" she asked while smirking.

"No", he answered honestly. "To be completely honest, you are still an extremely attractive woman. Like I said earlier I would swear in a court of law that you have not aged at all."

"Thank-you", she graciously accepted the compliment. She tugged on the bottom of the nightgown to provide only about a half inch more coverage. She said seriously, "Speaking of court of law, that is a pretty good lead into our conversation. I don't think we should start with the day we broke up quite yet."

He shook his head and she continued, "What do you recall from our time together?"

"Well, we partied a lot, or at least I did", he offered. "We went out to dinner a lot. You took me on vacation to Reno, Las Vegas, and New Orleans. We drank and gambled a lot. We had a lot of good times."

She nodded and pointedly asked, "How often did we have stimulating conversation."

"I don't think that was part of the equation", he honestly replied. "I also think it is safe to say that we had a pretty good sex life."

"I agree but I don't want to dive into that right now", she stated. "I don't want to sound like a bitch, but I have a lot of memories of you being drunk or high most of the time."

"That is true", he agreed. "I wasn't working during the time we lived together. At the beginning you guilted me to mow your yard, but I wasn't even doing that by the second summer. What the hell did you see in me?"

"I will get to that", she waved the topic aside. "Do you recall any of our disagreements?"

He thought for a second before he said, "The little odd things. This house always seemed to have something weird going on in it. I would tell you about something and you always quickly dismissed it."

"Now we are getting somewhere. Tell me about these odd things", she directed.

"You always blamed anything I saw or heard on the drugs", he offered. "Like the time I opened the locked bedroom door and you said you were rubbing yourself."

"Did you remember what you told me that you saw", she pressed.

"I don't remember the exact details", he lied. "I remember some sort of fog in the bedroom."

"At the time you gave me a real crazy story about another world and that I turned into some kind of monster", she replied staring hard at him.

He swallowed and said, "Like you said, I always had drugs in my system at the time. Maybe it was a bad trip."

She seemed to accept the answer. "Anything else that caused tension in the house."

"A couple. You were insane about the letters that you mailed on a frequent basis. You were so…so anal about them and you would not tell me anything about them. You made me jealous every time you went through the whole production of sealing them and putting them into the mailbox. You always gave me a warning to stay out of the mailbox. To be blunt, you were mean about it", Greg told her.

"Fair enough," she said acceptingly. "Almost all of them involved business dealings and you simply did not have a real need to read them. At times you had a warped sense of humor and I just did not want you messing around with them."

As she explained the purpose for the sensitivity to her mail, a bunch of memories jumped into his head involving, "Lights."

"Yes, the lights. You frequently claimed to see these flashes of light, like tiny lightning strikes", she replied.

"Yes, YES", he excited recalled. "I would tell you about them, you would ignore me and claim I was high. I would get angry and argue with you. Sometimes I let it go, but I also remember pressing you at times till…you…you."

"Go on", she said.

He remained quiet and she answered for him, "Till I exploded and screamed at you like a crazy woman."

"More than just that", he timidly said. "Your reaction scared the hell out of me."

"I don't know about scaring you…" she started.

He interrupted, "I can't explain why but I remember that you seemed positively evil."

"I won't try to change your impressions on twenty-year memories", she said a little snappy.

She took a drink from her glass and continued to hold it in one hand, "Do you remember my two friends both named Danielle?"

He slowly shook as vague memories awakened. "Yes, but not a lot of detail."

"You met Danielle Woo only a couple of times. She was the really tall and thin Asian girl that went to high school with me. The other Danielle, Danielle Dudek was here at the house a lot, especially at the end," she explained. "We became friends in grade school. She was my best friend."

He shook his head and shrugged. She curtly said, "Come on, you mean you don't remember the Danielle who was, as you always said, 'built like a brick shit house'." She set her glass on the floor and used her hands to simulate quotation marks around this description of the second Danielle.

He spoke as if in a daydream, “Double D.” As he said the nickname out loud, the image of five-foot seven-inch blonde woman jumped into his vision. She had long legs with thick thighs and a heavy bottom. Her arms and legs were toned, and her belly was flat. She had enormous breasts, hence Greg’s nickname of “Double D”. Long straight platinum blond hair fell around a round face. Her eyes were a bit too close together and she had an irregular pug of a nose. Fresh acne or acne scars covered her cheeks. She had a very wide mouth with a noticeable overbite. When she smiled, she revealed a mess of crooked and discolored teeth. She often walked around the house in daisy dukes and halter tops regardless of the season. Many times, she came into the kitchen in the morning in just her bra and panties. Greg gawked and Cynthia scolded her to put on more clothes. Greg once told Cynthia that ‘her body is banging but her face is brutal’.

“Greg Palmer, are you sitting on my couch and fantasizing about Danielle? What are remembering?” she demanded.

“You know that is exactly the issue that I discovered after I drove up here”, he flatly replied. “I remember Danielle, now, after you mentioned her. I can picture her, but I do not remember anything more specific. Much of my two years with you is like Danielle. I feel as if those few years were whitewashed away but pieces are starting to appear through the light coating. Nothing is connected together, just bits and pieces. Some are vivid while others, like Danielle, are just spotty.”

“You are telling me that you can’t remember Danielle walking around the house in just her under clothes?” she prodded.

“Yes, but not a whole lot else”, he honestly answered.

She crossly asked, “What about you two either always grab-assing or fighting? You two drove me crazy.”

“No”, he said, “Wait…yes. She always suggested that we have a threesome and then you would become furious with me.”

“The threesome was always your idea”, she retorted.

“No, it wasn’t,” he defended himself. “Let’s not argue about threesomes with Danielle. Why are you asking me about Danielle? What does she have to do with the flashes of light?”

“Hold on just one more minute”, she replied as she held her hand at waist level. “One more thing, or in reality, three more things. Do you remember my rules of the house?”

“Uhm...I think so. No heroin and don't mess with the mail”, he answered.

“Which you broke many times. What about the third rule?” she pressed.

He thought for a moment and then jumped up, “Holy shit, I cheated on you a bunch of times.”

She calmly replied, “I let you have sex with those sluts, so you weren't really cheating. You were not really a solid citizen back then; matter of fact, you were a miserable boyfriend. You were, if anything, like clockwork so I could tell when you were going to stray which was about every two months. The total was eleven times you fucked another woman.”

“And the rule was not in our bed”, he recalled. He paced the living room in front of her love seat.

“Yes, not in my bedroom”, she agreed. “Sit down, you are making me nervous stomping around the living room.”

“Oh, sorry”, he said as he sat in recliner in the corner. “I remember them now, each and every one of them. Maybe not their names or details but I remember bringing them here, and never going to their places. I made love with each of them in the small spare bedroom."

"My ass," she said icily. "You were not *making love*, you only wanted them to blow a load. I often had to show them out of the house because you passed out soon after you were done."

"I am not trying to mince words here", he interjected. "The point is I fucked almost a dozen women and I DID NOT REMEMBER TILL JUST NOW." He stood up again and paced out of the living room into the kitchen. He roughly pulled open the refrigerator door and snagged a beer. He absentmindedly slammed the door shut and quickly twisted the top of the beer. He threw the cap into the stainless sink which ricocheted out and hit the backsplash. The cap skipped twice off the granite countertop onto the floor. He downed half of the beer in a long swallow, quietly burped, and stared down at the bottle cap on the floor. He did not hear or detect Cynthia until she was right next to him.

She gently pressed against and softly said, "Ok, I can see this is upsetting. Try not to yell and throw things off my wall."

He pulled away and yelled, "THIS IS FREAKING SCARY. HOW CAN I NOT REMEMBER THIS SHIT?"

She aggressively pulled him into her for a hug. He started to wrench away from her, but he was shocked by how strong her grip was on him. She softly nestled into his neck while steel like arms clamped him to her. She quietly cooed, "Let's go sit down. I don't know why you don't remember certain things. Maybe if we talk it out, I can figure it out."

The arm holding the beer was free of her embrace. He lifted the bottle to his lips and finished the rest of the beer in a second-long gulp. He set the bottle on the counter and replied, "Let me get another beer first."

She released him and said, "Ok, but don't get shitty one me."

The morning Greg and Cynthia broke up, he woke up feeling horrible. His head was pounding, he was covered in a light coat of sweat, and he was nauseated. He looked at the clock radio and saw that it was pushing close to 11:00 AM. He zombie walked to the bathroom to urinate and splash water on his face. Last night was an especially wild night of steaming that ended with him sneaking some H into his body. He was pretty sure that he had not tricked Cynthia, but she did not bitch about it, so he considered the night a victory. On the other hand, he was feeling exceptionally rough today.

He kept trying to pinpoint a rancid smell in the bathroom. He turned his head several times before the lightbulb in his head illuminated. He was the source of the terrible odor. He laughed at himself, turned the knobs on the shower, and brushed his teeth while waiting for the water to come to temperature. *I wonder where Cynthia is at this morning. Did she try to wake me?* he wondered.

He took a long steamy shower and then splashed on an excessive amount of cologne. He still had a headache, so he swallowed three Tylenols in an attempt to fix. He put on clean clothes and headed towards the kitchen. He felt a thousand times better than the minute he woke up. His mind was greedily anticipating a fresh cup of coffee, an afternoon in the pool, and a night of more hedonistic joy. *Today is going to rock,* he gleefully thought as the rounded the hallway into the kitchen.

Danielle was seated at the kitchen table reading a magazine. She was dressed in tight pink sweatpants and an oversized Mariner's jersey. She was shoeless but a pair of Birkenstocks were piled under the table. One foot was on the table and the other was tucked under her thigh on the chair. She lifted her eyes from the magazine and beamed, "Well, look what the cat dragged in."

"Where's Cynthia", he asked starting to feel slightly annoyed.

"Good morning to you too", she replied. "You need to stop with the heroin, or she is going to boot you."

He lied, "I don't know what you are talking about. Where is Cynthia?"

"She had to go to Seattle today for some sort of business. She will be back before dinner. She would like you to mow the lawn," she answered. "Did you want a cup of coffee."

Feeling irritated that his afternoon of laziness was possibly going to be intruded he snapped, "How do you know that?"

She pointed to a piece of paper on the table, "She left you a note. Again, I made coffee, would you like some? And when was the last time you actually ate something? Do you want me to make you some breakfast?"

The idea of coffee did ease the sting of a ruined afternoon a little bit. He replied a little less irritated, "Ok, thanks. Coffee sounds great."

She bounced from the chair to the counter while he walked over to the table and picked up the note. She asked, "Cream and sugar?"

He answered while reading the note, "Yes, please."

He needed only a few seconds to digest the contents of the note. Danielle's summary was exactly correct. She scolded him for using last night, said she had to run to Seattle, and then directed him to take care of the yard work. He let the note float back onto the table. He looked up and his eyes settled on Danielle stirring the coffee at the counter. He focused on her round and firm bottom showcased in the very tight sweatpants.

With her back still to him, she teased, “Greg, are you staring at my ass?”

“No”, he denied, “Why would I do that?

She looked over her shoulder, wiggled her hips back and forth a few times and bragged, “Because I have an awesome ass and you know it.”

She fully turned around and handed Greg the cup of coffee. He mumbled a thank-you and blew onto the top of the liquid several times before taking a small sip from the cup. The coffee was still scalding, though his efforts were good enough to allow him to swallow the first sip. He wordlessly repeated the cooling actions and took a second larger sip. The coffee was good.

She watched the routine before asking, “Is it good?”

“Yes”, he replied.

“Thank-you. And what about the coffee”, she cooed with a devilish smile.

“I just…oh, you think I complimented your rear-end,” he said as he sat down at the table. He changed the subject, “Were you here when Cynthia left?”

“No”, she relied.

“How did you get in here”, he demanded.

She laughed, “Are you kidding me? You two are the most irresponsible people I know when it comes to locking cars and houses. I just walked right through the open garage into the open house.”

“Regardless I don't think Cynthia wants random people to just barge into her house,” he returned.

“Random people. You mean like you? I have known her almost my whole life. If anyone is welcome in here it is me”, she volleyed.

“Alright. So why are you here today?” he asked.

"I am going to go swimming", she pointed towards the outside deck. "I would invite you, but you have work to do first, lawn boy."

He gruffly retorted, "Shut the fuck up."

"Oooh, aren't you surly", she teased. "Before you start on your chores, the offer still stands. Do you want me to make you some breakfast?"

"I don't know if I am going to do the yard work", he retorted, "But I am a little hungry."

She found frozen sausages in the freezer and eggs in the refrigerator. She fried up a couple of eggs and the sausages in a pan. She filled a large glass full of ice water and set it down on the table while the food was still cooking. She told him, "You need to drink this. You have to be dehydrated. If you are going to work outside today, you need to drink some water."

He was going to argue about the idea of yard work, but the wisdom of hydration made sense. He gratefully accepted and finished the glass before the food was finished. She set the plate of food on the table and refilled his glass. She said, "If you are set for now, I am going to change into my bathing suit."

"No, I am good", he replied. "And thank-you. I am not always the sweetest person in the house."

She laughed and said, "We know." She passed by his seat and gently ran her hand across his shoulders. She leaned over, gave him a quick peck on the cheek, and bounced down the hallway to one of the spare bedrooms before he could react.

He mindlessly ate his breakfast while attempting to push aside the thoughts of doing the yard work that Cynthia requested. He found his efforts were not being very successful. He contemplated the heat and the grass, the raking and the weeding. The more he thought, the less happy be became. By the time he finished breakfast, he was quite furious. He decided that he was going to spend the day at Marco's and *fuck her work lists.*

He pushed his seat from the table right as Danielle entered the kitchen in a bright yellow two-piece bikini, with sunglasses sitting on top of her head, and a large bath towel thrown over her shoulder.

"You finished", she asked as she passed the table. She picked up his plate and deposited in the sink. "I am not going to do your dishes for you. Do you want a water bottle filled? I am going fill one for myself?"

He curtly replied, "I don't need one."

She laughed and said, "Oh, going to defiant today. Oh well."

She turned and opened a cabinet. She searched with her eyes till she located the water bottles. She leaned and stood on her tip toes as she reached to grab one off the top shelf. Greg once again found his eyes drawn to her arching back and backside.

She pulled a bottle down and remarked, "Greg, quit staring at my ass."

She turned around and before he could respond she continued, "For once do me the courtesy of not denying it."

"You are a conceited bitch", he grumbled.

She took two large steps toward the kitchen table and looked down at Greg. She replied, "Look at me. You know what I am Greg Palmer? I am not a conceited bitch. I am an ugly bitch."

"What?" Greg stammered.

She ignored him and continued, "Greg I know who and what I am. I faced the truth long time ago. I am not an attractive woman. I have two very great attributes that make me a special woman. And do you know what they are?"

Feeling flustered at her outburst, he could only grunt a few unintelligible words.

Becoming louder she continued, “The first is my mind. I am a bright woman, Greg. I bet you didn't know, but I finished high school when I was fourteen. I earned a BA at U-Dub in mathematics by the time I was eighteen. I went down to Stanford and earned a master’s in advanced mathematics on a full ride. I write algorithms for computer software companies that become the basis for many of those stupid video games you waste your time. I have made an ass ton of money which I have properly invested. I project that I can retire from working by the time that I am thirty-five if I so desire. What do you think of all that, Gregory?”

“I did not know. Is that true?”, he weakly replied.

“Every fucking word of it”, she angrily replied. “They throw such words as prodigy and genius. I look at problems that others say are near impossible to solve and the answers just seem to come to me. I love being ‘smart’, but no one even takes a second to wonder about my intelligence because they cringe from my facial features.”

He offered, “You are not really ugly. You are not a beauty queen, but I would not say that you are ugly.”

She yelled, “Fuck you Greg. I know what you say, ‘banging body but brutal face’.”

“Oh”, he said averting his eyes, “You know I am high most of the time, so I don't really know what I am saying. I say things to try to be funny.”

“Fuck that”, she hissed. “You know what you are saying. You are speaking from your heart. So, don't patronize me right now by denying your own words.”

He did not respond so she continued, “You know what my second unique attribute is?”

The question hung in the air for an uncomfortable minute. She pressed, “You know what it is. Say it.”

Reluctantly he offered, “You have a banging body.”

Triumphantly she announced, “I have a banging body.”

He saw her eyes were moist with tears. For once in his life he felt empathy towards another human being. He felt drawn deep into her eyes. He was pulled inside of her and felt her soul. He witnessed her pain though her eyes. Ashamed of himself for his part, his own heart ached. Her trials and tribulations were real and honest and beautiful. He mumbled an almost incoherent, “I am sorry. I was so mean.”

She lowered her voice but kept a sharp edge, “I don't want your apologies or your sympathies. What I want is honestly from you. When you are staring at my body and I call you on it, I want you to admit it. Knowing that a man, any man is looking at me in that way is important to me. Can you do that simply human act of kindness?”

“Yes”, he quickly replied.

“The second thing I want from you is for you to try to have a real conversation with me and not be so damn condescending,” she pressed.

“Ok”, he answered.

“Third thing”, she continued, “I want you to tell me the truth right now. Have you ever fantasized about me? Does my ass turn you on?”

Without thinking he admitted, “Yes.”

She smiled, stepped away from table and walked to the counter. She spun around and ran her hands through her hair. She quickly pulled her bikini bottoms down to her feet. She kicked them aside and stepped back to the table where she pushed every item on the table onto the floor with a crash. She bent over the table and said, “The last thing I want is for you to fuck me right here, right now. Take me from behind and FUCK THE SHIT OUT OF ME.”

Without a second thought of location, morality, or Cynthia, he ripped his shorts down to the floor and obeyed her demands. He managed to last for two minutes before he grunted, swore and finished inside of her. He wasn't sure but he thought she said something about 'gaining the power'. He was too involved in his own orgasm to try comprehending her words.

She promptly said, "You are not off the hook that easy mister. Let's go to the bedroom where *you can have it all.* Hell, maybe even give me mine!"

Alarms and warnings went off in Greg's head as he followed her into Cynthia's bedroom. A calming voice entered his head and said, *it is gonna be fine, just follow that delicious ass.* He lowered his vision and watched her bottom swaying in the hallway. He thought, *yep, everything is going to be OK.*

They took their time exploring each other's body with their hands and then their mouths. Each was only interested in the intense pleasure the other was currently giving. He was not known for long, romantic interludes, but that afternoon they enjoyed each other.

Cynthia returned home shortly after three o'clock. The first thing she noticed was that no yard work was accomplished. Her meeting in Seattle did not go as planned and she left the city irritated. The journey on I-5 made her absolutely cranky. The site of the unkempt lawn sent her boiling. As she neared the garage, she saw Danielle's car and some of the pressure building up inside her seemed to dissipate. She knew that she was going to chew Greg's ass and then end up being held by Danielle while she cried. Danielle was the only person in the world that understood why she dealt with Greg's daily bullshit. She was mad when she walked into the house from the garage door, but it was a calculated anger. She did not plan to completely blow up.

She saw the mess on the kitchen floor and said, "What the fuck?" She walked around the kitchen table in dismay. She long accepted that Greg was a slob, but he usually did not create a mess like she was seeing. She dropped her purse on the counter and walked to the back door expecting to find him lounging by the pool. She was surprised that he was not passed out on one of the adjustable teak chairs or floating on an inflatable chair in the pool. As she looked around, she had another thought pole vault into her mind. *Hey, where is Danielle.*

She stormed back into the house and immediately saw the clothes on the floor. At first she was amazed that she did not see them when she originally walked into the kitchen, but amazement quickly transformed into outright rage.

They are fucking in your bed right now, the wicked part of her mind inflamed the situation. She raced down the hallway and kicked open the partially open door expecting to catch them in mid-stroke. They were not actively engaged in a sexual act, but they were laying naked together. After their last mutual orgasm, she produced a small bag of coke. She allowed him to make lines on her butt and he snorted the drug right off her fanny. He enjoyed the buzz and drifted into a light nap with his head resting on her bottom like a pillow. Cynthia's screaming quickly ended the good feeling.

Her piercing wail broke the silence like an atomic bomb. Danielle seemed startled and unsure. She sat in the bed clutching a blanket around her body. Greg, on the other hand, took immediate action. He knew the source before he actually turned to look upon Cynthia. He hurriedly grabbed some clothes and his wallet. He understood that she was ending the relationship right on the spot. He tried to push past her into the hallway, but she blocked the doorway. He did not want this to become physical, so he slumped and listened to her ranting.

Surprisingly her volume actually lowered. She calmly said, “Why would you do this Danielle?”

Somewhat startled, he stepped to the side and looked upon the bed. Cynthia continued in an eerily mechanized voice, “Greg, you need to leave right now.” She stepped into the bedroom and he saw Danielle was now also getting out of the bed. He decided to take advantage of the opportunity to escape relatively unscathed. As he stepped past her and was about to pass through the doorway, he heard her say, “Greg.”

He thought, *Keep going Greg. Let’s figure this out later. Don’t turn around.*

He ignored his own mental advice and slowly turned to face the woman that he clearly wronged. He was not prepared for the sight and actually gasped out loud. Danielle was now out of the bed and standing next to Cynthia, though they seemed a hundred feet away instead of just the few feet. The green and purple haze he swore that he once saw in this room had reappeared. Each woman had an amazing array of colors surrounding their silhouette. Cynthia’s body trace was bigger than Danielle’s and seemed to be at least double her regular shadow. Danielle’s only exuded from her body a few inches, but the colors in hers were twice as bright and sharp. Greg saw that Danielle’s crotch was pulsating like a heartbeat with a thousand colors forming and changing per second. Cynthia spoke again in a hollow, far away voice that echoed throughout the room. He shifted his eyes to her as she spoke and was terrified of the image.

Her facial features no longer seemed human but instead made up of pure pulsating lights. The place in her head where her eyes should have been located now contained jagged and oversized holes of pure black. As she spoke, a voluminous crater stretched and closed to the rhythm of the words being spoken. A color wheel of flashes escaped with each word that was so carefully being enunciated to Greg.

She said, “You…could…have…had…it…all. I…would…have…freed…you.”

He literally rubbed his eyes to make the images disappear to no avail as she continued, “You…could…have…been…with…me…for-ever…You…could….

You could have it all,
But you are beginning to fall.

have…could…have…but…you…crossed…a…line…br oke…rule…

By valuing the crank,
And dropping the gloves,
You have lost my love.

Your…your…and…Danielle…the…drugs…do….nothing…over….now…leave.”

He did not wait for a second invitation. He turned on his heels ran out the door. He paused only long enough to grab a bag of dope that he hid in the garage. He ran to the end of the driveway and suddenly stopped because he was winded. He bent over with his hands on his knees trying to catch his breath and understand what he just witnessed in her bedroom.

Another example of crazy shit with that crazy broad, he thought as he punched the air. He began walking down the long driveway doing mimicking the song stuck in his head from the zombie movie. He bellowed, “You could have it all, but you are beginning to fall.” *I have it all alright. Let’s get down to Marcos’s and screw this crazy scene.* By the time he reached the overgrown tangled portion of her driveway and began his usual rendition of “Wrecks the Day”, he forgot everything that occurred that morning.

Chapter 10:
A nail and a hammer…

Cynthia only had to drop a few hints before Greg recalled the tryst with Danielle. He did not recall the details of their confrontation, but he also was content to leave that memory in the past. Cynthia did not press. He apologized profusely and sincerely. She laughed and suggested that water was long under the bridge. In his middle age he clearly recognized that his penis forced a woman that he did not deserve to end the relationship. That idea sparked curiosity.

"Why were we together", he asked. "I don't see what you saw in me. I was a train wreck and I did not treat you well at all."

"You know", she began, "I am on my third glass of wine. I am feeling kind of buzzed. To be honest, I don't think we should get into that tonight. How about we just enjoy each other's company."

"That is probably a wise suggestion", he agreed. "Want to watch a movie or something?'

"I would love that as long as it is not one of those weird space movies you like", she poked.

He turned on the television and began channel surfing. "Let's see what we can find." He turned, grinned, and said, "This is a good one."

"*Guardians of the Galaxy*? This sounds like one of your dumb movies", she cautioned.

"You'll love it", he chuckled.

On that warm summer day in 1996 Danielle and Cynthia faced each other like ancient gladiators. If someone peeked into the bedroom on that day, they did not see the distorted features that Greg saw. Instead the voyeur saw two women standing frozen in the middle of the room. One was completely nude and the other was clothed. Both appeared to be holding an invisible ball in front of their stomachs. They were motionless, but a close examination revealed trembling in their arms as if they were curling a massive weight. Both had perpetual matching scowls and no verbal communications were passing between them. They were, though, having a violent exchange of thoughts.

I will ask again, how could you? Cynthia demanded.

I could lie and tell you that fucking him is actually a good thing for you. You have thrown him out and you should stick with that plan, Danielle started.

FUCK YOU, YOU UGLY BITCH, Cynthia screamed.

Danielle continued calmly, *I said I am not going to lie to you. I looked at his aura this morning and I WANTED it. I feel so alive.*

Cynthia demanded, *how did you get him in bed with you?*

How do you know that I am at fault here? Danielle mockingly replied.

Tell me how, Cynthia pushed.

I pulled my bathing suit down to my ankles, bent over the kitchen table, and told him to fuck me right there. Let me tell you, he did not hesitate, she proudly proclaimed.

Who does that kind of thing? Nobody acts that way even without an aura in place. I can't believe you, Cynthia responded in disgust. *Besides, we agreed.*

Yes, we did. On the other hand, he is actually starting to weaken you, Danielle countered.

No, he is not, Cynthia disagreed.

Oh yes, he is, she remarked. *You have visible streams of grey in your aura. Yes, your power is bigger than mine. But...I see lots of strands of grey. It is only a matter of time.*

Cynthia started to argue but momentarily focused on her energy. She reluctantly acknowledged that Danielle was right. Her arms dipped just slightly, and she sensed Danielle's attempt to steal her energy. She violently restored her arms and howled, *NOT TODAY DANIELLE YOU UGLY BITCH!*

Danielle was stunned by the quick response, though she rapidly recovered, *Is the attack on my appearance really necessary?*

Cynthia did not respond as she considered the status quo and the future. She did not want to admit that removing Greg from her life was probably the right answer, at least for now. He has issues he needed to resolve before their connection could occur as she desired. He needed to quit the drugs and she wasn't sure if she could compel to get clean. His habits and behaviors had worsened tenfold in the two years they were together.

Several minutes passed as she pondered the past and the future. She was thankful that Danielle allowed her time to think and not bombard her with either questions or another attack. This lull in their interaction was just a few seconds to the two women, but nearly a half hour of real time actually passed. This lapse in time corresponded to Greg's visit to Marco's and Marcia touching herself.

Cynthia could always sense Greg's location and feelings. As she considered the wisdom of finally letting Greg go, a surge of energy jolted into and out of her invisible ball. Her eyes turned black with rage and jealousy. She strengthened her grip on the mental ball, and snarled at Danielle, *what did you do?*

Danielle mock innocently relied, *what do you mean?*

The frozen scene finally ended as Cynthia doubled over as if punched in the stomach. Danielle nonchalantly broke her poise and folded her arms over her exposed breasts. She retorted, "Oh I see the issue now. I had nothing to do with this, though I do think it is so funny. Will Greg fuck two UGLY women in one day."

Rational thought left Cynthia as she grabbed Danielle by the upper arms. She intended to toss her out of the bedroom so that she could produce an aura sphere and prevent a disaster at Marco's. She thought, *all my beautiful colors will escape if he even touches that beast. NO, NO, NO.* Her next thought was, *oh my God, I can't move Danielle an inch.*

Danielle stood solid as a statue and laughed purposely and rudely in her face. "Is someone weak?" she mocked.

Cynthia released her and ran out of the room. She yelled as she passed the doorway, "This is not over today."

"Oh, I will be here waiting. Maybe I will play with myself to pass the time…on your bed", she obnoxiously retorted. She took two steps and launched herself into the bed. She rolled in the rumpled sheets and pillows laughing hysterically. After a few moments, she nestled into the center on her back. *Oh, I am going to sap into you and Greg just a bit more*, she grinned as her hands rubbed her breasts working their way down.

Cynthia spun into one of the spare bedrooms and locked the door behind her. She sat on the floor with her back to the bed and closed her eyes. As angry and anxious that she felt, she forced herself into a yoga slow breathing technique. She needed only a few seconds to locate Greg in her mind as well as detect Marcia in the bathroom. She lifted her hands from her lap and held them in front of her stomach. She concentrated and poured her inner strength into releasing the energy from her body. A light immediately appeared under her shirt at the location of her belly button. This light evolved into flashes of various shades of blues. As sweat broke her brow, every color of the rainbow erupted from her midsection and wrapped around her hands. These streaks of light coalesced into a thousand strands of flying lights, like electrons orbiting a nucleus. She opened her eyes and the streaks froze leaving a blinding solid sphere of numerous shades and colors. She frowned at the size which was clearly diminished in her mind. She could not deal with the size right now. She spoke and Greg heard her in the store. She told him to get home before he crossed a line. She saw the door form in Greg's mind. She screamed out loud when she saw that he was going to open the door. She guessed that he would find a path to Marcia and all of the energy that she had pulled out of Greg would turn grey. Too much grey would crack her aura sphere and render her powerless. She broke the connection from Greg before that could happen. She reabsorbed the sphere into her body and slumped over onto the floor.

She spoke to herself, "I cannot do anything about Greg now. How did this all happen and so quickly."

A voice jumped into her head that she had not heard in almost a decade, *quit feeling sorry for yourself. You know what needs to be done and you cannot wait a second longer.*

The voice was like a brutal slap in her face. She blinked at the sudden surprise, shook her head as if actually struck, and jumped to her feet. "You are right", she exclaimed. "I cannot wait for her to become stronger."

She leapt to her feet, unlocked the door, and literally ran back into her bedroom. Danielle was waiting for her. She stopped masturbating and sat on the edge of the bed anticipating her entry. The speed and aggression surprised her, though, and she was knocked flat on the bed by the flying Cynthia. They wrestled, clutched, and scratched each other until

Danielle was able to free herself. She rolled off the bed and faced her sweating antagonist.

"Are you sure you really want to do this?" Danielle smirked. "You are not as strong as you think."

She cocked her head and added, "Ooh, power is going into Marcia as we speak."

"I have cut off that connection. Greg is a loss. You leave me no choice", Cynthia grimly stated. "This is not about a one-time pilfering from my sphere. I trusted you but I think that was a mistake. I think you have just been waiting for this very moment. For that reason, I will never be able to relax which will slowly grey my sphere and weaken me further."

"You could just walk away. Give me what you have and just leave," Danielle countered.

"As I said, I have lost Greg and that will take time to come to terms. I will lose no more", she defiantly stated. She did not wait for Danielle to respond. She instantly summoned her sphere from her body and pointed it in Danielle's direction.

The aggressive and rapid move took Danielle by surprise and her defenseless body was thrown violently off the bed and against the far wall. She struggled to put her hands up as Cynthia attacked a second time and then a third time. Cynthia was weakened from the events of the day, but Danielle had grossly underestimated the power that Cynthia had stored. She could do nothing but limply attempt to defend herself. The coitus with Greg had given her a significant burst to her sphere but that was no match for Cynthia. They both understood that Danielle's one-time connection was not enough. Her demise was only a matter of time. This understanding enabled Cynthia to momentarily focus on Marco's and manipulate an aura. Satisfied with the events at the convenience store she put all of attention back onto Danielle.

Cynthia was not a sadist, though she gradually achieved a sense of satisfaction as Danielle weakened. She would not allow herself to smile. She did grunt in contentment each time another layer was pealed from Danielle's orb and added to her own. The deeper Cynthia probed, the longer the process took. Cynthia was able to settle into a steady routine and to actually check on Greg as the destruction of her one-time best friend passed into minutes and then hours. By midnight that night she was able to leave the bedroom and still continue the battle. One day turned into two and days transitioned into weeks. After a month Cynthia paused to consider stopping the attack and banning Danielle from her life forever. She could never be a threat to Cynthia again. They truly loved each other at one time and her resolve weakened. She focused her attention on Greg by turning on his mental radio and making him experience raining blood. Danielle was the culprit, but Greg could have his kept his cock to himself. Cynthia allowed him to fool around with any number of dirty cunts, but touching Danielle was the one and only taboo. He broke the cardinal rule and so he paid for his indiscretion by having his music turned against him. Sadistic Arch perfectly captured her black anger she felt when she imaged the two of them wrapped together.

In the meantime, Danielle did not move and lay prone on the floor only partially out of injury. Mostly she reminded motionless out of pure fear. She dared not to move a muscle. Her physical body attempted to deteriorate from lack of food, water, and sleep but she skimmed the tiniest amount from her minuscule sphere to keep herself alive. The attacks stopped but the waiting was pure torture. This was not Cynthia's intent. She simply could not make up her mind. Her heart strings continued to evoke sympathy and warm memories. Danielle lay motionless day after day for over a month.

Cynthia spent more time watching Greg go through the worst mental horrors imaginable. She also observed that despite the horrendous mental anguish, he was actually becoming healthy. He weaned off the drugs, started eating better, and took up a little bit of exercise. His invisible sphere was becoming amazingly pure to Cynthia. One night she mentally sat in his cell for hours simply watching him breath and become more beautiful by the minute. She cried at the turn of the events and the terrible losses they all suffered. She made up her mind.

She returned to her house and turned off Greg's radio. She then applied her full attention to ending Danielle's existence. With the exception of a short trip to the courthouse to see Greg's innocent verdict in person, she spent the next ten years completely absorbing Danielle's aura.

The morning after Greg rediscovered his numerous infidelities, he woke early and hungry. He opened his eyes, recognized the unusual be room, and felt oddly content. He slept in the spare bedroom a few times during his time living with Cynthia. These were not especially good memories. When he especially out of his mind on heroin and sick, she banned him to one of the spare bedrooms. He usually awoke feeling like death. Despite the craziness of the past few days he felt energized.

He excitedly got of bed, took a long shower, and skipped into the kitchen. The curtains and shades were still pulled shut leaving the room still barely lit. When he lived with Cynthia he never rose before her, so this was a new and an exhilarating experience for him. He pulled the strings on the blinds and let the bright summer morning flow into the kitchen. He mindlessly made coffee and rifled through the pantry and refrigerator looking for stuff for breakfast. He did not find any meat but lots of fresh vegetables and eggs. He decided to chop up a few mushrooms, a green pepper, an onion, and an avocado to make an all veggie omelet. He found a cutting board and began his culinary operation. He repeatedly hummed a tune while he cut each vegetable and tossed into a skillet. His humming grew louder, and he started bouncing from foot to foot in rhythm. Next his head joined the party swaying left and right matching his feet and vocals. Finally, he took exaggerated downward strokes of the knife. When he flipped the vegetable towards the pan with a flourish, Cynthia giggled, "I don't know what song is in your head, but that was SO adorable."

He flinched as he replied, "How long have you been standing there?"

"Long enough", she answered while pulling a coffee cup from the cabinet. She filled her cup with coffee and sat down at the table. "Looks like I am getting breakfast."

"Just a few more minutes. You look nice this morning", he complimented.

She wore a loose, mid-thigh length, blue and white sun dress that flattered her figure. The dress's large checkered pattern resembled something that a fifties television mom would adorn, though a high leg slit, and low-cut front pushed her appearance a thousand miles away from Mrs. Cleaver. She wore simple matching flats and he noted a matching pocketbook was on the counter.

"Thank-you. I have an idea for today after we eat breakfast. Since you still have a few days before you have to drive back to Sacramento, lot's go do something fun. I was thinking that we can catch the ferry and spend the day in Seattle. I have not been to the Jimmy Hendrix museum yet. We could go up to the top of the Space Needle for lunch. If you want, I know that I can get us really good seats for the Mariners tonight. What do you say?" she cheerfully inquired.

"Mariners game. Since when do you like sports?" he teased.

"Oh, I know all about all the Seattle sports teams. King Felix is on the mound tonight", she remarked.

He chuckled, "You know who King Felix is?"

"I have no idea other than I hear his name on the news and the radio a lot", she admitted. "So, are you interested?"

"That all sounds great," he replied, "Though I haven't really followed sports since I left Washington. I heard the new park is beautiful so that will probably be fun."

"Great. Let me make a few phone calls and set up a few things", she said while getting up from the table.

"What do you have to set up?" he inquired.

"Being wealthy has its perks", she laughed. "Don't you worry your pretty little head about what I am going to do. Let's just say that I am going to call in a few favors."

She left the kitchen while he continued with the large omelets. By the time she returned, he was setting the plates on the table and partially singing the song that he was humming earlier. She eased into a chair and aid, "This looks great. I honestly do not remember you ever cooking for me. Did you?"

He shook his head and she continued, "Hey what are you singing now?"

He sat down opposite of her and shook his head again, though this time in frustration, "I honestly can't pinpoint it. I have bits of one lyric and the rhythm, but I can't bring the tune out into the open."

"What do you have?" she asked while scooping a large pile of omelet onto her fork. She took a small bite off the large forkful and motioned with her other hand to continue the song.

He swallowed his first bite and leaned back in his chair. He looked up towards the ceiling deep in thought. He slowly swung his hand in front of his chest and hummed a note. He stopped and said, "Ok, bear with me. I think it goes something like this...

NA, na, na, na, na, na
NA, na, my maker
NA, na, na, na, na,
NA, na, na, na, na, na, na, NA"

He stopped and saw that she was smiling. He took a small bite, quickly chewed and swallowed. He said, "You're laughing at me because my little soliloquy doesn't register a bit with you. You have absolutely no idea what I am trying to sing."

She placed a large forkful of food in her mouth and held up one finger. She chewed in mock bliss, swallowed, and replied, "On the contrary. I know what it is."

She took another large bit and he stared at her with a stunned gaze, "You are fucking with me."

He had to wait while she purposely slow chewed her food. She followed the bite with a drink from her coffee and then stared directly into his eyes, "Wouldn't you like to know. Oh, and nice language at the breakfast table."

He impatiently replied, "YES. Not knowing a song always drives me crazy. This one is right on the tip of my tongue."

She slid her chair back and reached over to her purse. She pulled out her cell phone and began typing into the keyboard. She set the phone on the table and used her right thumb to click the volume button on the side several times. She deliberately used her right pointer finger to press play.

As the first notes sounded out of the phone, he dropped his fork and exclaimed, "Oh my God, that is the song. It's, its's…"

He snapped his fingers a few times and she smirked, "'I Need Your Help'."

He slowly repeated back each word, "I…need…your…help. You are right."

"I know I am right", she smugly acknowledged.

"You don't know music", he argued.

"True, but I know this song", she continued to smile.

"Ok, Ms. Smartypants, who is the lead singer and what is special about this particular song?" he pressed.

She sighed and said, "I have absolutely no idea."

He triumphantly said, "I am redeemed. This is Rhino Din and the singer is Jack Zee. This album came out in '96. This single, though, was not released to early '98. The day after the song was released Jack Zee was killed in a car accident that was not his fault."

She lightly murmured and resumed eating her breakfast. He tapped his foot and mouthed the lyrics until the chorus began. He set his fork down and boldly sang along with the late Jack Zee,

A nail and a hammer,
Gifts from my maker.
I can't build this cross alone,
I need your help in this endeavor.

She did not interrupt but the second he finished singing along she quipped, "His version is better."

"You are so mean sometimes", he pretend pouted. "But you are taking me to see King Felix pitch so I guess it all evens out."

"I am not mean at all", she defended. In her mind she thought, *you really have no idea.*

They both thoroughly enjoyed the day and evening spent in Seattle together. The favors she called in included a private tour of the Jimi Hendrix museum, a private driver through the city, and box seats right behind the Mariners dugout. They talked, laughed, and shared a connection that their previous relationship never experienced. The unspoken negative things were left at the house and no effort was made to bring to light those memories. On the ferry ride back, she leaned against him and he wrapped his arm around her. She reached for his hand and he willingly gave it to her. Neither gave this closeness a second thought.

He drifted into a light nap as a driver took them from the ferry terminal back to her house. He seemed to sense that she was staring at him the entire ride. A rush of warmth spread throughout his body with this thought. She gently woke him, and they watched the car slowly drive out of the long driveway. Once the car made the bend to the left, they turned to each other and simultaneously stepped toward each other. They gently but firmly leaned into other for a quick kiss. Each was lost in thought as they stared into each other's eyes. They connected again for a longer a kiss. He felt her tongue gently probe the edge of his mouth and he readily accepted and reciprocated.

They broke naturally and he said, "I think we need to complete our discussion that we started last night...and maybe not here on your front porch."

She grinned, put her key in the lock, and said, "Ok, Mr. Palmer. Would like you like to come in for some stimulating conversation?"

Greg guided the Honda onto I-5 south for the ten-hour trek home to Sacramento before 6 AM the next morning. He needed time to think and the five hundred plus mile journey promised to provide just the space he needed. Almost all of the trip was highway driving. He anticipated that the Accord would go into cruise control and his mind and body would soon follow. The previous night became way more complicated than he could've ever imagined. Her explanations were hard to believe at a minimum; in some instances, simply downright frightening. She claimed total honesty and he had no reason not to believe her. The pragmatic side of him shunned her stories of "aura spheres" and "aura manipulation" into the same category as ESP and the paranormal. He could not accept most of her story. The non-rational side of his brain screamed for him to not ignore the things that he remembered. He kept going back to his drug use and wanted to compartmentalize each issue as part of his lifestyle. The argument continued in his head as he recalled that he thought he heard Monica's voice come out of the housekeeper. Not only did he think that he heard his deceased love, but she issued a warning.

Another facet that played a piece into his decision to drive away that morning was fear. When he heard Monica's voice, goose bumps covered his body. He suffered some sort of panic attack the afternoon he drove into Remington. Always on the outside promising to leak into his status quo was an ocean of fright. He could not explain why or pinpoint an exact source. He just felt for the last three days that he was on the verge of yelling in terror the same way someone felt going through a haunted forest. Your body expects the chain saw wielding maniac to jump out around the next bend. The chemicals have flooded the brain and the blood stream in anticipation of the upcoming act. The fight or flight is in full motion. He truly enjoyed spending time with Cynthia. On the other hand, his body's automatic systems were in overdrive.

Adding to the maelstrom of emotions was the overwhelming feeling of confusion. He could not fathom any scenario in which Cynthia sat down and invented all of the things that she told him just to mess with him. That type of behavior did not fit her personality at all. Even if she had a streak of prankster or psychotic, he was sure that she did not dust off the rola-deck to bring him up to Remington for a lark. He was not a psychologist, but he was pretty sure that she was not crazy. He believed that she *believed* every word that she said the previous night. Her impossible abilities were as real to her as the GPS system on his phone. He did not completely understand the technology, but it was tangible and real. He used the tech every day and that rendered the unknowable as unimportant. She shrugged her shoulders to many of his questions. She could not delve deeper into "the whys"; she could only state the end results. He concluded that she was telling the truth in her mind; on the other hand, he distinctly gleamed that she purposely left some pieces out of the puzzle. He could not fathom the things she willingly, or unthinkingly, avoided. This detection planted a seed of distrust that was blooming into more fear. He tried to fudge the truth to himself and say that he left in the early AM because he was becoming more and more alarmed. That feeling definitely played into his decision, but the emotion that was closer to the mark was one of bewilderment. Their conversation weighed heavy, but the tipping of the scale was due to the fact that they made love again.

Their kiss outside was exhilarating but Greg had no inclination when he stepped inside the house that they would soon find themselves in her bed. Most of the thoughts in his mind focused on the unanswered questions. Again and again he asked himself, *why am I here?*

He did not make the first move. He was distracted by the random questions in his mind and getting a beer from the refrigerator. She lightly touched his back while he opened the bottle and took a deep swig. As the story always goes, one touch led to another, and they ventured down the hallway to her bedroom. They did not act like hormonal teenagers unable to keep their hands off each other. Instead they calmly acknowledged their mutual desire and they wordlessly walked hand in hand into her bedroom. They made love with excitement but also with a sense of composure. In the car the next morning, he classified their lovemaking as *right,* but he also had to use another adjective. That word was *troubling.* Sex with Cynthia was always extremely fulfilling, and many powerful memories and feelings were reawakened. This time, though, he had to ask himself, *why?*

She explained her interest in him the first time around. He did not necessarily buy her reasons because he could not get past some of the supernatural elements. Despite the reservations, the attraction was plausible. The first thought that raced through his mind the next morning when he woke up was *what does she see in me this time around?* He classified himself as a "decent looking guy" and a "pretty good guy." He had enough girlfriends to feel fairly confident, but Cynthia was different. She was out of his league. By the time his feet touched the floor, he knew that he should leave. Less than 20 minutes later, he was in the Honda battling the shrubbery to get to Pleasant Avenue.

He set the cruise control seven miles higher than the speed limit. He could never explain the reason for exactly seven miles. He was a creature of habit and when he pushed the set button on the steering wheel, he breathed a sigh of relief. Something was now back to normal. He was in control again. Since he opened Cynthia's card, he did not perceive that he was actually managing his decisions. He was not sure if "aura manipulation" played a factor, though she denied that she had done anything except send a letter. He was very troubled by her repeated denials that she could not do anything like that anymore. He did not have the special gift of reading people, but he was sure that she was lying.

He discovered that Rhino Din's album from '96 was sitting in the pile of CD's on the passenger seat. He carefully steered with two fingers of his left hand while he used the other fingers and right hand to open the case. He lifted the CD out of the case and pushed into the CD player. As the opening notes to the first song, "Pure Noise", started, he nestled into his seat. He had the music provide the background distraction, many miles in front of him, and the car in cruise control. He thought back to the previous evening after they dressed and ventured back into the living room.

Greg sat down on the couch and sipped on his beer. Cynthia walked in a few minutes later holding a glass of wine and a large bowl of popcorn.

"Do you want some?" she asked.

He started to decline but the aroma changed his mind, "Alright."

She went back into the kitchen and returned with another bowl. She poured half the popcorn into the second bowl and handed it Greg.

"Thanks", he said as he took the bowl.

"No problem", she replied as she took a seat on the love seat opposite of Greg. "You think you want to watch television."

"No", he sighed. "I think we should have that stimulating conversation. Tell me the truth, did you think we would end up in your bedroom this evening?"

"Well no…and maybe", she flip-flopped. "The second I saw you walk onto the patio; I had a flash of our past. I understood a possibility existed, but I did not plan or see this evening unfolding as it did."

"Ok", he answered. He carefully thought about the direction he desired the conversation to trend. He tentatively stated, "I think I have a bunch of questions, but I am not really sure where to begin."

She nodded in acknowledgement and he continued, "Why were a couple? What did you see in me? Do you remember the first time we met? You mentioned something about being sure about something about me."

"A conversation from twenty years ago. I don't remember specifically what I said to you, but I think I can start to explain some things," she carefully said.

She chuckled for a second and said, "We actually had this discussion once before. It did not go well."

"We have", he stated in surprise.

"Yes, we did. Maybe about four to five months before we separated. Right about the time that the heroin became a prominent problem", she returned.

He shrugged his shoulders and she continued, "No matter. Maybe it will come back to you, maybe it won't."

She dug into the popcorn bowl and tossed a couple of kernels into her mouth. She followed with a sip of the wine and then half a handful of more popcorn. When she finished chewing, she began, “Greg, did you believe in things that you cannot see? Do you think that we may have more around us than meets the eye?”

“I am not sure how to answer that”, he slowly said. “I was raised in a religious home and so I do hold some tenets of Christianity in my life. I am not sure about stuff like ghosts and aliens. Is this what you are hinting?”

“Hmmm...sort of”, she hummed. “Remember when Esperanza called me la bruja?”

“Yes”, he replied after pushing a handful of pop-corn into his mouth.

“I have been called various names in my life. Bruja, mekhasheyfe, sorciere, strega, sahira and of course, plain old witch,” she explained. “The people that are calling me these names are always women and none of them have any idea why they do it.”

“People randomly call you a nasty name?” he scoffed.

“Yes”, she firmly replied. “I have even asked a few of these accusers why they did it and do you know what they say?”

He shook his head and she replied, “Not a damn thing. I am telling you that they don't have a clue. I have an inkling, though.”

“Ok what is your theory?” he asked.

She confidently replied, “They are touched a little bit.”

“Touched with what?” he asked while raising his eyebrows.

“That is where this becomes a little tough”, she slowly replied. “What if I told you that I know the world is full of things that you have never seen?”

He gave quick nod of his head, “Alright.”

“I can see some of these things. Seeing is kind of a bad word. I can sense some of these things and if I close my eyes, I can picture them”, she replied.

He leaned forward on the couch and queried, “What kinds of things?”

“All living things emit a kind of light source, like an invisible energy. Danielle and I used to call it their aura,” she explained.

“Wait, Danielle could see this stuff too”, he quickly asked.

“Not as well as me, but yes she could. That is one of the reasons why she wanted to seduce you”, she answered.

“She wanted to screw me because of my aura”, he sarcastically replied.

She put the bowl of popcorn and wineglass onto the end table. She stood up from the love seat and sat down next to Greg. She gently took his and hand looked pleadingly into his eyes.

“This is where this gets really tough. Like I said, the last time I tried to explain all of this you were not super receptive. Just hear me out for a few minutes before me condemn me as a liar or crazy”, she urged.

Greg reacted with dejection as he shook and said, “I remember this conversation now. You wanted me to stop the heroin for good. You said it was putting grey into my aura and then you tried to explain auras and aura spheres.”

“What more do you remember?” she excitedly pressed.

“I don’t really recall your explanations”, he said while rubbing his temples. “It is like the whole conversation is right there, but I can’t get it. I remember calling you Samantha.”

“Samantha”, she looked at him curiously.

"Yes, from the television show *Bewitched,*" he said. "I told you to wiggle your nose and have a beer brought to me from the kitchen."

"Uh-huh, anything else", she said.

"You don't remember do you", he stated. "I then invited you to perform oral sex and when you wiggled your nose I would give you a big surprise."

"Oh, you ass, I do remember that now. That was when the fight started, and I gave up on trying to explain it to you. At that time, I thought I could nag you into giving up the heroin", she admitted.

"Ok I remember a fight. I need you to go into detail on this aura stuff again. I don't understand how any of this has to do with me, or with Danielle or why I am here", he said a little harshly.

She rubbed his hand with hers and tried to sooth him, "I know, I know. Let me jump into it right now."

He gently pulled his hand from hers and gestured for her to continue. She stayed on the couch with him but leaned back into the corner. She lifted her legs to sit cross legged and faced him directly. He also maneuvered to be more directly face to face with her.

She spoke, "Every living thing emits an aura. I can see it. I thought everyone else could as well. I really frustrated my father as a child. He tried to be very patient, but he eventually started to classify my sightings in the same vein as an invisible friend. He assumed this was my way of reacting to the disappearance of my mother. None of my friends seemed to see the things I saw either, so I learned to just keep my shut about it. That is until Danielle accidentally mentioned seeing a blue glow surrounding their house cat. I jumped because I saw the same glow. Her parents also did not believe the things that she claimed to see, and they actually started disciplining her every time she said something. She tried to act like that she did not say anything about a glow, but I pressed her till she cried. We spent the rest of our childhood and early adult hood trying to figure this out. You couldn't actually go to the library and check out a book on the subject. I tried doing a google search a few years ago. I assumed I would get a hit or two, but nothing. I don't know if we are the only two people in the world that have this ability."

He interrupted, "Hey, where is Danielle."

"We stopped being friends the day you two slept together. She left the house shortly after you did that afternoon and I have never talked to her since", she replied with no emotion.

"You guys ended a lifetime friendship over a guy", he asked in a surprised tone.

"Yes, let me continue and you should understand why in a little bit", she justified. "We stumbled along seeing colors and pointing them to each other. Everyone's aura has different colors and different patterns; sort of like colorful snowflake. We learned that I could sometimes see different shades that she could not. We also discovered that not all auras were pleasant to view. Really sick people have grey or blackish auras. She went to the hospital to see her grandfather when we were about seven or eight. He was dying of cancer and she instantly knew he was going to die soon even before her parents told her. Pure blackness was emitting from every pore in his body. She came to my house that night in pure terror. When he died a few days later, we understood. Another time we were riding our bikes from her house to mine when a car slowed down next to us. A man started talking to us from the car. He said that he was lost and was wondering if we could help him. His aura had violent bloody red streaks and black flashes. We did not answer him but instead took off as fast as we could on our bikes. We were not smart enough to tell our parents. We should have. A few years later I saw him on the news for kidnapping and murdering a couple kids in Tacoma. Like I said, no textbook exists on this kind of thing."

She paused for a moment to stand and retrieve her glass of wine. She finished the glass with a large gulp. She motioned that she needed more and pointed at his beer. He shook the bottle indicating that it was empty. She went to the kitchen and then returned with a fresh glass and a new a beer.

She returned to her spot on the couch and spoke again, "In junior high we discovered that we could touch other people's auras. Hmm…touch is not really the right word again. I am inventing language for what we figured out. We could capture a piece of aura and add to our own. Imagine a colorful shadow behind you and having a handful taken away. Your shadow immediately fills in the blank, but I then have a handful of colorful flashes and lights. The closest thing I can describe would be holding a really colorful palm sized atom. This was really just a game to us. We picked people and borrowed some of their aura and then laugh about it. We did this until we accidentally discovered the next important feature. We were partners for a science project. We worked on this stupid thing really hard but when we got our grade, we had the lowest the grade in the class. We talked to the teacher, Mr. James about the grade after class. Danielle was an emotional wreck and was crying while I calmly asked about the grade. To our eighth-grade minds, our work was just as good as everyone else. I can't honestly tell you if our project was good or not, but in our mind, it was. As I talked to him, I unintentionally touched his aura with my mind, but I didn't steal it so to speak. I just turned one color to match one of my own. Again, this wasn't on purpose, it just happened. I was mad and I wanted him to see our way and it just happened. Danielle immediately stopped crying and she purposely reached and touched the aura and changed one of the colors to match one her own. We started with our mouths open as his aura became an amalgamation of the two of ours. Mr. James stopped in mid-sentence explaining why our work did not meet the objectives and instead completely reversed. He said he would re-grade the project."

"Touching his aura somehow influenced him", Greg asked.

"Yes. We didn't get an A but he did bump the score a little bit. For us, the project was no longer important. The discovery changed our lives. To be blunt, we became little bitches. We abused the ability. We made popular girls have break downs at school and we tricked good looking guys to ask us out. We turned them down just to be mean. We were teenagers, full of hormones, and had an unusual ability. We were not trying to figure out how to take over the world or even how to possible use it for good. We were just using it for fun. The next big step was also discovered by Danielle. She was always so self-conscious and whenever any boy showed her the least little bit of attention, she gave him whatever he wanted. Do you understand what I am saying?"

"I think you are saying that she was easy", he offered.

She continued, "Unfortunately, yes. She fooled around with a lot of guys in high school. She gave a lot of hand jobs and blew several guys. When she lost her virginity, we discovered that is the most powerful way to mimic someone's aura. You don't take the entire aura from the other person, but you can copy the entire thing and add it to your own. When I lost my virginity, I recognized that carrying the aura attached to our own was sort of unwieldy. I actually told her that I wish we could store it. She asked why we couldn't. We experimented with a bunch of crazy ideas, but I finally figure out that if I just concentrated, I could push some of my aura into a sphere and that sphere could be stored inside of me."

She stopped talking and studied Greg for a moment. He was not trying to hide his disbelief. He looked at her as if she was selling the worst tall tale of all time. She motioned, "Go ahead."

He shook his head and said, "I don't know what you want me to say. This is…is the craziest thing I have ever heard. I just don't know how to act."

She shook her head in agreement, "I understand. I wish I could show but I can't. If I brought out my aura sphere you would not see anything or feel anything. I have only a few more things to get out in the open."

"Well, let's hear it all", he flatly replied.

She continued, "Some people have special features in their aura. I do know what makes them special and most of the time I do not know they are special until I have touched them. These unique ones seem to give more power."

He interrupted, "Snagging someone's aura give you power?"

She waved her hand to indicate patience, "Power is such a difficult word to qualify. I found the larger my aura sphere, the easier it was to manipulate someone's aura to carry out my will. Early in my twenties I came to the conclusion that I am not an evil person. I have no desire to control the world or to do nasty things to other people. I used my abilities to make assholes easier to deal with and I admit that I used my special influence to maintain my wealth. Other than that, I was content to live a lazy life and occasionally influence someone to make my life easier. The DMV has no idea what hits it every time I renew my tags."

They both laughed at the idea of manipulating the DMV. A few minutes passed while she took a few drinks from her wine glass and he finished his beer. He motioned for her to continue while he rapidly retrieved a fresh one from the refrigerator.

"I am glad you could see a little humor in all of this", she replied.

"I am still not real keen on all of this", he honestly retorted. "I wonder how many more shockers you have."

"Just one", she began, "And it involves you."

"Me?" he asked in surprise.

She finished the wine in her glass and said, "You have asked several times why were we together? One-night Danielle, another girlfriend of ours named Sandy, and I went for a night of bar hopping and men teasing. As we drove past some dump, I had such a surge of warmth go through me like I never experienced. I had no idea what it was. We rented a limo that night and I immediately told the driver to stop. The girls overrode me, and we continued our trek to a nicer establishment. I had this weird feeling for weeks. I decided one night to go out without the girls, and I found that dive again. The minute I walked inside my whole body began tingling. I grabbed a drink and sat down. I had no idea who or what I was seeking. Then you stumbled in front of my table and stared into my eyes. I hate to use the word orgasm, but I experienced something so deep and so wonderful. You were the reason."

"Why am I so special?" he inquired with both a touch of sarcasm and curiosity.

"I had no idea until we got into the car. Your aura was SO bright, but it also was marred with a lot of grey and black. In aura terms you blinded me, but I could not really detect what you made you special, as you say, till later. Remember when you became excited about a song on the radio and started singing along with it?" she prompted.

"I sing along to a lot of songs but for some reason, I think it was the song, 'Radiate' by Tackles the Mute", he offered.

"Sounds right but I am not sure. Of course, the actual song is not the important part. When you started signing, you transitioned. Your true and innocent personality poked through the drugs. All of a sudden your aura revealed itself to me", she said with growing enthusiasm.

"And what makes it special", he pressed.

"Your aura is a mirror image to mine. I did not completely understand at the time why that was so special. I just knew that I felt SO AWESOME just looking at it. I snatched the tiniest piece and felt so surreal. I felt like I needed your aura to somehow complete me. I was able to study you and your energy in depth, especially after we made love and you fell asleep. Even when you were completely fucked up, your inner child cleansed the damage aura while you were sleeping. I was so amazed. I often found that I was holding my breath at the majestic beauty of it all. We were together for almost a month before I figured out that our auras were mirror images. Imagine two powerful magnets of opposite polarity. I was so drawn to you because my energy was pulled towards yours. I made a couple of poor assumptions though," she paused.

He raised his eyebrows and guessed, "You mistook that connection for some kind of love."

"Exactly", she threw her hands in the air. "I assumed we were going to be boyfriend and girlfriend, soulmates, lovers and be together FOREVER. To me, it was all inevitable. You, though, did not feel the type of connection that I did. You were in it for the sex and drugs and easy life. I think you cared for me in your own way, but we were never destined to be a couple connected by our auras because we could not be connected as human beings."

"I did care for you, though not as you deserved", he acknowledged. "What about Danielle?"

"She just wanted you for the energy you exuded, nothing more", she shook her head. "She recognized the truth about our relationship over a year before we ended the relationship."

He leaned back as a thousand disparate thoughts and questions raced through his head. He tried to sort them into a usable and coherent series of questions. His pragmatic side was attempting to put rationality into an unreal scenario. He needed to have something tangible and concrete that his mind could grasp before he could take a leap of faith.

For the next few hours he carefully asked questions. Some attempted to discover a scientific and rational reason for her claims. Others related to her use of the auras that she added to her own aura. Many of his inquires focused on himself and Cynthia's interest in him both past and present. She patiently replied to each of his queries, but he was not satisfied that she actually answered his questions. He felt that many of her explanations were maddeningly vague. A few she sidestepped and tried to distract him. Most troubling were the times that he sensed that she was lying to him. That avalanche of fear that hung on the cliffs threatened to loosen when he was sure that she was not being truthful.

As the evening passed into the next day, she repeatedly yawned and stretched. He understood the hints, but he really thought that this would be the last time that they had this discussion. He wanted to get everything out in the open and all of his questions answered. As the clock passed one in the morning, he recognized that he could gain no more useful information that night. He was now going to have to choose what to do with this experience.

He abruptly ended the probing and stood up, "Well, I guess we should call it a night."

"Oh, I am so glad you said that. I am super tired," she exclaimed as she also rose. "This is a little awkward, but do you plan to join me in my bed?'

"I think that maybe I should go to the spare bedroom", he replied.

"I understand", she sighed. "I want you to know that you are welcome. You need to decide for yourself about everything that we discussed tonight." She leaned and gave him a quick peck on the cheek, rubbed his bicep, and headed towards her own bedroom.

He walked into the kitchen and filled a glass with water from the faucet. He took a couple of drinks, leaned back against the sink, and stood deep in thought. His rational thought was screaming in protest. He knew that he needed to grab some sleep, but he was not sure if could get any REM that night. He felt overwhelmed with disbelief, curiosity and a touch of edginess. Greg never prayed for guidance, but he was sure that he needed help.

He pondered, *I wonder if spiritual guidance can help me.* The thought took him by surprise but also was reassuring. He finished his glass of water and slowly ambled towards the spare bedroom. He momentarily looked in the direction of her bedroom. The door was cracked slightly ajar. He turned back towards his own room and began humming,

A nail and a hammer,
Gifts from my maker.

He gently but firmly shut the door behind him. He sat on the bed and mulled the lyric. *I have no idea what to make about all of this crazy bullshit. I need help figuring this all out.*

I can't build this cross alone,
I need your help in this endeavor.

Part III:
The Second Verses

Chapter 11:
Hear me, love me, rock it tonight...

The morning that Greg stole out of Cynthia's house, he did pause to consider leaving a note. He felt that taking off without saying goodbye in person was already in the category of extreme rudeness. He tried to locate a pen and paper in the kitchen without making any noise or turning on a light. He discovered that she already left him a note.

Her short letter explained that she knew that he would go back to Sacramento before she woke up. She let him know that she understood and was not angry. Her hope was that after some time Greg could consider just being her friend again. Her cell phone number was printed in large clear numbers on the bottom of the note. She pleaded for him to at least send a text once he returned safely back to Sacramento.

For the entire five-hundred-mile trip every train of thought he developed ended with her requested text. He went through the gambit of emotions including anger, fear, and curiosity. He tried to rationally analyze the past, the present and potential future with the knowledge he gained. This effort was a waste. Every plausible and sane explanation or consideration was eradicated by memories of flashes, her admittance of a power to influence, and the outright outlandish story of auras and aura spheres. He always ended up back at square one. Two questions were constantly present; what he would do with the knowledge gained from the trip and would he send her a text once he was home.

He honestly did not know until he dropped his bag on his kitchen table. His cell phone appeared in his hand and before he gave it another thought, he typed a quick text. He read and reread the simply and short text that let her know that he was back in Sacramento. He thanked her for the invite and the day in Seattle. He avoided all mention of events and conversations that made him decide that he needed to return home. He decided to erase the message, but before he could he sent the text. He stared at the screen and asked out loud, "Did I really send that text?"

Before he could ponder for very long, she texted back. Her text read, *I am glad you made it safe. I loved seeing you again, even if just for a short time. Thx for coming. I needed to see you if even just one more time. Please call or text anytime you want. I think that I probably will not reach out to you till you reach out to me first. Again thanks and love you, Cynthia.*

He felt purged and in control. He understood that he would spend a significant amount of time going over and over the events from twenty years ago and the trip. He could, though, at least start to do "normal" again.

He unpacked his bag and dropped his dirty clothes into the laundry basket. He defrosted a small package of boneless and skinless chicken breasts in the microwave. He sliced the chicken into strips and sprinkled with garlic salt, pepper, and a dash of Old Bay. He pulled out a food steamer from a bottom cabinet and filled it with water. He placed the chicken into the basket and started the timer. When the chicken had about six minutes left, he tossed a bag of frozen green beans into the microwave. He pulled the chicken and beans out at the same time and then warmed a leftover cornbread muffin for a few seconds in the microwave.

He set down at the small kitchen table and suddenly had the urge to do something that he never did. He bowed his head and quickly gave grace and thanks for being home. He wasn't sure what possessed him to do perform that act, but the prayer simply felt right. He looked around the familiar walls and belongings and a sense of security and calm became his predominant emotions. His mind almost completely shut down with virtually no thoughts as the familiar filled his sight and sound. He was almost finished with dinner when a thought completely destroyed his tranquility.

His mind screamed, *What the fuck happened to Luke? Did you shoot Luke?*

He then chocked on a piece of chicken and the frantic rush of adrenaline that always occurs when one's windpipe is blocked by food spiked into his system. He stood up and put his hands around his throat for the international signal of a choking victim. He recognized the uselessness of that act with no one in the condo to help him. He remembered reading that people can give themselves the Heimlich maneuver. He grabbed the back of the chair partly out of measurement for attempting the maneuver and partly out of angst.

The movement caused him to cough slightly, but that was enough to loosen the chicken. He purposely hacked the rest up out of his mouth onto the floor. For a moment he feared that he would follow the spit up chicken with vomit, but his stomach held. He slumped into the chair and ignored the glop on the floor. He noted a slight sweat on his brow, and he used a napkin to wipe his brow. As the chemicals in his body that were released due to his choking dissipated, he returned to the original thing that broke his calm reverie.

Who killed Luke? he calmly asked himself.

Cynthia heard Greg leave that morning. She already left a note and decided that it would be better to just let him go unmolested. She was certain that the seed was planted to complete her plan. She felt that she had an ace in the hole and if Greg did not come around as she desired, she would set the hook to reel him, regardless of his desires. She rolled over and slept till early afternoon.

When she woke she felt anxious but extremely energized. She anticipated a lazy day by the pool and maybe a few phone calls to Bill. *He* was a situation that needed rectified soon, but she hoped to delay just a little while longer.

Her afternoon was proceeding exactly as anticipated when she felt a rush of blackness strike her deep inside her stored energy. She sat up in her pool chair and clutched her abdomen as if she was slugged by a heavy medicine ball. She struggled to her feet and limped towards the house.

Once inside she was able to catch her breath and rub the soreness out of her belly. She gingerly walked to her bedroom, slowly removing clothing along the way. She completely disrobed and she slid onto the floor with her back to her bed. She sat cross legged and closed her eyes. Her breathing slowed to a minimum and soon her sphere appeared. She opened her eyes and examined.

She frowned in slight confusion. Her orb looked perfect and full of delicious energy. She felt sexy, in control and most importantly, very powerful. Yet, a tiny doubt was crossing her threshold.

What was that feeling? she wondered. *My energy is pure. Could have that been a premonition? Am I gaining a new level?*

She closed her eyes and the thinnest of layers slowly peeled itself from her sphere and wafted into the room like a solar flare. Once a few feet away from the orb the barely visible layer coalesced and darted out of the bedroom at the speed of light. She opened her eyes and understood that she had a problem if she did not intervene.

She closed her eyes and slowed her breathing this time to almost nothing. Her pulse could be measured in single beats per minute and the temperature in the room slowly raised. She would be patient no matter how hot her environment became. She slightly arched her back when the temperature exceeded 100F. By the time the room was over 125F, she was somewhat desperate for a connection. She was not sure how much she could take but she feared to stop and miss the predicted event.

She never knew exactly how steamy the room became, but she guessed around 135F when Greg's mind unleashed the idea of Luke being murdered. She immediately understood this was the warning. She opened her eyes and lifted her sphere to the front of her face.

The edge closest her body instantly began to elongate and reach towards her body, or more specifically into the pendant around her neck. The sphere touched adornment by the thinnest of webs, but that was enough to visible diminish the size of her sphere. The pendant began glow blood red and then rapidly pulse. She had to be sure, so she allowed almost half the sphere to enter the pendant.

With a quick flick of her wrists the sphere both broke connection with the pendant and was reabsorbed into her body. She clutched the pendant and the entire room filled with a blinding light as if a flash grenade exploded next to the bed. The temperature broke and returned to normal leaving her body covered in sweat and exhausted. She lifted herself to her feet stepped out of the bedroom with the intention of jumping into the pool. She felt serene and sure, though she would have to wait to see if her influence was successful.

Greg was on the verge of asking a third time, this time out loud, about his friend Luke. The words seemed to get stuck in his throat just as hard as the food was a few moments earlier. He cleared his throat and he spoke, "I need to clean up this mess on the floor." He stepped around the small pile of chewed up food to grab a few paper towels off the roll under the kitchen sink. He no longer was wondering about Luke. That entire line of thought simply disappeared and would not reform for a long time.

Greg returned to his daily routine of working and living. A few days turned into a few weeks. He rarely dwelled on his trip to Remington, or his past. Thoughts usually emerged while eating his dinner by himself. He turned music on his phone for a distraction or surfed the internet on this computer while eating to distract himself. These memories ceased to be as vivid the moment Cynthia unleashed the energy from her pendant, but they were not gone. They were faded, or more like pushed into the recesses of his mind. The difference from before the trip to after the trip was that if he pressed, he could bring those memories into the light. He usually chose not to force them. He was content to avoid truly facing the situation.

On a bright but unseasonable cool fall Sunday morning, Greg literally leaped out of bed full of energy. He considered returning to routine a good thing, but he was becoming bored with his life. He needed a new distraction and that afternoon he was going to meet up with a few friends from work at a nearby sports bar called Whistles to watch the afternoon football games. This was going to be the second trip in three weeks. In the past he usually declined this kind of invitations, but he knew he needed to get out of the condo. The excitement stemmed from the fact that he hit it off with a divorcee named Sheryl. She was somewhat plump and not a great beauty. She was though, incredible sweet and her charming personality convinced Greg that she was someone that he would like to know a little better. He kicked himself for not asking for her out for some coffee or at least getting a phone number. He felt somewhat redeemed when he found her on Facebook, and she accepted his friend request. They made generic friendly comments on each other's walls. Greg learned through Facebook that she would be at Whistles that Sunday. Vanity was not one of Greg's vices, but that morning he spent extra time ensuring his appearance was as perfect as possible. He left the condo anticipating a great afternoon.

He returned before the end of the football game. He threw open his front door and whipped his keys across the room, ripped off his jacket, and threw that on the ground. He desperately wanted to scream in anger, but he held his tongue. Instead he dinosaur stomped around his living room seething in frustration. Everything went wrong right from the start and quickly spiraled out of control.

Sheryl was not the passive and demure lady that he remembered from two weeks ago. She was obnoxious and fairly insulting to him right off the bat. He was taken aback, but he continued to stay near her and attempt to chat. When she was not dramatically ignoring him, she was tossing verbal taunts in his direction. At half time he wondered to a different bar stool, made small talk with some of the guys from work, and pretended to be watching the game. He kept one eye on her when he could. He noticed in the middle of the third quarter that she disappeared from her seat. He scanned the entire bar and assumed that she left.

At the beginning of the fourth quarter she reappeared with a vengeance. He did not even know that she was behind him until she startled him and everyone on that side of bar.

She yelled, “HEY, ASSHOLE!”

He involuntary ducked his head and quickly turned around. She was ready for his movement and timed throwing a drink directly into his face.

“Take that you dick,” she yelled. “Fuck you and all of your stupid fucking questions.”

He could merely stutter, “What?”

She shot back, “Don’t act like an idiot. You know what you did.”

The alcohol in the drink was stinging his eyes. He turned to grab a napkin to try to dry his face. He winced in pain as his left eye burned. As he turned around holding the napkin against that eye, she punched him squarely in the stomach.

He doubled over and slipped out of the bar stool. He saw that her violent outburst had attracted a lot of attention. As he struggled to stand back up and hold himself up on the edge of the bar, he saw a large semicircle of people out of his one good eye. He again managed a feeble, “What?”

She began rapidly yelling curses and incoherent ramblings. She stood on her toes and leaned into him as he his back bowed against the bar. He saw several employees step through the throng of people and maneuver to get between the two of them. She was pulled aside, and two employees stood between them. A third, giant of a man entered the scene. He pointed a ridiculously large finger in Greg’s face and demanded, “What did you do to her?”

“What did I do to her?” he asked incredulously. “Are you freaking kidding? She came over here and thew a drink in my face and hit me.”

Someone from the masses through out, “He has been bothering her the entire game.”

A second voice offered, “Yea, she tried to be nice, but he has been a dick the entire time.”

The giant gave him an evil grin, “Oh, you like to bother the ladies.”

“No”, he defended himself. “I have been sitting here since half-time with my friends.”

The bouncer pointed towards his co-workers and snarled, “You know this asshole? What do you know about this?”

They timidly shook their heads affirming that they knew him. An awkward moment of silence occurred, and Greg wondered why they were not defending him. One shook his head and quietly stated, “Well he did spend a lot of the game on her side of the bar.”

Greg managed to get out a third, “What?” as the bouncer grabbed him and commenced roughly escorting him through the bar. People booed and threw drinks and food at him like a convicted felon in the middle ages. Greg was so shocked by the turn of events that he did not offer the slightest resistance. As they rounded the bar and headed towards the front door Sheryl and a couple of her girlfriends managed to push through the crowd and get between him and the door. The bouncer violently pulled Greg back and wrapped a muscular arm around his neck.

Greg’s windpipe was squashed shut and he felt like his head was going to explode from the pressure. The giant seethed, “Do you have something that you want to say to the lady?”

Even if he wanted to speak, he could not due to the chokehold the bouncer had on him. After a few silent moments, the bouncer gently said to Sheryl, “This asshole is not worth your time, Ma’am.”

An evil smile broke across her face as she stepped up to Greg’s face. She then spit directly into his face. Greg reacted for the first time and attempted to break free from the grasp. The large arm fell away for only a second and returned along with a violent smack to the back of his head. Greg swooned and the edges of the one good eye greyed. The friends joined Sheryl and launched spittle in this direction. The ladies then stepped aside, and the bouncer pushed him through the front door and launched him headlong into the parking lot.

Greg needed a few moments to gather his senses. When he rolled over onto his side, he saw several people were milling outside, but they were starting to turn their backs to him and head back inside the bar. He looked up and saw that a police officer was standing over him. Greg moaned and said, "I am glad so glad to see you."

The cop bent down on one knee, "Well, that is interesting. Why are you glad to see me?"

"I need to report an assault", Greg explained as he sat up.

"Are you reporting on yourself?" the police officer asked with a smile.

"What?" Greg asked in confusion.

"I have a bar full of people that are willing to testify that you are drunk and physically bothering one of the female patrons until the staff got involved. You went berserk and struck the staff members several times until they were able to subdue you and get you out of the bar", the cop replied. "The amazing thing is that the young lady and no one from the staff wants to press charges. They just want you to go home."

He hung his head and thought, *Cynthia La Bruja.* He meekly said, "Ok, can I go home?"

"Sure, but you are not driving since I already know that you are drunk", he sternly replied.

Greg did not want further confrontation. He pulled out his phone and searched for an Uber. He entered his information and told the police officer, "Should be here in about five minutes."

The cop snorted and walked over to his cruiser. He got inside, started the engine but leaned back in the seat ensuring Greg understood that he wasn't leaving until Greg was gone. Greg used Uber a several times previously, but he was never so happy to see his ride pull into the parking lot. The police officer followed them for a few miles before he got bored and headed back to his station. Greg was thankful that the Uber driver was not interested in starting a conversation. He gave a friendly wave to the driver away and stormed into condo.

He took a long shower in an attempt to wash away the physical mess from the food and saliva as well as the fresh memory of being incredibly wronged. No amount of water and soap could easily erase those memories. He stepped out of the shower and no longer felt that he would yell in absolute indignation. He was, though, still thoroughly infuriated. As he dressed, he plugged his phone into his stereo and selected the hard rock station on the Amazon music station. The last few notes of a Godsmack song ended followed immediately by the opening notes of an old rock rap song, "Tragedy" by S. Mint. Greg sang along to the rapping opening lyrics,

Hear me, love me, rock it tonight
Touch you, beg you, caress it just right.
Can you feel the energy in the air,
Now our time is freaking rare.

The music continued but he did not. He was in the process of pulling up his sock, but he ceased that action was well. He frowned and slowly repeated the first line out loud again, "Can you feel the energy in the air. What the fuck happened to me today? That was absolute bullshit."

He reached back down, finished pulling on his sock, and roughly put on the other sock. He clenched his fists open and shut and marched into the kitchen while S Mint was telling him that he could rock the world, love all the woman, and simply have it all.

"I don't want it all", he barked at the stereo. "I just want a life."

He hit stop on S. Mint in mid-rap and pulled out the connection cord. He scrolled through his contacts and aggressively hit dial. He waited as the phone began to ring on the other end. Once, twice, three and then four rings occurred before the call was answered.

An irritated Cynthia said, "Hello."

Greg replied, "Cynthia, this is Greg."

Her tone instantly turned friendly as she exclaimed, "Oh, my God, is this really you. What a surprise? How are you doing?"

Silence filled both ends as Greg simply breathed and boiled. After a few seconds she said curiously, "Hello....hello, are you there?"

He slowly vented, "Yes, I am here. I had something very bizarre happen to me this afternoon."

"Oh", she remarked with a note of wonder in her voice.

"Yes", he flatly returned.

Another moment of silence passed before she stated, "And?"

He carefully said, "The kind of really weird event that does not occur naturally."

Her voice indicated a sense of surprise and a touch of anger as she spoke, "I gather that you think I had something to do with this unusual event of yours."

Before he could respond she continued in a mocking tone, "Yep, I have nothing better to do with my life than to try to influence someone hundreds of miles of a way that crept out of my house in the middle of the night after I had shown them nothing but hospitality. And let's not forget that I shared my bed with that person and only wanted to rekindle some friendship. You are full of yourself Gregory Palmer."

Her response stunned him and left him speechless. She asked, "What happened today and why do you think I had something to do with it? Are you starting to believe in aura spheres?"

"I do not know what I believe", he honestly returned. "Does seem pretty far-fetched."

The edge came out of her voice as she said, "Well since you have me on the phone why don't you tell me what happened."

He gave a small laugh and said, "I feel kind of embarrassed and I think reliving what happened today will only make it worse. I am sorry that I bothered you."

"I was actually excited to hear from you so don't beat yourself up too bad. Do you have some time to tell what has been going on with you?", she replied.

He chuckled again and said, "Sure."

He spent five minutes giving her vague details of his dull life and she countered with an equally mundane summary, though she expressed frustration with the failings of Bill the financial manager. He moved to end the conversation and she quickly cut in, "Greg, I think you need to understand a couple of things. My days of stealing auras and storing in a sphere are over. I have what I need to live extremely simple and comfortably. The second thing you should understand is that even when I was heavy into dabbling with this ability, I could not reach out hundreds of miles away. Anything that happens to you in Sacramento is a result of the mixing of auras in that city. Maybe you crossed the wrong bitch."

He let out a loud roar of laughter and said, "You have no idea."

A few minutes later they hung up their phones in somewhat different tones. Her voice oozed with happiness and warmth while his was guarded and tentatively relieved. She was honest when she claimed to be thrilled to hear from him. He was still not sure if she played a part in the afternoon fiasco. Most of him wanted to chalk it up to a series of unfortunate events. He lied to himself and said *could have happened to anyone.* The small but rational side of his brain screamed foul. He thought that maybe he detected the slightest tic in her voice. Did she lie? And if so, exactly which part? After several minutes of deliberation, he eased into his new routine of ignoring and denial. He turned S. Mint back on and unabashedly sang along the rest of the song.

In Remington Cynthia clicked the red off button on her phone and held it tightly to her chest. She breathed out a large sigh of relief and whispered, "Ok."

From behind her Esperanza scathingly remarked, "You are such a bitch sometimes."

Cynthia spun around with her a face a picture of anger. She started to retort in kind, but instead humor spread across her face, "Oh, you adorable old hag."

She gave her housekeeper a quick hug and giggled, "I don't know why I keep you around. I should have gotten rid of you years ago."

Esperanza glared and remarked, "You tried once and if you remember, that did not go so well."

Cynthia gently pushed Esperanza to arm's length and evenly said, "I remember. I think you need to remember that *I* invited you back here. How about you just stay out of my business."

Esperanza huffed, turned, and slowly ambled out of the room with a bowed back. Once out of Cynthia's vision her back straightened and she rapidly scooted to the front door. By the time she was underneath the overgrown hedges that blocked the sky she appeared fifty years younger. She turned back to the house with a troubled look on her face, "Before this is done you will need me on this one."

A few days later Greg was deep in concentration analyzing a ledger of financial transactions. He did not notice that his immediate supervisor, Anthony Fabrini, was standing in the doorway to his office for several minutes. When Greg finally broke from his study Anthony cleared his throat which caused Greg to slightly jump in his seat.

"How long have you been standing there? "Greg chuckled.

Greg quickly noted the blanched look on Anthony's face and asked, "Is something wrong?"

"Greg, you and I need to grab Derek and head upstairs", he coolly replied.

Greg stood up and said, "Alright. Who are we seeing upstairs?"

Anthony already was exiting his office and only offered, "Derek will explain."

The trio made an odd sight as they stepped into the elevator to go up to the executive suites. Greg of average height and weight for the typical middle-aged white man severely contrasted against his two closest supervisors. Anthony was a tall and muscular black man in his early thirties. He was brought on from outside the company to replace Derek when he was promoted. Anthony was given the job over Greg despite Greg's long history with the company. Greg actually never gave that a thought until he stepped into the elevator behind his two bosses. He gazed upon the well-built Anthony who always brimmed with confidence to the polar opposite which was Derek.

Derek Richards was a short, extremely overweight, bald white man. A light sweat coated his forehead from the short walk from his office to the elevator. He exhibited little of Anthony's exuberance and constantly asked his subordinates for their inputs. Many viewed this a positive that he wanted the team to participate in the decision-making process. The truth of the matter was that Derek was over his head in this position. He barely managed to stay afloat for the past three years. He started at the firm five years after Greg and the two of them competed directly against each other for Antony's position almost five years prior. Greg never gave a second thought to Derek being selected over himself till that moment. A rush of conflicting thoughts and memories violently invaded his head causing him to scowl. He angrily evaluated Derek's two promotions as a travesty. He looked down at the sweating incompetent man and wondered about the companies' promotion and hiring decisions.

The elevator door opened, and Derek took the lead. Anthony gently waved and Greg followed Derek down the hall to a seated executive assistant. The thin elderly lady looked above her wide framed glasses and said in a high-pitched voice, "They are waiting for you. You can go right inside."

Derek opened the door and motioned for Greg to go inside first. He tilted his head in a curious manner but followed his boss's non-verbal direction. Greg nervously stepped into a large and lavishly decorated corporate office.

A thick cobalt blue carpet covered the floor while rich mahogany wood tiling graced the walls. Inlaid intricate cobalt blue swirls accentuated the chair rail and crown molding. The mammoth matching mahogany desk was pushed all the way to the rear of the office against a completely glass back wall. Two leather chairs rested in front of the desk. Two people that Greg had previously met at company functions sat in the chairs. He currently could not remember their names. The desktop was inlaid with leather and undecorated. The only item on the desk was a phone, a name plate, and a computer.

The man seated behind the desk and gazing at the computer screen appeared to be in his seventies. He was thin with a full head of snow-white hair. Greg noted his expensive handmade suit. He also could not help but to note the expensive watch that adorned the man's wrist. He read the name plate, *Lawrence Van DeCastle, Executive Vice President.*

Greg never met the man sitting at the desk and his slight nervousness transitioned into something more severe. His mind raced as he desperately tried to figure the reason for being in this man's office this morning. The seconds ticked away as neither Anthony or Derek nor the people seated made any motion to introduce or grab Lawrence's attention away from the computer screen. Greg thought about lightly clearing his throat when Lawrence finally spoke, "Mr. Palmer we have a big problem."

Greg quickly replied, "I did not know we have a problem. What can I do to help?"

Lawrence looked up from the computer screen to harshly answer, "For starters you can keep our company name out of your personal affairs."

As Greg started to ask a question the seated female spoke, "Greg we have seen the video."

Greg closed his mouth and became distracted trying to remember where he met this lady in the past. Lawrence stated, "Mr. Palmer, do you remember Mrs. Gaylish? She is the head of our HR department and she is the one that brought the issue to our attention."

Mrs. Gaylish clarified, "Actually my daughter found the video online. She simply asked if the disgusting man in the video actually works here."

The seated man whose name still escaped Greg spoke, "We then did a quick search and found some really scandalous posts on Facebook. What is your relationship to Sheryl Anderson?"

Greg coughed and stated, "I don't have a relationship so to speak with her. We met one time a few weeks ago at Whistles. We became Facebook friends but the next time we met up at Whistles did not go well."

"Mr. Palmer, that is a gross understatement of the facts", Lawrence rebuked gruffly. He turned his computer screen to face the group and hit play on a YouTube video. They watched the scene from Whistles be replayed starting at the point that the bouncer was guiding Greg to the front door. Greg winced in horror as the video's fuzzy images sharpened to show the girls spitting at him and the bouncer punching the back of his head. The crowd erupted in cheers as Greg was thrown through the front doors.

Greg feeling of vindication was instantly erased as group started chastising him for his behavior. He stood in shock as Anthony joined the seated people in questioning his behavior. After a few minutes Lawrence held up his hand to silence the group and asked, "Well, Mr. Palmer?"

"As you can see, I was roughly escorted out of Whistles. Sheryl told the bouncers that I was harassing her, and they never gave me a chance to defend myself. The crowd quickly turned into a mob", he replied.

From behind him Anthony sarcastically spat, "Are you trying to defend your actions?"

Greg turned and gave him a curious look. He said, "You watched the video. All you can see is me being tossed out. Yes, I am defending myself."

The group erupted again in tirade. This time Lawrence waved the storm of anger and interjected himself, "Yes, Mr. Palmer we watched the video and your behavior is despicable."

Greg opened and then closed his mouth looking for the words. From behind him Derek spoke for the first time. He timidly offered, "I agree this whole thing is terrible, but I didn't see what Greg actually did to warrant being removed from the bar."

The tension in the air changed direction and swooshed toward Derek with lightning speed. Greg could not help but to smirk slightly at the turn of events. Derek innocently expressed his exact thoughts, though the rest of the team was not having none of that apparent common sense. They took turns ridiculing his lack of attention to the details of the video. Lawrence cleared his throat and announced, "Derek thank-you for coming up here this morning. I do not think we require your presence here for the rest of the things we need to discuss with Mr. Palmer. You can go ahead back to the second floor."

"Oh, ok", Derek fumbled. He wiped his again sweaty brow and made an awkward act of leaving the office. Greg felt a moment of pity for the man especially after he stepped out of the door.

Lawrence spoke to himself but loud enough for all to hear, "I am not sure how long we will require your services at all." He turned to Mrs. Gaylish and directed, "Show Mr. Palmer those posts that you found."

She nodded and pulled out a tablet. She rapidly scrolled and typed into the electronic device. She waited a few seconds for the feed to appear. She then handed the tablet to Greg and said, "The problem we have is that Ms. Anderson keeps linking you with the company."

Greg took the tablet and scrolled through the web page that Mrs. Gaylish opened. He read though several of Sheryl's Facebook posts which damned Greg and the company in vitriolic tones. Greg was shocked by the vicious accusations that were stated as facts. The more he read the angrier he became.

He lost his cool and spat, “This is total bullshit. I NEVER said any of those things to her and I most definitely NEVER tried to touch her in any way. Every one of these posts is an outright lie. This defamation of my character.”

Anthony said pointedly, “The video supports her accusations.”

Greg aggressively turned and shot back, “That video shows nothing of the kind. All you can see is me being spat on, punched, and hurled out of the bar.”

Anthony took a step back and the other two men stood up. The three of them simultaneously ordered to Greg to calm down and don’t do anything violent. The situation struck Greg as ludicrous and ironic. He could not but help to laugh and say, “I am not sure how you expect me to act with these ridiculous accusations.”

Lawrence said, “I expect you to not become violent with my team. They are doing their jobs. I can see that this is not going to accomplish very much. I will tell you that you are still employed for now, but I will also tell you that our legal team is analyzing this entire situation. You can consider yourself on a type of probation period.”

He let that sink in for a moment before he continued, “You have been at our firm for a very, very long time. That is something that we don't take lightly. Unfortunately, this situation is adding to another problem.”

Greg asked, “What other problem?”

“Your performance records”, Lawrence said flatly.

“My performance reviews have always been very good. I have never once received negative feedback”, Greg retorted.

Lawrence gave a subtle flick of his wrist. The seated people rose giving indication that the meeting was soon ending. As they gathered themselves,

Lawrence continued, "That is another issue we are having our legal team review. Anthony recognized what I will label as discrepancies. To be blunt, many of your decisions concerning financial accounts have consistently been below the mark for a long time. We are not sure how or why your immediate supervisors have incorrectly elevated your performance reviews. As I indicted earlier, we are going to take a hard-long look at Mr. Richards performance reviews. Thank-you for your time today."

Lawrence turned the computer back around to face him and start typing on the keyboard. The other members gently but quickly escorted Greg out of the office. Once outside the office the HR personnel vectored away from Greg and Anthony. Greg silently followed Anthony to the elevator and then all the way back to Greg's office. Anthony wordlessly deposited Greg and turned away without a second glance. Greg slumped into his chair in a daze. In less than twenty minutes his whole work life was turned upside down. He started down a path of self-pity when a mental slap stopped him cold. He thought, *Not here. They are watching you and now you need to be the world's greatest employee until this shit is resolved. Fucking Sheryl. I met you only once…who does this to another human being?*

He slammed his back into the seat like a steal rod. He bulldozed all distractions from his mind and fully concentrated on the work that his employer was currently paying for him to accomplish. Deep inside he thought the entire situation was bullshit but he was not going to go out without a fight. He hummed as he worked,

Hear me, love me, rock it tonight
Touch you, beg you, caress it just right.
Can you feel the energy in the air,
Now our time is freaking rare.

Chapter 12:
Let the faith touch you…

A month later Greg sat uncomfortably on the raised examination table of Dr. Howard's office. Greg was generally blessed with good health, and even though Dr. Howard was his doctor for over a decade he visited this office only twice. Today he sat in discomfort and impatience waiting for the physician to enter the room. Greg used WebMD to self-diagnosis himself, but he needed the doctor to confirm and help alleviate his symptoms. He leaned over to put his weight fully on the right side of his rear and winced in pain as his left side sent waves of shooting fire.

Dr. Howard entered while reading his case file. He spoke, "Good morning Gregory. Looks like it has been a few years since I saw you last. Looking through your file you have indicated to the staff that you think you have shingles. Have you ever had the chicken pox?"

Greg replied, "Yes."

"Have you experienced any flu-like symptoms", the doctor inquired.

"Yes", he answered. "A few days before the rash and pain."

The doctor pulled out a set of examination gloves from a box and donned them. He said, "Ok, let's take a look and see what we have."

Thirty minutes later Greg was driving to the pharmacy to fill two prescriptions. One was to help with the pain and the other was an ointment to help prevent infection of the blisters that were starting on his lower back and rear. Greg rarely missed a day of work due to illness, but the flu-like symptoms knocked him on his butt. He was now on the second day off of work due to the outbreak which was painful and left him completely miserable. The doctor advised him that the medicine would take a day to take affect and that unfortunately the virus had to run its course. He could be out of commission up to another five days. He thought that his illness could not have occurred at an absolute worst possible time.

The atmosphere at work drastically changed since his visit meeting the executive vice president. Greg was never overly involved in workplace drama, and he mostly kept to himself over the years. He always wore a smile and had a friendly greeting for everyone at the firm. He usually took his lunch in his office preferring to eat and work on a few minor things such as answering emails instead of venturing to the cafeteria. On the few days a month he opted to join his peers he was always welcomed to join a group already seated at one the tables.

The tension around his office was palpable and the shunning in the cafeteria was blatantly obvious. No one would make eye contact and his conversations with co-workers de-evolved into short exchanges that were only directly related to work matters. The absolute minimum to answer a question from Greg was verbalized. All inquiries to Greg now came via email. The usual chatter of people conversing and joking outside his door ceased. The twenty feet before and after his office became a dead zone of social interaction. Greg was especially hurt by the avoidance of the few employees that worked at the firm as long or even longer than him. He attempted to ignore the whole situation, but he grew suspicious of the work of the “legal team”.

He confronted Anthony once a week and was given curt, almost categorically rude responses. His supervisor claimed that he had no knowledge of the legal department’s review and that Greg should concentrate on his clients. Greg was positive that Anthony was lying, and that he knew the exact status of the so-called investigation.

Fortunately, Sheryl moved on and was no longer posting abusive attacks on him and the firm, but the damage was already done. Greg came to this conclusion the previous week after he cornered Derek in his office. Greg was technically not following protocol by going to Derek, but he hated the feeling of walking on eggshells. The unknown was driving him crazy and causing him to second guess every decision he was making. Derek gave the same rote answers as Anthony, but his flushed appearance indicated to Greg that he knew more than he was letting on. Greg morphed into a mode of extreme thankfulness for Derek's honest answer (though he knew he was not being completely truthful). He artfully used verbal judo to relax Derek, and soon the boss gave up a few tidbits of information. The issue was indeed not over, and the company was lining their ducks in a row to fire him. Greg thanked him and carefully made his way back to his own office. For the first time in his twenty years as an employee Greg spent the afternoon doing personal work vice furthering company profit. He searched the internet and then made several phones calls to locate and hire a lawyer.

He was able to arrange a meeting that evening at the law firm of Johnson, Soble, and Tiant. A paralegal named Sue jotted many of the details over the phone and met with him when he arrived at the firm. She verified the information from their phone call earlier, set him up in conference room by himself, and gave him a few papers to fill out. Greg was almost completed with the paperwork when Barbara Johnson entered the room and introduced herself. Greg explained the situation at work and his concerns. Sue was able to locate both the video and Sheryl's

Facebook posts to show the attorney. Barbara expression never changed throughout his explanation or her viewing of the video. She simply nodded, took notes, and maintained a professional attitude. She agreed to take Greg on with a retainer. She told him that she needed the company personnel handbook while she did a little research. She concluded by saying, "I expect that you are not going to need my services. These things have a way of fizzling. Based on the information I have right now I do not see a legal reason for them to let you go."

Greg left her office and felt good for about six hours, then the first symptoms of the shingles hit him. As he sat waiting for his prescription to be filled, he wished he could be at work for damage control purposes, but the words of his attorney kept his spirits buoyed. His phone buzzed and he was surprised to see a call coming in from his work.

Greg answered, "Hello."

"Greg, this Anthony from work", his supervisor began, "we need you to come into work today for a meeting upstairs."

"I am out on sick leave", Greg responses. "I have the paperwork filled out by the doctor's office which I intend to scan and email to HR this evening."

Anthony persisted, "You still need to come into the office."

"This is not really the company's business, but I have shingles. I am in a lot of pain and pretty miserable right now. I am waiting for a couple of prescriptions to be filled, but I am going to miss a few more days", Greg responded.

"No", Anthony replied sharply, "You must be here at 4 PM for a meeting to determine your employment status."

"Let me get this right", Greg began angrily, "You expect me to report to work when I have a legitimate medical issue to discuss my employment. That does not sound right at all."

"The decision was made to have the hearing today. If you do not show I can only guess how the board will react," Antony jeered.

"So, this is a hearing and not a meeting. This sounds like I have to defend myself. Give me five minutes", Greg seethed as he hung up the phone. He rapidly located Sue the paralegal's desk number in his phone and dialed. He explained the situation to her. She said that she would try to interrupt a meeting that Barbara was currently attending at the firm. He was on hold for several minutes before Barbara picked up the phone.

"Gregory, this is Barbara Johnson. Sue was telling me that your company is going to have a hearing. Did I understand all of this correctly?" Barbara asked.

"Yes", Greg replied. "They just called me. I am sitting at a CVS waiting to have a couple prescriptions filled because I am sick."

"Have you followed your company's sick days protocol?" she inquired.

"Yes, to the letter", he confirmed.

"This is highly unusual", she said out loud to herself. Greg could hear Sue talking to Barbara in the background and the attorney asked several questions. He could not hear any of the specifics and was left in the dark while holding his cell phone to his ear. After a few minutes Barbara returned and said, "Gregory, can you give me the number to your boss or more specifically, the person that called you and told you to go to work."

He provided the attorney both the name and the phone number and the call ended. His prescriptions were ready a few minutes later. He could not wait till he got home so he took the pill for pain with a swig from a bottle of water in the car. Greg was almost home when the phone buzzed again from his attorney. He shifted the call to blue tooth and answered, "Hello."

"Gregory this Barbara Johnson calling you back. I spoke first with Mr. Anthony Fabrini and then was transferred to several people within your firm. I explained to each of them that this hearing that they intended to conduct was not in accordance with their own employee handbook or the laws of the state of California. Greg you have two issues going on. The first is the negative publicity from the video and the internet posts. That is a grey area that *potentially* could have caused you to be released based on the negative publicity. Your handbook is vague on that merit. The other is their claim of invalid performance reviews. This does have a very detailed process. I am assuming that they have not provided you with each review and a detailed summary of each issue in each review."

"No", he answered, "I have even asked, and they said legal was still reviewing."

"As I figured", she replied. "You are entitled to have those provided to you at least ten days before a hearing can even be considered. In those ten days you can provide a written reclama to each alleged mistake in the reviews. Those must be reviewed separately and if your counter points are weak then they can inform you of a hearing. You again are entitled to a minimum of ten days to prepare. I need you to call your supervisor and authorize your company to send these review mistakes to Sue at my office. They have the number."

"Ok I can do that", Greg responded.

"And Greg", the attorney continued, "they are not really happy right now. I understand that you have been with them for a real long time, but I am not sure if that is going to be good place in your future. You may want to consider starting a resume."

Greg sighed, “You probably have a point.”

Despite feeling poorly Greg forced himself to do internet research on resume writing over the next three days. He called a friend from the animal shelter named Lynsey that worked in an HR department. She said that she would be glad to take a look at his resume and provide feedback. She nonchalantly offered that the idea of leaving his current company with all the benefits at his age was a risky proposition. He completely understood and agreed with her point of view. He was vested in the company and was still under the old fixed pension plan. Like many other companies in the country he was grandfathered in the old plan when the company shifted almost a decade prior to a 401K type plan. He was able to shift some money into that plan as well and he felt that he was right on track for retirement when he approached sixty. He was still fifteen years short of that target and the idea of starting over did not thrill him. He was pretty sure the writing was on the wall based on the vicious response he received when he called Anthony to forward the performance review paperwork to his lawyer’s office. On Friday afternoon his suspicions were confirmed with a buzz at the front door.

He looked through the peephole and viewed a UPS delivery person standing on the other side of the door. Greg unlocked the door and saw that the man had a rather large box sitting at his feet.

“Mr. Palmer?” the delivery person asked.

“Yes”, Greg responded.

The UPS man pulled out a tablet, scrolled a couple of times, and said, “I need you to sign for receipt of this package, Sir.”

“Who is it from?” Greg inquired.

“Not sure”, the man replied as he handed the tablet to Greg.

Greg groaned when he saw the sender was his work. He scribbled his name with his finger on the tablet and handed it back to the delivery person. He absentmindedly said, “Thanks.”

The UPS man responded in kind while Greg lifted the fairly awkward sized box and carried it into his house. He felt a rush of blood slam through his body and a light sheen of sweat broke on his body. He was guessing that he knew the contents and that he was going to become extremely pissed.

He set the box on the small kitchen table and aggressively cut through the packing tape with a small pocketknife. He pulled the top open and used one arm to sift through the items in the box. He angrily flipped over the box and dumped the entire contents onto the table which overflowed onto the floor. He whipped the empty box across the condo and spatted, “Fuck” while he stared at all his personnel belongings that were in his work office.

He kicked a few loose desk items and clenched his fists open and closed. As he stared at twenty years of his stuff on his table and floor, he noted a large sealed envelope on the edge of the table. He snagged it and tore at the taped edge. The wrapping would not give so he grabbed the pocketknife and cut through the tape. He looked at the stack of papers inside the envelope and hesitated. He thought, *I am pretty damn sure that I am not supposed to mix alcohol with my medicine, but I am also sure that I cannot read whatever this shit paper has to say without a beer.* He set the envelope back on the table and felt a flare of pain from the blisters on his lower back. He winced and hobbled toward the refrigerator with the intent to grab a beer. His phone rang and he stopped him in his tracks. He surveyed his kitchen trying to locate where he placed his phone. A second ring reminded him that he left the phone on the nightstand next to his bed. He rambled over the debris on the floor and answered on the fourth ring.

"Hello", he said hoping the call had not already went into voice mail.

Sue's voice came on the line, "Greg this Sue from Johnson, Soble, and Tiant. How are you today?"

"Well, I have had better days. Still under the weather", he honestly answered.

"I am sorry to hear about that", she said sympathetically. "Unfortunately, I don't think I am going to make your day any better."

Greg chuckled to himself and said, "Oh."

"Ms. Johnson wanted to call you herself, but she will be in court for the rest of the day. She said that she can call you tomorrow to answer any of your questions. In the meantime, she wanted you to know that we received a packet of papers from your employer. She has not had the time to thoroughly review but the papers indicate that they held a hearing anyway. They altered at least five years of your performance reviews. Your employment was terminated on Tuesday."

She paused to let the information register with Greg. He retorted, "So that explains the big box of my personal stuff from my office that was just delivered. I am guessing that the sealed envelope of papers is the same information that was delivered to your office."

This time it was Sue's turn to be surprised. She uttered a simply, "Oh."

He actually laughed out loud at the absurdity of the situation. She recovered and directed, "Greg, we are going to need you to scan the paperwork you have and email to us. Ms. Johnson will compare to what we have here to make sure they are the same. I think you should sit down tonight and develop a list of questions to help Ms. Johnson determine the path that is right for you."

He grinned broadly but did not laugh directly into the phone towards the lady that was only trying to help him. He knew any questions or paths were probably going to be fruitless. What recourses did he have? Would any of them matter? The bridges were not just burned but blown the fuck up. Instead of reading the papers in the envelope, he spent the afternoon working on his resume. *So, life has thrown me a curveball,* he thought, *just have to ride this downward spiral out. Things will turn soon.*

In Remington Cynthia and Esperanza sat across from each other at the kitchen table. Cynthia was clearly aggravated with Esperanza and beginning to raise her voice.

"I need you to stay out of my business", Cynthia spoke in a loud tone. Esperanza held her hands out and shrugged her shoulders.

Cynthia continued, "Don't patronize me."

Esperanza slowly rose from the table and quietly remarked, "I think it is time for me to go."

Cynthia quickly stood up and moved between her and the hallway to the front door. She said with venom, "Stay…out…of…my…business."

Esperanza shook her head and replied, "Too long, too dangerous."

Cynthia eased her tone and acknowledged, "I know that it has been a long time. This will be worth it."

"We shall see", Esperanza murmured and pushed herself past Cynthia into the hall. She did not try to stop her again but simply watched the elderly women struggle with the multiple locks and finally pull the heavy door open. She exited the house without either women saying another word to each other. Cynthia followed and pushed the front door all the way shut but did not bother with the locks.

She turned around and leaned with her back to the door and muttered, “I hope you do not interfere.”

Nearly eight weeks passed before Esperanza returned to Cynthia’s house. This lengthy absence was not unusual, and Cynthia did not give it a second thought. She went about her daily and weekly life attempting to control her excitement. She let her guard down and therefore was not prepared for the possibility of any unexpected events. A couple situations arose rapidly that turned her world upside down.

When Esperanza opened the door after her lengthy absence the first thing, she noticed was an overwhelming stuffiness in the house as if the doors had not been opened in weeks. The house was deathly quiet and dark as she made her way down the hallway. The kitchen table and sink were littered with a mass of unwashed dishes. The garbage can was overflowing and two large full garbage bags were sitting next to the can. Esperanza twitched her noise at the rank odor emanating from the kitchen. She clutched her small bag and called out, “Cynthia.”

A weak voice returned, “In my bedroom.”

Esperanza slowly shuffled down the hallway and pushed the partially open bedroom door. The bedroom had the same unkept and cluttered appearance as the kitchen. Clothes and dishes littered the floor and end tables. She spotted Cynthia lying flat on her back in the middle of her bed.

“Señorita?” Esperanza gently called. She took a few steps towards the bed and gazed down upon the prone figure. She gasped slightly and then deeply frowned. She set her bag on top of a pile of clothes on the nightstand. She sat down and said, “You look horrible. You look like you have aged forty years. What happened?”

The haggard figure struggled to push herself up and lean against the headboard. Her face was creased with lines and her long beautiful black hair was thinned, white, and stringy. Her eyes were sunken and her normally glowing skin was pallid and dotted with liver spots. She lifted a misshapen, arthritic claw of a hand and set it on Esperanza's upper arm. The statement about aging forty years did not appear to be an exaggeration.

Cynthia wheezed, "It looks worse than what it actually is. I am conserving energy."

"For what? To turn into a mummy", Esperanza quipped.

Cynthia ignored the jab and continued, "I made a mistake. I need your help."

Esperanza raised an eyebrow and asked, "What kind of mistake?"

"I underestimated the human condition", she sighed.

For the first month after Greg was fired, he kept himself very busy. Unfortunately, most of his experiences fell solidly on the negative scale. Just as the shingles started to clear they reappeared with vengeance. He returned to the doctor's two more times and a befuddled Dr. Howard prescribed different and stronger medicine. The side effects included sensitivity to light and nausea. For someone who rarely became sick he suffered a lifetime of illness during that month. Not only did he fight the shingles and the side effects from the medicine he had a few other random issues that shook him to his foundations.

He worked and reworked his resume for four straight days right after he received his box of personal items. Lynsey provided a lot of input. She also gave him dozens of tips for searching and applying for jobs on-line. She actually met up at Starbucks to help him create a LinkedIn account. He was going full bore with finding new employment and keeping his lawyer at bay in regard to a lawsuit. He knew that he was morally in the right and his lawyer was certain that the law supported him. The question he kept asking himself was the worth. He just felt that the sooner he found a new job the better his life would be.

He was surprised to get a call only a week after he was fired. The phone call was a simple check to verify some of Greg's information. He could not believe it when the company asked if he could come in the next day. His back and bottom were just starting to feel better from the first flare up, but he jumped at the opportunity. He did not think that the job was going to be a great one, but he was excited for the chance to at least have an interview. He figured that he would need the practice. All in all, he went to bed thinking that the situation was a win-win and maybe things were turning in the right direction.

He woke at 2:30 AM with a start. His mouth was watering, his stomach was on fire, and he was gagging. He scrambled out of his bed hoping that he could make it to the toilet. He did not. He made a terrible mess of the bathroom sink and floor. He had to kneel in vomit the second and third time he regurgitated. He broke into a shivering fit and all he wanted to do was climb back into bed. Instead he got into the shower and commenced spraying the vomit off his knees and ankles. He carefully stepped around the pile on the floor when he felt his stomach lurch again. He was able to slam his butt onto the toilet as the other end got into the act with a vengeance. He gagged from his own smell and feared that he would throw up while sitting on the toilet. He physically pinched his nose shut in an effort to not smell the horrendous odor now in the bathroom. The waterfall from his butt stopped and his stomach wrenched in pain. He doubled over and threw up once again on his lap and floor. He spent the rest of the night alternating between trying to clean up a mess and being sick. He was not sure if he had food poisoning or some kind of flu, but at that moment he simply wanted to die. The thought of getting up for a job interview did not cross his mind till two days after the fact.

Once he got the hang of the modern job search, he flooded companies with his resume, reached out to many contacts on LinkedIn, and tried to have conversations with as many past clients as he could. He was optimistic despite some of his health issues. One week turned into three and he still did not receive a second call back. Lynsey urged him to be patient. She understood that very few people were able to instantly jump for one place of employment to another. He could afford to be fairly patient as he had stashed several months of pay in the bank. The one facet of being unemployed that he did not consider until it was too late was the loss of health insurance.

Two weeks after his bout of gastroenteritis he was back at the nearby CVS filling new prescriptions for his return bout of the shingles. As he painfully approached his car door an ancient and decrepit Ford Crown Victoria swung into the parking spot next to Greg's Audi. The driver unfortunately misjudged the angle and speed. Greg was not fast enough to jump back as he was pinned between his car the Ford's front passenger panel. He heard the snap of his femur and fell to the ground in agony while the driver of the Ford slowly backed up. The ninety plus year female driver had not possessed a valid license or insurance for at least a decade. Those facts did not help Greg as an ambulance rushed him to the emergency room. The ER doctors said that he was lucky in that it was a clean break in his thigh bone with no other major damage occurred. Greg was not feeling lucky at all.

The lone bright spot in Greg's life for the first few months after being fired was his volunteer work with the animal shelter. As horrible as felt he still managed to go on a couple of Saturdays to clean kennels and walk dogs. A husband and wife team, John and Sandy Beyers ran the local no-kill shelter. One of them usually called him by Thursday to let him know if they needed his help that weekend. Needing help was always a given so the call was really just a recruiting tool for the weekend. He always promised at least one day a month and more if he did not have other commitments. On the Thursday after his accident Sandy called just like clockwork. He apologized that he would not be able to help because of the broken leg. She wished him better health and promised to call the next week.

By the time John picked up the phone the next week to go through his list of volunteers Greg experienced another bout of gastroenteritis. The second time around was just as violent and exhausting as the first time. The only positive was that Greg managed to avoid having to clean up any unplanned messes. He once again found himself praying for relief, but for the first time since his childhood he seriously wanted a connection with a higher authority.

Greg once again declined to help when John called. His voice cracked during his apology for not helping for a second week. John picked up on the unusual tenor and asked, "Greg, are you alright?"

Greg chuckled a little and realized that his eyes were a little watery, "Oh, yes. Just had a couple of rough weeks. I would like help, but I can't drive right now."

"Greg you have done so much for us over the past decade. If you want to help let us come get you", John offered.

"Oh, that is so great of you guys, but even if you came and got me, I will not be much help with my leg. Besides I also have a few other health issues that I am battling", Greg explained.

John quickly explained, "Oh, Greg. We always asked you to do some of the manual labor because you physically could. We have lots of other jobs that you can still do that will be a big help to us."

Greg deflected, "I still don't think that this is a good weekend."

"Greg, let me ask you one more question before you say no", John pressed. Before Greg could respond he continued, "How are things going for you right now?"

Greg defensively responded, "What have you heard?"

John laughed and said, "I have not heard anything other than the life in your voice. Or more precisely the lack of it in recent weeks. Even when you not could support us in the past you always had a spirit that I could detect in your voice. That has been missing recently and tonight you sound outright like you are down in the dumps. I am probably way out of line for even mentioning anything, but you have done so much for Sandy and I and our animal sanctuary that I would be remiss as a Christian if I did not try to at least reach out."

Greg did not immediately respond but he did have a tingling warmth inside that he had not felt in quite a while. He mumbled, "No, things have been kind of awry."

"Then let us come get you. I don't really need you do any kind of work. I just want to give you an afternoon to forgot about whatever is ailing your life", John enthusiastically responded. "Plus, I think I have the perfect job for someone with an aching soul."

Greg quietly accepted the offer and hung up. His misty eyes morphed into actual tears. He sat in silence and sobbed. He wiped his face and wondered if he was crying for the misfortunes that had struck him or the simply act of kindness from John.

A thought struck him that sent a flush of embarrassment up to his cheeks. He always considered himself a "good guy'. He never hurt an animal or another human being. He was conscious of other people's feelings, he was a defensive driver, and he could not remember a time in which he purposely screwed someone over. He realized, though, that he could not consider himself a good "Christian" in the manner in which John demonstrated. HIs friend reached out to him in Greg's time of struggle without a selfish agenda. Greg strained his memory to recall one time that he did the same. He liked to help at the animal sanctuary but that did not require diagnosing another's situation and trying to be empathetic.

He got up and hobbled to the shower. He suddenly did not feel like a good human being. He was afraid to examine his past in too great of detail at that particular moment. He needed to be physically and spiritually cleansed.

John and Sandy arrived at Greg's condo promptly at 8 AM on Saturday with sunny dispositions and a box of Dunkin Donuts coffee. They also had three large boxes of donut holes and insisted that Greg try one from each box as well as pour himself a cup of coffee before they would let him into the van. Once sugared and caffeinated they helped him into the van. Their natural exuberance brought a small smile on his face. Sandy talked excitedly about the "special" job they had lined up for him.

They drove fifteen miles outside of the city limits to a rural farm. The animal sanctuary sat on twenty acres of land that John inherited from his grandfather. The moderate unassuming 2000 square foot ranch was dwarfed by two large barns that flanked the house. The barn to the left was for the dogs and had a holding capacity of thirty. Fencing connected to this barn gave the dogs almost three acres to run and play. The other barn was for the feline rescues and it was equipped to house about fifty cats. A small outside carpeted area was connected to this barn. The Beyer's ran their sanctuary strictly off of donations and volunteer work. Sandy held a full-time job as a nurse and John was a part-time handyman. Most of the hours in the day he spent cleaning kennels and litter boxes and taking care of the nearly eighty animals that they sheltered. Greg had toured the establishment during his first day volunteering. Since then he always worked on the canine side of the property. Today they drove him towards the cat side.

"You are not allergic to cats, are you?" John quizzed.

"No", Greg answered as he scooted to the end of the seat while setting the ends of his crutches to the ground. "I guess I am with the cats today."

Sandy laughed and said, "You will see."

They entered the temperature-controlled building to the sound of dozens of cats meowing in different tones. A few younger volunteers that Greg had previously met already had selected cages open. They exchanged friendly salutations and fell back into their tasks.

The lay out inside the barn consisted of three long rows of cages. Each row was eight cages long and stacked two high. The volunteers were working on the left-hand row first and had all sixteen cages open. He watched the assembly line procedure of dragging out a litter box and emptying into a large garbage can. A few others were then taking the empty boxes to a back room for scrubbing. While the boxes were cleansed the cages were vacuumed and disinfected. The owner or owners of the cages were free to roam the barn or the enclosed outside area. Most of the cages held only one adult cat while several kittens may share a cage together.

Greg asked, “How many do you have right now?”

Sandy replied, “We have two litters of kittens right now. One set has only three left and the other has six, though they are still too young to adopt. We have thirty-seven, no wait, thirty-six adults right now.”

“Man, that is a lot of litter”, he laughed.

John pointed to a corner which held a pallet of boxes of kitty litter, “That is one of the most expensive part of this operation. We have a handful of vets that will come out here periodically and provide services at no charge. Almost all of the cat and dog is donated. The litter though is right out of our pockets. We could not do this if Sandy was not working full-time. The donations just don't cover enough.”

Sandy piped, “But we would not have it any other way. The Good Lord decided not to bless John and I with the ability to have children and these animals are our lives. Turning this property into an animal sanctuary is the best thing that we ever did.”

John was hauling boxes of litter to the back room and echoed her sentiments, “Amen.”

“Ok, am I scrubbing poopy boxes?” he asked.

Sandy laughed and called out, “Bring out the chair.”

Two twenty-something ladies reappeared from the back pushing a large decrepit leather chair. The positioned it at the end of the rows of cages near the open door to the outside enclosure. The taller women smiled, “You get to be Dr. Evil today?”

Confused Greg said, “What?”

John returned to grab another load of litter, “I used to call it the Ernest Bloefeld chair but none of the kids got the reference, so I changed the name to the Dr. Evil chair."

"I have to admit that I don't understand either", Greg shook his head.

John stopped and said, "Ernest Bloefeld from the James Bond movies. The head of SPECTRE guy."

"Sorry, not a Bond guy", Greg apologized. "I have seen a couple of the movies, but I don't remember any of the characters."

One of the men hauling boxes of litter stopped, put one his pinkies to his lips, and squeaked, "Sharks with frickin' laser beams attached to their heads."

The group all laughed including Greg though he offered, "I don't know what that was, but it sounded funny."

Sandy teased, "You mean to tell us that you don't know the cinematic classic trilogy of Austin Powers International Man of Mystery, The Spy Who Shagged Me and Goldmember?"

"Uh…no", he answered.

"I usually tell these kids that they need to get off their computers or turn off their tv's and go outside and meet the world", John began, "But in your case, you need to spend some time on Netflix watching Bond movies or Austin Powers movies."

They all laughed, and Greg asked, "Are the Austin Power's movies spy movies like the James Bond movies."

The circle roared in laughter again and John said while wiping an eye, "Just do me a favor and watch one and then you tell me. In the meantime, will one of you be so kind to explain to Greg what Dr. Evil and Bloefeld have in common."

A heavy-set man that was in the back scrubbing boxes chimed in with his impersonation of Dr. Evil, "Mr. Bigglesworth."

He laughed at his own mimicry and continued, "Evil villains, man. Evil villains that pet cats. Have a seat Greg."

"I am going to seat in the chair and pet a cat?" Greg replied with a pinched look.

Sandy urged, "Sit, please, just sit."

Greg shuffled his crutches and plopped into the ancient chair. He looked around the group with a confused look and said, "Now what?"

They began to disperse to their own tasks. Sandy simply offered, "Just be still for a second."

Within a few moments one of the elder statesmen of the shelter slowly meandered in the general direction of Greg's chair, but once within a few feet homed in like a torpedo to his lap. He laughed and stroked the aged grey cat. The animal arched its back and pressed its nose aggressively into his hand.

Sandy remarked, "That is Maxine. She is the old lady of the sanctuary. She has been here since day one. We do not definitely know her age, but she is at least eighteen."

The cat moved onto the arm of the chair and laid down with her paw tucked under her body. Greg remarked, "What's up with her eye? Is she blind in her left eye?"

"Yes", Sandy replied, "That is probably the reason we were never able to adopt her out. She is a permanent fixture and of the few cats that we let wonder the barn out a cage. She is such a sweet-heart".

Maxine purred as if she understood that the conversation centered around her. Before Greg could ask a follow up question a scrawny orange cat launched itself onto Greg's lap.

Greg remarked, "What do we have here?"

“That one is Tigger”, Sandy laughed while walking towards the back of the barn. “You are on your own for a while.”

One by the one the cats that were out of their cages found Greg and visited him. A few stayed just long enough for just a few quick strokes of their head. Most circled on his lap and happily accepted the attention provided by Greg. As silly as he felt playing the role of “Dr. Evil” instead of actually performing his normal manual labor he had to admit to himself that he enjoyed his task. Maxine stayed close the entire time while the others took turns ensuring that he was never left without attention for more than a couple of minutes.

John ventured by and handed him a cup of coffee when they started on the second row of cages. Most of the first group were shepherded back towards their cages and the new cats soon found their way to the chair and Greg. John watched the interaction with Greg and his charges for a few minutes and commented, “May not seem important but with so many cats it is hard for us to give each of them human interaction on a frequent basis. Almost all of our rescues are really friendly and just want to be around us. It becomes super difficult to get the cages cleaned with them seeking attention.”

“Well it is a unique way to help the shelter”, Greg chuckled.

At that moment a large white cat with black feet and tail sat at Greg’s feet looking up at him. John commented, “No way. Isiah here is very, very skittish and has never been interested in humans.

All eyes fell on Greg and the newcomer. Isiah did not appear to be in a hurry and simply laid down staring into the distance. One of the volunteers said, “He doesn’t appear to want to humor us.”

John smiled as he walked away, “Typical prima donna cat.”

Maxine still sat on the left arm rest and he was able to use his right hand to turn his phone onto the Facebook app. He scrolled through a day's worth of entries before Isiah jumped onto his lap. The cat froze and appeared caught between deciding to make friends or bolting out of fear. Greg remained calm and the cat leaned forward and rubbed its chin against his chest. He lighted ran his hand across the animal's back and remarked, "See, I am pretty good guy.'

Isiah vaulted off of his lap and literally bounced off the walls in hot pursuit of some unknown enemy. Another cat quickly took Isiah's spot and the afternoon continued. Greg shifted between apps and cats and was surprised that two hours had passed. He took a moment to amble to his feet before another feline came to visit. He crutched his way to the front of the barn and the rest room. He relieved himself, washed his hands, and looked into the mirror. He thought, *For the first time in several weeks I feel pretty…I suppose the word is good. I am glad I came now. This place, the cats, John and Sandy have…I guess sort of touched me…sort of renewed some faith.*

The rest of the afternoon passed in similar fashion. One by one volunteers arrived, performed some task, and headed back to their own lives. John and Sandy always provided pepperoni or cheese pizzas to the team on Saturdays. Greg wolfed down a couple of slices between cats pressing against his hand. This held his stomach at bay till dinner time. By this time all the cages were cleaned and the glow of sitting around and petting cats all afternoon had worn off. Greg left the chair and limped around the barn trying to help reload the last of the cages. When the last volunteer said good-bye John offered, "Greg we would love for you to stay for dinner with us before we drive you home. What do you say?"

“You guys have already gone out of your way. I don't want to be more of an inconvenience”, Greg deferred.

“Don’t be silly”, Sandy chastised. “I already have a roast in the crock pot that is going to be too much for just the two of us. Please join us for dinner.”

“Well, if you insist”, he returned.

The trio made small talk with Greg resting on a kitchen chair. John and Sandy worked together to set the table, fill drink glasses, and bring the food to the table.

When all three were seated John said, “We are going to offer a quick grace.” He held out one hand towards Sandy. She clutched his hand and offered her other hand to Greg. He put his hand in hers and then gave John his other hand to complete the circle. John gave a short but sincere offering of thanks. Greg found himself muttering *Amen* but inside he did indeed feel a sense of thankfulness.

Their dinner conversation revolved around the animals and the sanctuary. Greg inquired about several of the dogs that he remembered. He was pleased to learn that many of his favorites were adopted since his last visit. He learned over the years that life on an animal sanctuary was cyclical; always new rescues and always new placements. The conversation eventually stalled.

“You know Greg”, John began, “our life revolves around these animals and a lot of times I don't do a great job of trying to connect to people. I don't think I have ever really asked much about you. What kind of movies do you like? What are your hobbies? Hell, I really don't remember what you do for a living.”

Greg choked out, “Well I enjoy biking when the weather supports.”

The husband and wife duo both noted the crack in Greg’s voice. They exchanged a silent look that spoke a thousand words. Greg continued, "I guess I like sci-fi or fantasy type movies. When I go to the theater I like to be awed and entertained."

John shook his head and softly said, "I think I have touched a nerve somehow. I am sorry if I made you uncomfortable in any way."

Greg shook his head and said, "No, no you did not". The light glaze in his eyes gave away the emotions the he was struggling to stifle. He felt a hand touch and looked down and saw Sandy gently holding his hand in hers.

She spoke, "Please let us know if there is anything we can do."

Greg wiped his eyes and laughed, "Well, I could use a job."

Greg watched as their jaws literally dropped and now, he made an apology, "I am sorry, that was kind of blunt. I am not trying to cause you discomfort."

"The human condition is not discomforting", John replied thoughtfully. "Can I assume that your employment comment is true."

Greg nodded his head and John continued, "You are not causing us discomfort at all Greg. We fail on a daily basis, but we do try to be good Christians. If we can't handle a little bit of solemn news, then how can we help. Please, why don't you tell us about your employment situation and anything else that has caused one of our family members to be so obviously tore up."

Greg looked from John to Sandy and then back to John before he said, "Family member? Tore up?"

"Greg you have been part of our animal sanctuary family for years now. You come here and help us live our dreams of saving these beautiful creatures. You have given us thousands of hours of free labor. We have broken bread together at our dinner table. You seem to be on the verge of breaking down. Something has not been right in a month or so. We both picked up on it immediately. Maybe if you tell us we can help", John counseled.

Greg chuckled, "I had no idea that my misfortunes are so apparent in my voice and face. Well, I have not really told anyone about the stuff that has been happening. If you guys really want to know..."

They gently urged Greg to tell his story and to not leave out any warts. He started with the day that he met Sheryl all the way through his most recent bout of food poisoning. They mostly kept silent and only interrupted a couple of times to clarify a few points. He finished and grinned, "And that is the whole horror show. Have you ever felt like God was toying with your life?"

John and Sandy gave each other a long stare. John carefully said, "Why don't we grab a beer and sit on the deck."

Greg shrugged and agreed. Once comfortably seated on the cushioned outside chairs with beers close by John spoke, "Greg I am sure you are familiar with the story of Job from the Bible. I will not say that both Sandy and I had God messing with our lives, but we had some detours down wrong paths. God actually put us back on the right path."

Greg silently nodded and John told his own personal tale of woe. His father left the scene before he started school. His mother drifted from one bad and abusive relationship to another in order to maintain her insatiable drug habits. He was unsupervised and undisciplined throughout his formative years. He discovered drugs and alcohol at an early age and soon thereafter petty crimes to support his recreation. He was arrested more than once and bounced from one foster house to another and then eventually various juvenile detention halls. At nineteen he OD'd on heroin.

He came critically close to dying. At the time he was not afraid to die. He considered his life useless until the day he met Sandy.

The future love of his life walked an almost identical life path as John. She became promiscuous at a young age resulting in a couple of unwanted pregnancies and subsequent abortions. The last procedure rendered her unable to ever have children. They walked into each other's lives shortly after each one of them escaped their near-death drug trips.

They met (and grew to love) Reverend Leonard who they always referred to simply as Joe. He saved their lives. Individually their cases were separate but intertwined due to the relationship that they quickly forged. He considered himself moderately successful in helping young people whose lives were off-track. Sandy and John were two of his greatest successes. Initially he was able to get them to walk away from the drugs. They then went one step further and became happy and productive human beings. As their animal sanctuary idea became reality Joe's age and health forced him into retirement, but they still maintained a relationship.

When Greg asked how they did get from point "A" which was their past to point "B" which was their present contentment, they simultaneously answered, "Joe."

"Joe must be some kind of miracle worker", Greg responded.

"No, not a miracle worker. He just gave our lives focus. He gave us something to envision for the first time in our separate but equally miserable lives. He gave us something to hope for, something tangible we could envision", Sandy corrected.

"What did you envision?" Greg asked.

"Life beyond our current situation. We grew to understand that the human condition is tractable.

Things occurring today do not have to define the future", John chimed in. "For me personally, he offered a path that I never considered."

"And the path was?" Greg asked.

"He was able to connect us first to each other and then to the rest of the human condition. He did that through a simple connection of faith", Sandy answered. "That faith was missing from both of our lives."

"I reached out in an entirely new direction and let faith touch us", John emphasized.

Greg smiled and said, "You let the faith touch you."

They simultaneously responded, "Exactly."

Greg internally debated for moment in telling the couple that he was connecting the path that changed their lives to an old blue grass song that his parents used to frequently play on the home stereo. He hated their music and he was sure they played this particular song just to torture him. The thought felt inappropriate, so he chose to bury the smile. The song continued to sail through his mind as John spoke again.

"Greg, with your permission I would like to do a couple of things for you", John offered. Greg did not respond affirmative or negative as John continued. "We know a lot of folks in this part of the state. I would like to semi-advertise for you that you may be available for hire."

Greg broke from the blue grass song as the words registered with him. He quickly nodded approval and said, "Thank-you. Any help is appreciated."

John rubbed his hands and excitedly replied, "I think we have better connections than the typical monster.com. I have helped a few folks in the past. Now as far as the second item do you have anything going on tomorrow?"

"More unemployment and more pain and itching", Greg joked.

"Glad to see you are trying to find some humor in your situation. I would love to come pick you up in the early afternoon and take you to meet our friend Joe", John replied.

"I appreciate the offer, but I am not sure that is necessary", Greg stated somewhat standoffishly.

"I understand your hesitance. Please think of Joe as a human being and not so much as a retired preacher. I just think his words have had a way of helping people whether from the Bible or from the deep recesses of his mind", John explained, "And before you say no, I want to offer you one more observation."

Greg evenly said, "Ok."

"Greg that is one helluva story you told us. Pretty amazing string of bad luck over the past couple of months. But I have to tell you that something seems amiss. I can't pinpoint or explain it, but I feel like that this story has another chapter that you have not told us", John said.

"I agree", Sandy concurred.

Before Greg could respond John continued, "And I am not sure we are the right ones to help with that other chapter."

For a split second a rush of anger raced through Greg's body. He thought, *What the fuck is this psychological bullshit. I told them everything.*

Another voice from the back of his mind jumped in forebrain, *you have not told them anything about Cynthia.*

She does not have anything to do with the stuff happening to me, he argued with himself.

She doesn't? the other voice asked.

He could tell John and Sandy were studying his expressions. *So much for having a poker face,* he grimly thought. He realized that on the surface he was purposely refusing to connect the recent events with Cynthia. The deep and primal side of him that ran the fight or flight neural network kept her mental image just below his denials. The last time that they talked she flatly refuted his accusations. That was the crux of his inner turmoil; on one hand she made sense but on the other he did not know what to believe.

Several seconds of silence passed as Greg mentally argued and contemplated ideas that he previously buried. John spoke, “Greg, are you ok?”

Greg let out a deep breath that he did not realize that he was holding. “Let’s just say that maybe you are not too far off.”

“Pick you tomorrow about noon then”, John said. Sandy then artfully shifted the conversation to the mundane topic of upcoming weather before Greg could change the plan. She continued to skillfully navigate harmless topics for the rest of the visit including the drive back to Greg’s condo.

Greg thanked them and hobbled up the stairs to his apartment. Once inside he absentmindedly plugged his phone to his stereo hit play on the Spotify app. He was thinking about his parents’ blue grass song when the music started. He laughed out loud when the Marilyn Manson version of the Depeche Mode song “Personal Jesus” filled his apartment. Much different in tone from his parent’s blue grass song, but both urged an engagement with faith. He shook his head and sang along.

Chapter 13:
Had confusion and darkness for years…

The next day John picked up Greg and drove him an assisted living residence in the suburbs. The meeting between Greg and the aged Joe Leonard set off a chain reaction of events hundreds of miles to the north.

Bill "the financial advisor" took a phone call from Cynthia. She directed him in not-so polite terms to report to her house that afternoon. He responded with an equally direct vigor. He refused her demand and then subsequently suggested that more than likely he would not be able to make time for her for the entire upcoming week. His response was only the beginning of a two-week path of insecurity and rage for her. By the end of the day she was cognizant that she lost several layers from her aura sphere, but she was also pretty certain that she had enough conserved until Esperanza returned. On the other side of the coin, Bill felt completely triumphant. He also unknowingly sealed his own doom.

Greg's phone was connected to his stereo while he showered and dressed. The sounds of the blues drifted into his bedroom as *The Blues Brunch* churned out of the phone app. He unconsciously sang along to a familiar Stevie Ray Vaughn song and then one he knew from Kenny Wayne Shepherd. The opening notes of the third song were slower, somber, and seemed to emanate from the darkest of places. The crying vocals of an old deep south bluesman from the thirties were full of anguish. Greg was not familiar with this song and he listened as the singer moaned,

Had confusion and darkness for years,
You know the truth I speak is filled with tears.
A lot of rumors and whispers but I can excite,
The essence of a woman is not from the light.

Greg paused from brushing his teeth. The primal side of his mind tried to connect the dots. He buried the developing train of thought and recommenced scrubbing his teeth. As the old blues man's woeful gasps created a soundtrack for a hellish broken heart, Greg refused to allow the tone to set the mood for the day. He ignored the warnings and instead allowed excitement to build towards his meeting with John's mentor.

Joe had numerous physical ailments though most of them were simply related to age. His movement was ungainly and full of pain. His clothes seemed to just hang on his frail limbs like a child wearing his father's suit. His sparse hair was unruly, and a razor had not touched his face in a week. Overall, he simply did not look healthy. On the other hand, his heart was still incredibly strong, and his mind was even sharper. After a quick introduction John excused himself. Joe asked Greg to help him to a common sunroom in the complex. His feebleness was on full display, but Greg could not help but to note a spark in the old man's eyes. Greg estimated that nothing escaped the former preacher and life saver of John and Sandy. He wondered if some of the frailness was a facade to give a false impression of weakness.

They exchanged pleasantries and small talk for a few minutes before Joe bluntly remarked, "John rarely asks for me to meet with someone. You are the first one he has brought to see me since I moved into this home. You must be special to them."

"I have helped them on the animal sanctuary for years", Greg replied.

"Do you have animals yourself?" he queried.

"No. I simply stumbled onto them via a work friend. I volunteered one Saturday and just kept going back", Greg replied.

"Uh-huh", the old man thought. "You must also have something very troubling for them to bring you out here. John and Sandy are pretty resilient, and they know how to help folks."

"I am not too sure what John or Sandy mentioned to you", Greg began.

Joe interrupted, "They have told me nothing. John simply asked if I could talk to you. So, he we are. I have occasionally been able to help people that allow me to help them. Do you want me to help you?"

Greg smiled, "That is a little bit of a loaded question. I recently had several things not go very well in my life. These events have caused me to be a little...not even sure of the right word."

"Confused", Joe offered.

"That is probably a fair statement", Greg admitted.

"So back to my question. Do you want me to help you; help you with your confusion?" Joe asked.

Greg gave him an odd look and replied, "Sure. Who wouldn't want help with some sort of problem?"

"Ahh...you would be surprised. For example, people with substance abuse problems will often say they want help, but deep inside they really do not. They are not ready to be helped. They know that beginning the path to recovery puts certain obligations on themselves. I have spent sixty plus years listening to folks and determining if they really desire help. I am too old and cranky to have my time wasted so I will be direct and ask you again, do you want me to try to help you", Joe pressed. Before Greg could answer Joe asked, "Do you have a substance problem?"

He replied, "I did. I have been clean for over twenty years."

Joe stared at Greg with weary but keen eyes for a few minutes. His age made his eyes appear rheumatic and tired but within seconds they laser focused into Greg's own eyes. He prompted, "Why don't you tell me about that period of your life before we jump into today's issues."

Greg talked for a few minutes providing a general overview. He did not intend to go into great detail, but before he realized he was deep into the raw and unpleasant part of his life with drugs. He included his unusual relationship with Cynthia, the murder of his friend Luke, and the new beginning in Sacramento. When he paused the elderly man peppered him with questions that revealed his astute detection of missing details. Greg answered each query with the unaltered truth. A nurse walked in as Joe asked, "Have you had any contact with that Cynthia girl since you left Washington?"

She brightly said, "Mr. Leonard, your visitor has been here an hour. Are you ready to rest for a little while?"

Joe said to Greg, "These girls are always trying to get me to rest. That is all I do anymore."

He then turned to the nurse, "No, I am good. This young man here is telling me a really good story…the kind of story that gets my blood pumping. Please give us some time."

She smiled at Greg and said as she walked out, "Well don't get his heart pumping too much. Keep it G rated."

"I get your heart pumping?" Greg teased.

"Around here everyone's problems involve weak bladders, bad hearts, and erectile dysfunction. Your conundrum is a breath of fresh air", Joe joked. "Now back to my question. Did you ever see that old girlfriend again?"

Greg sighed and replied, "Yes."

He brought Joe up to date with his most recent visit to Remington. He skirted the supernatural discussions as well as some of the visions he had when they were together. He summarized by stating that she "dabbled in things that he did not understand and made him uncomfortable". Greg was somewhat surprised that the old man did not press for more details. Instead he simply asked, "Is this why you are here today?"

"No. Well, yes…sort of", Greg stammered. "Can I tell you about the last month or so?"

Joe waved a hand indicating that he should continue. Greg rapidly described each of the recent events without leaving out any details. He finished by explaining that John and Sandy noted a change in his demeanor and became worried.

"As they should have. I would have been upset with them if they had not tried to pry some information out of you", Joe replied. The retired reverend closed his eyes in apparent deep thought. After a few minutes Greg wondered if the man had drifted into a slumber.

"Joe", Greg prodded.

"Yep", Joe replied opening his eyes.

"Just checking", Greg stated with a little embarrassment.

Joe sat up straight in his chair and firmly explained, "Greg I was not taking a little snooze. You couldn't see the smoke but the gears in my head were turning. I have spent my life studying the Bible and using my knowledge to help people with their problems. The Bible is the great underutilized Google. Today people use Google to answer all their questions. Many of the burning questions in their souls don't need Google. They need to seek the answers in the good book. You know what made me a little different from my peers?"

Greg shrugged his shoulders and Joe continued, "I have a voracious appetite for learning. I read and learn for the simple fact that I love new knowledge. Besides theology I have studied anthropology, psychology, philosophy, ancient history, political science, and cognitive function to name just a few disciplines. I use all gathered knowledge to booster my understanding of the word of God to help people that want to be helped. I am educated in all, but I have to caution that I am a master of none. That fact should make me dangerous, but I have found that that this diversity allows me to see problems from different angles and offer alternative solutions. For some people a simply psalm out of the Bible is not enough. My wheels were turning because my senses are tingling. My hack understanding of therapy and counseling makes me think you are deflecting. I could just concentrate on the last six weeks of your life, spout off some passages from the Bible, tell you to give me three Hell Mary's, and send you on your way."

Joe's last words hung in the air like the undeniable elephant in the room. Greg realized that he was fidgeting in his chair and several thoughts streaked through his head while Joe seemed content to watch him be unsettled.

"What say you?" Joe prodded. "What are you not telling me?"

"Do you believe things exist in the world that we don't understand? Have you ever witnessed something that your mind tells you should not be?" Greg cautiously asked.

Joe replied, "I believe in the Resurrection and the Holy Ghost so sometimes we must face the realization that some things are beyond our comprehension."

"Has anyone ever come to you with stories of unnatural powers?" Greg queried with visible nervousness.

"Let me put it this way", Joe smiled, "You ever see that movie *Rudy*? The movie about the twerp that gets his ass kicked year after year on the Notre Dame football practice team."

Greg nodded affirmative and Joe continued, "In the movie that Rudy is at a crossroads and he is discussing his situation with the Father…I think his name was Provsky, but don't quote me on it. Anyway, Rudy has asked Father Provsky if he has done enough and the Father says 'In my thirty-five years of religious studies I have come up with only two concrete pillars of truth. The first is that there is a God and two, I am not him."

Greg smiled while Joe roared at the movie quote until that morphed into a coughing fit. When his laughter and choking subsided he continued, "The point is that many answers are somewhere between those two great truths, God exists, and I am not God. I may not have familiarity with your particular story of 'unnatural power', but my experiences are vast and in a few cases, pretty deep. Why don't you fire away and let me figure out on which spectrum your troubles lie."

Greg was normally a calm and deliberate speaker. When he told stories he often had uncomfortable pauses as he tried to select just the right adjective or adverb. Today his story spilled out like a runaway freight train. He barely stopped to grab a breath so even if Joe wanted to interject for a question he could not. Greg raced through getting the twenty plus years of unsettled memories purged from his body. When he finally stopped, he was curiously surprised that he was slightly out of breath.

"Son, that is one heckuva story", Joe said flatly. "I tell you what we are going to do. We are going to hobble down to my apartment. You with your crutches and me with my eighty-six-year-old legs. To be blunt, I have to piss like a racehorse and can't risk holding off any longer. Growing old sometimes really sucks. I could use the restroom right around the corner, but I have something in my apartment that I need before we continue."

Greg followed the elderly man through the common areas of the assisted living home to his own personal apartment. Ten minutes later he was sitting at the small kitchen table while Joe relieved himself. Joe slowly returned from the bathroom and plopped himself into a recliner in the combined living and dining area.

"Go inside the refrigerator and grab me beer. You can help yourself to one as well. I do have a couple of bottles of water in the back", Joe directed while pointing towards the refrigerator. Greg found the bottom shelf was completely filled with Bud Light cans neatly lined up in rows with the labels all facing outwards. He grabbed a beer for Joe and a bottle of water for himself. He delivered the beer to the seated former preacher while twisting the top on the bottle of water.

"I usually don't imbibe on Sunday even during the football season", Joe lamented, "But today is a special occasion. In case you are wondering the beer is what I needed to get. Some folks get uppity if you drink a beer in the common areas, especially on Sunday."

Greg took long swallow from his bottle and wordlessly nodded in understanding. Joe spoke again, "As I mentioned I have never been formally certified as a psychologist or a therapist but over the years I have picked up a few tricks of the trade so to speak. I can always tell within two minutes if someone is lying. Greg, I am convinced that you believe every word you said to me."

Greg stood up an began to pace, "That is exactly the problem. I should not believe any of it. This whole thing is bat shit crazy. Oh, sorry for my language."

Joe chuckled and said, "If you only knew how much trouble my mouth has caused me over the years. I believe I am effective at helping people change their lives because I speak to them in the language that they understand. You just continue to say what you need to say in the manner that suits you."

Greg nodded and continued, "Every rational fiber of my brain wants to reject everything she told me and everything I think I may have seen. I want to believe that the recent events in my life are just a crazy coincidence. I should be solely focused on just finding a new job, but I CAN'T. Is my past somehow connected to my present, or more specifically is Cynthia somehow putting a voodoo curse on my ass? I just want to feel...I don't know the right word."

"Many people would offer the word saved", Joe replied.

"Am I crazy, Joe? Should I really be seeking medical help instead?" he honestly pleaded.

"No, I don't think you are crazy as you say. I think you are confused, and we established that fact an hour ago", Joe answered. He took a large gulp and finished the can of beer. He held it towards Greg and said, "Be a good lad and get me another. I am now going to tell you a story. Not as good as yours but a story. Then I think I have three different paths from three different fields that I think may help with your confusion."

Greg fetched the beer and Joe began speaking before he returned from the refrigerator. He said, "When I was in my early twenties, I did a lot of mission work. Almost all of my trips were to central or south America. I often ended up in very rural settings with the absolute minimal technology... minimal technology even for that day and age. Running water was often a luxury. Anyway, one year I was assigned to a tiny dot of a village in Peru. I honestly don't recall the name of the spot, but I can actually still remember the faces of a couple of the nice folks that lived and struggled there. Didn't take long in those little burgs to figure out who was what and what help you could provide. The setting was beautiful as all get out, but the poverty was extreme. Me and two other fellows were assigned to that particular village at that time. Like I said, you quickly learn who all the people you are assigned to help so after six months of being with them we were stunned one morning to see two extremely beautiful young ladies that we never saw before suddenly appear. They didn't approach us right away but just intermingled with the locals as if they were in the village the entire time. They stuck out like a sore thumb. They had what I guess they used to call natural beauty. They were simply stunning. The next day I asked one of the local elders about them and he became awful jittery. We often had a language barrier during these mission trips. We usually only knew the basics of the hometown language and they likewise with English. On that day Ol' Boy gets super excited and completely digresses out of English. We try to get him to slow down and he does only long enough for us to gather that he wanted us to stay away from those girls. I shrugged it off as simply being protective, so I questioned another guy closer to our age. He also became excited, but we were able to interpret a few ideas from him. The villagers truly believed that they were some kind of sorceresses. They could seduce a man with a look, steal their souls, and keep the souls in a kind of magic ball. Sound familiar? They believed that the soul could be used to cast a spell for the purposes of evil. I was a little more adventurous, or more of a dumb ass, than my compatriots. I approached one of these ladies with the simple intent of saying hello, getting a name, and making my partners envious. We were devoted to spreading the word of God, but we still had human hormones racing through our young bodies. Let me tell you that up close that this young lady was the kind of woman that make all men forget whatever vows they had. She may have been the sexiest women that I actually ever spoke to. I was instantly smitten. I don't remember what exactly she said. Heck I don't remember if she spoke in English. It wasn't the words that I still recall. She had sweetest sounding voice. Just like an angel. But underneath that siren call I swear to my dying day was the epitome of evil begging to be unleashed. The voice was harmonious on the surface, but I heard a terrible shriek hidden inside of it. I know that sounds crazy for a person to speak and have two voices come out of one mouth but that was what I heard. The other crazy thing I witnessed involved her eyes. I later explained away what I thought I saw as tricks of lights. Her eyes changed colors right before my own eyes while she spoke. Not just a shade but from deep brown to the brightest of blues. This amazing young woman instantly scared the living crap out of me. I did not answer her or wait for her to speak again. I did not go pass go and collect two hundred dollars, but simply got out of her presence. I must have sounded like an absolute idiot because I went back and begged the other fellows that we needed to leave the village right then and there. I remember them scoffing and saying the next village was something like fifteen miles away. They refused to leave but I did. I don't know exactly how far the next village was, but I completed the trek late that night. I stayed there for two days and started to feel incredible foolish so I headed back. The other missionaries were gone. So were the girls. The villagers said that they thought that the guys left with me. This was long before the advent of cell phones and such and so I had to hike three villages over to get to the one with the working radio. It took a month before the response came back from the church that I should close out and return to the states. I went back to the village and said my good-byes. They were all very sorry to see me leave and wished me the best of luck. I arranged to ride a mule back and while they prepped my ride, the old man suddenly appeared at my side. He startled me when he spoke. He simply said that he tried to warn us. He slipped away from my side just as quick as he appeared. I rode the mule back to the radio station village and came back to the states. I fudged the story that I told the church. I told them that we separated to try to help more villages. I did not want to sound like an insane person. I figured they would launch some sort of investigation, but they did not. They accepted my story that the men disappeared and that no one had any idea as the cause. They simply and quickly closed the case. That gnawed at me for years, but time has a way of making things fade. Greg, I have never told another living soul about those girls until today. Your story about, as you called them 'aura spheres', slammed the memory back into me. So now comes the million-dollar question. What do we do with these stories?"

"I don't know", Greg honestly replied.

Joe took a large drink from the beer, shook the near empty can, and replied, "This one is almost dead too, though it is a bit early to tie one on. As I said before I started my story, I have three things for you to consider. The first is your faith. Greg, are you a religious person? Do you consider yourself a Christian?"

"I grew up attending Sunday services. I suppose I am by definition a Christian because I believe Jesus died on the cross for our sins. I have to admit, though, that is the extent. I have not been inside a church in almost thirty years and I can't say that I ever give it any thought", Greg answered.

"Fair enough", Joe said. "I think you need to give it more thought. I am going to recommend to you that next Sunday instead of playing hooky I want John and Sandy to take you to that little church a few miles from their house. That is where I preached and helped people for a long time. The new preacher has continued with the tone that I set all those years ago. The exact denomination is not important right now. I will just say that we are maybe a little unorthodox, but I feel truly effective. I always wanted my congregation to walk out on Sunday mornings feeling like their faith batteries have been recharged. Human beings suffer many angsts and troubles on a daily basis that drains them and leaves feeling discouraged. They forget their faith and they become confused. I truly believe that faith is like a battery. Go sit on just one Sunday morning and I bet you come away feeling something and that something is energy being put back into your faith battery. I want you to promise me that you will at least *consider* going one time with John and Sandy."

Greg stated in a noncommittal tone, "Alright I will consider it."

Joe slapped his hands on his knees and stated, "Good. I think you need to restore the faith in your life that was introduced to you at a young age. The reason is tied to the recent events in your life. Let's forget about our questions regarding our stories of frightening females for a second. These other worldly events have left you drained and feeling confused. Confusion is the work of Satan and not of God. I could spend several hours giving you multiple sermons on that very topic. When things are not right in your life and you become confused that is the work of the devil. He is the author of chaos and disorder. His goal is to make you forget your faith. Does that make sense to you?"

Greg nodded and Joe continued, "Now I need to make a confession. I did know a little about you before you walked in the building today. I did not want to know the problem, but I did ask John about some of your background. You know one of the things he told me that I found really interesting?"

"That I have never seen an Austin Power movie", Greg smirked.

"No, he didn't mention that fact. You aren't missing much. No, he said that you constantly hum and sing while you are working. He said that he thinks that you know the lyrics from every rock song from the 1970's and 1980's."

Greg chuckled and said, "I don't know about every lyric, but I will agree that I know way more than the average person."

"And I suppose you have one of those fancy phones that you can ask it questions?" Joe pressed.

"Yes, I have one of those fancy phones too", Greg smiled.

"The Bible is like those rock songs you like. You remember lyrics because they have meaning to you in some way. You connect with them. The Bible is the original album liner", Joe pointed out. "I am going to give you couple to ponder just for starters. Corinthians I says 'For God is not the author of confusion, but of peace, as in all churches of the saints'. The second one comes from Isiah and that one says 'And the spirit of the Lord shall rest upon him, the spirit of wisdom, and understanding, the spirit of counsel and might, the spirits of wisdom. Image those verses to your favorite guitar riff. Then imagine the words as related to your life."

Greg spouted, "You are not what I expected. Rock lyrics and Bible verses!"

"Yea, yea. I take that as a compliment", Joe brushed aside Greg's outburst, "I am not done with you yet. We need to get your butt in a pew on Sunday and I get more conviction from a drug addict that we all know is going to relapse than I do with you. So, here is what you *are* going to promise me and this time I won't accept just a consideration. I want you to promise me that sometime in the next few days you will pull out that ridiculous expense toy you call a phone and I want you to talk to it. I want you to ask it what the Bible has to say about confusion. I think you are going to find several hits very interesting. I believe you will see that you are not alone, and your troubles are not new and are discussed in the Bible. I think if you do this that you may seriously consider joining Sandy and John. Will you humor an old man and promise me that you will talk to your phone?"

Greg could not help but to feel amused. He agreed and felt strangely serene with the idea. He began to wonder what he may find on the internet when Joe brought him back to the current conversation.

"We are not done solving all of your problems yet young fella", Joe scolded. "We need to talk about that ex-girlfriend of yours and I am going to lean on a different discipline to help you with her."

"I am all ears", Greg said with somber enthusiasm.

"Are you familiar with the principle of Occam's razor?" Joe questioned.

Greg thought for a moment before he stated, "I have heard of it, but I do not remember what it says."

Joe explained, "It is a problem-solving principle. In essence, the idea is that if you have competing hypothesis, the one with the fewest assumptions should be selected. The solution that is the easiest with fewer difficult assumptions should be used. Yours is not the first case of unexplained occurrences that I have ever heard. I have utilized this principle when dealing with things that seem unnatural. Let's start with my own experience in Peru. I know that I left two young men in a tiny village where two exotically beautiful women suddenly appeared. One of the young ladies gave me a good case of the heebie-jeebies. I left for a few days and when I returned all four were gone. Those are the facts. The questions become what happened to the four young people. I suppose we could image a thousand different scenarios. I want to focus on just a couple. Let's say that hypothesis A is that these young ladies had some kind of power, they stole the souls of the young men, and left the village. We must make some complex assumptions for that theory. We must assume that this kind of witchery is real. We must assume that they were able to steal their souls. We are left with no bodies so we must conjecture on what happened to those. Now I thought I heard something very evil when I spoke to one of these girls. That adds a level of believability to theory A. Now let's assume for theory B that these were just normal young ladies. Their appearance in the village was odd and they were strangely attractive. I hear a story about these young ladies having powers. Did I hear the young women speak in some kind of twisted tongue or is it possible that my mind decided to be imaginative at that given time and trick me into believing that she spoke in some kind of horrible language. Is it possible that these young people simply ran off together to do whatever young people do? Have young men forgot about their obligations by the first affections of the opposite sex? What if these ladies were ten out tens on the sexy scale? How often do young people find the new people strangely exciting and attractive. While these fellows were no Tom Cruises, they were not grotesque. Which theory now has less difficult assumptions and which one is more likely? "

Greg waited a second assuming the question was rhetorical. He finally accepted, "I see your point for your situation. I assume that the idea is to apply your process to my own experiences."

"Exactly. But not here", Joe sighed. "You must think long and hard and be honest with yourself."

"Are you convinced that hypothesis B is the right one in your case?" Greg tentatively asked.

"Don't be shy. You want to know if I practice what I preach. Fair enough. For a long time, the answer was no. I would not let myself believe in stealing souls and storing in a ball, but I could also not accept more plausible situations. I am not going to tell you that every supernatural occurrence that has ever happened is an outright lie. We are only human and many, many things are beyond our comprehension. Some of that craziness may exist. I am just convinced that my own experience was not one of those."

"What do you think about mine?" Greg asked.

"Doesn't matter what I think, only what you conclude. I will offer that I think that your experiences have more to do with illegal substances than actual substance", Joe replied.

"Hmm...the part that confuses me is that she herself told me about her powers", Greg said thoughtfully out loud. "How do I resolve that part of the story?"

"Same way. Use Occam's razor. Make an assumption that every single thing she said to you is one hundred percent true. Then make a second one where you provide a counter to her claims. When dealing with the idea of that ex-girlfriend I am also going to advise to you use a third discipline to help you. Remember this is all about trying to help with your confusion. With confusion at bay your faith is strong which enhances your ability to think and be resilient to obstacles. I will acknowledge that the bad things that happened to you recently are a bit in the strange category. On the other hand, millions of people have suffered worse and overcame. You ready for a math lesson?" Joe said with a smirk.

"A math lesson?" Greg repeated.

"Well not really", Joe continued to grin, "I am going to show off a bit."

Puzzled Greg said, "Uh?"

"I told you that I am continuously learning. Over the past few years I have started learning computer science and algorithms. This discipline has theorems and laws like other forms of learning. Men of extremely high intelligence contemplate extremely advanced problems and then try to develop ways to solve them. Some of these problems become famous and are passed down for generations. Today these math wizards have actually developed algorithms to determine if a problem can even be solved. If that problem can be solved using an efficient algorithm, they say that problem is *tractable*. If it cannot then they say the problem is *intractable*. Not bad for an old preacher man wouldn't you say", Joe bragged.

"Never heard those terms before, but I believe you. How do algorithms and problem solving help me?" Greg pressed.

"Know what those brainiacs do when they figure out that they have an intractable problem?" Joe leaned forward. Before Greg could answer he triumphantly responded, "They relax the damn thing."

Greg raised an eyebrow, "Relax it. What does that mean?"

"It means that many times these problems have too many variables, too many constraints. Relaxing it means simplifying it by removing constraints. They have developed formal processes for this idea. These math problems become simpler and often they can become closer to being solved. The solutions are not one percent accurate, but the answers are close enough to be usable. After studying these concepts for a little while I decided to try to apply this ideology to our everyday problems. I tell people to try to remove a constraint from their problem and see if it gets easier."

"My constraint in your analogy must be Cynthia", Greg surmised.

"Son I know this is really simplistic but believe it or not I know several folks that latched onto this idea. Changed their lives. They were forced to recognize the truth. Your ex-girlfriend is a constraint that complicates your life. Try to image your life without all of...well you the stuff that has your troubled", Joe expounded.

Before Greg could reply his phone rang. John was calling to tell him that he was ten minutes away and was wondering if he was ready for a ride. Greg told that he was and that he would be waiting outside. He clicked the phone off and said, "John is inbound."

"I figured. Pretty good timing because I have to admit that I am getting a little tired. I am glad you decided to let me hear your story today. I hope that maybe some of the ramblings of this old man may help you a bit", John replied.

"Gave me a lot to think about", Greg responded.

"I am sure I did. I want to talk about one more thing before you leave. The idea of using algorithmic relaxation techniques to help solve your life problems is simply an interesting view. I introduced you to that discipline to make you think about that lady of yours. Those powers that your witch lady described to you are pretty concerning. Maybe there is an ounce of truth in it. Probably not but I can't help but to advise you to really think about it. If she does have powers, they are not a gift from God. Do you want to be involved with something that could risk your eternal soul? If she is not being truthful than I have to ask what is her game? Whatever it is, you probably do not want to be involved", Joe paused.

"These thoughts have run through my head a few times", Greg admitted.

Joe said with earnest, "You really need to completely remove her from your life. I am old as you can see and some of my beliefs are not exactly in tune with the modern times. Some of my thoughts in regard to women could be considered old fashioned at a minimum. Feminists would lose their shit if they could read my mind most of the time. All I have is a life worth of experiences and I have seen the evil that women can wrench on a man. Eve was the original antagonists. I have always had an uneasy feeling that women were put on this earth to test men. And our dumb asses usually fail. They have an essence deep inside that was not created out of goodness."

"You saying women have a wicked soul?" Greg asked with a touch of surprise.

"Maybe not that but I will say that the soul of a women is different from that of a man. Your ex-lady friend has something that you really need to avoid", Joe concluded. "Now I don't want to sound rude, but you have provided me more excitement than I get in a month combined. I am going to say it was a pleasure to meet you and please don't be shy. I would really like to know how things are going in a few weeks or so. I would like to rest here in this chair so if you don't mind letting yourself out."

Greg quickly stood and warmly shook the man's hand. "Thank-you for your words. I will reach out some day to give you an update."

He left the apartment with his mind mulling all of the words that Joe bestowed upon him. He only had to wait a few minutes before John pulled up in the sanctuary van. John helped him into the van and tossed the crutches into the back. John pulled away from the retirement center and quizzed, "Well what did you think? What kind of stories did he tell you? What type of advice did he offer?"

Greg chuckled, "He is definitely one of a kind. I will need some time to fully compute all of his ideas."

"I bet one of his suggestions was that he wants you to tag along with Sandy and I to the little church by our farm", Joe guessed.

"Yep", he replied. "And you know what? I think I want to go with you guys if you don't mind.'

John exclaimed with excitement, "We would really enjoy having you go with us. Don't worry about if you still are not up to driving. I will be glad to come get you. This is really a great surprise."

A few minutes later John queried again, "Did Joe bestow any pearls of wisdom onto you that you don't mind sharing?"

Had confusion and darkness for years

Greg carefully replied, "We talked about confusion and some ways to work through the confusing things in my life. He suggested using Occam's razor and algorithmic relaxation techniques. These were new concepts to me. I let him know about of a couple of things that I haven't really shared with anyone.

You know the truth I speak is filled with tears.

He also gave some real direct advice. He skirted on brimstone and fire kind of stuff if you know what I am saying. I will say, though, that he did offer a unique hypothesis on dealing with the fairer sex. I can't say that I necessarily disagree with him."

A lot of rumors and whispers but I can excite,
The essence of a woman is not from the light.

Part IV: The Chorus (The Title)

Chapter 14:
"Fire Woman"

Esperanza finished scrubbing the kitchen, taking out all the trash, and preparing an elegant lunch meal before Cynthia emerged from her bedroom. She was freshly showered and dressed in a form fitting but conservative pin stripe business skirt and jacket. Her hair was up in single beret and short heels matched her suit. She was absent makeup or jewelry with the exception of her starburst pendent which appeared lighter than usual in color. The lengthy time she spent in her bathroom took days of sweat off and years of aging. Esperanza took one look at her, focused on the necklace, and flatly remarked, "You look better."

"I cleansed off my self-pity, and I am now able to focus. I have a plan now", she excitedly remarked.

"I hope your plan doesn't involve leaving the house", Esperanza chided.

"Why not?" Cynthia asked. "You know it does."

The housekeeper sighed and remarked, "I said you look *better.* I did not say that you look like are ready to be seen by the public. Where are you planning to go?"

"Well that is a rude thing to say. I need to go see Bill and restore some order", she retorted.

Esperanza motioned and said, "Sit. I have lunch ready for us."

Cynthia obeyed the elder woman's direction and was served a bowl of tomato bisque and an extravagant three cheese and bacon grilled cheese sandwich. Cynthia did not hesitate and began to wordlessly devour the meal. Esperanza set a small bowl and half a sandwich down on the table for herself. She took a few small bites before she remarked, "I was not being rude. You still look too old to go see Bill."

Cynthia asked with a mouth full of food, “How old?”

“At least sixty. You are not ready”, Esperanza replied.

Cynthia set down her half-eaten sandwich, wiped her hands on a cloth napkin, and stood up from the table. She walked over to the counter and opened a large purse. She shuffled a few items inside the bag and produced a makeup mirror. She gazed at herself through the miniature mirror. She frowned in agreement with Esperanza. She pulled out compact and brush. She lightly dusted a layer of blush onto her cheeks and used the brush to spread. She set the instruments down and used her hands to pinch and tug at her face for a moment. She pulled the clip from her hair and allowed her long hair to flow freely around the side of her face. She bowed her head causing her hair to momentarily hide her facial features. Her head momentarily glowed with a blinding light. She vigorously shook her head several times before reaching up and reapplying the clip.

She turned to Esperanza and said, “What do you think now?”

She remarked, “You need to go to the bathroom and properly fix your hair now.”

Cynthia snapped, “I know that you are an annoying old hag. I am talking about the age problem.”

Esperanza nonchalantly acknowledged, “Yes. You look normal.”

She at back down and silently finished her lunch. Esperanza was only halfway through her own meal, but she immediately stopped her own lunch to take the empty dishes to the sink. Her own soup she dumped into the sink. The sandwich she wrapped in Saran wrap and left on the counter. She lightly wiped the table and said, “You said something about needing my help in the bedroom.”

Cynthia was reading email on her phone. She did not lift her eyes from the device but did respond, "Yes."

She continued scanning the emails for a few more minutes before she closed the email messenger, clicked the phone off, and set it on the table.

She announced, "Like I said earlier I am going downtown and see Bill. Removing him was part of my plan anyway, and with his recent behavior I might as well cross that bridge sooner than later."

"When you say plan…", Esperanza murmured.

"Yes, I mean with Greg. You were right that this has been too long of a process. We are going to push things along."

"To what end?", Esperanza reacted with an icy tone.

"You know what end. He is going to move back to Remington", she replied.

Esperanza sat silent for a moment before she quietly stated, "I am still not sure that this is going to work out the way you envision. I have known you too long to try to talk you out of going down this path. What do you need from me?"

Cynthia gave a devilish smile and replied, "You are going to Sacramento for a few days."

Bill opened the door to his upscale high-rise condo located only a few blocks from the downtown Seattle business center. He paid an outrageous monthly rent because of the majestic view his living room offered of Mount Rainier. The first time he walked into the unfurnished condo his eyes were instantly drawn to the view. He walked right over to the sliding glass door and stepped outside on the deck. A light misty rain blew right into his face and the mountain view was partially hidden by the heavy cloud cover. Despite the weather his breath was taken away. He told the agent that he wanted the condo without seeing the rest. Every day for the next ten years that he occupied the condo he absolutely treasured walking into his residence. He always left the curtains open to the sliding door so that the first thing he saw was the magnificent view. Those first few moments always sent a rush of good feeling soaring through his body no matter how bad the things were with work, with traffic, or with other human beings. He took the first few steps into his condo and the flash of good feeling that he was expecting was instantly swept away.

His heart skipped a beat and his throat closed shut as he saw Cynthia standing in front of the sliding door. Her stiff posture and fine clothes radiated power and anger. For a second her appearance sent a wave of shivers through his body. He shook the feeling away and angrily reacted, “What the hell are you doing in my house?”

“Your house?” she laughed.

He took an aggressive step forward and pointed a finger, “You are going to get out of here right fucking now and maybe, just maybe I won’t call the cops on you.”

“Don’t be silly”, she scoffed. “Your name might be on the rental agreement, but this condo, your cars, your clothes, and all your assets are yours because I gave them to you.”

“I don't know what you have been smoking, but you are out of your mind”, he rejected. “Yes, you gave me a break with your portfolio, but I have worked my ass off to earn everything I have. You are one narcissistic bitch to think you had anything to do with my fortune.”

“No, everything was set up and handed to you. A trained monkey could have managed the assets provided to you, but I required someone that could actually write their name. You have accomplished nothing except sign the papers I ensured were pushed in front of you. No matter. I do not need you to believe me", she sneered.

"Alright I have had", he began.

Her voice boomed, "Stop talking." The force of words caused him to literally take two steps backwards. A picture fell off the wall with a crash and the glass front shattered across the tile floor. The sound echoed and reverberated as he involuntarily cupped his hands over his ears.

In a calmer tone she said, "I am bored with this. I have too much to do to dumb things down to a point that you can understand. When we first met you confided to me that you grew up in extreme poverty. Your only desire in life was to never know that kind of lifestyle again. You said you wanted to be wealthy. I told you that I could set you free from your past. Do you remember that conversation?"

She took several seductive steps toward and purred, "Don't you remember."

When she was inches from his face he stuttered, "Maybe. Vaguely. So what?"

She interrupted him, placed both her hands on his shoulders, and stared into his eyes, "Just answer my question. Do you remember that conversation?"

"Ok, sure. Again, so what?" he asked.

She swung her body behind his and wrapped her arms around him. Her hands came up rested on his chest while she slowly grinded her pelvis into his back. In a raspy tone, "You are so close from being truly free. I want to set you free RIGHT NOW."

Her hands rubbed down his stomach while she slinked around to his left side. She deftly sent her left hand under his waist band and rubbed his crotch. He instinctively sucked in his gut to give the hand easier access. In his mind he thought, *this is absolutely fucking nuts. Kick this wacky bitch out of your house before something really insane occurs.*

Instead he moaned, “Yes.”

She pulled her hand from his pants and swayed back to the glass door. She turned and faced him with a lustful gaze. She ripped her jacket open sending buttons flying across the room. She dropped her skirt to the floor revealing a garter and thigh highs and seductively pulled her shirt over her head.

He stuttered, “Oh my God.”

“God has nothing to with this”, she winked. He watched as her hands came together in front of her stomach and slowly spread apart as if holding an invisible object. “Tell me that you want to be free.”

This is the craziest thing I have ever seen, he thought. He kicked his shoes off and began pushing his pants to his ankles. He thew out, “Fuck yea I want to be set free.”

He watched her blow him a kiss and the room filled with a blinding light and obscenely loud cracking sound. He was attempting to pull the last leg from his pants when she sent him the kiss. He was caught off guard by the light explosion. He lost his balance fell backwards onto his butt. When he lifted his head and the illuminance subsided his perception of his apartment changed.

All the walls were pushed well into the distance giving the illusion that his entranceway was the size of a football field. Phosphorous green and purple fog floated along about foot above and down to the floor. The air seemed stale and sickly hot. He no longer felt the rush of lust, but a spear of panic pierced his body. He frantically looked around the apartment while he tried to stand. He moaned, “What the hell is this?

Cynthia was leaning against the sliding door with one hand inside her panties. Her breathe was ragged as she answered, “This is setting you free.” Her body froze and then racked in apparent orgasm. At the same time, she blew him another kiss.

A visible wave of energy parted the gaseous haze and raced toward Bill like a torpedo in the water. Before he could react, he felt the wave wrap around his body like an invisible hand and slam him to the floor. He watched as tendrils of colors peeled from his body and raced back towards Cynthia. She was now calmly sitting with her legs crossed on the floor. Her head was bowed but angled so that she could make eye contact with him.

He struggled to make his vocal cords work. The misting from his body was not painful but he felt bound and almost paralyzed. He finally was able to force a few words, “What…colors…move.”

She did not speak but in his mind, she said, *Relax this will be over soon. This is what you wanted, to be set free. Your aura is melding with mine.*”

He croaked out loud, “Aura.”

That is what I call it. I guess it may be your life energy. Or could possibly be your soul. I don’t know, she mentally responded.

He gave forth a maximum effort to lightly rock back and forth. He used his last strength to yell, “Soul?”

She chided with irritation, *I don't know if it your soul. I just know that you will be just a shell of your former self left. Right…NOW.*

Bill’s condo distorted dimensions sprang back to normal and the hazy fog instantly vanished. The shell of Bill flopped over onto his side. She slowly dressed herself and found each of the buttons from her jacket. Bill remained motionless and she honestly did not know if he could recover and return to “normal”. She also did not care because that was not part of her agenda. She had his aura and now she wanted his position that he held managing her estate.

She opened her purse and produced a rubber strap, a small bag of heroin, and a needle. She tied the band on his upper arm and gave him the injection of the drug. She murmured to herself, "This amount will kill an elephant." To be sure she loaded the syringe two more times and roughly injected him. She then gathered all of her belongings and sat on the Bill's couch channel surfing. When she was certain that he was dead she called Esperanza.

When she answered Cynthia said, "I am done with my meeting. How about you?"

Esperanza gruffly replied, "Give me a break, I am not as young and spry as you. I just got into town. My meeting isn't till later."

"Don't give me any age excuses. I need you to do this. Have you started making the plans for the second meeting?", Cynthia retorted.

Esperanza laughed and said, "You really are a bitch. I have been in town for literally twenty minutes. So, NO. I have not started on the second project. I will call you in a couple of days."

Esperanza ended the call and Cynthia stared at the cell phone screen for a moment. She grabbed her bag and quietly left the condo. She made herself small and inconspicuous as she clung to the shadows all the way to her car that was parked four blocks away. As she drove back to Remington she said to herself, "I hope I do not regret bringing her into this."

Joe Leonard woke from a late afternoon nap with a start. He often had difficulty sleeping a full night in his bed due to various pains. The worst was in his hip, and when the joint began to flare up no position in the bed could relieve the discomfort. He always gave up trying and semi-rested in his easy chair in the living room.

When he had three or four bad nights in a row, a nap in the middle of the day was inevitable. He faced a grim reality a few years back that no surgeon would be willing to touch him at his age and that he could spend the remainder of days in pain or doped up. Neither prospect was very appealing. He hoped to be called to heaven before he deteriorated too much.

On this afternoon he was not surprised to find himself reclining in his chair, though he could not figure out why he was so startled. A woman's voice made him jump.

"Good morning Glory", an attractive young Hispanic woman said to him from a kneeling position a few feet from his chair. She slowly stood while using her hands to evenly spread out her knee length skirt.

"Who are you? How did you get in here? You are not one of the staff members", Joe said with a note of concern in his voice.

"My name is not really important. This is your lucky day because I am here to help you", she cheerfully replied.

"Now listen here lass, whatever you think you are going to sell just stop. I want you out of my apartment right now", he snapped.

"You silly old man", she giggled, "Don't you want help with the pain in your hip?"

He grunted, "How did you know about my pain. Never mind, never mind. I want you to leave."

Joe used the lever on the side of the chair to lower the footrest section. He then started to pull on the armrests to push himself out of the chair. She leaned over and lightly pushed him back into the seat.

"Where are you going? I haven't helped you yet", she grinned.

He loudly exclaimed, "I don't like this one bit at all. I don't know who you are or how you got into my house. I am going to call for security if you don't leave at once."

She sighed and said, "I told you why I am here. If this will make it easier, you can call me Sofia. You are Joe and I am Sofia. We are now met so now you can relax and let me help you."

"This is nuts", he said in an exasperated tone. "How do you think you are going to help me?"

She clapped her hands and sang, "I am going to set you free, set you free, set you free."

"Set me free?" he questioned.

"YES", she exclaimed. "From your pain. Wouldn't it be nice to be able to sleep through the night without that horrible piercing sensation?"

He quietly admitted, "I would love to have this pain go away." He deliberately shook his head in an attempt to refocus and sniped, "Hey, how in the hell do you know so much about my ailments?"

She leaned over and placed both hands on the arm rests. She stared deeply into his eyes and seductively said, "Just tell me you want me to set you free, Joe."

In his mind Joe thought, *this woman has the soul of the Devil. I have no idea what she is trying to pull but I am not going to be part of it.*

Instead he said, "Young lady you are intoxicating."

She pressed, "Tell me to set you free."

He laughed and said, "I am too old for this horse shit but what the hell. Sofia set me free."

She stood straight up and blew him a kiss. The apartment filled with a momentary blinding light. She looked around and noted that nothing appeared different. She looked down at Joe and angrily spat, "Oh you son of a bitch."

She kicked his leg and stormed out the apartment muttering, “You had to go and die before I could get anything out of you.”

Greg walked out of the apartment with a handheld Dirt Devil and a garbage bag. Earlier in the day he took the Honda through the carwash and now he intended to give the inside the once over. He opened the driver side door and plugged in the small vacuum into the lighter plug. He switched on the cleaning device and began sucking up dirt and crumbs off the floor mats and seats. He did not intend to scrub it like new, but he did want to make the car a little more presentable. He finally broke down and put the car for sale. He did not go all out and advertise in multiple places. He put a notice only in his condo association flyer the previous day. Within a few hours a few people called to inquire. That morning a lady told him that she wanted to come see if the car would be a good car for her teenage son.

He finished with the driver front and back seat and moved on to the passenger side. The floorboard with littered with empty water bottles and snack wrappers. He started to fill the garbage bag with the trash from the floor and then he emptied the glove box of twenty years of old receipts, maps, and other assorted junk. The passenger seat still held the two dozen or so CD’s that he took with him on his trip up to Washington. He opened each case to verify a CD was still inside and then set the case on the ground outside the car. Each CD sparked a host of memories.

The first Rage Against the Machine album, Alice in Chain’s *Dirt* and White Zombie’s *La Sexorcisto: Devil Music Vol. I* were CD’s of choice after high school but before Cynthia. Soundgarden’s *Superunknown* had heavy play in his stereo and on the radio during his time with Cynthia. He involuntarily shivered and quickly shuffled the discs to look at another title. Each one brought a flash of recollection. Most of these thoughts seemed warm to him even though more than one was reminiscent of the time when his life was out of control. The very last disc held his attention a little longer. He swung around and sat down on the passenger seat staring at the cover.

The album depicted a guitar wielding blond man wearing tight leather pants and a leather vest exposing his bare midriff. The man's legs were spread, and the guitar was held parallel to the ground with the left hand while the right hand was straight over his head. His head was down, and the long hair covered the face. His posture gave the appearance that he was getting ready to bring the hand down and strike a massive chord. In the background a reddish blurry image of man holding a microphone melded into the overall brownish backdrop. The image of the guitarist was sharp and clear and contrasted the broad paint stroke vision of the singer.

He instantly identified the guitarist as Billy Duffy and the singer as Ian Astbury. The silver block letters at the top and bottom of the CD named the band as The Cult and album title as *Sonic Temple.* Cult fans may recognize this one of their best efforts. He considered *Sonic Temple* as their absolute best. He also linked the album to extremely significant memories from his life.

In the spring of 1989 Greg was excelling at school and failing at life. Only a few months prior his best (and really only) friend Josh Walters was whisked out of his life down to Texas. His parents were oblivious to his inner turmoil. Other than the actual education he had zero interest in any other aspect of his school. He was a social pariah and was becoming clinically depressed. He found refuge by flipping through the album racks in the town's two records stores.

This was a period of time in which the format of music was transitioning. He mainly owned music on vinyl and still continued to purchase some on the older format, but others were becoming prominent. In junior high his parents gave him a Walk-Man for Christmas and so most of his most recent music purchases were in the form of the cassette tape. During the last holiday period his parents added a compact disc player to their home stereo. He owned only a couple of CDs' and these were really his favorite albums. He had to wait till his parents were not home to be able to listen to them on the home stereo so most of the time he still stuck with vinyl or tape.

He ventured into Rock Steady Records on a Wednesday afternoon after school and saw posters of *Sonic Temple* plastered across the entranceway to the store. He was mesmerized by the image, and he instantly had to own the album on vinyl. He held and stared at the cover for hours as he lay on his bed listening to the album over and over again.

He connected with the lyrics and made them his own. He found the slow ballads such as "Edie (Ciao Baby)" and "Soul Asylum" soothing and others such as "Sun King" and "Medicine Train" absolutely energizing. The song that helped him with cope with the absence of his only friend was "Fire Woman". Lyrically the song had no identifiable clues that should make him think of his old friend. The video for the song was dark and full of fiery images. Greg connected this with Josh, and he convinced himself that Josh would love the video, love the song, and the album as a whole. He was sure that any time that he was listening to the album that Josh also having the same experience. He stared at the album cover pretending the images were him and Josh vice Ian and Billy. These thoughts comforted him and made him feel like he still had a connection with his missing friend. He never found out that his intuition was correct. Josh was spellbound by the video and embraced the album.

Greg actually broke from his shell about a month after purchasing the album. The teacher in charge of the yearbook pestered thought the school year to join the yearbook staff. He finally relented and agreed to be one of the photographers. He was tasked with trying to capture on film as many of his grade mates as possible before the end of the year. Narcissistic teenagers, even ones that claimed that did not want their pictures taken, were instantly drawn to him when he entered a room with the school's camera. Over the next few months of school he was able to put Josh out of his mind and actually started to enjoy the social aspects of high school. Unfortunately, tragedy struck during his last week of school. His parents were killed in an automobile accident on the way home from the movies.

He regressed into full blown and undiagnosed depression while the state inefficiently tried to figure the best course for him. The foster parents attempted to help but he was not at a stage for strangers to reach him. He bought *Sonic Temple* on cassette tape and proceeded to continuously listen to the tape in his Walk Man. For a year he bounced from one counselor to another while the state shifted his foster parents half a dozen times. He ignored them all and found solace only Ian Astubury's vocals and Billy Duffy's guitar solos. He still frequently ventured into the record stores, but even if he had money in his pocket, he did not purchase any new music.

On a Thursday afternoon almost a year to the date of his parents' untimely deaths he strolled into Rock Steady Records, and he was intrigued by the neon green posters plastered all over the walls. These posters were advertisements for the new Motley Crue album, *Dr. Feelgood.* He was fascinated enough to buy the new offering from the L.A. bad boys. He walked outside the store and wrestled with the plastic wrapping which he let litter the ground. He popped out The Cult, slipped the tape into his pocket, and inserted Motley Crue into the portable tape player. The new tunes broke his daily addiction to The Cult. He moved on to other bands and other albums. This also marked the time in his life when he transitioned from an experimental drug user to an abuser. As drugs and new music filled the rest of his high school years, *Sonic Temple* stayed figuratively in his pocket. He often paused to gaze intently at the album cover, but he felt no urge to ever play again. The album and tape remained in their covers until he moved in with Cynthia.

He actually brought very few possessions into the relationship. Material things did not matter as much to him as a steady supply of party materials. He did try to keep a close eye on his music, but he lost more than he purchased in the first couple of years after high school.

She teased him at the meager few boxes that he carried into the house from the car. She insisted that all of his clothes go straight into the washer before filling one of the empty dresser drawers. While he sorted the box and bags of clothes, she noised through the other boxes. A majority of his belongings could be classified as junk and was roughly thrown into the boxes. She quickly bored with rifling through those boxes. She was, though, fascinated with how meticulously he packed the album and tape box. He respected his efforts and carefully removed each album or tape. She was not familiar with almost all of his collection. She read the back of each to see if she recognized any of the song titles with little luck.

As he walked into the kitchen back from the laundry room, she pulled the *Sonic Temple* album from the box. She ran her hands over the album cover and was oddly intrigued with the imagery. She flipped it over and once again failed to recognize any of the songs. She asked, “What is this?”

“That is *Sonic Temple*”, he off-handedly replied.

“I can read, you shit. I mean is this any good?”, she pressed.

“I think so. I have not listened to it in a freaking long time. Probably been five years since that was on a record player”, he answered.

“Well, that sounds like a good reason to check it out”, she cheerfully said.

“Shoot yourself”, he replied while grabbing a beer from the refrigerator. He plopped down onto the couch while she pulled the disc from the cover, set on the stereo turntable, and hit start. She set the volume to six out of ten and joined him the couch. She took his beer out his hands, took a drink, and nestled into his body.

As the opening notes filled the room he remarked, “This is not exactly cuddle music.”

“I will be the judge of that”, she cooed.

They sat in silence while the first song reverberated from the speakers. He occasionally mouthed the lyrics or bobbed his bed while she thoughtfully listened to lyrics. As the last note ended, he remarked, “Great shit isn’t it.”

“Mmmm…not like the stuff you normally play for me. Different”, she carefully replied.

“Different as in awesome. Check out this next song, ‘Fire Woman’, best song on the album”, he excitedly returned.

The first notes began, and she responded with, “Ok just one more.” A few seconds later she remarked, “Oh, I have heard this song.”

As Ian Astbury kicked out the opening lyrics she jumped up from the couch and began dancing to the music. She swayed her hips to the rhythm while circling towards the kitchen. His eyes were glued to her torso as she erotically matched the driving beat and vocals. She danced around the kitchen while simultaneously filling a glass full of wine. During the second half of the song a bridge progressed of slower rhythms and close to spoken vocals. She stopped her prancing and downed the entire glass of wine in three large gulps. A rapid fire of drumbeats broke the bridge and sped the song to the climax. She ran back into the living room, pulled her shirt over her head, and dropped her pants to the floor. The lyrics joined the rush of guitars and drums and she wildly sang along, swinging her body back and forth while whipping her hair to the rhythm. She climbed on top of him, pushed his head back and aggressively kissed him full on the mouth. As her tongue pierced his lips, she ground her pelvis onto his. He reacted by grabbing her butt, running his hands up her back, and returning the kiss. Astubury finished the song by repeating the lyric over and over again. They were now oblivious to the actual lyrics to the music as they locked together in full primal passion. She managed to pull her underwear to the side, and he lowered his shorts to his knees. She mounted and rode him with an unbridled flash of energy. He did not try to change position or even match her intensity. He let her control the situation and she very quickly drove him to the point of no return. He started to warn her that he was close when she arched her back and yelled for her own upcoming climax. He grunted and finished as she pressed herself down onto his member with such force that for a split second, he feared that she would actually break the appendage. They sat in that position for a few minutes, each breathing heavy, and sweating lightly. He managed to croak out, “What was that?”

She bounced off of him as easy as a gymnast and bounced toward the bedroom. She laughed and spouted over her shoulder, "I like that song. I will always be your fire woman."

He took several large drinks off his beer with his pants still pulled down. He closed his eyes and let the magic of the moment fill him with contentment. He wondered what Cynthia was doing in the bedroom, finished the beer, and let the thought fade out of his mind. In truth he really did not care what she was doing or her happiness.

At that moment she was directing the aura that she stripped from him during their loving making. She experienced a surge of contentment and was positive that she needed him in her life for the unforeseen future. She also did not care about his satisfaction.

These memories flooded into Greg's mind as he sat on the ground next to his Honda. The force of recollection surprised him. He took a deep breath to steady himself and said out loud, "I don't need you fire woman."

He pulled open the garbage bag and dropped the CD into it. He slammed the door shut to the Accord and decided the car was clean enough for a teenager. He hummed an unknown tune and headed back into the condo.

He followed Joe's advice almost to the letter. His first visit to Joe's former church had indeed "recharged" the faith batteries as promised. John and Sandy taught a Bible class on Thursday evenings. They did not so much teach as facilitate a small group of friends and the occasional guest. The gathering shared life experiences and then tried to expound upon those situations with similar events found in the Bible. They left each evening promising to further the lesson by reading select passages during the upcoming week. Greg participated in the past three Thursdays and he still had to complete the reading for this week.

In Remington Cynthia felt another pain surge through her stomach. She recognized the symptom and this time was able to deflect the strike into dozens of pins and needles until all sensation subsided. She closed her eyes and concentrated. The thinnest of layers escaped from her aura and streaked outwards in all directions. Within a few seconds a return vibration similar to a sonar wave echoed in her brain. She physically turned towards Sacramento. She mentally broke the connection with the searching streamers. She did not hear Greg's thoughts or vocalizations, but she completely understood the sentiment.

Her eyes lit with rage and she spoke with venom, "Oh Greg, I will forever be your fire woman." She snapped her fingers and her home stereo turned on and immediately the sounds of The Cult and the chorus to "Fire Woman" echoed throughout her house,

Chapter 15:
"Welcome to the Jungle"

Greg sold the Accord to the single mom and her teenage son for an absolute steal. The lady brought a mechanic friend along to check out the car because the deal just seemed too good to be true. The auto expert declared the car in great condition and then expressed some suspicion on the reduced price. Greg honestly answered that he simply needed to sell the car. After exchanging money and a notary signed the title over to the new owner, they all departed feeling satisfied. The mother felt that her son now had a reliable vehicle without breaking her bank. Greg wondered if he would feel some sort of heart ache when his long-owned car pulled out of sight. He felt nothing.

Later that afternoon he received a call from the HR department of one of the places that he submitted his resume. The lady on the other end of the call apologized for not getting back to him sooner, but she wanted to know if he could come to an interview the next morning. He affirmed that he could be at the interview at the requested time.

The company was located in the heart of downtown Sacramento in an upscale and modern new building. He recognized several attributes that labeled the company as being "green." He was ushered into a small but elaborately decorated waiting area with five other people. One by one each person was pulled out of the waiting area and did not return. Greg was the last to follow the assistant out of the waiting area. He was led to a large conference room where a team of four interviewers sat at a long table with a singular chair centered in the front of them. They quickly provided Greg their names which he concentrated to lock the name with the face. Their intros were pretty succinct and noticeable gruff. The two men and two women appeared tired and aggravated.

Despite the initial reception Greg felt that he knocked the interview out of the park. They thanked him with little commitment. He was escorted to a different waiting area where two men from the first group were seated. He was asked to wait with the others. He thought this procedure was a little odd, but he went ahead and confirmed that he had the time.

A few minutes a man and a woman entered the room. The former called out the names of the other two applicants. They acknowledged and he gestured for them to follow him.

The woman spoke to Greg, “You must Gregory Palmer.”

He stood and confirmed, “Yes, I am Gregory Palmer.”

She nodded and replied, “If you would please follow me.”

They wordlessly walked her through the maze of office spaces and up three floors via an elevator. He was deposited into an empty but plush conference room. She told him to have a seat and then announced that she would return momentarily. He pondered about this chain of events. He did not have to wait long as she returned with a large stack of papers.

“Mr. Palmer”, she carefully began, “my name is Rebecca Johnson and the position you applied is going to be filled by someone else.”

“Oh, I see”, he stated evenly while trying to not sound disappointed.

She nodded and said, “With that said, we may possible have something different for someone with your qualifications. Do you possible have another hour to spend with us this afternoon?”

“I do”, he said enthusiastically.

She dumped the pile of papers on the conference table in front of him. She also set down a notepad and a handful of pens and pencils. She explained, "This is the portfolio of a recently signed client. We have redacted the identification but left the raw numbers. We would like to you to examine them over the next thirty minutes or so. We understand that this is not normal procedure and we in no way expect to be able to produce the type of professional analysis that you normally would. We just want you to give us your initial thoughts."

Greg visibly exhaled and said, "I have never done anything like this."

She held her hand up and curtly replied, "We understand. Please indulge us. We may have something that may be mutually beneficial to both yourself and the company."

He smiled and said, "I need to get started then."

She quickly exited the conference room and he immediately opened the folder on the top of the stack. He tried to be both meticulous and expeditious as he examined the lines and lines of financial data. He jotted down several notes. He recognized that his handwriting was degrading at a rapid rate, but he wanted to get through as much of the pile as possible. Instinctively he felt that the portfolio had a story hidden and he wanted to flush it out. He was not even a third of the way through the stack when Rebecca Johnson returned with a group behind her. He silently counted as three men and three women walked around and sat down at the conference table.

Rebecca was the last to take a seat. She instructed, "Mr. Palmer could you please tell the team your initial thoughts on this portfolio."

Three hours later Greg sat at his small kitchen table with a large contract. The company was impressed with his review despite such a short period of time to review. He was immediately offered a contract but the job offer had several strings attached. The portfolio was recently sent over to their company from a gold star client. This particular case was owned by client in another city and up until recently had been managed by another agency. Greg's review identified minor discrepancies but ones that could accumulate. The contact was a short-term deal. He would be hired on for a six-month period to specifically work with this client. If things went well, they promised that he would be given serious consideration for a permanent position in the company.

The first half of the contract was highly intriguing to him. He would make more money in six months then he earned in the last three years at his last job combined. They were offering a full year of premium health and dental insurance benefits as well as a bonus calculated on a full year of work. He almost signed the contact on the spot. Then Rebecca nonchalantly mentioned the fantastic high-rise apartment with an impressive view.

The client had large interests throughout California, but the home base was in Seattle. The client desired to have close and frequent contact with Greg. If he signed the contract, he would be required to relocate to Seattle for the next six months. His hesitation seemed to agitate several people sitting at the conference table, but they reluctantly agreed to give him until tomorrow morning to decide.

He read the contract thoroughly while drinking a beer. He repeated these actions two more times. He knew he was simply avoiding making a decision by scrutinizing the legal document. The temporary relocation was not the real issue. If the job were in any other major city in the country, he would not have hesitated. Seattle was simply too close to Remington. And Remington had Cynthia.

He pushed the paperwork aside, stood up and paced the floor. He ran his fingers through his hair and grunted out loud, "This is crazy."

He thought about Joe, John and Sandy and his recent visits to church. He stopped pacing and literally dropped to his knees. He never before actually prayed on his knees, but on this evening he did. He wanted guidance. He wanted some kind of sign. The job offer was gold, but he kept hearing Joe's advice about relaxing his life's problems and removing the constraints. He felt that he took the steps to remove that constraint from his life. The job was putting that constraint only an hour away from his place of employment and apartment.

He did not hear golden trumpets or receive mystical revelations. He started to feel foolish after a few minutes on his knees. He stood and sighed. While he did not feel God sent a positive confirmation, he also did not sense a warning. He turned, bent over the table and rapidly signed the contract.

The next two weeks were an absolute whirlwind for Greg. He successfully managed to move his belongings and his life to the upscale apartment in Seattle. As promised the dwelling had a sensational view and was clearly the nicest place he had ever lived. He arrived to Harris Financial early on Monday morning and was quickly ushered through the HR process. By lunch he was escorted to a sparsely modeled conference room. Two other people were already in the room opening boxes.

He quickly learned that he was not going to be working alone on this project but as part of a team. The woman momentarily lifted her eyes to give a quick greeting and say that her name was Mary Chambers.

She went back to unloading the boxes without waiting for a response.

The man stepped around the table and offered his hand, "Well there you are. I am Simon Troutman. We are in this together, but I am sort of the lead, at least until we get roles clearly divided."

Mary grunted as she slammed a large stack of papers onto the table. She aggressively broke down the box. Simon chuckled and continued, "Miss Congeniality may not win any personality awards, but she is REALLY good at what she does. We will need her for this project."

She stopped for a second to glare. She started to say something, but instead shook her head. She refocused her attention on a new box.

Simon smiled and said, "This is the team. Welcome to Harris Financial, welcome to Seattle, welcome to the jungle."

Greg shook Simon's hand and said, "I am really glad to be here". As Simon started to explain the rough plan the company had developed for the project, his mind drifted to the opening cords to one of his all-time favorite albums. He could hear Axl Rose singing "Welcome to the Jungle" intermingling with Simon's chatter. Greg forced the song to stop and thought, *what kind of games am I going to get into here in Seattle.* Simon droned on while Greg continued, *I need to focus for six months and get back to Sacramento. The only thing I want to do is work, enjoy the view from the apartment, and sleep. Repeat. No trouble.*

The thought that he buried and would not allow to surface was, *No Cynthia.*

At the exact same time that Greg was hearing Guns 'n Roses in his head, Cynthia was sitting alone in her living room holding a tablet. She used a remote to hit play on her sound dock and the sounds of the same opening cords from *Appetite to Destruction* filled her living room. She sensed Greg's thoughts and smiled. She typed onto her tablet and a list began to grow. She sang along with Axl as her fingers rapidly typed several names on the electronic document. All of them female.

She smiled and said out loud, "Mr. Rose, I know the names and have the money."

She jotted a few more names and paused to study the list. After a few minutes she smiled in satisfaction with the length and quality. She reached for her phone to start an afternoon of phone calls. Everything was proceeding as planned except for one minor irritation. Esperanza had not returned since her trip to Sacramento.

Greg kept the promises to himself for the first couple of weeks. Eventually Simon began suggesting that they all grab some dinner and drinks after work. Greg politely stiff armed the suggestion and Mary disdainfully waved away the offer. After a particularly productive Friday she actually smiled and agreed before Greg could decline. Her unexpected agreement boosted Simon's enthusiasm for the idea and he playfully pestered Greg until he agreed.

They met up at a local steak house and walked around the corner to a club for drinks. Greg stressed that he was going to have just one drink. A tall, elegant forty-something brunette named Shannon altered his plans.

To say they hit it off was a massive understatement. They laughed and flirted and before the night was done, they shared a bed in nearby hotel. The next morning she abruptly thanked him and more or less explained that she was in town only for a conference. She added that she was not looking for a relationship. She left without the two exchanging phone numbers.

Part of him wanted to spend the afternoon Facebook stalking her, but he was already committed to helping at a local pet shelter. He realized that he needed something to fill the time on the weekends and Google provided him with a list of potential shelters. He found a no-kill dog kennel twenty minutes outside of the city that was desperate for funds and volunteers. The two women that ran the shelter, Bonnie and Sarah, were apologetic but they simply needed manual labor that afternoon. After hours of picking up dog feces and spraying down kennels, the memory of the previous night faded. He was exhausted by the time he returned to his high-rise apartment. He opened the curtains fully to look at the nighttime silhouette, flopped on his couch, and immediately crashed out. The next day he did reminisce about Shannon (the sex was really good) but he did not dwell nor attempt to find her on-line. By the end of the day on Monday things were back to norm and the one-night stand was the furthest thing from his mind.

The next Friday was a repeat of the previous start to the weekend. He reluctantly went out with Simon and Mary (and a few other people from the office). He insisted he would stay for only one drink but had several. He met a woman and like the previous weekend, had a one-night stand. The coincidence should have triggered warnings in his head, but he made no connections. He failed to see anything unusual as this pattern repeated a third, fourth, and fifth time. After the sixth consecutive Friday of sex with a stranger he was once again at the shelter. Bonnie watched him for a short period before pulling him aside.

"Greg", she began with genuine concern on her face, "you look a little rough today."

Greg chuckled and replied, "I had a late night. I met someone."

"Oh", Bonnie replied looking away with slight embarrassment, "again."

The word "again" was like a slap in the face. He instantly connected the dots of the previous six weeks. He was shocked that he had someone managed to "forget" about each of the women shortly after they separated. His surprise gave way to venom laced anger. The expressions on his face told a story.

Bonnie involuntarily took a step backward and asked, "Greg, are you alright. You look mad enough to tangle with the devil."

Greg spat, "I am mad enough, and I *do* intend to tangle with the devil. I am sorry but I need to jet."

Bonnie cautiously put his hand on Greg's shoulder, "I have no idea what has you so riled, but I want to caution you to be careful. Sometimes things are better off left alone."

Greg walked away and threw over his shoulder, "I need to go into the jungle and flesh out a snake."

In Cynthia's bedroom she sat cross legged and naked on the floor. The dimensions of her room seemed distorted giving the impression of a wall less canyon. A green and purple fog floated around her as she held her aura sphere in her lap. The size of her sphere had multiplied to the size of a large medicine ball. A massive golden scaled snake towered over her from behind her back, the beast's foot long tongue flicking the air to the left and right of her head. She knew the dimensional creature was to her back, but she was not concerned. Her focus was on the rage she sensed in Greg.

She opened her eyes revealing orbits of immense brightness. Her lips did not move but her voice filled the room, "Come to my jungle Greg."

Part V:
The Bridge & Searing Guitar Solo

Chapter 16:
"Rock and Roll Machine"

Greg slammed the car door shut to his audio, put his foot on the break, and punched the start push button. His intention at that given moment was to drive straight to Cynthia's. He was going to have it out with her once and for all. He was determined that she would not fuck with his life anymore. He thought, *this ends NOW!*

Somewhere deep in psyche he heard a giggle. The kind of snicker that indicates that your words, your plans, and your ideas are nonsense. He then heard the voice of the deceased Joe Leonard, weak in tones but strong in determination. *This does end, but it ends badly for you.*

The anger meter came off the peg just long enough to begin thinking about a different course of action. His fight or flight instinct was activated, and the chemicals were still coursing through his veins. If given more time the odds were high that he chose's a different path. Instead of putting the car in gear he grabbed his iPhone and called her.

She picked up on the second ring. She sounded out of breath as she answered, "Hello."

He curtly replied, "Cynthia, this is Gregory."

She pleasantly asked, "Gregory who?"

He snapped, "You know which Gregory. The one that you are playing your mind-fuck games. The one you told about aura's and other mystical magical bullshit."

"If it is such mystical bullshit then why are calling? Are you telling me that you believe in the things I have tried to tell you?" she icily responded.

"I don't know exactly know what I believe. I do believe that you can and have done things to affect my life", he said with his voice rising with each syllable. "I want to know why."

"I told you a long time ago that you are important to me in a way like no other", she answered.

"You have not been exactly truthful throughout our entire relationship", he accused.

She sighed, "That is true."

"The job here in Seattle and all the women. You caused those things to happen", he spoke looking for justification.

She succinctly replied, "Yes, all of it."

"What about those issues I had in Sacramento? The loss of my job and the streak of bad health", he asked.

"Yes", she said.

He took a few seconds to process these confessions. She left him alone with his thoughts as he saw Bonnie and Sara approaching the car from the shelter. He started to put the window down when Cynthia spoke with urgency, "Greg you need to put the car in gear and drive away RIGHT NOW."

Her angst took him by surprise. He looked down at the iPhone screen and back out the window. He simply asked, "Why? Give me the truth for once."

Without hesitation she answered, "Because I am pretty sure that they will talk you out of the car. All these plans I set in motion for the last few months will come crashing down."

"You mean you would never bother me again?" he asked.

"No", she responded. "I would just be back to square one for today. I would try to coax you again and again, but I am not too sure if I will have a better opportunity than today."

“The opportunity for what?” he asked with a tremor in his voice.

“I want to meld our auras together”, she stated.

He could hear the concerned women through the window. He could not decipher the words, but he understood their meaning. They did not understand the change in Greg, but they inherently sensed danger. They did not want him to leave.

He looked down to the phone and said, “That sounds selfish.”

She frantically yelled, “Oh, Greg, it is so selfish, but I cannot live without trying to tie yours to mine.”

“Why should I help you get this unnatural thing you so desire?” he said while moving his hand to shut the car engine off.

“I told you on the very first night in the car. You spoke about a song called ‘Confusion’. I told you that I could set you free. I asked you and you said that you wanted to be free”, she desperately offered.

“What does being free entail in all of this craziness? Are you saying that I will be free from confusion?” he asked.

Bonnie pounded on the passenger window with Sara just a few feet in tow. He looked into her eyes and saw great fear in them. He heard Cynthia say, “Yes, in a way. You will achieve a whole new level of enlightenment. But that is sort of a guess. I do not know for a fact what will lie on the other side for both of us. The only thing that I am positive is that you will free from me for all of time.”

The words put Greg in motion. He gave the ladies a thumbs up and a hearty smile. He put the Audi and gear and carefully pulled away from the women. Once he was clear of the couple them punched the gas. The car fishtailed in the gravel and dirt driveway. He accelerated off their property and the car went momentarily airborne as the Audi launched onto the main road. He yelled like a foolish teenager and jammed the gas pedal to the floor once the Audi regained the traction. The motion momentarily pinned him to the molded leather seat. He quickly passed over 100 mph as he flipped through the satellite radio. He stopped searching when he recognized the song "Rock and Roll Machine" by Triumph. He used the radio controls on the steering wheel to max out the volume when the bridge in the middle of the song transitioned into the long guitar solo. He played air guitar on the steering wheel as the solo accelerated to the blistering end. His car rocketed down the road uninhibited as mysteriously the route was free of all other traffic, only green lights shined, and police were absent. By the time the guitar solo wound down to the last vocals Greg was oblivious to his actual speed or his surroundings. He shouted the final lyrics at the top of the lungs as the Audi raced up the hill towards Pleasant Ave. The tires squealed and smoke erupted from under the car as he made the left like an Indy Car racer. He thought with satisfaction, *Today I am a fucking rock and roll machine.*

Part VI: The Final Lyrics (The Title)

Chapter 17:
"Highway to Hell"

Cynthia was outside waiting for Greg as he parked his car next to her Tesla. The final notes of one his favorite AC/DC songs was blaring through the closed windows. He enthusiastically sang the final lyrics to "Highway to Hell" oblivious to her presence in the driveway. He exited the car and recognized that she was standing on the walkway with a wide smile. Despite the unbridled excitement that he had just shown he now looked troubled. Her smirk faded and she took a few small steps. They slowly closed the gap between each other. The awkward silence lasted a few more moments before she smiled and said, "Ok, welcome to my humble abode."

He could not but help to smirk and shake his head in acknowledgement at attempt to ease the mood. He asked, "Thank you. Do we shake hands, and this is all over?"

She laughed out loud which made him join her. She leaned into him and let the humor fully engulf her. He did not push her away, though he also did not go out of his way to embrace her. Spasms of laugher racked her for several seconds before she gently pushed herself off of his chest.

"No", she began. "I am afraid not. This will take a little while."

The truth was that Cynthia did not know exactly how to accomplish what she desired. Her plans had involved getting him voluntarily to the house. She did not calculate beyond getting him in front of her. Instinctively she understood that this would not proceed in the same route as her former financial consultant. In that case she simply stripped his aura away. The goal was more complex with Greg. She craved an intermingling vice a simple addition. She knew that they had to mutually desire this conjoining, but she felt unsure of the necessary steps. She also had a strong intuition that she only had one attempt. He would be free of her regardless of the outcome. A shiver of nervousness ran down her spine as she suspected that her time was limited as well. She surmised that she had only a few days to dwell and act or the opportunity would be lost forever. Her previous ventures into this realm always revealed the tactics she needed to take well in advance. He was now standing in front of her unintentionally questioning her next steps and she was not prepared.

"What is a little while?", he questioned.

She sighed and said, "I am not positive. Maybe a night, maybe longer."

He gave her a hard look and said, "I am going to need you to explain what is going to happen, or otherwise I am going to get back into my car and head home. This is absolutely insane."

She gently replied, "I know. Will you come inside and try to relax? I know *that* is a critical first step."

He turned away from her and stared at the apple trees in her yard. A thousand disparate thoughts raced through his mind, all of which gave conflicting recommendations. She lightly put her hand on his arm and said, "If you come in, I will make you tacos for dinner."

He shook his head and said, "Are you serious? We are talking about dabbling in the unknown and you want to talk about tacos. This is so absurd."

He paused and she silently looked into his eyes. He sighed, "You know it is so absurd, that I feel compelled to stay and have tacos with you."

She quickly grabbed his hand and led him into the house. Once inside she played the role of the perfect hostess. His reservations were momentarily kept at bay as he drank a bottle of water and listened to her bright chatter concerning recent changes in her investments. She suddenly changed the subject and said that she had something to show him. They went into the living room where she revealed a new Onkyo sound system that included a new turn table. She pointed to a shelf which held at least 500 vinyl albums.

"I have not had the chance to play most of those yet", she explained. "Why don't you find something to put on the record player while I put together some lunch for us. It is too early for tacos."

He did not look back at her as he said, "Never too early for tacos." She laughed lightly and said something that he did not hear. He was too focused on the rows of vinyl albums, many with the plastic wrapping still intact. She yelled from the kitchen, "I am now a believer. Vinyl sounds so much better. I have been a fanatic buying new remastered classics on 180-gram vinyl."

He still did not respond as he flipped through the albums. He muttered to himself, "I don't know where to start. If this is meant to distract me, it is working."

He pulled out the Doors first, self-titled album. He turned on the stereo, selected the turntable, lifted the dust cover, and carefully laid the album on the player. He hit the button to lift the arm and watched as the needle made contact with the record. He set the volume in the middle and scrambled to the couch. As the opening notes of "Break on Through (To the Other Side)" filled the room, he settled into the couch and let the pure sound of the vinyl wash over him. He closed his eyes and carefully listened to each note and tone. He became so enthralled with the sound emitting from the surround sound that he felt that he was being transported to another time and place. When the second song, "Soul Kitchen", began he felt her slide onto the couch next to him. He opened his eyes momentarily as she leaned into him. He thought, *Again this is fucking insane.*

She seemed to read his mind and whispered, "Great album, relax and just enjoy it."

When the first side ended, she left the couch to flip the album to the second side. As she closed the dust cover, he asked, "Why now?"

She looked at him inquisitively and he continued, "I mean why reach out after twenty years in the first place. What is different? You said the aura stuff is not as important to you."

"I have no nice way to say it other than I lied. Your aura is important to me. As far as the reasons for the timing that is harder to explain", she replied.

He gestured that she should elaborate. She said, "I think I once told you that you can't exactly Google this sort of thing. I have learned as I aged. When you and Danielle left my life, I had a lot of anger. I guess that fueled my aura needs so to speak. My aura sphere does not grow fast...I don't feel a need to expose it very often. As I hit my thirties and forties the desire for that matched the need for sexual intimacy. I still want sex, particular good sex but I think about sex and the aura sphere less and less as I age."

She paused and he asked, "Ok so why am I here?"

She bit her lip and concentrated. She slowly answered, "You are different. You always have been. My anger really lasted for over a decade but as I learned to forgive and move on a new feeling moved into my life. At first the feeling was just that, a feeling. Over the past few years that feeling has morphed into something...something...I can't seem to live without."

"Like an addiction?", he offered.

"I suppose that analogy is as good as any other", she answered. "The thought of you almost became an obsession."

"For addicts there never is an end", he cautiously said. "An obsession is spooky enough without unexplainable supernatural elements."

"I know I have not been entirely truthful about all of this. On this one point I am asking you to believe me when I say that this melding, this joining of auras is a one-time event. I don't know how but I just know that I will no longer need you in my life. You are like that life-long goal. You are my Mount Everest", she said.

"You may be satisfied so to speak, but you could still manipulate my life just like you manipulate others", he said while pointing at her.

"No. You will be free from me forever. You can see me or not see me. That will be your choice", she responded. "Let me ask you a question. What was your drive like on the way here today?"

"Easy, no traffic", he replied.

"No, I mean how did you feel? Did you have any feeling of excitement", she expounded on the question.

He chuckled and said, "I drove like a bat out of hell. Seriously, I have not driven like such an idiot since I was in my early twenties."

"Why?", she asked softly. "What were you feeling?"

He stared into space for moment as he struggled to answer her question. Twice he opened his mouth to answer and twice no words were uttered. Finally, he simply stated, "That is a good question. I am not sure."

She stood and said, "Think about it. I have to use the bathroom. I will be back."

As she exited the living room into the kitchen area he blurted, "I just had this feeling that I had to be with you."

She turned and said, "Like lust."

"No", he answered, "And not like love either. A strong feeling. A magnetic feeling is the best I can answer."

She smiled and said, "I did not manipulate anything for you to feel what you feel. I guessed a long time ago that you wanted to be with me for more than just the sex. I think the drugs numbed you to the pull and the distance kept the attraction hidden until I reached out to you. I think you may be touched in similar way but also very different way than I am. You sense it. You want something that you can't quit grasp." She turned back again and headed towards the back of the house leaving him to contemplate her last words.

He thought, *what do I feel? Rationally, I think I should leave. I don't want to though, that much I do know. I want…what is that I want? I feel, well shit, I feel aroused. I want to touch her in that way but…is that all? No, I don't think so. I have this undesirable need. If I was younger, I would define it as love. I loved Monica. Hell, I still do. I never wanted anything more in my entire life than to spend my life with her. Oh God I still wish…*

He leaped off the couch and violently spat, "No fucking way. NO FUCKING WAY!"

He ran out of the living room towards the bath-room. He pounded on the door and yelled, "Get out here right NOW!"

She opened the door and he roughly grabbed her by the arms. He pushed her back and slammed her into the towel closet door. She left out a surprised yelp and then squeaked, "Greg what are you doing?"

He leaned forward a few inches from her face and growled, "Tell me that you had nothing to do with Monica's death. Tell me right now. If you did, I swear to God…"

He shoved her into the wall a second time causing her head to bounce off the door. She let out a cry of both pain and fear. She cringed," Monica who? Greg what is this…"

"Don't mess me Cynthia", he interrupted, "Monica my fiancé who suddenly died and very shortly thereafter you SEND an invitation after twenty fucking years."

Realization sprang onto her face and she urgently said, "No, no, no. I had NOTHING to do with your relationship or with her passing."

He gripped her shoulders tightly and she cried out, "Greg you are hurting me."

He snarled, "Your invitation was just merely a *coincidence.* You just *suddenly* needed to see me."

"No. I sensed your immense pain", she meekly replied.

He let go of her and shed slid down to the floor in a heap. She covered her head with her arms and tearfully moaned, "I did not know exactly what happened. Yes, I had been obsessing over you and wondering almost daily about your life. Then all of a sudden, I got this flash from you. We always had to be connected through sex for me to feel that kind of pulse. What you sent out was so powerful. You hurt me. Bad. Worse than just now. It took me a couple of days to figure out that your pulse was a thousand times more powerful. I had no idea that you were engaged or that someone had died. I just knew you were in immense pain and your presence was like a giant beacon. I waited for several months but the feeling from your pulse stayed strong. One day I just said, 'fuck it' and reached out. I had to know. I had to know if you would come see me."

He wordlessly left the bathroom. She listened trying to determine if he was leaving the house. When she heard the door to the back deck open and close, she slowly stood up. She rubbed the back of her head. She did not feel a knot, but her head still rung from hitting the door. She went to the sink and splashed water onto her face. She looked in the mirror and viewed the reflection of a truly frightened woman. His violent outburst took her completely by surprise. At a moment she thought that he was going to seriously hurt her. A thought zipped into her head and the face in the mirror morphed a devious smile. She knew that she needed to see.

She headed to her bedroom removing clothes as she walked. She shut and locked the door, finished removing her clothes and dropped everything in a pile. She sat down and within seconds she produced a dazzling bright ball of energy the size of a small boulder. The radiant object dwarfed her in size, but she did not struggle in the least to manipulate. She understood that after decades that she still did not understand all of this power. His outburst revealed a startling but terrifying new level of potential power. She inhaled the sphere back inside of her. She quickly re-dressed and thought, *I was not sure the steps I needed to prepare when he got of his car. This afternoon I thought I was starting to see a path open in the fog of my mind. His outburst has changed everything. He could drain me if I am not extremely careful. I never imagined that to be possible. But his anger also revealed to me something much deeper than I ever detected in him. I am still on a tight timeline. The question is how am I going to set this up in such a short period of time?*

As she approached him by the pool he stood and meekly apologized, "I'm sorry. I have never acted that way towards another human being much less a woman. They talk about seeing 'red' and losing it."

"I am not going to say it is alright and that it is water under the bridge. Things have changed now.

Everything just feels…different…faded so to speak", she replied. She down on a chair next to him and continued, "I will just say that I think that I can understand."

"What now?" he asked.

"You hear stories of people preparing for years to climb Mount Everest. When they get to the mountain the weather suddenly changes and they are forced to cancel their attempt. They can't just wait a day and try later. If they miss that window, they must wait for quite a while for another attempt. I think some weather has moved in on my mountain", she said.

He shrugged his shoulders and said, "So…should I leave and go about my life until your window opens again so to speak."

"No, not yet", she quickly responded. "I would like you to stay here with me for the next couple of days. We can run to your apartment and grab some things that you will need but I would like for us to remain in close contact for a few days."

He shrugged his shoulders again, "Today and tomorrow are no problem but what about Monday? Are you asking me to skip work? I am under contract", he replied.

She smirked and said, "I own that contract. You are working for me. I will make the appropriate phone calls. I will have you back on the job no later than Wednesday."

He gave her a cross look and asked, "Are those accounts all manipulated too?"

"No", she sighed. "Those are the result of me not being intrusive enough. I manipulated the hiring, but I really do need that portfolio independently researched and managed."

"Well I expect a big bonus at the end", he flippantly replied.

"I see that you have your humor back. Does that mean you will stay?" she inquired.

"You did promise tacos", he reminded.

She leaned over, hugged him, and planted a wet kiss on his cheek, "Thank-you." She felt a jolt of energy that made her toes curl and squeeze her thighs together. She leaned back into her chair and let the warmth fill her.

The rest of the afternoon was spent listening to records and light conversation. She broke out a thousand-piece puzzle of snow-covered mountains. He never put together puzzles, but he went along with the suggestion. They sat side by side on the couch peering over the pieces, making small talk, and avoiding any discussion of the reason for his presence in her house. After a few hours he inquired about missing work on Monday. She left the couch momentarily to make a phone call in the kitchen. When she returned, she informed him that he was "excused" from work on Monday and Tuesday.

"I will be back to work by Wednesday", he confirmed.

She wordlessly nodded and sat back down. She gently leaned into him and said, "Don't worry about work for now."

He grunted for an answer. He thought, *I should be worrying but I am not. I feel like I am speeding towards something unseen just beyond the horizon.*

The puzzle was half finished when they broke for dinner. He sat at the kitchen table and watched her prepare the meal. She suggested that he open a bottle of wine for them. He pulled a bottle of Robert Mondavi Cabernet off her wine rack. He uncorked the bottle and poured her a full glass. He inquired if she had any beer in the house. She smiled and pointed to the refrigerator where he found three different six packs from local breweries. He selected a double IPA and watched her finish making the meal. She lined up several small glass dishes of taco toppings on the counter. He made two large overflowing tacos and sat down. He waited till she made her own before he started eating.

After his first bite she asked, "Is this worth staying a few days with me?"

"These tacos are top notch", he admitted. "I am still not sure why I am here. I mean more specifically why I *allowed* myself to drive here or agree to stay."

"Eat your tacos", she directed. "We can talk about that after dinner."

They finished dinner with little conversation. She quickly cleared the dishes. He suggested to go sit outside by the pool. He opened a second beer and she said, "Go ahead I will be out shortly."

She watched him settle in a lounge chair before turning towards her bedroom. She shut and locked the door and quickly undressed. An idea formed during the dinner, one with risk. She decided before he finished his second taco that the gamble was worth the potential calamity. She sat and concentrated.

Like earlier in the afternoon the room distorted and filled with a discolored haze. She spoke in low whispers in a rhythmic chant. Unlike earlier she did not draw out her aura sphere. She understood the status of her power. She needed answers that the sphere could not help her answer. She chanted faster and hoped Greg would be patient and not seek her. She sensed Its alertness. She knew It would appear at Its own pleasure. She waited.

The snake's curiosity overpowered Its normal sense of detachment. It normally appeared only when It sensed impatience in the summoner. None was detected but It also felt something vastly different. *No magic protection encircled the summoner!* The beast raced through the ravaged dimensions with full intent of devouring the fool. The entirety of the massive being suddenly appeared and poised to swallow Cynthia in one bite. The demon did not detect any fear and in mid-downward strike darted to the corner. She opened her eyes and communicated via her mind,

Thank-you powerful and magnificent golden demon for graciously accepting my invitation, she elegantly and formally announced.

The beast wrapped around her without touching her. The foot-long tongue flicked the air before it returned her hail, *You have no protection.*

She pointed to her stomach and replied, *I have it in here.*

The snake thrashed around the room destroying all physical objects. As the bed and dresser drawers were crushed into splinters and the mattress shredded to dust the demon raged and yelled, *YOU DARE THREATEN ME.*

She calmly replied, *Beast, do you know me?*

The snake flicked the air several times and said, *La bruja. You carry the magic sphere.*

Cynthia sensed something extraordinarily rare in the ancient being. The beast was uncertain, and she knew that she must act quickly. She spoke in a confident voice, *you are most powerful. We have met before but always with my sphere at the ready. If I summoned, you in that manner I feared that you would not trust me. I am before you requesting a boon.*

The snake produced its version of grotesque laugh, *No one in all the millennia that I have lived ever did something so foolhardy.*

It is a risk I agree. We both know that I can produce my sphere. The question is who is faster. My guess is that it would be a draw. We would only succeed in destroying each other, she explained.

You foolish witch, the snake sickeningly screeched. *But we will not find out today. Your stupidity has piqued my curiosity. I have not been so entertained in an age.*

I like to think my actions are of courage and not stupidity, she corrected. Before the snake could react negatively, she said, *my vision is clouded, and I know you are mighty enough to free me from my confusion.*

The snake haughtily replied, *I can grant anything your weak human form can imagine. Why would I spend even one tiny second considering your request?*

The snake finished the last syllable by spraying venom over Cynthia. She felt the liquid pierce and burn her skin like acid. She swallowed a scream of pain and yelled; *I ask for nothing for free. I have a proposition that you may just consider interesting.*

The snake cackled so loud that she was certain that her ear drums would rupture. She sat motionless despite the pain in her head and melting skin. The snake spun around Cynthia in a flash and all the venom was removed from her body. She desperately wanted to see if the spray left marks, but she dared not move a muscle in front of the unpredictable demon.

After several agonizing seconds the snake spoke, *you are indeed a rare, rare entity. If I do not devour you, I will be watching you very close across the dimensions. I know what confuses you. I grant you ONLY the opportunity to make your offer to reveal your path.*

She made the offer. The beast accepted.

Greg was patient and deep in thought. Every time he convinced himself that he was flirting with something beyond his comprehension he felt a bolt contentment. He could not pinpoint the reason, but he simply felt *happier* than he had in years. He did not view the past twenty years as miserable. He just felt that he was home. After thirty minutes his mind tired of arguing with himself and he started to ponder Cynthia's absence. He purposely stayed put but after another five minutes he found himself standing up. He justified to himself that he was only getting up to get another beer.

As he reached the French door Cynthia opened it and stepped outside. She said while handing him an open beer, “I figured you needed another.”

“Perfect timing”, he acknowledged.

They sat down and he took a large gulp from the bottle. He casually scanned her and noted that she was drenched in sweat. He gazed again and said, “You are covered in some kind of spots.”

He leaned forward and exclaimed, “They look like blisters.”

“Oh, don’t worry about those. I have some great news”, she excitedly reported.

He curled his eyebrows in concern, but before he could speak she announced, “I know how to blend our auras.”

He momentarily forgot about the blisters and said, “What? How?”

“I needed some time alone to figure a few things out. We need to take a trip first”, she informed him.

He yawned feeling suddenly very tired. He slurred, “A trip?”

“Well sort of. I need to find someone”, she said while standing up. She took the beer out of his hands the second before he passed out.

She struggled with his dead weight but after a few minutes and several curse words she was able to lay him flat on the pool chair.

She spoke to the unconscious figure, “I’m sorry I had to drug you. You will be fine here tonight. I will get you up in the morning and into the house. I am not really leaving the house for the trip. I need you to stay here until I am done, and I think this will take a lot longer than just a few days. I am sorry in advance for keeping you drugged.”

He grunted and then farted as if in response. She laughed and said, “Did you say something?”

His lifeless body suddenly flailed his arms and he mumbled something unintelligible. She looked down and mockingly asked, “Yes, dear? Are you trying to say something?”

He lay perfectly still and started snoring. She turned away from him and he started sleep talking, or more specifically sleep singing AC/DC’s “Highway to Hell”.

Chapter 18:
"The End"

He woke the next morning by her gentle prodding. He stirred but resisted completely waking. She persistently said his name and shook him till he finally opened his eyes.

"Well good morning sleepy head", she cheerfully said.

He sat up in the lounge chair and said, "How did I end up out here? Last thing I remember was talking about a trip."

"I don't know what you are talking about", she lied. "Your dead soldiers have something to with your camping out."

He looked to where she was pointing. Several beer bottles cluttered the table next to the lounge chair. He rubbed his eyes and said, "I drank all of those?"

"Yep", she replied. "How do you feel?"

He stood up and said, "Actually pretty damn good for the damage that was done. I have to take a piss like crazy."

"Not in my pool", she jokingly warned. "Are you hungry? I have breakfast ready."

"Starving", he answered as he headed towards the house and to the bathroom.

He ate the hearty breakfast with little conversation. When he finished, she urged him to go watch some television while she cleaned up. She brought him a large bottle filled with ice water. She said, "You probably need to hydrate. Drink this water."

"You are bossy this morning", he teased.

"I just don't want you getting sick", she defended. "Just drink the water."

"Ok", he said after taking a large swig. "I swear you said last night that you know the plan and we have to take a trip?"

"Sorry, you must have dreamt all of that", she replied.

"Then what is the plan for today?" he asked.

"I am going to clean the kitchen than take a shower. I think we will head to town today", she answered.

"Sounds good", he said after taking another drink. "Man speaking of dreams, I had a wacked out one last night. You know what I dreamt?"

"I have no idea", she said while rinsing the plates.

"I normally don't remember my dreams but his one was so vivid. The thing made no sense but as I ate breakfast, I connected it to a song", he said through a long yawn.

She waited a few moments before she responded, "Oh yea. What song?"

She continued washing the dishes while the living room emitted silence. She assumed he fell asleep when he said, "Do you want to hear about the dream?"

She shut the water off feeling slightly irritated. *You should be sleeping by now,* she snapped in her head. Out loud she announced, "I am all ears."

He yawned loudly but mumbled, "That last song on the Doors first record, 'The End'. Remember we listened to it yesterday."

"What about it?" she asked. "We listened to a lot of songs."

He continued to struggle talking but she could still understand his words, "The lyrics say something about a snake, like a really long one. I think miles long…do you remember?"

"I think that is probably some sort of metaphor", she said feeling a shiver go down her back.

"You are probably right", he murmured. "Must have been that lyric."

She looked into the living room and saw that his eyes were barely open.

He said, "I feel really weird. Do you feel alright?"

She walked into the living room drying her hands on a dishtowel. She replied, "Yes, I am fine. What about your dream?"

"Oh yea. I was on top of the snake. Well...maybe I wasn't. I dunno...it was freak...so huge...I dunno miles. It...the snake was gold....that much I remember real clear...weird, huh?" he finished before falling into a deep slumber.

She visibly shook and clenched her fists. She knew the beast could and probably would be a problem. She did not have time to dwell on the potential damage It could cause. She knew that she needed to calculate for Its unpredictability. That problem was for another day. She left the living room towards her bedroom and the project that she started the previous night.

The next couple of days were a repeat of Saturday night and Sunday morning. She drugged him, woke him, fed him, got him to use the bathroom, shower, kept him confused, and drugged him again. By Monday evening she recognized that the "drugging" plan was not going to work for the length of time she needed. She used more of her aura sphere than she wanted but she essentially put him into a kind of coma. All of his vital functions infinitely slowed. He could be kept in that condition for months without food, water, or having to relieve himself. She knew the task at hand would not take months to complete but would take more than a few days. Without having to tend to him every 12 hours or so would allow her to concentrate and quicken the pace. She literally rolled up her sleeves after coma sleeping him in the spare bedroom and confidently marched into her own. She felt excited with her progress.

When he finally woke, he felt incredibly weak. He struggled to get to his feet. His muscles were strangely lethargic to respond to his mental commands. He recognized that he was in one of Cynthia's spare bedrooms. He also remembered agreeing to stay with Cynthia for a few days. He was, though, confused about the exact day. This thought faded as he struggled to stand for what he was sure was the longest pee of his life. He opened his bedroom door and the natural sunlight blinded him. He zombie walked into the kitchen and saw two figures through squinted eyes.

"Well look what the cat dragged in", Danielle teased.

He took a second to register the fact that Cynthia's one-time best friend was sitting at the kitchen table with one foot propped on the table and the other under her bottom. Her shorts were too short, and her top was too tight. She smiled at him through her bad teeth and too close together eyes. Danielle was present in all of her glory.

"Danielle?", he questioningly stated.

Before she could respond he looked in the direction of Cynthia and asked, "What day is it?"

She partially told the truth. "It is Monday, silly", she teased. She did not mention of which month. He was in her magic coma for almost three weeks.

He grunted at her response and stumbled towards the kitchen table. Danielle reacted with lightning quickness and grabbed before he fell to the floor. She eased him onto the chair that she recently occupied.

"What is going on honey?" she gently soothed. "Been a little while".

She leaned over and firmly embraced him. She gave him a quick peck on the cheek and stood up just enough to bury his face between her breasts. She quipped, "Did you miss me."

He heard Cynthia warn, "Danielle."

Danielle immediately let him go and pulled out another seat. As she sat, he quickly glanced her over and said, "You look remarkably like I remember you. You have not aged at all."

She leaned over and patted his arm, "You are SO sweet."

He shifted his gaze to Cynthia and asked, "I don't want to sound rude, but why is she here."

"Well that was rude", Danielle play pouted. "Next you will be saying that you don't like my ass."

"Danielle", he carefully said, "A lot has happened, and I feel really out of sorts. The last time I commented about your butt a lot of things happened. I am not sure why you are here, and I think I need a minute with Cynthia."

Cynthia nodded at Danielle. Surprisingly she left the room without further comment and outside to the pool. Once the French doors were shut behind her, he gave his full attention to Cynthia. He closely studied her features and said, "You don't look too good. Have you been sick?"

"No", she answered. "I had use part of my sphere to manipulate her to come here. Not making fun of you but it was way more exhausting than you."

"Why is she here? To be honest I was actually feeling very content here, like I belonged in this house with you. My reservations were fading. I feel like I am in fight or flight mode right now. She makes me feel...", he struggled to complete the sentence.

"Like her presence is antagonistic", she offered.

“As good a word as any”, he accepted. “How does she fit into the plans? Do you have a plan worked out? How much longer? I go back to work on Wednesday. And why do I feel like a just ran ten straight marathons?”

“Ok one thing at a time”, she said while standing up. “Let’s get some food in you to recharge your battery. She is needed for the plan, though, she does not know the extent yet.”

“What does she need to do?” he asked.

Cynthia smiled, “Just be herself. No more on this subject till after breakfast.”

The morning and afternoon progressed with an uneasy feeling filling the air. Greg and Cynthia walked on eggshells while Danielle kept up her easy going and flirtatious persona. They ate dinner predominately in silence until Danielle spoke, “So what is going on? Cynthia you were a mile a minute until Greg got out of bed. And Greg, you are super stand-offish. What gives?”

Greg looked to Cynthia first and then said, “I recently got back into contact with Cynthia. We did not talk for over twenty years and the reason we separated is that you and I fooled around. I am not sure how to act around you when I am still figuring how to act around Cynthia.”

He looked at Cynthia and asked, “When this is done, do you think that you will want me in your life? When that special hunger is satiated will you find me compelling at all?”

The question startled Cynthia. She slowly replied, “I have honestly not thought it. I believe we both will be changed forever, but I can’t predict in what ways. I think I will want you in my life. I do enjoy being with you.”

Danielle teased, “You are so sappy.”

She ignored her female friend, “Why would you ask that question?”

He pointed at the two women and said, “You two are yin and yang. You two are so different. I was stoned most of the time twenty years ago to see the real differences. Within a handful of hours, I can easily see the vast differences. I am actually surprised that you two were so close at one time.”

“What does us being different have to do with anything?”, Danielle defensively questioned.

He looked to Cynthia while pointing towards Danielle and said, “You told me that she just needed to be herself.”

“Be my normal sexy, intelligent and vibrant self”, Danielle announced. “Again, so what?”

“I agree with her, Greg”, Cynthia frowned, “where is this heading?”

He smiled and said, “Yes, Danielle, you are all of those things. You are other things that Cynthia is not, and Cynthia has an essence that is not you. Watching the two of you together was like opening a door to my psyche. The things that make Cynthia, Cynthia are many of the things that register deeply to me. The long answer to that simple question is that when this is done, I want to be in your life. I don’t know if like boyfriend and girlfriend or soulmates, but I feel like I am home.”

No one spoke for a few minutes with each person deciphering Greg’s confession. Cynthia heard an audible click in her mind. Another piece just fell into place. She studied Danielle because she was the next key step. She just needed her to be herself. She had no doubt that Danielle would play her part, but she wasn’t sure of the timing. *I think soon, very soon. Maybe even tonight,* she thought.

Cynthia spoke, “Greg that is extraordinarily sweet. I am humbled that despite everything that has occurred that you have those feelings. I think I need some wine."

She stood and Danielle said, "Bring me some too."

Greg said, "Are you any closer to figuring out what you need to do now that Danielle is here?"

Cynthia sighed, "No. All I can tell you is that we, including Danielle, will know when the time is right. I believe all will be revealed to all us at the same time."

Danielle laughed, "Cryptic as ever."

Greg looked thoughtful and said, "Please bring me a beer."

After drinks were handed out and the gas fire pit was lit Greg started to speak, "So Danielle..."

He could see through the flames and detected an instant change in Cynthia's expression. She visibly shook her head in a negative motion. Greg changed the question on the fly, "Do you like that wine?"

She giggled and said, "It is made of grapes and has alcohol. Of course, I like it. What about your beer?"

Greg intended to ask about Danielle's life since they all separated but he guessed that Cynthia did not want him to broach that subject. As the flames danced around the fire pit Greg noted Cynthia's approval. He remarked, "Hops, water, barley and alcohol. Yep, it is pretty good. I joke but I like IPA's, and this is a pretty good one from a local brewery."

"Whatever", she replied waving her hand. "What do you guys want to do tomorrow."

Over the next few hours the sun set, and wine glasses emptied. The conversation was dominated by Danielle on topics of various degrees of unimportance. Greg observed that she finished two glasses to one of his beers and that Cynthia was still nursing her first glass. When he finished his second beer he stood and announced that he was going to go to the bathroom and grab another beer. He inquired if anyone needed another. Danielle handed him an empty glass and Cynthia declined with a wicked gleam in her eye.

He felt a pulse race through his body and goosebumps broke out over his skin. He never felt so in love and aroused. He feared to look and see if an erection was showing. He took a few large steps around the fire pit out and put his back to the women. He felt his heart racing and his hands were shaking. He also realized that he was terrified.

He dropped the empty beer bottle into the garbage and set Danielle's wine glass on the counter. He headed to the bathroom and relieved himself. By the time he finished he could feel his heart slowing. As he washed his hands he stared into the mirror. He was confident but a glow of nervousness was evident on his face.

He thought, *how many times have I stared into this face and asked myself what am I doing? Greg, she is dangerous.*

He splashed water on his face and continued, *But I am here till the end.*

He lightly sang the lyrics to 'The End' as he dried his hands. He was genuinely startled when the door opened, and Danielle staggered into the room.

She already poured herself a giant glass of wine and was drunkenly waving it around in front of her. She drank half in three large swallows and then slurred, "Leaving already."

"I finished going to the bathroom and I need another beer", he answered looking over her shoulder for signs of Cynthia.

She noted his searching, closed the door, and leaned against it. She set her glass on the counter and purred, "I have something I need to show you."

He shook his head, "No I don't think you do."

By the time he finished his sentence her shirt and bra were already on the floor, "I think the girls look good tonight. What do you think?"

She rubbed her breasts together in an attempt to be sexy, but the drunken motions made her look ridiculous to Greg. He started to tell her in a tone that was far from pleasant when he heard a clear voice in his head. Cynthia urged, *Wait.*

"Cat got your tongue?" she giggled. "Maybe it is not the cat, but maybe the pussy got your tongue. Maybe the pussy is in that devious little head of yours."

Greg said nothing in confusion and then Cynthia calmly said to him, *let her continue.*

Danielle took Greg's lack of response as an indication that he was interested. She pinched and teased her nipples to hard points and slyly asked, "Do you want to see more? Do you want to see all of me?"

Greg started to say no, but the voice urged otherwise. He simply nodded up and down. She pulled her shorts and underwear to her ankles and tossed them into the sink. She lifted one foot up and rested it on the edge of the sink while grabbing his hand. The voice coaxed, *don't resist.* Greg allowed Danielle to rub his hand on her wet womanhood. She moaned slightly and turned around. She pleaded, "Rub me from behind."

The voice was silent, but Greg was sure that he should continue. He was sure that he could feel the presence of Cynthia, maybe even detect her aura. She was now in the house and walking down the hall.

Danielle writhed against his hand and hoarsely pleaded, "Put your cock inside of me."

The voice in his head violently yelled, *No.*

He repeated the direction, "No."

She pressed harder on his hand, "Please."

He remained silent waiting on further instruction. He felt her aura pass the bathroom and go into

Cynthia's bedroom. Danielle abruptly turned around and demanded with a violent zeal in her eye, "Why won't you fuck me?"

Cynthia, *you have not showed me all of you yet.*

Greg repeated verbatim. Danielle drunken eyes narrowed, "What the fuck do you mean? I am naked."

Cynthia squealed as if in ecstasy herself, *I want to see your aura sphere.*

Greg repeated, "You have not shown me your aura sphere. I want to see that."

She giggled and slurred, "Silly goose, you won't see it even if I did bring it out. It is invisi, indivis, vis-solable, whatever. You can't see it."

Tell her you can. Tell her that I taught you, Cynthia commanded.

Greg confidently replied, "Oh yes I can. Cynthia showed me the secret."

Quickly Greg, grab her hand and rub your crotch. Tell her you want to be inside of her while she is holding her aura sphere, Cynthia raged.

Greg did as directed both physically and verbally. Danielle teetered and he was sure she was going to fall. She held herself up with one hand on the wall. She smiled wickedly and said, "Get that cock out because here it comes."

She slid to the floor and closed her eyes. She placed her hands in front of her lap and concentrated. Greg looked around the room as if looking for some kind of confirmation, Cynthia cooed, *just wait a few seconds…and keep your penis in your pants.*

Despite the crazy situation he smiled at the clear note of jealously in the voice. He watched in silence as she hummed a chant that eerily seemed to match the melody to 'The End'.

He gasped in amazement as her aura sphere became visible to him. He took a step backwards and yelped, "Holy shit, I can actually see it."

She opened her eyes and her hollow voice echoed in the room, “My sphere is so beautiful, isn’t it.”

He nodded simply out of confusion. She demanded, “Why are you still dressed.? You wanted to get inside of me with my sphere exposed. Do it!”

Greg heard the voice direct, *Step into the protection circle behind you.*

He looked down at his feet and saw glowing runes emerging from the stone tiles. They wrapped themselves together forming a rough four-foot diameter circle. He carefully stepped over the runes creating the circle. As soon as both feet were within the protection ring the reality changed.

The first thing that occurred was a blinding light erupted. The concussion forced him backwards with a thud onto his butt. He heard Cynthia urge, *Stay in the circle.*

The light lasted for several seconds burning his eyes. The flash completely vanished as quickly as it formed. He first verified that his body was completely within the protection circle then he examined the landscape.

The house was gone, and they appeared to be in rocky valley void of vegetation or other life. He recognized the purplish green fog and the streaks of harmless lightning exploding from the haze to the ground. To his right his saw Cynthia standing naked holding her exposed aura sphere. He was stunned to see that hers was smaller than Danielle’s. He turned to where Danielle sat in what was once the bathroom. He involuntarily shrieked.

Cynthia mentally calmed him, *the beast is here at my bidding.*

The gigantic golden snake completely wrapped itself around Danielle. Only a portion of her hair and one foot were visible. In the neck of the monster a brightness emitted the same size as her sphere.

Excellent, the thing purred. *Actually, better than expected.*

Greg spoke verbally, “What happened?”

The thing twisted in blink of an eye and was upon Greg. The thing kept Danielle wrapped tight but still circled the head near Greg’s circle. The tongue seemed to be tracing Greg’s body without breaking the boundary of the rune circle.

The snake shrieked in apparent laughter, *Oh how precious. You did not know!* The beast twisted the massive head towards Cynthia, *Bruja you are so full of surprises.* It turned back to Greg and slowly said, *I ate her sphere. Oh, what a delight.*

Horrified Greg stammered, “What about Danielle.”

The snake commanded, *you will stop communicating with me in such a primitive and vulgar manner.*

Cynthia warned, *don’t talk to It at all. You cannot trust anything It says or does.*

Greg shouted out, “What about Danielle?”

The snake thrashed and convulsed before, *one more insult to my being and I will crash that circle.*

She warned, *Mentally, Greg. My sphere is drained from the last few days of effort. Please be quiet while I dismiss It.*

Greg meekly thought, *Danielle.*

The snake snarled in horrible laugher, *you can have this back. It is broken and of no use to me any-more.*

The snake unfolded itself and flung the bloody and battered rag doll of a woman across the landscape. The body lay with the head twisted to the back. The eyes were open and seemed to be resting on Greg. He shivered in disgust and felt bile in the back of his throat.

Do not vomit, Cynthia warned. *That will amuse the demon and entertaining the beast will only make it more powerful.* She turned and walked directly to the snake. The beast towered over her but she powerfully commanded, *you have had your fun and I have fulfilled my end of the agreement. Unveil the secrets hidden from my gaze.*

Greg thought, *Agreement?*

She hissed, *SHUT UP, GREG!*

She continued with the beast, *Honor the deal and do it NOW!*

The snake appeared nonplussed by the demands. Each scale on the monster seemed to shiver in a manner similar to a cat purr. It began to slowly and leisurely slide in the canyon between Greg and Cynthia.

ENOUGH STALLING, she screamed.

The beast stopped and icily warned, *Be careful Bruja. I have tolerated some of your insolence because you have been so entertaining.*

Calmly she said, *I am ready for you to bestow your ancient wisdom upon me.*

Of course, you are, the snake patronizingly responded. The thing spoke an unintelligible phrase. A golden cloud appeared around Cynthia's head and the snake announced, *your ignorance is cleared.*

The cloud slowly faded from around her eyes. She gasped slightly, immediately recovered her composure and announced, *your wisdom is passed on to me. I can see the path and the words that have eluded me. I have struggled for years to learn on my own but in an instant your power gave me all that I seek. I thank-you mighty demon.*

The beast shimmered in the flattery. *Your frail presence is almost amusing to me and honoring the agreement was but a tiny hint of my power. Your praise is well-targeted.*

Mighty beast, she bowed, *our pact is now complete, and it is time for you to BE GONE!*

Ahh! snickered the snake. *You did not actually command my banishment. Before you do, I have an offer for you. You are compelled by honor to at least hear my proposition.*

As powerful as you are I fear to trust you, Cynthia flatly stated.

Ha-ha you should fear me in all aspects and be suspect of trust, the beast replied. *I, though, am bound to honor all contracts.*

What is that you want? she said impatiently.

Upon your demand, I will clear your vision for a future problem. All you have to do is bring me to this dimension and I will instantly honor the debt. No questions asked and no problem is too big for my magic, the snake offered in a boastful pride.

I have no doubt of your abilities, she began, *but what is your price for this future gift.*

I want to simply watch. That is all, to merely observe your melding. I know the spectacle will be less than satisfying, but your magic does offer a minuscule possibility of a few seconds of entertainment. Your effort to contain this power offers some humor to me, the snake insulted.

Your half of the deal is mighty indeed, but I am loathed to let you stay. You will interfere in some way. Therefore, I must send you back, she determinedly said.

WAIT! the snake yelled, *let me clear your vision again.* Before she could respond another gold, cloud appeared around her head. The fog instantly dissipated, and she wiped her eyes.

You have shown me how to bind you away from us in this arena, she said with some amazement.

Yes. When you cast the spell, I will be unable to cross the line you set. The only direction I can go will be back to my dimension, the snake explained.

This is indeed a powerful ability to possess, she said thoughtfully.

Before you count it as a permanent, I am also bound to inform that you will forget the spell once it is used, the snake admitted.

She crossly asked, *How long will the bounding last?*

As long as the melding takes, the snake assured.

She closed her eyes and said the magic phrase. A clear but apparently solid wall emerged from the ground infinitely into the sky. The opaque wall separated the beast from Cynthia and Greg.

Will that hold him, Greg inquired. The beast demonstrated by launching the entirety of its body at the wall. The beast violently slammed repeatedly with no apparent damage to the transparent structure.

It slithered backwards and appeared to take a resting position, *I believe my demonstration suffices, though my word is all that you truly need.*

She snorted, *we both know your word is tentative at best unless involved in actual compact. With that said I accept your offer.*

The beast laughed hideously and sprayed venom all along the wall. *You have made a wise choice.*

Probably not. Greg, to be on the safe side do not leave your protection circle, Cynthia cautioned.

Throughout the events of the previous several minutes Greg forgot about the runes on the bathroom floor. He looked down at his feet and saw the symbols vibrantly glowing in the dull, gray rock. He was still firmly in the middle, but he still spaced himself to ensure that he was as close to the middle of the rune-formed circle as possible. He looked back to her. He saw that she had her eyes closed and appeared to be in some sort of trance. Every fiber in his body urged him to stay silent but the broken body of Danielle was still visible and unnerving.

What about Danielle? he asked.

She did not answer him, and he pressed, *Cynthia did know the snake would kill her to get to her sphere?*

Her eyes snapped open and she raged, *Greg, we will talk about Danielle when this is finished. I need to concentrate. The snake has shown me the way, but this will not be easy. I must say the phrases exactly as It revealed them to me. So, I need you to SHUT UP!*

The last words came out as a growl and for the zillionth time in their relationship, his body broke into a cold sweat. He nervously swallowed and simply nodded.

The snake roared in sickening laughter and thrashed around in apparent humor. She gave the beast a hateful look but quickly recognized that the snake was not even looking in her direction. She figured any chastisement would only humor and encourage the beast. She frowned and wondered if this was an attempt to distract her from the forthcoming enchantment.

She turned and put her back to both Greg and the snake. She concentrated and repeated the first part of the magic phrases in her mind. When she was certain that she could repeat the words she confidently spoke them out loud.

Greg heard her speak but could not decipher the words. She turned around to him and smiled. She announced, *the pre-staging is complete. The air is ready for us.*

He lifted his arms up in confusion and said, *I can't feel a difference.*

She excitedly replied, *I can. We are ready.*

The snake gruffly announced, *to my great dismay she has indeed cast the first half correctly. We are waiting on you now.*

She ignored the snake and gently said to Greg, *the time is now. Remember earlier this evening you described why you would return to me when this is complete? Those are the feelings that has bond us together. Those are the feelings that brought you back to me. Those are the feelings that make you want to join with me on a level even deeper than spiritually or sexually. We have something vastly more complex and stronger than love. I promised you the first night I met you that I could free you. Do you want me to free you? I need you to say it out loud after I utter the next part of the enchantment. Are you ready?*

He did not agree nor disagree. He simply stood frozen in the center of the protection circle. She closed her eyes and rehearsed the next phrases in her head several times. She re-opened her eyes, nodded in his direction and spoke the words. The snake howled and thrashed at maximum decibels preventing him from hearing anything she said. He felt nothing difference with the scene, but Cynthia was viciously swaying back and forth. He took a deep breath.

John and Sandy yelled simultaneously in his head, *NO!!*

Joe Leonard calmly urged, *No.*

The long dead voice of his parents followed, *No.*

Danielle squealed, *No.*

He spoke loud and clear, "Cynthia, free me."

A bright red flash erupted from the pendant on her neck into her aura sphere. The brilliant blue orb absorbed the ray and a slightly reddish hue covered the sphere. The thinnest of threads emerged from the side closest to Greg and crossed the space towards him. The snake and Greg both gave out mental gasps.

Greg then saw that his own body had a silhouette of dazzling colors. He held his arms and hands in front of his face in amazement. As the thread from Cynthia's sphere approached, his own color pattern pulsed and stretched towards hers.

The two auras spun around each other like magnets of opposite polarity. Greg heard her mutter something that he was sure was in Latin. The colors conjoined and spun in a slow circle. The two tendrils fed the small ball and within seconds Greg understood that the ball was growing in size.

She soothed, *Greg, do not be afraid. Nothing will harm you.*

I'm not afraid, he responded. He flicked his wrist to put a ripple into his part of the thread. The wave traveled down the tendril and bumped into their conjoining ball with a small burst of light. He laughed and said, *did you feel that? That kind of tickled.*

She did not answer his question but instead stated as a query, *you can move?*

He waved at her, twisted his trunk, and lifted one foot up and down. *Yes. Did you think I would not be able?*

I thought it was a possibility. I think we need to be careful until this complete, she answered.

He asked, *how long and when will know that it is complete? What will I feel?*

She shrugged slightly and said, *I am not sure how long? Not too much longer. We will both simply know. Now please be quiet and be still. I still have to concentrate, or the spell will be lost.*

He apologized, *I'm sorry.*

He spent the next few minutes studying the conjoined sphere. He watched as each layer was wrapped tight like the center of a baseball with the threads from their auras. The sphere was visibly growing larger every few wraps and he noted that the colors leaving from him were not as vivid as in the very beginning. He felt nothing different, but he was sure that was important in some way. Regardless, he still felt relaxed and mesmerized by the event unfolding in front of his eyes.

A voice crashed into his head and interrupted his trance, *You and I have met before today.*

The words broke his reverie. He looked around as if expecting someone else to be in the canyon with them. The voice continued, *we met in a jungle on the other side of the door in your mind.*

Greg grasped when he figured out that the snake was speaking directly to him. He looked towards the beast who was pressed tightly against the magic wall. The head was staring straight at their conjoined sphere and was not giving any indication that It was involved with anything but the spectacle in front of It.

Do not look at me, the beast admonished. *You can simply think towards me and I will understand.*

Greg cautiously sent, *I do not think I should communicate with you at all. I am sure Cynthia will be angry with me.*

The beast agreed, *Oh, she most definitely would and more than likely immediately banish me back to my plane.*

Greg's curiosity overwhelmed the prudent side, *why speak to me at all?*

I just had to be positive, It chuckled. *You and I did meet on that path on that day.*

Greg mentally shook his head and the snake murmured to Itself. Greg said, *I think you should stop talking to me.*

I agree, the beast said with a hint of excitement, *but first let me clear your vision.*

A golden fog engulfed Greg's head for a split second. The haze formed and vanished so quickly that Cynthia did not notice and Greg barely had time to register the event himself. He demanded, *what did you just do?*

Cynthia had questions, very hard questions that were hidden from her view. I made a pact with her and my breathe revealed the secrets she wished to know. You have a question, a question that you do not even know that you want to know. I have given you the ability to understand the question and the path for it to be revealed, the snake said with glee.

What question? Greg asked.

You have to ask yourself and not me, the beast replied. *But if you want your secret revealed, you must act quickly. The spell is rapidly reaching the climax.*

Greg saw that their sphere had doubled in size and was rotating faster than his eyes could physically see. His thread was now almost gray with only specks of brightness. He said to the snake, *you only give something when you want something. What do you want from me?*

From you, nothing, the snake hissed. *Don't take my act as some form of benevolence. I risk the gift to you in hopes of something grander, of something that leads to unexpected twists. I exist and hope for chaos.*

Greg understood that the beast spoke the truth. He was fearful to look inside his mind because he could guess what he expected to see. He also knew that when his thread no longer had any color that this opportunity, whatever it may actually be, was lost forever. He tentatively looked and was not surprised.

A wooden door appeared solidly in the center of his mind. He did not hesitate but instantly reached out and opened. He expected a repeat and find himself on a jungle path. Instead he was in a brightly lit room. As his eyes adjusted, he discerned that he was holding a Twixt bar in his hand. He glanced around and he quickly understood that he was standing in the middle of Marco's of the nineties. He looked towards the front counter and watched Luke hand an elderly black man several lottery tickets. The man haphazardly shoved several scraps of paper that contained long lists of numbers into various pockets of his overcoat. He then very gingerly and carefully deposited the lottery tickets into the front pocket of his button up shirt under the overcoat.

He realized that he was watching the events of over twenty years ago. He tried to move but found he was frozen in place.

He thought, *Did I time travel? Am I really back to 1990 something?*

The snake's voice echoed through the door in his head, *you are still in the now. I have just provided a path to answer your question. I have unveiled memories.*

What question am I seeking? Greg thought.

Again, only you can answer that question, the snake replied. *You need to hurry.*

Greg watched the old man slowly shuffle out of the convenience store while Luke stowed the money into the register. He felt the body he was sharing drop the candy bar and turn towards the counter. As the figure of himself retraced steps from over twenty years ago, his current self-struggled with deciphering the cryptic message from the snake. He wrestled with the mystery and the question that the beast offered.

The old man suddenly returned into the store. Greg was still several feet from the counter, and he could not hear the exact words spoken by the old man. He could, though, detect a tone of anger. Luke looked surprised by the man's outburst. The clerk held his hands to his sides in a gesture of sympathy.

The conjoined aura sphere began spinning at even faster rate. The rotation was starting to wobble causing violent reverberations along the threads. He faintly heard Cynthia sigh, *we are almost joined.*

He returned his focus to the store from the past. He watched the old man frantically patting the pockets of his overcoat as if searching for something misplaced in one of the numerous pockets. He was muttering to himself and becoming more agitated by the second.

Greg intercepted a thought from the self of the past. The Greg of the Marco's era finally noted, *What a weird little dude. Man, it is freaking summertime and he is wearing that ridiculous overcoat.*

The Greg of today howled in understanding, *Who the fuck killed Luke?!*

Cynthia instantly noticed a change in Greg's demeanor. His eyes were closed, and he was visibly shaking. She glanced to her right and saw the snake writhing in apparent ecstasy. She was not positive if the boundary could actually keep the beast contained but she was now certain It was somehow interfering. She opened her mouth to banish the creature back to Its own existence.

Greg screamed, *NOOOO!!!* in all time and places. The body in the convenient store simply watched in horror unable to speak as the old man pulled out a handgun and shot Luke. The first bullet lodged itself in the clerk's right shoulder. The force of the bullet sent him backwards into the shelves of cigarettes. He instinctively reached up to grab the wound and slid against the shelves to the ground. Dozens of packs of cigarettes crashed around him as he fell behind the counter and no longer visible to Greg.

The old man looked down at the wounded clerk for a few seconds. He then calmly lifted the gun and with a downward aim pulled the trigger two more times. Luke made no sound from behind the counter. The first bullet hit him in the center of his chest while the second pierced his throat. He was dead before he slipped over onto his side.

Greg could not see the damage done by the second and third bullets, but he understood that his friend was no more. Shock gripped his body and he was unable to move. The Greg of the past tried to order his legs and arms move to tackle the murderer, but he was frozen in place. The old man gently set the handgun on the counter and with a limping gait exited the convenient store. The store cameras failed to operate that day and no witnesses saw him enter or leave the store. Greg somehow felt removed from the situation and he sensed that he was struggling with something else other than the scenario directly in front of him.

The two minds of the same person scrambled across the decades to act or make sense of the situation. The Greg facing Cynthia seemed to sense that he was missing some key piece. The snake yelled across the eons, *THE REFLECTION!*

Cynthia knew that she had a very untenable situation. She did know the reasons for Greg's sudden change of demeanor. He was visibly agitated, and she sensed on the verge of something irrational and potentially violent. She did not need to know the thoughts racing in his mind to know the snake was behind the change. She was faced with a choice; either banish the snake, which will further weaken her, or focus on Greg, which could allow more mischief from It. She chose the snake.

She uttered the magic words and verbally announced, "BE GONE BEAST."

It hated the assault on Its senses by the spoken words. The snake twisted in anger but was more incensed by the banishment. The thing tried to launch Itself against the magic border, but It was being pulled away. It heard her order him back to his dimension a second time. The snake desperately wanted to view the showdown between Greg and Cynthia. It was sure that they were on the verge of destroying each other. Against Its wishes It returned to Its own plane of existence.

Greg forced the body of his twenty-something version of himself to look at the glass door of the convenient store as the old man exited. For the briefest of seconds, the old man's features reflected back into the store. The image was not of an elderly black man in an overcoat. Instead Greg saw the clear vision of the upper body of Cynthia. She was wearing the suit that she caught him and Danielle in bed just an hour earlier. She also wore a mask of pure hatred on her face. He understood all of this in a span of milli-seconds. His rage erupted like a volcano. Not only had she hid her part in the murder, she managed to keep the memory of the murder out of his head.

His mentally raced through the wooden door back to the reality that contained Cynthia and their conjoined sphere. He spread his arms out wide and verbally yelled, "You are the one that murdered Luke."

He saw that her sphere was half the size than when they arrived at this place. He wrapped his hands on his thread and pulled. He screamed, "You bitch. You are not getting my aura. Fuck you."

The orb tottered on its axis but visibly inched towards Greg. He guessed correctly that he could move the sphere and keep it from her. He gave a victory yelp at the recognition that he was right. He tugged harder and the orb leaped a foot closer to him.

She pleaded, *Greg no! You don't understand. Just let this finish and it will all make sense.*

He laughed at her and pulled again, "I don't think so. I have allowed you to manipulate me for over twenty years. I think if I get this orb then I will be free on my *own* terms."

He spoke the truth of the spell. The sphere was now only a few feet from Greg. She sighed and pointed at him. She said, *I am truly sorry, but I cannot let that happen.* She spoke in tongues and pointed at him.

He felt like he was hit with a wall of heat. He let go of his thread and fell to the ground. He found that he could not move a single muscle. He mentally fought with his body to respond but the binding spell would not allow him to even blink. He heard her ask, *are you hurt?*

I can't move, he returned.

Are you in pain? she asked with compassion

No, he crossly replied. *Why do you care?*

Oh, Greg I do care about you, but I simply have to have this. I am sorry that this must end this way, she said with remorse.

The sphere moved back to the center and then inched slowly in her direction. His thread was now completely black and seemed to be fraying and stretching. He frantically thought, *what happens when my thread breaks?*

I had to use the binding spell. I am not completely sure, she replied.

He watched his thread stretch and thin to the point of being almost non-visible. He gasped in panic. His body felt hollow to him and he was now sure that he would simply become a shell of himself. His aura was more than just a color silhouette but somehow was connected to his soul. His body may live but his life would soon end.

A voice shifted his attention from his inner turmoil. *Lying to him till the very end.*

He was able to focus his vision to a figure standing behind and slightly to the right of Cynthia. The image of tiny but fit Hispanic woman filled his view.

She was dressed in an odd form fitting, blood red, one-piece suit that revealed shapely legs and a flat stomach. The younger woman had her left hand in the air holding an aura sphere. Greg thought, *I think that is Sofia, but she is younger than Cynthia.*

Cynthia spoke out loud, "Well now you decide to show up, Esperanza. A little late to help now."

Greg thought, *Is she crazy? That is not Esperanza.*

The new arrival calmly replied, "I came exactly at the right time. I warned you about this one and this path."

A vibrant, aura sphere colored sword suddenly emerged through Cynthia's chest from her back. As his tormentor slipped to the ground Greg saw a solid two-inch strand coming out of the bottom of Esperanza's sphere and formed into a glowing sword which she held in her right hand. Esperanza ripped the sword out of Cynthia and with a quick flick of her wrist cut Cynthia's thread to the conjoined sphere.

Cynthia wailed, "Why?!"

Esperanza walked towards the sphere now spinning in a slow, downward swirl towards the ground. She remarked, "You have become too dangerous. You risk much and your obsession potentially puts us all in great harm. Damnit, you bargained with the snake."

Esperanza made a movement similar to a swashbuckler sheafing their sword but in this instance her sword slid into her sphere. She used the line coming out the bottom to tie her sphere around her waist. She then carefully stopped the conjoined sphere from spinning on the ground and held it up to her face. She carefully studied and appeared to be seeing directly inside the object.

"I will give you this", Sofia said with a low whistle, "this is absolutely remarkable. I have never seen anything like this in my entire long life. I now understand why you took the chance."

Cynthia moaned in pain and Esperanza viciously spun and hissed, "But your actions have simply been too outrageous and dangerous to allow you to continue. You were once one of my brightest and I hoped you would stand next to me as one of my lieutenants. You are now my greatest failure. I cannot risk anymore of your antics. I am so sorry that we failed each other, but your time and the time of this connection that you have tracked for decades must cease. I have to destroy this conjoined aura sphere to prevent beings such as the snake from attempting to escape their planes to possess. You foolish girl. You have created something that is pulsating across the eons and dimensions. You couldn't just take his aura; you had to go and create this absolutely beautiful but insanely dangerous weapon."

She slowly turned to Greg and said, "I am sorry, but your time is now done." She reached for the hairlike strand that still connected him to the sphere. Cynthia yelled to Esperanza in a language that Greg had never heard. Esperanza hissed in anger. She spun around, pulled an aura knife from her sphere, and flung it straight into Cynthia's heart. Greg watched as the most significant person in his entire life breathe her last breath.

VII: The Ten Seconds After the Last Song Ends on the Vinyl Record

Chapter 19:
Subliminal Messages

Greg woke with absolutely no understanding of his situation. Every muscle and joint in his body ached. His eyes were so blurry that he was almost blind, and he felt as if he had plugs shoved in his ears. He tried to stretch, and pain ripped through his body. He tried a second time with more success, but a wave of horrible nausea gripped him. He stayed perfectly still for several minutes. Eventually his eyesight cleared enough to allow him to look around.

He was sitting in the driver seat of his Audi. He gazed out the windows which were hazy and incredibly filthy. He strained to see through the grime. He understood that his car was parked in a filthy and rundown alley, but he had no familiarity with this alley.

He started to ask himself out loud about his current situation but only a slight wheeze left his throat. A voice said, "Speech is going to take a few days to return correctly."

He shifted in his seat and viewed the woman that Cynthia identified as Esperanza sat in the passenger seat in the same one-piece outfit that she wore during their confrontation. She sent a mental communication to him, *don't try to talk. Communicate with your mind.*

Who are you? he asked.

You already know, she responded with a bit of irritation.

She thought you were Esperanza, he noted.

She gave him a thoughtful look before she said, *I was Esperanza to her. I hid my true identity from her. I hated to do it, but I needed to get close to watch and make sure that she did not continue with the folly that was you.*

You are young but I thought you once told me that you were her mother, he remarked.

I used the word mother because that was the simplest thing to say at the time. I did not give birth to her in the sense that you know. For a lack of better word, you could say that she was one my proteges. I exposed her to the beginning of her powers, she answered. *I am also much older than I choose to appear. I like this young body.*

The stories she told me about learning about her abilities as a child were all lies. Everything she probably told was a lie, he sullenly stated.

She waved away his whining, *it is very complicated, and I do not have the time nor the inclination to explain our coven to you. When it comes to her childhood, let us just say that she mostly told you the truth as she saw it.*

Coven? Your proteges? How many do you have? How big is your coven? he inquired.

She aggressively snarled, "That is absolutely none of your business. I think you should stick your own concerns because I only have a few more minutes. Then you will be left on to your own devices."

He thought and asked, *Where the hell am I parked?*

She laughed and answered, "You are in the reality of Cynthia's property. She hid the house from the surrounding areas but once she died her spell ended. This lovely shit hole of an alley is right off of Pleasant Avenue. I think you know that you are not in a good part of town. Once I leave this car my masking spell will make you and your car visible to the felons that rule these streets. You just need to drive straight ahead for one block and turn left onto Lazarus Street. I assume you remember how to get the hell out of this part of town once you get onto Lazarus."

Ok, Greg answered. *What day is it? Things have blended together from Saturday. I don't feel right at all.*

She laughed, "It is Wednesday but that is not really the question you need answered. You have been out of it longer than you know."

How long? he asked.

"Three years", she answered.

Three years! Are your freaking serious? How is that possible? he asked in shock.

"Time is not the same in another plane. I needed time to study your sphere before I destroyed it," she explained.

Why am I here? I thought you were going to kill me too, he carefully inquired.

"I was. I have no bond to you, and you are really just a complication. Did you hear Cynthia at the end?" she asked. Before he could respond she continued, "Those were power words. She made an offer to spare your life. She did actually care for you and in the end, she proved it beyond a shadow of doubt in my mind. And don't even think about asking about her sacrifice. That is also none of your business."

Ok, where do I go from here? he asked.

"Not my concern. I spared your life and hid you in this car until I completed what I needed to do", she scornfully said. "Once I step out of this car you are on your own."

He felt into his pocket and found his cell phone. He pulled it out and thought, *after three years, this is dead. The authorities probably assume I am dead. I have no job and no place to live. Hell, I don't even know if I have money.*

He pulled his wallet out of his back pocket and counted $43. He laughed, though no noise actually left his mouth.

He thought, *this is fucking crazy.*

"Don't curse at me", she warned. "You are the fool. I have no idea why you let her lead you by your noise for over twenty years. You brought this on yourself. Here is a little bit of money I found in the remains of her spell house. You can have it because I have no need for it. Do you have faith, Greg?"

He shrugged and she continued, "You should consider finding faith and maybe someone from your path separate from Cynthia that may be willing to help you in your time of desperation."

He took the cash and quickly counted. He now had $2000 give or take. He nodded in appreciation.

She announced, "Our time is done. Maybe next time you will listen to that little voice in your head in regards to women. Probably not."

She got out of the door and slammed the door shut. She went between the fence line of two back yards and rapidly seemed to blend into the overgrown grass and trash.

He started to press the start button for the engine when he thought, *been sitting here for three years, not gonna start asshole.*

He pushed the button anyway and to his great surprise the car started. He viewed her advice as sound. He left that alley and soon merged onto the highway heading south and out of the state of Washington.

He could think of only one place to go. He prayed that John and Sandy would have sympathy and help him rebuild the life that he destroyed. He had some faith in that regards. He tensely drove in silence trying to imagine a reunion with them. He tightly gripped the steering wheel and intensely focused on the road. He could not wait to be out the state.

He did not pull over until he crossed the border into Oregon. He stopped at a busy rest stop to fill the gas tank. He went inside and purchased several bottles of water and a pile of junk food. He sensed the people staring and stepping away from him. He understood. He looked like the living dead and he could smell himself. He stank like the living dead. Once back on the highway he wolfed down two power bars and a bottle of water. He started to relax. He loosened the death grip on the steering wheel. He reached over and turned on the radio. He broke out in laughter as rock guitar riffs and drums filled the front of the car. A raspy voice belted the lyrics,

She was a wicked sorceress…

Made in the USA
Columbia, SC
13 September 2020

20591183R00200